GROWING UP FILIPINO

STORIES FOR YOUNG ADULTS

Collected and Edited by
Cecilia Manguerra Brainard

PALH

GROWING UP FILIPINO: STORIES FOR YOUNG ADULTS

Collected and edited by Cecilia Manguerra Brainard

Published by PALH
Philippine American Literary House
P. O. Box 5099
Santa Monica, California 90409
USA
palhbooks.com; palh@aol.com

Library of Congress Control Number: 2002104406
ISBN 9780971945807 (softcover)
ISBN 9781953716002 (hardcover)

Contents

LOVE

HOME

Preface

I am happy to present *Growing Up Filipino: Stories for Young Adults*, a collection of twenty-nine stories by the same number of writers. Susan Montepio and I have collaborated on this book, I as collector and editor, and Susan as book producer and designer. This is not the first book Susan and I have worked on. As co-founders and members of PAWWA (Philippine American Women Writers and Artists), we edited and published two children's books and a Directory of Filipina Women Writers. In addition Susan, Edmundo Litton, and I worked on PAWWA's final book project, *Journey of 100 Years: Reflections on the Centennial of Philippine Independence.*

This time, Susan and I have thrown our energies into this book, which is published by PALH (Philippine American Literary House). Since 1995, PALH—a business that I own—has been engaged in making available select Philippine and Philippine American books and ephemera in the United States, primarily via the internet. *Growing Up Filipino: Stories for Young Adults* is PALH's first publication.

The idea of this book began with my earlier editing projects: *Fiction by Filipinos in America* and *Contemporary Fiction by Filipinos in America*. Editing those books was an extension of my own writing efforts. It had been my search of my "writer's voice" which made me realize the scarcity of Filipino American Literature, and which in turn led me to editing the two books. Now it is the realization that there is a scarcity of Filipino young adult books that has spurred me to edit and publish this book. I recall my own growing up and the only books available to me then where the Nancy Drew and Emily Loring type of books. While I enjoyed those books, I would have wanted books with Filipino protagonists, heroes and heroines who could have taught me how to negotiate life as a Filipina youth.

The readers of this book, as I see it, are not limited to Filipino (or Filipino American) young adults, but to those interested in the lives and negotiations that Filipino (or Filipino American) young adults have to make. Parents, teachers, and those who wish to recall their own coming-of-age will find the book a fascinating read. Most certainly the stories in this collection are as a whole sophisticated enough for an adult readership; it is the subject matter that defines more the book's category as "young adult." Those who know Filipino or Filipino American literature will recognize many of the contributors of the book, for indeed the book includes a fair number of established Filipino writers.

Special thanks to the contributors, Roger Buckley, Rocio Davis, Vince Gotera, Susan Montepio, Veronica Montes, and Marily Ysip Orosa.

Cecilia Manguerra Brainard

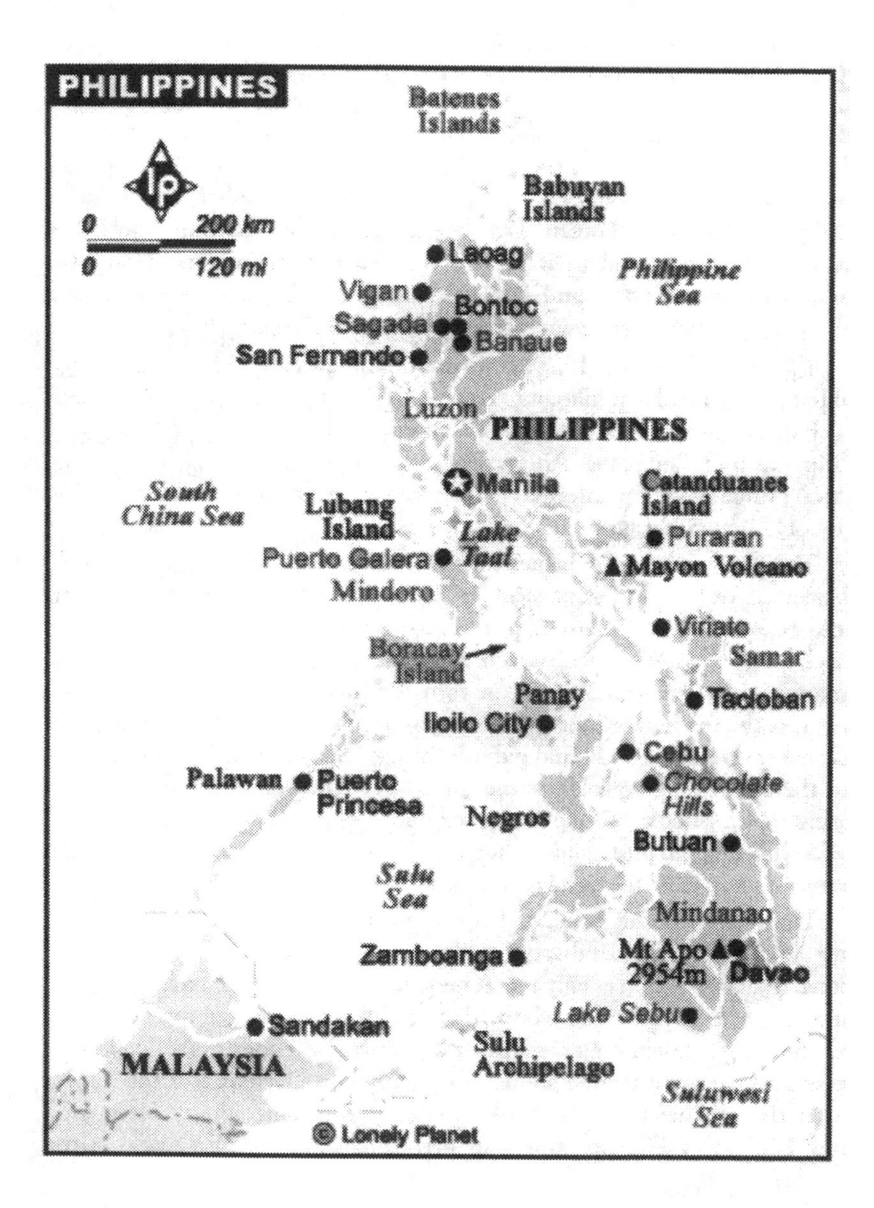
PHILIPPINES
Batenes Islands
0 200 km
0 120 mi
Babuyan Islands
Laoag
Philippine Sea
Vigan
Bontoc
Sagada
Banaue
San Fernando
Luzon
PHILIPPINES
Manila
Catanduanes Island
South China Sea
Lubang Island
Lake Taal
Puraran
Puerto Galera
Mayon Volcano
Mindoro
Viriato
Boracay Island
Samar
Panay
Tacloban
Iloilo City
Cebu
Palawan
Puerto Princesa
Chocolate Hills
Negros
Butuan
Sulu Sea
Mindanao
Zamboanga
Mt Apo 2954m
Davao
Lake Sebu
Sandakan
Sulu Archipelago
MALAYSIA
Suluwesi Sea
© Lonely Planet

Introduction

On the Edge: Paradigms of the Filipino and Filipino American *Bildungsroman*

— Rocio G. Davis

The process of establishing Filipino and Filipino American subjectivities from within—foregrounding creative imagination as a vital part of the process of self-identification—has reached a turning point clearly resonant with the phenomenological reality of the Filipino/American. Cecilia Manguerra Brainard's compilation of short stories for young adults addresses the layered complexity of Filipino and Filipino American writing that engages the definition and the process of growing up Filipino. This ground-breaking anthology invites the reader to immerse him or herself into the multifariousness of the Filipino experience, a palimpsest of races, religions, languages, customs, allegiances, and affiliations. The intense world of childhood and the passage into adulthood protagonizes these stories of family relationships, rites of passage, friendships, war and loss, adolescence, romance, sexual awakening, and immigration, disclosing the characters' haunting insecurities and reveling in moments of pure joy. In the contexts of traditional extended families, convent schools, rural villages, wartime cities and towns in Manila, and cosmopolitan settings in the United States, the protagonists of the stories undergo processes of maturity that involve self-identification and make choices that determine their positions. The stories repeatedly highlight diverse metaphors of Filipino-ness, as they suggest that growing up Filipino implies negotiating the consequences of history and family eccentricities, navigating cultural contingencies and personal choices, and enacting individual strategies of self-formation and self-representation.

The collection represents the scope and diversity—and, importantly, suggests renewed possibilities and an auspicious future—for Filipino/American writing today. As Sau-ling C. Wong points out in her recent review of Asian American literary anthologies, the current proliferation of specialized anthologies linked by genre or theme may be considered "a measure of the field's professionalization" (237); the addition of *Growing Up Filipino* to the group of existing anthologies of Filipino and Filipino American writing makes a significant statement on the vitality of the field.

The contributors to this volume—Filipinos and Filipino Americans, established writers and emerging voices—confirms the stimulating development and increasing maturity of Filipino and Filipino American writing in English, as each creatively engages the shifting ground between self and culture, questioning notions of purpose and belonging, using humor and pathos to formulate the nuances of the Filipino personality acting upon the world. Moreover, to publish writing by Filipinos and Filipino Americans in the same volume stresses the continuity of Filipino writing in English, and the emergence of mutually enhancing forms of discerning and articulating the Filipino experience. This strategy also highlights the fluid nature of the Filipino/Filipino American divide and allows individual writers to dialogue with the community of voices assembled by the anthology: the resulting polyphony offers a kaleidoscopic vision of the Filipino psyche.

The stories are driven by their writers' attempts to organize and make sense of personal and collective experiences that are often contradictory, vexing, and paradoxical. They repeatedly demonstrate how Filipinos cross the boundaries of unity and diversity to claim multiple and complementary relationships to distinct communities, languages, and cultures. As Eric Gamalinda points out in the introduction to another anthology of Filipino writing, *Flippin': Filipinos on America*:

> Philippine writing remains one of the most vibrant in the world, an on-going tradition that can no longer be contained by the strictures of language or even of geography: for Philippine literature is a complex, multifaceted, multilingual organism, written in various dialects (and in English) in the archipelago, in Australia, in Europe and America, by people who have never seen America, people who have never seen the Philippines, or people who have seen one or both, but who feel continually called upon to make sense of this unique and sometimes flabbergasting culture. (4)

These texts confirm Gamalinda's claim to the continuing resonance of writing by Filipinos, in particular through the appropriation and manipulation of metaphors specific to the Filipino/American experience. Relatives, rites of passage, food, and language are among the most loaded metaphors. By highlighting these metaphors, the writers construct texts that emphasize their own awareness of the multilayered nature of Filipinoness. In particular, for instance, the negotiation with the languages spoken by Filipinos and Filipino Americans becomes one of the recurring issues in many of these texts. Because of the critical position of language as a means of self-expression and empowerment, identifying the discursive realm as one of the terrains of oppression or personal insecurity or as a means for agency allows writers to successfully examine their protagonists' process of socialization.

Brainard's specific focus, narratives of childhood, makes this anthology an important contribution to the field by filling a space that was clamoring for recognition. This collection is the first anthology that focuses exclusively on children and adolescents, and is directed towards a young adult audience. By addressing the issues of childhood and adolescent culture, aside from ethnic affiliation, the anthology can also speak to a wider audience. The diverse stories demonstrate how the child archetype, one of the most recurrent themes for many important ethnic writers, can be a powerful means of defining the responses of a country's artistic minds to its evolving socio-cultural climate. Literary texts are emblematic of the structures that generate or manipulate meanings at specific historical moments, by presenting a larger critique of culture and ideology, of the manner in which the inscription of the experiences of particular children bear on or illustrate the development of contemporary societies. Texts that privilege the child character bear a special burden in negotiating the representations of the palimpsestic societies within which they are set. By collecting texts that span decades and cross oceans as they deal with the representation of childhood, this anthology highlights innovative or even subversive perceptions, approaches, and representations of the Filipino's necessarily transcultural identity. The stories collectively attest that the Filipino identity is not unitary—that it is in constant flux and is subject to being written and rewritten in literary terms. They also explore the fragmented nature of the Filipino collective self, as they examine the limits of history and ethnicity. The vision represented, in highly individual ways, consistently challenges accepted versions of the child character or the form of the child's involvement with the world. The manner in which the child's self is constituted and the process of meaning, therefore, stress the child's subjectivity, as determined by social formations, language, and political or personal contingencies. What is consistent across these stories is the manner in which considerations of the figure of the child, or the child as primary audience for the text, nuance our view of representations of society. The passage from subject to individual becomes a central theme for many of these texts, as the children begin to impose themselves upon the world, transforming themselves into active participants in their stories, protagonists of their own lives.

The engagement with childhood and the contingencies of history, ethnicity, family, and social class are highlighted by the stories' status as *Bildungsroman*, the classic narrative of formation, which, as Lisa Lowe argues, is "the primary form for narrating the development of the individual from youthful innocence to civilized maturity, the telos of which is the reconciliation of the individual with the social order" (98). The traditional *Bildungsroman* functions as a strategy for identification with the accepted social order and value system, as it chronicles the protagonist's assimilation of his or her society's values. The ethnic *Bildungsroman* departs dramatically from the traditional pattern, to engage the individual's process of awareness of particularity and difference, and the choice of identifying with or rejecting the models society offers. The stories in this collection manifest this singular approach: rather than merely appropriating accepted societal perspectives, the protagonists explore the nature and predicament of the child on the cusp of change. This renewed position postulates an identity that is self-defined, rather than merely a product of traditional influences; it makes reevaluation as important as learning. As such, these stories can also be read as strategic interventions in psychological or literary constructions of ethnicity, gender, and culture. The process of selfhood and the Filipino or Filipino American child's evolving subjectivity are the covert themes in much of this fiction, and the politics of identity and self-formation find in these writings fertile ground for discovery. The focus is on the process of becoming, rather than on the act of being; a program that cannot be divorced from the act of representation.

The recurring theme is evidenced in the title of the anthology: the stories are about "growing up." Interestingly, substituting the preposition with others multiplies meanings, and reflects some of the stories' central concerns, while challenging conventional limitations and exploring diverse themes and approaches. The stories in Brainard's anthology are not only about "growing up," but also importantly engage the process of "growing into" Filipino-ness, "growing with" Filipinos, and "growing in" or "growing away from" the Philippines. Two oftentimes complementary, but sometimes oppositional, processes are enacted in this anthology: the natural biological/psychological journey from childhood to adolescence to adulthood; and the process of becoming Filipino, awakening to and integrating the specificities of one's cultural milieu or heritage. If a literary revisitation of the time of childhood means, in a sense, re-creating that childhood, then revisiting the complex manifestations of Filipino culture as apprehended by a child or adolescent becomes a creative journey into identity and self-formation.

The twenty-nine stories in the anthology are divided into five sections, "Family," "Angst," "Friendship," "Love," and "Home." The first section explores a variety of family relationships and cultural norms and expectations. Grandparents are the focal point of several stories, such as

Paula Angeles's "Lola Sim's Handkerchief," where a sixteen-year-old Filipina American whose relationship with her grandmother had soured as she became more and more Americanized, chooses to keep only her grandmother's handkerchief after her death, a memento of their most harmonious moments together. In Libay Linsangan Cantor's "Tea and Empathy," a young girl recalls her grandmother's maid, who had taught her to drink tea and understand the insidious nature of class divisions. Veronica Montes's "Lolo's Bride" is a subtly humorous story about keeping up appearances, as the narrator's mother refuses to accept that her recently-widowed father has actually returned to the Philippines and come back to the U.S. with a new, very young wife. A young girl's true awakening comes in Marianne Villanueva's "Grandmother" when she understands her liminal position between her grandmother's frustration and her mother's tragic life. The experience of a deception played on an older relative is the theme of Ruby Enario Carlino's "Blue Fangipanis," where the narrator learns that her dying Aunt Julia has been tricked by a young man who has taken advantage of her loneliness. Complex family relationships are explored in both Linda Ty-Casper's war story, "In Place of Trees," and Gémino Abad's urban narrative, "Houseboy." These sophisticated stories center on young boys negotiating their family relationships, grief, and hidden secrets. Culture shock and inadaptability to the land of heritage characterizes Ricco Siasoco's "Deaf Mute," where an American-born boy about to go to college visits the Philippines for the first time and meets his family there.

The section entitled "Angst" suggests that loss, violence, and insecurity are constituents of the process of maturity. "Voice in the Hills," by Alfred Yuson, set in a rural village, recounts Bingo's several rites of passage: his circumcision, a growing awareness of the nature of violence, and lessons in loyalty. The violent nature of the racial divide that characterized the United States in the 1960s is the thematic center of both Vince Gotera's "Manny's Climb" and Oscar Peñaranda's "Day of the Butterfly," where groups of boys and young men, aware of the role of their race in their interactions with others, have to make decisions about where they stand. The effects of violence also surface in "*American Son* Epilogue," which begins where Brian Ascalon Roley's novel *American Son* ends. Here, the biracial adolescent Gabe negotiates the consequences of beating up a schoolboy, the lies he's told his mother, his brother's imprisonment, family and religious belief, and the hope for another chance to return to school. Alberto Florentino's young protagonist, Annette, in "Indian-Giver," cannot forgive God for taking her baby sister away. A mother's acceptance and support of her son's sexual orientation and his need to explore the limits of this choice is the theme of Joel Tan's "San Prancisco."

The stories in the section entitled "Friendship" highlight the idiosyncrasies of childhood or adolescent relationships, as well as the anguish and insecurity children feel. The need to be part of a group, to conform rather than to be different, becomes a driving force. Wanggo Gallaga's "The Purpose of Malls" is a slice-of-an-afternoon scene that reflects the pivotal position of the mall in the performance of Filipino adolescent's dating rituals, as well as the evanescent nature of those attachments. Gilda Cordero-Fernando's "The Eye of the Needle" and Cristina Pantoja Hidalgo's "The Magic Glasses" focus on young girls at school and their efforts to belong to the group. In the first story, the narrator allows herself to be blackmailed by another girl who threatens to tell the head nun about an episode of the former's "immodesty"; in the second, a girl experiments with strategies to become popular. Edgar Poma's story about differences in sexual orientation is set in a migrant camp and foregrounds the lives of the children of these workers. Mar V. Puatu's "It's a Gruen" centers on a boy's hero-worship of an older cousin, and the young adolescent's typical desire to be older.

The section entitled "Love" takes some of the issues of the previous one a step further by focusing on moments of defining relationships for the adolescent protagonists, and revising the question of attachment and identification. In M. Evelina Galang's "Her Wild American Self," the narrator recounts the story of her "wild" American-born aunt, who was sent back to the Philippines in disgrace, stressing a bond between them. In Cecilia Brainard's "Last Moon-Game of Summer," the narrator crosses the border between childhood games and adult relationships, knowing that things will never be the same. Marily Ysip Orosa's "The Curfew" is the interior monologue of a young mother who remembers dating as a young girl as she waits up for her daughter to come home from a prom. Though she promises herself that she will not commit the mistakes her own mother made, she finds herself falling into the trap. Consciousness of his lack of sophistication and his failure at speaking proper English does not prevent the protagonist of Anthony L. Tan's "Sweet Grapes, Sour Grapes," a village boy at University in the city, from dreaming about a popular girl. Ruth T. Sarreal's experimental story interrogates a protagonist on the nuances of relationships, and the reasons behind her choices.

The last section, "Home," focuses on specific metaphors and experiences peculiar to Filipinos in the Philippines, that make them reflect on attachment or being accustomed to a place. Rogelio Cruz's "Flooded," captures a typical experience after a typhoon, as Fritz and Jan try to make their way home after a flash flood in Manila. Connie Jan Maraan's "The Boundary" has the protagonist, a Filipina American living in the Philippines, contemplating the chasm between a Quiapo market and the sterile environment of an American hamburger chain, and reacting violently at the Filipino's obsession with American goods and mimicry of American accents. Alex Dean Bru's "The Spirits of Kanlanti" is a valedictory for one of the most important persons in a small town, the priest, told from the perspective of a young boy who later also joins the priesthood. In M. S. Sia's "Below the Belt," a biracial boy's friends come to his aid against another classmate who makes fun of him. Poor children singing carols in the streets, hoping for hand-outs from tourists evoke memories of his own childhood for a Filipino immigrant to Sydney returning to Manila with his wife in Erwin Cabucos's "I'll be Home for Christmas."

In diverse ways, the stories in this collection dialogue with Ricardo M. de Ungria's sentiments in his poem "Room for Time Passing": "Whichever side of the ocean I'm on / completeness will seek me and the world exceed / the surprises I spring on it with these same words." Negotiating the paradigms of cultural formation and singularity, these stories collectively identify and illuminate the metaphors writers today use to arrive at conclusions about the nature and possibilities of childhood within the multiple contexts of Filipino and Filipino American culture. Questions about self-representation are answered through narratives that articulate stories of survivors in a shifting world. The manner in which these writers have appropriated the child character and the characteristics of the *Bildungsroman* as a metaphor for the fragmentation and multiplicity of transcultural lives is itself an articulation of new awareness of subjectivity and the complex process towards self-identification. As such, the multiple impressionistic perspectives and formulation of the metaphors of culture emphasize possibilities of renewed insight into contemporary Filipino and Filipino American societies and children, engaged in the process of transformation and growth.

WORKS CITED

Gamalinda, Eric. "Myth, Memory, Myopia: Or, I May Be Brown But I Hear America Singin'." *Flippin': Filipinos on America*. Eds. Luis H. Francia and Eric Gamalinda. New York: The Asian American Writers' Workshop, 1996. 1-5.

Lowe, Lisa. *Immigrant Acts: On Asian American Cultural Politics*. Durham and London: Duke UP, 1996.

Wong, Sau-ling Cynthia. "Navigating Asian American Panethnic Anthologies." *A Resource Guide to Asian American Literature*. Eds. Sau-ling Cynthia Wong and Stephen H. Sumida. New York: The Modern Language Association, 2001. 235-251.

FAMILY

The present started a while ago,
long before men cried.

— Bienvenido N. Santos

Paula Angeles

Born 1973, Quezon City, Philippines; immigrated to the U.S. in 1986

About the Author

Paula Angeles has a degree in Secondary Education (English) from Temple University in Philadelphia, Pennsylvania. A self-proclaimed nomad and gourmand, she travels incessantly via land, sea, and air, all throughout the East Coast, West Coast, and Europe for the sheer pleasure of getting lost and eating regional delicacies. Her writings have appeared in *Disorient* 9 (2001).

Lively Philippine Markets

Even though there are modern supermarkets in the Philippines, the old-style markets called *palengke* continue to exist. These are huge sprawling areas that can accommodate numerous vendors' stalls. The old-fashioned market is not walled-in but has posts supporting roofing, usually of corrugated sheets. Some stalls are within this area, but more stalls spill out all around this central marketplace. This "open market" has different sections selling different things: fruits and vegetables, flowers, meat, fresh fish, dried fish, woven mats, clothing, slippers, grain, salt, seasoning, and let's not forget squawking chickens and live pigs. *Jeepneys*, pedicabs, and *tartanillas* hang around to take shoppers home. It's definitely a lively place where one must haggle—and watch one's purse because sometimes there are pickpockets in the area. In fact, for safekeeping, old-fashioned Filipinas will tie their money in a handkerchief and pin this small bundle inside their blouses next to their bosoms.

Lola Sim's Handkerchief

— Paula Angeles

When my Lola Sim, my mother's mother, died after my sixteenth birthday, no one wanted to open her armoire. After all, her death ended over fifty years of marriage with my grandfather. Our matriarch and patriarch endured volumes of life-shaping events: World War II, six children, my grandfather's long business trips, the diaspora of their children to places all over the globe, and finally, our family's reunification in America. Memories were crammed into the armoire, making it unbearable to look at during the days of mourning. No one wanted to touch it fearing it might open my grandfather's floodgates of tears.

Sometime after my grandmother was buried high atop a hill in Culver City, California, my mother, Lola Sim's eldest daughter, took it upon herself to clean out the armoire. For days, our relatives sat in our grandfather's apartment and divided the time between brooding quietly and reminiscing openly. But my mother had enough of the inaction.

"I know it's difficult," my mother Rebecca said to all who listened in the living room, "but we have to open her armoire someday. Her memories are in there. It's only right that we share them."

On the chosen morning, my mother, Aunt Rose, and I attended the opening ceremony. My grandfather, who could not join us, hung around the periphery. With much hesitation, we cracked the door open. The scent of loose make-up powder tinged with orange zest wafted and wrapped us. It was her scent. It felt as if she lived again. It was the same scent that clung to the green polyester dress she used to wear during sultry Novenas in the Philippines, Novenas which now hung prominently in front of the armoire. Yellowing pieces of paper with her scribbles, recipes, receipts, little notes she had given to her children and vice versa, slid to the floor. Boxes of unused So-en brand underwear were stacked five high. We craned our necks to view the landslide before us. My grandfather gasped and I turned just in time to see him walk out of the bedroom with a balled fist upon his lips. A loud sob escaped from him.

"*Hay naku*," my mother sighed and tried to laugh through the tears welling in her eyes. "Ma was a pack-rat, *talaga*."

It took a long time and much chattering, some happy, some sad, and some periods of heavy silence, for my mom and aunt to clean out their mother's closet. They recounted the stories behind the little objects they uncovered. The storytelling didn't end until dusk colored the sky outside. My mother chose some things including pictures and porcelain figurines. My Aunt Rose selected some articles of clothing and religious mementos. They then cautiously walked out of the bedroom, hiding their treasures in brown paper bags, for fear of upsetting my grandfather.

When my mother and I were finally alone, she asked me if I wanted to keep anything as a keepsake of my life with my grandmother.

I said no.

During my teenage years, my grandmother and I argued constantly, on subjects ranging from serious to trivial. We argued about my using the phone and my going-out privileges. We fought if I didn't want to help her cook. We fought when I watched television. Many of my recent memories of her were unpleasant.

"No," I repeated. I didn't want anything of hers.

"Are you sure?" my mom asked. "I'm sure she'd want you to have something."

Me? Have something of hers? I laughed.

My teenage years with my grandmother echoed with the volleys of words in our continuous argument game. One day, we had an especially heated argument about my wanting to go to the movies instead of helping her chop vegetables for dinner. She told me that even if I was one of her more accessible grandchildren, I wasn't one of the ones she liked. I was annoying, *matigas ang ulo*—hardheaded, disrespectful of elders, and Lola Sim threatened that my mother would hear about my horrible upbringing when she returned from work.

"No Filipino values anymore," she added. "You just came to America and made a few friends and now you think you can do whatever you want to do! The days of obedient granddaughters are gone," she said and walked away ensuring that she had the final word and the argument was now over. Still seething, I held my tongue and complained to my grandfather later.

"You know how she is," he explained. "She'll remind you that you're the eldest in your family and that you have certain things you have to do as *Ate*. Just do what she says and you'll be okay. Arguing will make her angrier at you and then you'll get nothing." There was something about the way he explained things that appeased my teenage soul unlike my grandmother's Vigan-Ilocana ways, forceful and single-minded. My grandfather's tone of voice and choice of words were diplomatic and not at all condescending, and they also carried sympathy, which was all I wanted.

"But it's not fair! I don't want to be *Ate* anymore if it means I have to give up my freedom to become her indentured servant. I didn't ask to be the oldest girl in the family," I whined.

"Ah, you can't do anything about that. Besides, you do have to pull your own weight around here. You can't have fun all the time," he explained. "Besides, *Ate* or not, you and your younger sister can do what you want as long as you know you what you're doing won't harm you. Just be good."

"Apparently, she doesn't trust me enough to be good while watching a movie with my friends. I'm not stupid," I sighed. It was then that my grandfather reached into his pocket, gave me money for a matinee and popcorn, and placed his index finger on his lips. At least someone in the family trusted me, I thought gratefully.

Afterwards, I went to my grandmother near the stove and helped her chop vegetables for *nilagang baka*: potatoes, carrots, and cabbage, while she cut the beef into cubes. She and I stood quietly beside each other, feeling the tendrils of our electric anger crisscross the air and then dissipate later with the sound of knives on the chopping boards. We normally ended our arguments this way—allowing the anger to dissipate and never talking about it again. It wasn't exactly closure.

My mind was swirling with all these thoughts when something caught my eye on my mom's pile of mementos. It was a neatly folded, thread-worn, plaid handkerchief under some of my grandmother's rosaries. It was pink and green, a horrendous color combination, with embroidered scalloped edges in an off-green thread. The color had faded over the years; some spots had turned white. I was much, much younger the last time I had seen that handkerchief. Six years old? Five? I rummaged through my memories. I knew it was back in the Philippines when I had last seen that handkerchief. I remembered seeing my grandmother's wiry, salt-and-pepper hair under that handkerchief on the hot afternoons she walked home after Wednesday Novenas. I recalled that handkerchief poking out of her dress pockets when she pulled out change to pay the jeepney driver for our fare to and from the *palengke*.

Lola Sim insisted on taking me to the market. I couldn't carry very many things for her. I hated the *palengke* mud as it crusted on my rubber slippers. Once there, I quickly grew impatient while she haggled with the vegetable vendors. Her haggling always lasted longer than my curiosity over the neatly piled, meaty chayote or jiggling tofu that lay before me. My squirming and whining forced her to settle for prices higher than what she wanted.

But there was a fascinating parade of many wonderful things in the market: prickly fruit; smooth-skinned fruit; wrinkle-skinned vegetables; sucking black mud with the distinct smell of rotting vegetation mingling with the sweet smell from cauldrons of shelled peanuts frying in oil and garlic; active, entrepreneurial boys around my age peddling plastic bags, flashing me toothy smiles. There were many times I caught her staring at me while I stood entranced at the visions before me. I thought the *palengke* was a magical place.

On one market day, we passed by neatly piled rows of cantaloupes and mangoes of different sizes and colors. My steps slowed as I looked at the tower of cantaloupes, wondering how the fruit vendors piled round fruit one on top of the other without the whole thing collapsing. My grandmother stopped, sensed my interest, and began to inspect one pile. She picked up a cantaloupe and sniffed the depression where the stem was once attached. I grabbed a cantaloupe and mimicked her, needing both hands to lift it.

"You see, you sniff the little hole here to find out if it's ripe. If it smells nice and sweet, it's ready to eat." She gave the cantaloupe hole a little squeeze with her thumb.

I smelled the greenish hole on the cantaloupe in my hands. I thought it smelled sweet enough, hinting of the golden flesh underneath. "Is this good?" I asked my grandmother as she returned the one she held back into the pile.

Her eyes brightened as she gave a quick sniff. "This is a good one. We'll turn this into a drink later. You know, if you keep on picking good fruits and vegetables, I think you might be helping me cook soon enough." My grandmother gave me the cantaloupe, fully paid for now, to carry.

At the market, or anywhere for that matter, there was no escape from the tropical Philippine heat. Sweat made my T-shirt stick uncomfortably to my skinny brown back while I carried small bags of produce. My grandmother would always take her pink handkerchief and sandwich it between my shirt and skin, so that only a little edge of the pink plaid showed on the back of my shirt. Yes, that was the one, the utilitarian handkerchief! When we got home, our house-servants scuttled about, putting away the food we had bought. Then I was shooed away from the kitchen, while my grandmother lectured that the blue flames from the propane gas stove were dangerous for curious little girls. I was very pleased with myself for the remainder of that day.

Soon after, she and my grandfather left for the United States, leaving their children and grandchildren behind. When she and I saw each other again, years later, I was already a headstrong teenager with cooking skills not worth a lick. And my grandmother and I did not see eye-to-eye.

With my mother beside me, I stared hard at the plaid handkerchief, the same handkerchief that lived many days stuck to my skin, drenched with my sweat, neatly tucked by my grandmother's knobby fingers at a distant open-air market many years ago and many thousands of miles away. Since then, the pink handkerchief had probably spent most of its time under the pile of rosaries in my grandmother's armoire. The last time I had seen that handkerchief, Lola Sim had looked upon me with approval and I was young and unschooled at throwing angry words at her. We had loads of fun at the market. She sparked my first curiosity about food, a curiosity that I still cultivate.

"Your Lola would really want you to have something," my mother repeated.

I took a breath. "Fine! I'll take that pink thing," I said, spilling pictures on the floor as I roughly grabbed the handkerchief. I walked away from my mom, placed the faded pink handkerchief in my pocket and smiled.

(2001)

Libay Linsangan Cantor

Born 1973, Quezon City, Philippines

About the Author

Libay Linsangan Cantor's real name is Olivia. She has a B.A. in Film from the University of the Philippines, where she is in the master's program in Creative Writing. Libay won two Carlos Palanca literary awards for her Filipino fiction in 1997. She also received an honorable mention award at the annual scriptwriting competition of the Film Development Foundation of the Philippines in 1998.

Libay served as the entertainment editor of the political tabloid *Pinoy Times* from September 2000 until it closed in December 2001. She is a freelance writer/editor/film reviewer/editorial consultant for several lifestyle and entertainment magazines, newspapers and web-zines. She is also an occasional director/scriptwriter/editor of video documentaries and corporate audiovisual productions.

In June 1999, Libay co-founded the U.P. Sappho Society, the first university-based lesbian organization in the Philippines, focusing on lesbian rights advocacy and student support in the University of the Philippines Diliman campus. Her position is the head of networking and promotions, representing the organization as an active member of Task Force Pride, a network of gay and lesbian organizations in the Philippines.

Household Help

"Tea and Empathy" started as a creative nonfiction piece about tea-drinking but evolved into a fictional story about a maid and her employers' child. It is set in Metro Manila, which is seen as a "place of hope" by the people in the provinces. They flock to Manila, the supposed land of dreams, jobs, and money, but not everyone succeeds. In the absence of lucrative jobs, many poor families end up placing their daughters and sons (aged 13 and up) as servants in middle- and upper-class Manila homes. These young servants generally become part of the families of their employers. To show respect, the children of the household call them *ate* (older sister) or *kuya* (older brother).

Tea and Empathy

— Libay Linsangan Cantor

I grew up in a house surrounded by plants. My Lola was the one who had the green thumb in the family. My dad wasn't around much; too busy at the office to play with me. Same thing with my mom. Me, I had a very curious hand, using my grandmother's garden as my pretend-market where I "bought" my veggies for the day. That was how I played when I was eight—no sister, no brother, always alone. I would pick leaves of different sizes and colors and harvest any weird-looking fruit from any of the weird-leafed bushes. I would then "cook" my harvest in my small *palayok* and other miniature terracotta cooking toys.

One of my favorite bushes was the small, spindly one that grew near the gate. The bush had small, round fruits the size of peppercorns; the leaves were pointed. I had fun playing with the leaves and more fun playing with the green fruit. I observed that the green fruit turned yellow as it ripened. When it was truly ripe, it became orange, the shade of sunset.

One day, our maid Teresa joined me when I was playing. She pointed out the different leaves, blades of grass, and fruits and taught me their names. She grew up in a farm in Ilocos Sur, which was why she knew all their names. She told me that my favorite weird bush was a tea plant. *Tsaa 'yan, eh*—That's tea. I thought she was speaking in Chinese, but she explained that tea is a drink that comes from plants. She said the leaves are the important part, not the fruit. She then picked some leaves and put them in a glass of water. *Ganito yan, tsaa, 'pag nagkakulay, iinumin na*—When tea gets this color, drink it. But Ate Teresa explained that was not the usual way it was done in the city. Tea, as we knew it, came in bags, and the bags were the ones you put in the water. That was my introduction to the world of tea.

I found all this fascinating, and every chance I had, I tagged along with Ate Teresa. I especially liked it when one of my aunts would ask her to make a cup of tea. My aunts always insisted that Ate Teresa prepare the tea because she was the best tea-maker.

In the kitchen, I would watch carefully as she steeped tea leaves in hot water. She'd pour the steaming golden liquid into a cup. Later, she'd drop a sugar cube in the cup, place the cup on a saucer, place a teaspoon and a lemon slice on the saucer, and the tea was ready for serving. There were no spills, ever, no mess whatsoever. I sometimes wondered if the other maids could make good tea like Ate Teresa. I decided that they probably couldn't, because Ate Teresa was special.

At that time, I thought tea—like coffee—was for adults only. This misconception started when I saw my grandmother scold Ate Teresa for buying the wrong item from the grocery. Lola was shouting at her, insisting that she read the label on the package. My hefty Lola's voice boomed. Ate Teresa's small frame trembled with fear. "*L-li-m-mon te-i-yaa . . .*"—Ate Teresa struggled to read the label but couldn't. She had never learned how to read English. My Lola shouted louder. I felt sorry for Ate Teresa, and I wanted to help her. I wanted to shout, "lemon tea, lemon tea!" Instead, my Lola shouted, "Lemon tea! *Tsaa 'yan! Sabi ko,* juice—That's tea, I told you to buy juice!"

My Lola was furious because I needed juice for my *baon* the next day. She sent Ate Teresa back to the store to get the juice. My strict Lola always displayed her bad temper to the servants, and nobody ever questioned her about it. I wanted to say something to her; I wanted to protest her unjust scolding of Ate Teresa, but I could not speak. All I could do was look at Ate Teresa, and ask her to play with me in the garden. I asked her to identify plants again; and we went from plant to plant, very sadly.

For some reason, that episode left me with the impression that children should never, ever drink tea. It was only when I was sixteen that I changed my mind.

In high school, I had a best friend, Christine, who was addicted to Wendy's lemon iced tea. Going to Wendy's was exciting because that meant we didn't have class and we were free to roam around on our own. One day, I accompanied Christine to the Wendy's branch in Cubao near Fiesta Carnival. She ordered two glasses of iced tea, part of the famous Wendy's double-iced-tea promo where you get one glass for free every time you order one. She gave me the second glass. Instantly I remember my Lola scolding Ate Teresa. I looked at the tea and squirmed at the idea of drinking an adult drink.

"Mmm, *sarap*. Lisa, try it. It's good. Very refreshing."

"Eecchh . . . tea? With ice? Isn't this supposed to be served hot only?"

"*Loka*! This is iced tea. Wendy's is famous for this. Come on, try it."

"Eechh, Christine, are you sure?"

"*Sige na*! Trust me. This is good, Lisa! Drink it!"

I liked Christine and so I did. The tea was rather sweet. What surprised me was that it wasn't as bad as I thought it would be. I actually enjoyed the lemon twist taste. It wasn't hard at all to gulp down this "new" beverage. It was great with french fries. And from then on, I was hooked. I never passed up the opportunity to drink iced tea. But always, whenever I looked at that cup of tea, I would remember Ate Teresa.

She continued working at my Lola's house, even after my parents and I moved out of that house and into our own. We visited Lola only during the Christmas holidays. I saw less and less of Ate Teresa, and I didn't even notice when exactly she left my grandmother's house. Years passed, and I learned she got pregnant by a man who wouldn't marry her. She was back in her hometown of Vigan and having a difficult time.

I was terribly sad when I learned this. I wished I could help, but I didn't know where exactly she lived. I had failed her when I was a child, and now I found myself in the same helpless position. All I could give this woman who took care of me when I was a lonely child, was empathy.

(2000)

Veronica Montes

Born 1967, San Francisco, California

About the Author

Raised in the Bay Area, Veronica Montes continues to live there with her husband, Andrew Wadhams, and their three daughters. She has a B.A. in English Literature from San Francisco State University (1988). Her short fiction has appeared in *Prism International* (Vol. 30, No. 2, Winter 1992), *Furious Fictions* (Fall 1992-Winter 1993), and *Contemporary Fiction by Filipinos in America* (Anvil, 1997). She was Corporate Writer for Banana Republic (1987-1989) and has been a freelance writer for a variety of museums, visitor centers, and retailers from 1994 to the present.

Filipino American Family

At my Lolo and Lola's small home in Daly City, California, certain things could be counted on: an abundance of food (naturally), a visitor or two from the Philippines, the fact that you would be forced against your will to sing in front of everyone, and—best of all—an ongoing undercurrent of drama provided by the strong, sometimes overwhelming personalities of certain women in my family. These adult dramas were none of my business, of course, but much to my nosy delight, I discovered that with a little subtle sleuthing I could unearth secret histories and family lore. This story is not autobiographical, but it did grow out of my eventual realization that though many things went unspoken in my Filipino American family, very little was private.

Lolo's Bride

— Veronica Montes

After my grandmother died, Lolo Ting spent three months blinking. He blinked slowly and frequently, as if thinking hard. He blinked twice before answering simple questions like "how are you?" and four or five times before tackling the more difficult ones like "where are you going?" Without the visual weight of Lola standing beside him, Lolo looked as if he might blow away on the slightest breeze.

As far as I could tell, blinking was all he did. He just blinked and looked small and one day, while I shared a french dip sandwich with him at The Roast House in the mall, I saw a pregnant woman's eyes fill with tears at the sight of him.

My mother does not like interruptions, but I took a chance and told her about the teary pregnant woman. Though she was staring intently into the mirror while plucking her eyebrows, she seemed to listen. "Crying? Why was she crying?" she asked. She said this not to me, but to my reflection.

"She was crying," I answered, "because it makes people sad to look at him." Then after awhile, "It makes me sad, too."

She didn't say anything else, but I could see her mind clicking away as she continued to pluck, pluck, pluck.

I didn't mention that besides making me sad, the whole situation embarrassed me. Not only was I fifteen years old and still not allowed to wear make-up, but keeping Lolo company forced me to endure even more taunting from the girls who wore cherries-in-the-snow lipstick and all the right clothes. "That your boyfriend?" they'd hiss as Lolo and I walked past. "Isn't he a little old for you?" This was always followed by an eruption of giggles that echoed in my ears for hours and followed me right to bed each night.

Soon, my mother had Lolo Ting's faded plaid wing chair and portable electric heater moved into our living room, and he was duly situated in the guestroom where he muttered obscenities to himself and looked stepped-upon. I knew he would never stand up to her because with my mother, as with any terrifying opponent, it is easier to submit than to fight. In the mornings, my father would read the weather report and Dear Abby out loud, and Lolo would nod and blink while eating dry toast. His hair, which popped up all over, made him look like a crazy person, so I stood behind his chair and patted it down. I don't think he ever noticed.

My mother pretends it never happened, but it did.

When I was eight years old, my dad left us without saying when he'd be back. After a week, my mother often forgot to pick me up at school and rarely left her room, so Lolo and Lola came to take care of me. They cautioned me in urgent whispers not to bother her, but one night I slipped into my mother's room and sat beside the bed, watching.

She was sleeping, but breathing in fits and tossing her head from side to side. Then suddenly she opened her eyes and locked them directly on mine.

"Mommy?" I said. "Why did Daddy go away?"

She shut her eyes. "Because you're boring," she said.

I began to cry, but she had nothing more to add.

Two weeks later, my dad came home tan and fat, and we all went about our business.

Lolo Ting allowed my mother to dress him, monitor his diet, and brush crumbs from his face for nearly a year before he broached the subject of a trip to the Philippines. "It's been fifty years since mango jam and *pan de sal*," he said. Then, like a poet, he added, "Since *santol* trees and *kundiman*."

"How long would you be gone?" my mother asked. She masked her annoyance by switching television stations furiously from the local news to public television, and then to music videos and Spanish-speaking programming.

"Eight weeks *lang*, sweetheart," Lolo said.

My mother let the matter float about unresolved until a big family dinner a few days later where, via stern looks and banging pots, she ordered her five brothers to voice their reservations about Lolo's trip. And for the first time that I could remember, they failed to comply with her wishes. Mommy scooped rice onto Lolo's plate. "Why do you have to go by yourself? Who do you know there? This is ridiculous. Who's left?"

We turned to him as one, our eyebrows raised. Lolo, prepared for the assault, cleared his throat and rattled off a list of cousins and cronies we had never, ever heard mentioned before. When he finished, it was quiet except for the dull sound of feet kicking beneath the table. My cousin Rica accidentally hit me hard in the shin and then apologized to someone else by mistake. Her boyfriend, who was sitting beside her, has skin the color of coffee with just the right amount of cream. If she were not my cousin, she would laugh at me at the mall.

After the footwork subsided, the not-so-silent silence broke. Brave Uncle Gregorio, my mother's youngest brother, said, "Great, Dad. I think that's great." And to my mother's horror, the others concurred.

That was two months ago and now my mother, my dad, and I are riding in our maroon minivan to greet Lolo Ting at the airport. Upon arrival, I see we're not the only people with this idea. Apparently everyone's Lolo was on an eight-week-trip to Negros Island. The fact that there are only three of us, while other people have brought along up to fifteen family members, makes me feel more like a loser than usual. "Stand up straight," my mother says. "What's wrong with you?" Out of the corner of my eye I see two airport security guards, one blond and the other red-haired, elbowing each other in that get-a-load-of-this way. There are little kids picking their noses; boys my age with hickey-covered necks; mothers clutching fake designer bags and looking down their noses at one another's children; fathers napping with their arms crossed over their chests; and, of course, the girls who roll their eyes at me because I am wearing a shirt with a collar instead of a scoop neck.

When the plane finally arrives, there is a rush towards the doors that lead out of Customs. It is a pointless move because before we even see any of the passengers, they need to claim their baggage and then chat for a bit with the Customs officials. This is the moment I realize that though my Lolo was gone for only two months, there are people who have waited years to greet this plane. Some of them are bouncing on the balls of their feet, checking their lipstick and touching their hair, clutching handkerchiefs, wailing softly.

I am the first one to see Lolo Ting, and because the sight of him renders me speechless, I just point.

"Oh my God," my mother says. She says it so loud that other people look at us. Lolo's hair is curly.

He has a thin moustache.

He's wearing tortoise-shell sunglasses.

And jeans.

And a San Miguel Beer T-shirt.

And (fake) Air Jordan sneakers.

"What is this?" my mother demands, putting a hand on Lolo's head. "What in the world did you do?"

"Oh, sweetheart, so many things," Lolo says, misunderstanding the question. He kisses her on the cheek. "But let's talk later."

"Lolo," I say, "she means what did you do to your hair and stuff?"

Lolo laughs and turns to look at a young woman who is standing behind him. Her dark skin is marked with pock scars, so I can't imagine what reason she has to smile, but she's smiling. She wears a long cotton skirt, dark pantyhose, and red plastic slippers crowned with large cloth daisies. She smells like baby lotion.

The young woman is called Cora. My mother clasps her hands together like a thrilled child and beams. "A maid? A maid! Are her papers in order?"

My dad and I look at each other and wonder why what is obvious to the two of us should be so blissfully unclear to my mother. Perhaps she is too busy envisioning herself enjoying *Ladies Home Journal* while Cora vacuums the bedrooms, steams fish, folds laundry, and disinfects the toilet. The silence that follows affords an opportunity to correct my mother's mistake, but no one does.

Cora is not offended. She walks behind us dragging Lolo's heavy carry-on bag along the floor, and my mother sneaks looks at other moms to make sure they realize that she has a maid, a live maid, in her employ.

On the drive home, I buckle myself in beside Cora and whisper, "How old are you?"

"Twenty years old, miss."

When we get home from the airport, my mother tells me to set up a makeshift bedroom for Cora. In the garage.

I drag my old twin bed into the space, being sure to place it as far away from the garbage cans as possible. I fashion a bedside table out of some boxes, and I cover them with a flowered tablecloth. Out of desperation, I grab some daisies from the yard and put them in a glass. I do my best.

"My God, she'll freeze in here," my dad says when I'm done. He looks around and shakes his head.

"Don't be a fool," my mother snaps. "It's probably better than what she had at home." She points at the sheets and looks at Cora, who steps over the oil spot in the middle of the floor and begins to make up the bed.

Lolo just shrugs and walks back into the house.

For two weeks, Cora dutifully sleeps in the garage and does everything my mother tells her to do. After that, she only *pretends* to sleep in the garage. And because Cora continues to follow orders, my mother pretends right along.

Cora can cook.

In the morning, she makes a plump omelet stuffed with sautéed potatoes, which Lolo says his mother used to make when he was a boy. For dinner, Cora makes *palabok* and *bistek* and *sinigang* and the kitchen smells like garlic and ginger, always. At every meal, she sets a little bowl of raw tomatoes and onions beside Lolo's plate. When she splashes it with fish sauce he smiles and says "*Salamat*, Cora." Thank you.

Cora will often squeeze my shoulder or gently tug my ponytail before retreating to the kitchen, where my mother insists she eats. Like Lolo, I smile. But I don't say my thank you out loud.

She only cooks jasmine rice, the scent of which promises, but never delivers, something far more exotic than the simple white grain that actually appears in the pot.

"Cora, why don't you just make plain rice?" I say.

"This was my mother's favorite," she answers. "She used to say it smells like angel's tears."

"Did you love your mother?"

"Dearly," she says.

I lift the lid off the rice cooker and let the steam hit my face.

At the next big family dinner, my uncles' girlfriends and all my aunties pile into the kitchen as usual to help slice and chop and gossip. My cousins like to stand outside and sneak cigarettes. Though it's my house, there never seems to be a place for me, so I sit patiently at the dining room table, waiting for the kitchen door to swing open so I can hear a bit of laughter or someone singing. My mother, who used to be at the center of it all, won't go in. Instead, she gives herself a manicure in the living room while the men watch football.

"You don't have to stay cooped up in the kitchen, Irene," Mommy says loudly to Uncle Gregorio's fiancée, who has emerged to set the table. Mommy blows on her wet thumbnail and surveys it at arm's length. "We have Cora now."

I find most silences uncomfortable, but this one is different. This one is right. Uncle Hector, who is a troublemaker, presses the mute button on the remote control so as to emphasize the absolute quiet. The men all look at one another.

"What?" my mother says. "What's going on?"

"For God's sake, Tess," Uncle Gregorio says. He looks at Lolo.

"For God's sake what?"

Uncle Hector is trying not to laugh. My dad hangs his head. Uncle Gregorio braces himself. Uncle Pidio puts his hand over his mouth. Another uncle leaves. Another one pretends nothing is going on and continues to stare at the television.

I'd like to grab a fork from Irene and throw it at my mother because the wide-eyed, innocent look on her face is too much to bear. But instead I'm biting down on my lower lip. I count to three, swallow hard and then, still sitting, I say, "Cora is Lolo's wife. His *wife*. Okay?" I say it slowly, as if delivering bad medical news.

Everyone looks at me, but nobody says anything. My father shakes his head to make me stop, but it's too late.

"I beg your pardon!" my mother screams. "What did you say, young lady? What did you just say?" She gets up from the couch yelling in rapid-fire Tagalog and waving her nail file in the air.

Doesn't she know I can't understand a word she's saying? I get up from the table and I calmly tell her. "Sorry, Mommy," I say. "I don't understand you."

(2002)

Marianne Villanueva

Born 1958, Manila, Philippines; immigrated *to the U.S. in 1980*

About the Author

Marianne Villanueva lives in the San Francisco Bay Area with her husband and son. Her short fiction has appeared in *The Three-penny Review, ZYZZYVA, The Literary Review, Puerto del Sol,* and several anthologies, including *Contemporary Fiction by Filipinos in America* (Anvil, 1998) and *Tilting The Continent* (New Rivers Press, 2000). Her short story, "Silence," was a finalist for the 2000 O. Henry Literature Prize.

Genesis of a Story

I wrote this piece very quickly, in the late '80s, when my son wasn't even in pre-school. At that time, I was a stay-at-home mom. Going to parks with my son, I noticed that the only other adults in the park would be young Asian, Hispanic, or African-American women. The children these young women were looking after were all white. It started me thinking about who was watching these young women's children, if they had any.

At that time, my sister in New York had just had her first child, and she was able to bring our cook from Manila to help her care for the baby. Our cook left two little boys at home so that she could go to New York to help my sister.

I thought about these women, and what they had to give up. I thought, too, of the children left back home in the Philippines. Out of these various thoughts, I crafted this story.

Grandmother

— Marianne Villanueva

They say my mother is crazy. They say she married my father when he was just eighteen and she was already an older woman of thirty-two. They say my father was no good, that he stole. He was in jail once, for stealing from a rich widow in San Pablo. My grandmother says, what did my mother have to get married for? She had a good job as a cook with a rich family in Manila. But she came home one year for vacation, met my father, and then had me.

My grandmother says my father was a devil. Where he came from, no one knows. He walked into town, barefoot, in the middle of the dry season. One of his eyes was all black, as though there were a hole there instead of an eye. He passed my mother as she was drawing water from the pump. She stared at him. From then on, my grandmother says, my mother couldn't get enough of him.

My grandmother says she tried to warn my mother, but my mother was stubborn. My grandmother and my mother fought about my father all the time, until finally my mother took my father with her to Manila, to work for the rich family. But they caught him stealing one day and threw him out. My mother followed because she was pregnant with my younger brother.

My grandmother is very old. Her face is dark and wrinkled, and if she were not my grandmother I would even say that she is ugly. The veins on the backs of her hands are like tree roots. Her eyes have a milky-white film over the black parts. She moves slowly, because of her lame foot, but she is still strong. Every day she sweeps the yard with her broom of wooden bristles, and takes our clothes down to the river where she washes them, slapping them against the smooth stones. We are afraid of her hard hands. Even when we are far away we hear her voice, sharp and angry, arguing with the neighbors. When she calls us for our supper, we know we have to come running, or she will twist our ears and perhaps give us a slap or two.

Before we came, she lived by herself in her one-room nipa hut way off the edge of San Ysidro. She doesn't even go into town much—only on market days—and even then she has a scowl on her face. I sometimes wonder why she is always so angry, but then I tell myself she can't help it; it is because she is thinking of my mother. Every day I hear her muttering my mother's name to herself. At times she spits it out like a curse.

My younger brother Ipe, who my grandmother says looks so much like my father, is always hungry. She doesn't give him as much food as she gives me. Ipe says he will run away as soon as he gets a little bigger. He says he saw our father once, standing behind the mango tree at the back of our hut. This man had one black eye and feet that were wide and flat, like lily pads. He called to Ipe and Ipe would have gone, only just then a big black dog came along and Ipe, remembering what my grandmother says about such animals, got scared and ran instead to the hut where my grandmother was cooking rice. When he told grandmother about the man, she grew angrier than she always is and grabbed her big wooden spoon—the one that she uses to ladle out soup—and said she would hit my father over the head with it if he came any nearer. Then she wouldn't let Ipe go out anymore, but kept him by her side all day, with her rosary around her neck as though to ward off some evil.

I know my father is dead, but I don't tell Ipe. They say it happened a long time ago, before Ipe could even walk. It was the time of the last drought, when there was no food and my mother had just left us to look for work in Manila. They say my father got into a fight with a man from the next town and that man stuck my father in the back with a big *bolo*. Then, since no one liked my father, they left him in the middle of the street until he died. They say he took a long time, and just before he went, he got to his feet, arched his back, and gave a howl that reached all the way to Cavite. Afterward, his back remained arched and no one could straighten him out enough to fit into a coffin. So they simply dug a hole in the ground and left him there.

People have started to say things about my mother—about why she has not come back to San Ysidro for so long. They say she has taken up with another man, that she has left Manila and now works in a bar in Olongapo, where the American servicemen are. They say she is touched in the head, man-crazy. It all began when she was fifteen and her first *nobyo*, the one she probably would have been happy with, the townspeople say, was struck by lightning as he was coming home from working in the fields. He was burnt black, as black as the statue of the Nazarene in the main altar of the parish church. Afterward, when my mother took up with my father, who had that one black eye, they said the ghost of her first lover was still haunting her, that she could never get over him.

I hear all these things from my grandmother. I wonder how she knows what she does, but I am afraid to ask. My grandmother, too, has no husband. Or maybe she had one once, but it was too long ago to make any difference. There are many women like her in the town, women whose husbands have left them to work in the big city, and whose children seem to spring—bones, skin, hair, and all—entirely from their mother's loins.

Yet my grandmother was a good mother. She was the one who watched over my mother when she nearly lost her mind over her young man, when he was struck by lightning. People said my mother couldn't be left alone, that she had to be watched day and night, because she had almost succeeded in drowning herself in the river. Then my grandmother brought my mother to an *herbolario* who made my mother lie down on a table and pulled bushels and bushels of dried brown leaves out of my mother's mouth, and after that my mother began to get much better. She stopped talking about her dead *nobyo* and found a good job in the city and my grandmother had no more trouble from her for many years.

That is why this thing with my father was so bad. My grandmother did not like my father at all, not at all. But what could she do? The more my grandmother talked about my father, the less my mother listened, until finally it was as if my grandmother were nothing but a rock or a tree, that was how little attention my mother paid her. My grandmother says that when my mother wanted a man, she was like someone under a spell. Her breath always came a little faster, she grew pale, she even gave off a smell. If you have seen the stray dogs wandering around our village, how they behave when they are in heat, going around all day rubbing against posts and scratching themselves, that was how my mother would be.

That was how she was when I was little, a very long time ago, before I even heard that my father had died. We were already living with my grandmother then, and my mother was going around San Ysidro in tight jeans and high heels, powdering her face even for trips to the pump. At Mass no one sat beside us in the pews, nor did my mother ask for the priest's blessing as we filed in front of him before leaving the church.

Nights were hard. My mother and grandmother would fight. They always stood outside the hut when they thought we were sleeping. But I would creep to the window and look out, and I would see them in the yard under the mango tree. It was mostly my grandmother who did the talking at such times. I tried to hear what she was saying, but even when I could hear, the words had no meaning. What did I know of such words, words like "morals" and "virtue" and "piety," words that could hurt my mother? Evil words—words that made my mother stoop, as though there were a great weight pressing on her back. Afterward, my mother would lie down on the mat beside me, and I would carefully pat the curve of her back, feeling the thin bones beneath her duster, and know that she was crying.

Now she has gone away again, back to the big city. Now when I go into town, people look at me and shake their heads. I see their lips form words: "Poor girl." It is as though they think my mother is not coming back. They say my grandmother is angry because my mother has stopped sending money. I used to see thin, pale blue envelopes, so light they seemed to be filled with air, behind the portrait of the Sacred Heart of Jesus on the shelf. Now nothing is there, and my grandmother beats Ipe almost everyday. Ipe cries, makes his hand a fist, and presses it against his mouth. Afterward, he will sit in the mango tree and look out over the fields. I hear him saying, as if to our father, "Come and get me. I am ready now."

(1991)

Linda Ty-Casper

Born 1931, Manila, Philippines; immigrated *to the U.S. in 1956*

About the Author

Linda Ty-Casper has published fifteen books including the historical novel *DreamEden* and the political novels *Awaiting Trespass*, *Wings of Stone*, *A Small Party in a Garden*, and *Fortress in the Plaza*. She has also published three collections of short stories which present a cross-section of Filipino society. In 1993, "Tides and Near Occasions of Love" won the Philippine P.E.N. short story prize; another at the UNESCO International Writers' Day, London; and the SEAWrite Award in Bangkok. "Triptych for a Ruined Altar" was in the Roll of Honor of *The Best American Short Stories*, 1977. She lives in Massachusetts and is an officer of The Boston Authors Club, founded in 1900. Her degrees are from the University of the Philippines and Harvard.

World War II

World War II in the Pacific began on December 7, 1941 with Japan's surprise attack on Pearl Harbor and the Philippines. Manila was declared an Open City but, daily, sirens signaled air attacks. As hopes failed, fuel and ammunition supplies were destroyed. Amid the chaos, the defenders and Commonwealth President Manuel Quezon withdrew to Corregidor and Bataan which fell in 1942. Soldiers died in the Death March and in concentration camps, from forced labor in Japanese mines. Civilians succumbed to brutalities, starvation and disease. The tide turned in October 1944 when General Douglas MacArthur and then Commonwealth President Sergio Osmeña landed in Leyte. In February 1945, Manila was liberated. In April 1946 elections were held. On July 4, 1946 the Philippine Republic was inaugurated, the first in Asia.

But the War and Occupation had changed the lives of the people and that of the country. The experience of lawlessness and violence and, in order to survive, of self-interest above national interest, gradually replaced genuine liberty with corrupting political license, requiring radical honesty to return the country to the prewar guidelines of principles, loyalty and honor.

In Place of Trees

— Linda Ty-Casper

He came out of the sun, onto the porch, with the shadows white on his dark face. "Where's your father, Boy," he asked, without telling me who he was, not making way for the woman who stood behind him on the lower step, a large man's watch on her right arm.

"He's not here," I answered, staring at him, challenging him to know my name.

"Your mother?"

I ignored his question. I was the only one home and I was wondering if I could grapple him to the floor if he forced his way. The war had just ended and houses left standing in Manila were being broken into during the day. Before the war, we never locked our doors.

Looking at my knee pants (I was not yet fourteen) the man took a step forward, allowing the woman to stand beside him on the porch. His face was long, too lean for his short body. It was easy to see that he would get fat again; that his dull skin would become shiny like that of wine proprietors.

"May I sit down?" the woman asked, after placing herself deep in the green wicker chair. She was wearing mauve canvas shoes, the kind being distributed by American relief agencies. Too big for her and obviously similarly acquired, her dress was a heavy black cloth beaded in front and at the pockets. My mother at least had the pride to make over the dresses she got from UNRRA.

After she sat down, how could I ask them to leave? They might have seen my mother leave—every Friday she and my sisters walked to Quiapo to visit the Black Nazarene and kiss its hand—knew I was alone, and had come to steal. They were now too far apart for me to watch their faces at the same time. I concentrated on him, searching for a distinguishing mark I could describe to the police. Acne pitted his neck with scars that looked like beach sand drying. The sleeves of his khaki jacket—surplus American Army uniforms were being peddled on sidewalks—reached halfway down his stubby fingers. I wondered where to hit him to repel his attack.

"There used to be a *kamachile* tree in that corner." The man turned to the front yard where months before antiaircraft and machine gun shells lay scattered like strange seeds. Several neighbors were hit. In places our roof was pierced. The sound of the corrugated iron tearing was the magnified screech of dog-fights in the sky.

"Yes, I remember," the woman said. "You're right." Then she turned to face the other corner. "Was there not a *mabolo* there? No. It was a paradise tree with sweet pulpy fruit."

How could they have known? Firewood was scarce during the Japanese occupation and, branch by branch, our trees were being hacked. We would wake up to find fresh sap dripping from wounded trunks and more sky visible from the windows, so that my mother decided to cut down the trees to sell at the gate in small bundles. Kindling was saved for our stove. . . How could they know these? Nothing remained of the trees, for we even dug the roots.

"And there was a guava tree in back, with small white fruits and pink seeds," the man said walking to the end of the porch to look around.

I felt displaced when they began talking about my brothers, wondering when they came back from Bataan, comparing them to their own sons and remembering how they all played together as children and how they fought. I could not recall the things they remembered about us. They could have been making it up, I thought, part of their game to make me trust.

But I knew my brothers went to war. Late in December of '41 we waited outside Intramuros until the red and black buses took them to the battle lines just before the Japanese entered Manila which had been declared an open city. I no longer recalled their names easily. It seemed so long ago since I called them Ben and Floro. The first time they went off to training camp they brought back stories about eating unwashed rice and burnt meat that floated in the sauce like beetles. Each time, they had returned blacked by the sun and hungry; but they learned to shoot, to clean and unlock real guns. At R.O.T.C. they had only wooden replicas to drill with.

While the sun shaped the man's ears, outlining them against the sky, I recalled that my brothers sat humped in the back of the bus that was taking them to war; that they smiled but did not wave; that I wished I were going with them. Everyone being left behind was crying. Their raised hands, intending to wave, clawed the air. When I raised my hand as my brothers' bus found its place in the long line, I found I was still holding on to the chicken *adobo* that was to be their *baon* in the war. We walked back slowly across the river. My mother appeared dazed walking on the Colgante that swung over the waterlilies flowing towards Manila Bay. The sun seemed to float on the round leaves.

Distracted by my memories I had failed to see the visitors move to the chairs set against the house. Could their accomplice have entered through the back porch? Without asking me to confirm their stories, the two mentioned the green sofa and the curtains my mother sewed, the Philco above which hung my parents' wedding pictures, almost life-size in their pose, their teeth hidden behind their smiles.

The man suddenly stood to walk to the top of the steps. Only then did I see my mother and my sisters at the gate.

My mother who no longer entered through the front porch hesitated. Her veil covered her narrow shoulders. The holes enlarged by sunlight made her look as if her hair had fallen off in those spots.

"Miguel. I'm Miguel! Don't you recognize me?" The man spread his arms out: but her stare stopped him from going down to where she stood. Dropping both arms to his sides, he looked back at the woman in the porch.

My sisters stood behind my mother, holding on to their prayer books covered with Manila paper to save the binding. Eleven and twelve, they stood almost as tall as my mother. Thick braids hung alongside their necks like heavy strings of beads.

Not wishing to be impolite, still trying to place the man's claim, my mother went up the steps of the porch halting as if she were the visitor. I could tell she could not recognize them as relatives for she did not ask us to kiss their hands; but eyes startled, she said, "I'm sorry I have nothing to offer you to eat."

"I understand," the woman said, smoothing the dark dress over her knees. "It's too soon to expect things to be good again." Then poised to reach, her hand finally pulled back and she held it on her lap. "I, too, had a devotion to the Black Nazarene," she smiled at my sisters who had followed up the steps. "It was He who saved Miguel from the war. Every Friday, I walked on my knees to the altar, not stopping to rest even once. But now my legs are weak." She stretched out her right leg, bent down to press it at the ankle. Her finger left a reddish indentation there. "Could I have a glass of water?"

Before my mother could reply, Alicia, the younger one named after my grandmother from Porac, went inside the house and soon returned with a glass neither sparkling nor cold. The icebox was the first thing sold during the war. In it we had cooled sarsaparilla for unexpected guests. On warm nights we shared a bottle while we sat on that porch, inhaling the *champaca* whose petals were still tightly curled after falling to the ground. I missed the odor of sawdust on which the block of ice rested, catching the drippings. I missed many things.

The woman drank half the glass, which she then gave to the man who drank the rest promptly. "Water is so scarce, it's a shame to waste a drop. Where we rent now there is no water in the pipes. Where do you get water?" She sounded simple and artless.

"Fermin fetches four cans in the morning. From the artesian well. Again in the evening." My mother looked up at me. I could not tell whether she took this opportunity to blame me for the visit, or to commend my efforts. Bullies were beginning to charge for the right to line up at the well, and there were no policemen.

"I came to see Antonio," the man cut through the small talk. He now sat on the edge of his chair. Like dark flowers, the leaves of the vine that bore neither fruit nor flowers dropped their shadow between his feet.

"Our house in Paco was burned. We are now renting a room at Callejon de la Fe." The woman pulled out a handkerchief from her pocket.

The man sat farther forward. "I want to rent a room."

"Not for us," the woman added. "But to use as his office. Miguel was a guerrilla, you know. He was called 'Colonel' by his men and they asked him to work for their recognition by the American army." She lifted her body proudly up, sitting taller than he. "Here, he can prepare their claims. I'm happy your house survived the war."

"The sooner we are recognized, the better. Fake guerrillas who never left Manila, who even bought and sold war materials, have put in their claims. As I see it, America knows exactly how many helped defeat the Japanese. If the fake ones get ahead, those who really served will lose out." At this he hung his head and waited for my mother's reply.

It did not come. Though she had been listening carefully, she could not decide without my father, who was in Porac to save the coconut trees his parents left him when they died in the war. My mother, who expressed an opinion on very few things, refused to sell the house and return with all of us to Porac. "Wait at least until the children have finished their education." It was a sly refusal to leave for it would take Alicia fifteen years to become a doctor. Anita who liked to read was to become a teacher. I was to be an engineer.

The man and the woman waited silently for the answer. They avoided each other's eyes, as if they wanted to save each other from my mother's decision.

Finally, my mother found the words she wanted to say: "Antonio is not here. He will return in two months." Then she looked down on the floor, which had dried and splintered by being long unpainted.

The woman dropped her shoulders and the beaded dress sagged with her body. The man reduced his plea for room. "Just this porch. The men will not enter the house. You can keep that door locked. Only this porch and I will pay thirty pesos a month."

The offer made my mother lift her head. Everyone turned.

She had always wanted me to study at the Mapua Institute of Technology, but until the coconut crop there was no money for tuition. "Only until Antonio returns," she said without smiling, a sigh escaping from her as if the decision was a rope being pulled out of her.

I did not question her decision, although it was not mine. Her character had always been enough to support our conscience.

"Is he in Porac?" the woman asked. "His mother, Mana Agusta, used to have us for vacations in her farm. I remember . . ."

Looking away from the woman and the man, my mother began to cry large solid tears that made her eyes bulge. "Stella," she called out.

The two held on to each other in the porch. Their dark clothes joined them as tightly as sap glued fighting beetles together back to back while children bet on which one would get itself upright and carry the other on its back. Mother broke away to ask, "Did you kiss your aunt's and uncle's hands?"

"He already has," the man said, sparing me the act of humbling myself before I was ready for it.

Instead of being grateful, I was angry that he would speak for me, and lie.

"If it were Stella who had said she was your cousin, I would have recognized them," my mother was telling my father as they sat in the green wicker chairs in the front porch. "But it was he who said he is your cousin. Besides, you would not have recognized either one of them yourself."

My father rarely claimed relatives. When the Americans were liberating Manila from Lingayen and fighting was expected in our neighborhood, he still refused to evacuate to Taft Avenue where his own brother lived. Luckily for us, he stalled: for that was one of the places where Japanese soldiers burned people out of their homes, using flame-throwers on those who ran out. My uncle's family died that way.

Though his eyes were almost asleep, my father sat with us on the porch. It had taken him three days on an open boat—mostly standing by day, at night squeezed between the cargo—to come home from Porac. As if storing up our company for the next months when he would be away, he listened to us telling him what happened while he was away. I kept myself awake by listening to my sisters dropping cowrie shells on the *chongca* board, laughing whenever the other's last shell landed into an empty hole.

Without trees, the moon looked abandoned in the sky. On such nights before the war, we played in the streets, kicking an empty can of milk, or playing tag or *piko*. But during the war, Japanese soldiers stood guard at street-corners. Their heavy boots kept us awake at night.

During the day, the sentries forced people to bow low from the waist, even the old and women; as many times as would make them collapse. One day, searching for those who had escaped from Bataan and had become guerrillas, the Japanese brought the men in our street to the schoolhouse. My twin brother and I saw bodies hanging from the acacia tree where, before the war, flag ceremonies were held on Mondays. When I close my eyes, sometimes I still see the drops of blood below the men's feet.

Now the street was very quiet. People had no time to talk and visit neighbors. Everyone was trying to accumulate again what they had lost. I walked down to the yard, which was kept clear of grass. To keep the men from walking on that part of the yard, my mother had planted a garden of *rosals* and *sampaguita*, *azucena* and *pitimini*. Nothing ornamental, but flowers with sweet odors.

My mother walked down to where I stood. My father followed and both of them stood beside me, as if we were all there were in the world.

The light was falling softly, falling like rain where the earth was gently mounded.

"They will not step on the flowers, will they?" she asked my father. Then she began to cry, speaking my brothers' names. "I don't even know where they lie buried . . . "

Moved by what was happening, I offered to go to Porac with my father. "I don't have to go to school."

"No." My mother stopped crying. "No. Your father and I have had our lives and we must prepare for yours. I could also go to Porac but that will be the end of our dreams. The war took so much already . . . "

"Time will pass quickly," my father said. "I will come home every three months. We will not be long separated. If only the war did not come. If only the Japanese . . ." Like my mother, he spoke of the war that had just ended as if it was the source of everything that touched our lives.

I remained in the yard after they left to go inside, hand in hand with my sisters. Trying to fix a purpose in my life, to deserve my parents' sacrifices, all I could sense were shadows although the moon, having climbed as high as it could, was very bright. All their hopes in their sons had to be fulfilled in me, and I did not know if my character was strong enough for the burden.

At first it was only the Colonel and two men, and on the first day they brought an old desk as large as a bed with two drawers missing. They dragged it as if pulling a bull *carabao* by the horn. After it was carried up the porch steps, they could not decide where to place it. Finally, they centered it against the front door and there, in a swivel chair that did not match, the Colonel sat down to wait.

We referred to him as the Colonel, because he gave himself so much importance; and to deny the arrangement any hint of kinship or support. My brothers died in the war, yet we did not intend to make any claim for them. "My sons died for their country," my father said to those who suggested he accept payment for their lives. "I will not ask America for money."

While the arrangement had its novelty, my sisters walked slowly to and from the gate to watch the two men dusting the desk. They made a ritual of opening the drawers each morning, taking out pen and ink holder to center on the desk. By the time the Colonel arrived, the two had moved the swivel chair several times. The two also struggled over the right to open the gate for the Colonel, to take his briefcase, a battered one containing the Colonel's lunch which he shared with the two.

Other men started coming. My sisters saw them signing papers, taking oaths right there on our front porch. They lounged on the steps, stood about whispering or smoking American cigarettes. Some looked ill. One fainted in the yard and my mother brewed him ginger tea and lent him a blanket, because he shook from the chills in midday. He said he was in the Death March to Capas.

We soon enough got used to hearing strangers talking in our front porch, and stopped paying them any attention. But the man who fell ill often came around to the back porch. From him we learned what was happening. Noting the slow progress of my mother's garden in the front yard, he offered some tufts of Bermuda grass and, himself, planted these in the ground that was so hard it could hardly absorb the rain. Only later did he tell us he had taken the grass from the Chinese cemetery.

Intrigued by the scar on his chin, I finally asked him how he got it. A Japanese officer, he said, shot him in the face when he fell while being marched to a concentration camp after the fall of Corregidor, then Bataan.

Before we knew it, the Colonel had a jeep and a driver. Taller and younger men who spoke only English in the clipped accents of radio announcers flanked him constantly. They arrived and left with him. More men were coming. We could not close the windows to their laughter. My mother thought of erecting a fence along the front walk so they would not step on her garden. I was to strip bamboo for the fence.

One afternoon while I was stripping a length of bamboo with an army knife, the Colonel came to the back porch surrounded by his aides. His face was shiny. His cap was freshly braided and there were insignias on his shoulder straps. Proudly he offered my mother the use of his jeep and driver. "Don't hesitate." He urged her. "Any time I'm not using it."

Overwhelmed by this generosity, my mother started to brew coffee; but the Colonel said they were going out to Dewey Boulevard—across from the American Embassy—for coffee and sandwiches. "Stella is looking for a house to buy," he said.

Hearing this, my mother's face darkened. The rent was sending me to school, but she managed to ask, "How is Stella?" Then not knowing what else to say to someone so important that he always looked displeased, she offered coffee once more.

"Not too bad," the Colonel shrugged off my mother's concern. "Some days are better than others." A lot of things could be inferred from the remark, but the Colonel did not specify. He went on to list the day's schedule. "Today, back to Malacañang to see the President; then to Camp Crame, after that to JUSMAG . . . " his voice trailed off into a yawn. Then he saw me, "How's the Boy?"

"He's doing well," my mother answered. I let her speak for me, in case she wanted an opportunity to ask about the rent. She did. "When you buy a house, you will be moving away . . . ?"

The Colonel touched the end of his cigar to the heel of one shoe. A flake at a time, the ash fell; forming a small heap on the back porch. "Not at all. This place is good luck for me. We'll soon be recognized as a unit. A mere matter of days. Even hours. In fact I may know today. Tell Antonio to file his papers with me. I'll vouch for him. It's only fair for what you lost in the war."

"You are very kind," my mother said, without appearing to be grateful.

"One thing more, Cousin," the Colonel turned from walking away. "Perhaps you will let me stretch a piece of canvas from the front porch to the fence so the men can wait in the shade. I will have your flowers moved to the side of the house. My men will be careful."

My mother remained where she was standing, but to me it seemed as if she had run. Her eyes were bright and wet. Not able to speak, she turned around and pulled me to where she stood, strengthening herself with my body.

The Colonel took off his cap, trying to absolve himself for making her cry. "But it's only a garden. Tell the men where you wish to move it."

Looking at his aides, he smiled as if he had humored someone who was being unreasonable.

"My brother is buried there." I spoke head on, without bothering to consider if it was right to share my mother's secret. She had placed no cross on the mounded earth so the authorities, unaware of the grave, would not order my brother to be moved from our yard. I realized then, that it was not I, nor my sisters who kept my mother in that house.

"I didn't know." The Colonel put on his cap and, stepping on the ashes he had been dropping on the floor, left quickly with a trail of aides.

My mother did not turn to see them leave. She remained against me, holding me; but I knew it was my brother she was trying to hold as she had held him where he fell, struck by shrapnel in the front yard. I remember the way she had looked up at the uncovered sky, saying in a voice that asked for judgment, "If I had not cut down the trees . . . "

She had called me to get a priest, but my father would not let me go. His arms were strong about me when I struggled. She held my brother until his wound no longer bled, while shrapnel and empty shells continued falling; until my father took Justo from her, and with my help, buried him in place of the trees.

Though he was not able to get his shade, the Colonel added five pesos to the rent. His unit was not recognized that day, but it was as imminent as daybreak. More men came, willing to sign away part of their impending backpay. To ensure recognition important officials were being taken to nightclubs and bars, showered with imposing gifts—all paid for by the men's contributions.

While the Colonel's success was assured, we were begrudged our slight hopes. The first crop failed. My father had worked too long in Manila, teaching history in Mapa High, to know how to run his parent's farm. I began dreaming of giant beetles that blighted tree after tree after tree. Also, the army camp where I worked, from which we got fresh bread and butter in green cans, was being closed since the American soldiers were returning home or moving on to occupy Japan. I decided to ask the Colonel for help. With all the officials he knew, he could recommend me for a job. It was time to humble myself.

Then, no sooner did a thought occur to me than I acted upon it. With no clear idea of how to make the request or where to stand, I sought the Colonel in the front porch.

I was surprised to see the Colonel at the desk because his jeep was not parked by the gate. Only a handful of men were in the porch.

"Boy, how did you find out?" The Colonel's eyes were smudged with dust when he looked at me.

I turned to the men for clues, but they all looked away.

"I paid as much as the other units, threw as many parties. My aides, you saw them yourself, looked as smart as the best. Why then did we not get recognition? I love my country even more than the next man. If the Japanese had ordered me to haul down the flag, I would have refused quicker than Claudio, preferring to be shot." He turned in his swivel chair, keeping the arc of his movement tight. "The ones who knew me are dead. I helped blow the bridge at Santarem just as the Japanese were marching across, but the lieutenant who led us got killed there. How can I prove it, Boy?"

He said more things, cursing the men who abandoned him for other units. Words tumbled out of his mouth with such bitterness that he had to belch.

I stayed, out of respect, half listening and thinking of the opportunity I had lost by not asking for the favor while it was still in his power to grant.

The next day I expected the Colonel not to come anymore. But he did. So did the man who fell ill in the yard. For some time, every day, the Colonel continued to come, wearing his insignias and shoulder straps. The two spent those days in the front porch, their faces worn and silent, whispering some conspiratorial dreams; and I, passing, walked by as quietly as I could, trying not to disturb their hopes.

(1980s)

Ricco Villanueva Siasoco

Born 1972, Des Moines, Iowa

About the Author

Ricco Villanueva Siasoco received his M.FA. from the Bennington Writing Seminars (2001). He has a B.S. in Broadcasting and Film from Boston University (1994). His fiction and nonfiction have appeared in the *North American Review, Flyway Literary Review, The Boston Globe, The Boston Phoenix, The Milwaukee Journal-Sentinel,* and the anthology *Take Out: Queer Writing from Asian Pacific America* (Asian American Writers' Workshop, 2001). In 1998, he was selected to be a P.E.N./New England Discovery writer. He has received fellowships and awards from The L.E.F. Foundation, the Fine Arts Work Center in Provincetown, and the Institute of Asian American Studies. Ricco teaches writing at Boston College, and is finishing a collection of short stories.

Balikbayan

The term *Balikbayan* was coined when the many Filipino immigrants to the United States started visiting the Philippines, the land of their birth. *Balikbayan* literally means "Return to Your Country."

When I began working on "Deaf Mute," I was thinking about the Filipino notion of the *Balikbayan.* As an American-born Filipino, the idea of "returning home" always seemed strange to me. Where is home? What connections do second-generation Americans form with their parents' homeland? How do we "return" to a place we've never seen, much less experienced? At the time I wrote this story, in 1999, I had written a few other stories with these same characters, a middle-class family in Boston. In "Deaf Mute," I decided to focus on Noel, the youngest child. The idea of a *Balikbayan* seemed an interesting way to force this typical American teenager out of his relatively complacent environment—in which his personal problems were his only concern—and into a foreign place, where his daily life would consist of more than the usual teenage American angst.

Deaf Mute

— Ricco Villanueva Siasoco

Nancy had said the best fish and pork were sold five blocks from the Cathedral of the Immaculate Conception, so Noel Borgos followed his mother, his Tito Mario, and his teenage cousins Nancy and Claudine as they weaved through the wet, narrow aisles of the markets at Baclaran. Every so often a stray cat, thin and sickly but scavenging the rot left in the alleys, would dart from beneath a display of cheap handbags, splash in a puddle at Noel's feet, and then disappear just as rapidly beneath a table across the aisle.

Noel wiped the sweat from his forehead with his shirt sleeve. "How much further is it?" he asked. Nancy rolled her eyes. She was a slender girl who wore her long black hair in braids and, like Noel, had just graduated from high school.

"It's behind the Pizza Hut. *Naku*, you whine a lot."

Noel hated his cousin's smugness. She was less confident than pushy, he'd decided, like the gum-smacking girls in his graduating class; it was a trait he recognized in many of the Filipinos he'd met here in Manila, the cockiness that masked uncertainty. A few paces ahead, Nancy wrapped her arm around Claudine's waist. Claudine—shorter and heavier than her sister, with a thick melony face and horn-rimmed glasses—leaned into Nancy. The older girl whispered into Claudine's ear and they laughed.

Tito Mario made a guttural sound at Noel's mother, Teresa, and they waved at a dainty woman across the aisle. Noel's uncle was deaf, and signed to his sister with sharp, tossing gestures as if he were throwing unwanted items—spent lottery tickets or orange peels—on the ground. Teresa looked back at Noel and smiled.

Noel followed his relatives past a long row of vendors selling countless bolts of fabric, displayed on end like oversized crayons. It was both exotic and strangely familiar, and seemed to Noel to typify Manila in mid-July. Here he was, his first trip outside the U.S., traveling in the brief summer months between graduation and his first semester at Princeton. Before he'd arrived with his mother, he had imagined lilting palm trees, white-sand beaches, and grilled yellowfin steaks with mango salsa. That was what he hoped for, and what his single mother could not provide on her meager nurse's income: fine dining and expensive resorts; a trip to Europe instead of a *balikbayan* trip to the Philippines. Now that he had lived in the hard grip of Manila for a week, Noel realized how his notions had been flawed: before he arrived, he had always pictured objects, never people. The reality of the Philippines was, more than anything else, throngs and throngs of look-alike people. Brown arms, brown faces, hair wiry as his and dark as the Charles River at night. Beside a vendor hawking Chiclets and fragrant *sampaguita* necklaces, he watched his mother and Tito Mario bargain with strangers across the aisle. Mario pointed at a leather belt looped around a high bar, while his mother counted peso bills and sniped at her brother in Tagalog. He watched with strong indifference, as if he were watching a documentary in civics class. Around them, other Filipinos clamored for the attention of the vendor. Noel felt ordinary. In Boston there were other Asian kids, of course, but not in the multitudes he'd experienced in the Philippines. Here, he thought, touching a carved wooden spoon on a table, he looked exactly like everyone else. No white kids around to provide contrast or fill the space around him like Styrofoam peanuts.

His mother purchased the leather belt for her brother and trotted ahead. Noel hurried to catch up to her.

"Do you know where we're going?" Noel asked.

His mother scowled, "I lived here for thirty years, Noel. I haven't lost all of my memory."

Teresa approached a fat, bearded vendor behind a table of dead fish. Melting ice dripped from the corners of the table into the street.

"Tatay doesn't like to serve guests seafood. He thinks it's dirty." Nancy stood behind Noel and leaned collegially on his shoulder.

"Then why's he letting Mom buy it?"

"He can't control her anymore. She's too American now." Nancy pulled her sister closer. His cousins hovered on both sides of him, breathing lightly on his neck.

"Tita Teresa says Daddy always used to smell like fish. She called him her little *bangus*," Claudine added. In the shadow of a canopy, his mother and Tito Mario argued with the fishmonger. "*Bangus?*" Noel said, without looking at his cousins.

"Milkfish," laughed Claudine. "Don't you know any Tagalog?"

He smiled. His cousins reached around him and locked hands. Nancy pulled her portly young sister to her side and they ran up to Teresa and pointed out a purple spade-headed squid. Tito Mario whined, his lean-muscled arms crossed over his chest. Teresa nodded quickly at the vendor.

He reached across the table with great puffing noises, wrapping the fresh *bangus* and squid in the front page of *The Philippine Star.*

Tito Mario walked up to Noel and tugged the hem of his shirt. He signed angrily and made stunted, nasal sentences, but Noel couldn't understand.

"Why do you call Tito Mario a deaf mute, Mom? Isn't it just deaf?"

She looked at Noel as if he'd uttered an obscenity. "That's just what we called them, 'deaf mutes.' It's not meant negatively."

Teresa zipped her clear make-up bag and placed it on a *narra* bench at the foot of Nancy and Claudine's bed. Noel tipped his chair against the wall of the girls' bedroom, which they had cleaned and vacated for Noel and his mother.

Had he offended her? He knew his mother would sulk for days without saying a word, until he left a drawer open or a jar lid unscrewed, then explode in a careless rage. Just as well. Lately he had taken her moodiness as opportunity for sinking into daydreams about Chad Kline, the curly-haired captain of the wrestling team. He removed a soft black CD case from his backpack, and placed it on the painted dresser.

Noel looked over at his mother. "But he's not mute. He can speak—sort of."

"Ay, Noel. Don't ask me so many questions."

Teresa slipped through the thin mosquito net covering the bed and lay down. She rested her palm on her forehead, her elbow pointing at the low ceiling.

Noel chose a CD of deep house music and then wrapped his ear-held headphones around the back of his head. He pulled his chair up to the window and pushed "Play." The Hondas and crowded jeepneys were bumper-to-bumper along Roxas Boulevard. In the middle of the road a tricycle taxi with thin streamers flying from the antenna wedged itself between trucks. Noel closed his eyes and tried to feel the groove of the electronic music over the mid-morning traffic. With his own stereo in Boston, it would have been easy. But a week had passed since he and his mother sat on the floor of their living room, listening to the expensive speakers he'd set up in the four corners of the room. His mother had purchased a huge cardboard box with the word BALIKBAYAN printed in angled letters on four sides and was packing it on their colorful Himalayan rug. She was a small woman—a midget's wife, his brother-in-law Thomas joked—with dark, permed hair and a certain aloofness toward waiters and cashiers that embarrassed Noel. Scattered on the floor, Teresa had collected small plastic eggs containing pantyhose, dozens of bargain-bin lipsticks, reflective pencils and pens, and several 12-ounce bags of M&Ms.

"Why are you packing all this crap?" Noel had asked.

"It's not crap! This is *pasalubong.*"

She scowled, then opened a package of pastel-colored M&Ms and put Noel to work. He divided the candy into Ziploc bags while his mother wrote the names of his relatives on pieces of masking tape, and attached them to each bag. To Noel, the handwritten names were like generic "Hello, My Name Is" tags.

"This *pasalubong* is for your relatives. Tito Mario and his girls love knick-knacks; I haven't seen them in twenty years! It's tradition." Noel had packed his suitcase with items for his cousins as well: crisp new Levi's he intended to sell for a profit.

Filipinos had never struck Noel as people with tradition. The large Brazilian family that lived in the triple decker across the street, sure, but Filipinos? His mother and her girlfriends made greasy egg rolls or thick deviled eggs, and held potlucks to which they dragged their husbands and children on American holidays like Thanksgiving and the Fourth of July. On those occasions, they laughed at the same Tagalog jokes until dusk settled over them like a fine mist, and Noel was called to set kerosene lamps on the shaky railing of the Borgos's porch. Now he removed his headphones and stood in front of the window, inhaling the exhaust fumes and scent of fried bananas from the sidewalk in front of the house. What was Chad Kline doing right now? The time difference was exactly seventeen hours from Boston, and he imagined the red-haired boy at some party with a wine cooler to his lips, talking to another wrestler about their summer jobs.

His mother snored loudly. Nancy and Claudine shared a queen-sized bed, as had Tito Mario and his mother, in this same dilapidated room. Noel parted the mosquito net and sat on the edge of the mattress beside her. The heat and noise from the boulevard exhausted him.

He closed his eyes. A few minutes passed before Claudine knocked meekly on the open door. "Tatay asked for your assistance in the garden. Are you sleeping?"

He sighed. His mother rolled onto her stomach and mumbled for him to go. It was one of her tests, he knew. Either he heeded her wish or added to her long list of impertinences. What my father always taught us, she repeated when she was angry at him or his sister Maribel, was respect your elders. And then she would give in, unable to resist his attempt to make her smile. "You and Maribel never listen. When you were born, the doctor turned you over and stamped 'Made in the USA' on your *puwet.*"

Noel got up, tied the laces of his ragged sneakers, and followed Claudine down the back stairs to his uncle's scrubby garden.

The numbers were easiest to understand. When Tito Mario held out his hand and counted backward from three, both men lifted the heavy oil drum in the middle of the garden and carried it to an alley outside Mario's glass-sharded walls. Noel had difficulty putting together Mario's words, though before he left Maribel had showed him simple phrases like "How are you?" and "I am ready for bed." Noel had decided that reading his uncle's emotions—his withdrawn blankness, bright eyes, or tightly clenched fists—was easier than learning sign language.

He liked his uncle. Tito Mario was small and cagey, like his mother (Noel, on the other hand, was tall and studied, with careful gestures and an often-embarrassed face), though his Tito Mario also had a childlike whimsy that Noel admired. Once, unprovoked, he howled at an orange blimp in the hazy midday sky. When Noel's cousins opened their umbrellas and complained of the relentless heat, he tickled them until the two girls laughed. He guessed Mario was in his early fifties, a few years younger than his mother, and he knew he had maintained the pristine lawns at the Manila Country Club ever since his wife had left him and the girls a dozen years earlier. Nancy was the one who had kept Teresa Borgos apprised of her brother's life, and had kept the house together when Mario's wife fled with his best friend. Tito Mario was a stubborn man; he and his mother possessed the same proud chin and tight-lipped smile as their eight siblings, who seemed to stare at Noel each time he descended the back stairs of the family's crumbling, Spanish-style villa.

Now his uncle stood in a narrow sluice between hedges and motioned for Noel to come closer. He held the young man on the back and pointed to a withered bush. "Pull it out?" Noel asked, mock-pulling the bush with two hands.

His uncle shook his hands "no" and grimaced. He crouched down and lifted a long branch. On the tip was a single, dried-out leaf, brittle and yellow on the underside. Noel was hot and wanted to lie down.

"You want me to water it, Tito?"

Mario grabbed the boy by the wrist and pulled him to the clay ground. He squinted at the spot where his Tito Mario pointed a dirty fingernail. At the origin of the dead leaf, a delicate green bud was beginning to emerge. Tito Mario held Noel's wrist, silently meeting his eyes. Noel now wondered how to praise his uncle's careful work.

His mother called to him from an upper window. Tito Mario gave him a friendly push, and Noel ran up the stairs and joined his mother in the bedroom. His shirt clung to his chest, and he pulled it off and changed into a clean one while his mother scolded him from beneath the mosquito net. "He was trying to explain his dreams to you for the garden. You weren't listening." It seemed like a stupid thing for his mother to say.

In Tito Mario's humid kitchen, the whirring of electric fans—one slotted into the windowsill and one in the long cement hall—and Nancy's quiet knife-chopping made the afternoon feel languid and soft. Noel sat at the round plastic table and ate homemade pork rinds, watching Priscilla, the family's maid, stir a steaming pot on the stove. Behind her, Claudine labored over the sink, scaling his mother's *bangus*. In the way Claudine pressed Priscilla's arm to pass by her, he sensed the girl's affection for the age-spotted maid and conversely, Priscilla's amiable independence. His mother had told him that Priscilla had been with them since his Lolo and Lola—Noel's grandparents—had given birth to Mario. Then she remembered a tearful Priscilla on the day she left for the airport, holding out a bag of floury *polvoron* candy for Teresa during her long journey to the States. Noel had never met his Lolo or Lola. Old people were oddities to him, as disparate from his experience as a monsoon in December. Nancy and Claudine, however, were at ease with Priscilla, and Noel felt suddenly ashamed of the starched Levi's he'd planned to sell to his cousins for a profit.

Tito Mario banged the flimsy screen door. He'd been working in the clumpy garden the remainder of the afternoon, and his tank top hung like a dishrag from his back pocket. With another sharp cry he yelled at Claudine, who found a juice glass and filled it with water for her father. The bare-chested man drank noisily. When he was finished, he handed her the glass (she was waiting), and signed brusquely to her. Noel thought he was beginning to recognize patterns, certain chin-to-chest motions that kept recurring in his uncle's speech. Claudine frowned. She held the glass in her right hand. "But Tita Teresa asked . . . "

Her father hit her square across the cheek, the empty glass shattering as it hit the floor. Tito Mario scowled as he pushed the door open and returned to the fenced yard.

Nancy quickly moved to her sister, picking up the large shards in front of the refrigerator. Noel watched them silently. He wanted to be with his friends on the other side of the world, watching a horror movie in the cool lava-lamp glow of his bedroom.

"No fish," Claudine whispered to Priscilla, who stood over the girls. The old maid nodded, and removed a frozen pork rump from the freezer above their heads. She seemed to intentionally avoid Noel's gaze, as if to meet his eyes would be to acknowledge that she had witnessed all of this before.

Noel felt sticky and strung out after their dinner of roast *lechon*, steaming *sinigang* soup (without the *bangus*), and *leche flan*, which his mother had made with extra custard and chilled overnight in the refrigerator. Noel hadn't mentioned Tito Mario's violence to his mother. In the second-floor bathroom—which reminded Noel of a highway rest stop because of its cinder-block walls and high, unscreened window—he turned on the boxy water heater attached to the tub. Nancy had taught him how to operate the contraption on his first day in Manila.

Noel undressed and listened to the heater groan to life. His thoughts lapsed to earlier that afternoon, the sharp slap of Tito Mario's hand as it struck Claudine's cheek. Was this normal? His mother had never laid a hand on him or his sister Maribel (except in affection, of course), and he wondered how this small deaf man and his mother could have been raised by the same parents.

Cats mewed outside the high window. Naked, his teeth flossed, Noel climbed on top of the toilet seat and held the bottom of the sill. He peered onto the quiet clay yard where his mother, his Tito Mario, and their posse had once played, imagining not their *merienda* of RC Cola and garlic peanuts, but his young Titos and Titas playing hide-and-go-seek and chasing one another under the clothesline. No, not hide-and-go-seek; kick the can. He had no idea what they had played, really. They were frozen in his mind as adults, had never been eighteen or headed to Princeton; obsessed with a curly-haired boy on the wrestling team and clueless about a career—much less the contents of the following day. He wondered if Chad Kline was sleeping-in (it was already Saturday morning in Boston) or awake, figuring out how to waste another vacation day in Harvard Square. The mewing cat crawled along the shed's tin roof. Noel counted the row of spindly *kamachile* trees growing along its side. With a graceful leap, it jumped down and strode across the patio toward the house. Noel heard the fast, hollow clucking of a tongue.

When he raised himself on his toes, Noel saw his Tito Mario crouched on the stoop below, waving a chunk of *bangus* in the air. The pink, emaciated cat was just a few feet from him, and when it made its move Tito Mario pulled the piece away and ate it, taunting the stray with delight.

(2001)

Ruby Enario Carlino

Born 1963, Cebu City, Philippines; immigrated to the U.S. in 1995

About the Author

Ruby Enario Carlino has a B.S. in Commerce (Human Resource Management) from the University of San Jose-Recoletos, Cebu, Philippines, and had worked on an M.A. in Literature from the University of San Carlos, Cebu, Philippines. She has received writing fellowships from the University of the Philippines Creative Writing Center (1984); Silliman University Writers Workshop (1986); 4th Solidarity Southeast Asian Writers Conference (1990); Women in Literary Arts-Cebu Writers Workshop (1993), and the Cebuano Studies Center Writing Workshops. Her works have previously appeared in *Turkish Daily News, European Stars and Stripes, Tales From a Small Planet, American Diplomacy, The Foreign Service Journal, The Washington Post*, and various Philippine magazines and journals. She writes a monthly column, "Traveler Without a Luggage" for *Sun Star Weekend*, a Philippine magazine. Aside from being a wife and mother, she works as an independent writer/web designer based in Virginia, U.S.A.

Generation Gap

Filipino young adults are often viewed as children who should be seen but not heard. This premise makes it impossible for young people to have real conversations with their elders; makes it impossible to become friends or share secrets across a spectrum of age and emotions. Young people can only grow into maturity by living a full life, which includes making their own decisions, becoming independent, thinking for themselves, making mistakes, and learning from them. When in a quandary, a young person such as Emily in "Blue Frangipanis" is as capable of emotional depth and strength as any adult. Our wisdom lies in allowing young adults to be their own persons, even if they no longer agree with us, even if their opinions make us squirm, and even if they break our hearts and theirs, sometimes; to let go even as we keep them forever in our hearts.

Blue Frangipanis

— Ruby Enario Carlino

The sweet smell of frangipanis assaulted my nose when I opened the door. The room was dim and all the shades were drawn. Besides the air-conditioning unit that was humming on and off, the room was dead quiet and sterile. I walked to the bedside and gingerly peered down on the person in bed. I caught my breath. What was lying in bed was only the shell of a woman I used to know. Her long gray tresses were gone and her cheeks were hollow. She wore no make-up and her mouth was unsmiling, set in a worried crease. Years of battling breast cancer had certainly taken its toll. She looked frailer and desperately ill since I last saw her a year ago.

"Joe?" the woman moaned as if in pain. She moaned again and muttered something unintelligible. I put out my hand to hold hers.

"What is it, Aunt Julia? What can I get you?"

Aunt Julia's eyes opened quickly when she heard my voice. For a brief instance, I thought I saw fear in her eyes. Then it was gone and she gave me a weary smile.

"Why, Emily, what are you doing here?" she asked with genuine pleasure in her voice.

"I came to see you, my favorite aunt, what else?" I replied gaily as I kissed her wrinkled cheek. "How are you feeling?"

"Have you been here long?" she asked with that fearful look in her eyes again, ignoring my question.

"A few minutes," I said, a little puzzled.

"Did I say anything in my sleep?" she asked looking hard at me for the first time.

"Well, I thought you called a name," I replied.

"Ahh, I must have been dreaming," she said simply. "Come, sit down," she commanded as she patted the side of her bed.

Aunt Julia was my mother's oldest sister. She helped send my mother to a teacher's college by working as a dressmaker for the town's more prosperous residents. She, herself, had only the most minimal education. She married off my mother to the most eligible bachelor in town. When the children (the twins and I) started coming and my mother had to go back to work, Aunt Julia took care of us, too. My mother never had to discipline us. Aunt Julia was mother, nanny, grandmother rolled into one. Looking back now, I felt she could have breast-fed the twins and me. She doted on us, particularly me. She never married but I heard hush-hush stories from our nosy housemaids when I was growing up. A long time ago, she was supposed to have gotten married. The man asked for her hand in marriage but failed to show up in church. She never entertained suitors after that. In fact, she acted as if her heart had never broken.

This humiliating experience colored her view about the world. Unfortunately for me, I was the first teenager in the house. I could not even go to the movies with friends. There were many no-no's in those days. I could not walk home from school with my best friend, Ann Marie, because she laughed too loudly. Loudness in Aunt Julia's eyes was "calling attention." Loudness was equated to boys and boys meant major trouble.

She meant well, I knew that. But her life was us, she had no other. At that time, I had thought more than once of wringing her lily-white neck. She was devastated when we all went to college and she did not have anyone left to worry about except for the small farm and the dogs.

In the city, I often missed the smell of the old coastal town. I would dream about the sea and could taste the saltiness of the air in my sleep. Except for the last year when I was juggling part-time work and school, I had been able to return to Santa Elena as often as I could during holidays and school breaks.

"His name is Joe," she began. "I met him a year ago when he stopped by here to ask for directions. He is a traveling salesman," she explained quietly as if in a confession, her hands clasped tightly across her chest. "Please do not tell your mother," she begged.

"Of course not, I won't," I replied quickly. "Does he know you are here?" I asked gently.

She smiled and nodded towards the vase of frangipanis on her side table. "Yes, he knows—he came and brought those, my favorite flowers."

At that moment, fifty years disappeared and she looked like a young woman again. Her eyes sparkled like precious jewels and her face turned luminous with pure happiness. In all the years I had known her, I never saw Aunt Julia look like this. She raised one frail arm and in an almost girlish gesture, patted her thin hair in place. How happy she looked, I exclaimed silently to myself.

"That's really nice," I replied, not quite sure where this conversation was going. "When is he coming back?"

"He should be back soon," she answered. "I have not seen him in two weeks and three days," she added with a sweet smile. "But he must be very busy with his routes, and he is also starting a business, you see," she explained in a voice tinged with a shadow of uncertainty.

I could not help but stare at the fresh frangipanis.

"Actually, there is something I would like you to do for me," Aunt Julia said as she clasped and unclasped her hands. "Would you call Joe for me?" she finally asked without looking at me.

"Of course, Aunt Julia, anything," I replied. "And don't worry about mother," I added quickly.

She looked at me and smiled gratefully. Then she pointed at her pillow. "Look inside the pillowcase. Yesterday I stuffed a piece of paper there with his telephone number," she said. "I move that paper around, you know. I don't want anyone to see it," she explained as she watched me feel around for the paper with Joe's number.

I pulled out a carefully folded cigarette foil from her pillow. On it was a hurriedly scribbled telephone number in faded blue ink. The paper looked like it had been folded and refolded many times, a memento from a distant past. I could not say anything. I was afraid I might cry. I placed the paper carefully in my knapsack and saw my aunt's slight nod of approval. Then I hurriedly said goodbye and promised to call Joe at the first opportunity.

I walked from the hospital to Rizal Park, a five-minute walk through a strip of fruit stalls and 24-hour pharmacies. I tried not to think about Aunt Julia and the man she called Joe.

Traffic was horrendous, I suddenly noticed. Santa Elena had grown tremendously during the past year. There seemed to be more people in the streets. In addition to the tricycles and the horse-drawn carriages, there were now jeepneys and mini-buses in Santa Elena's narrow streets.

I passed a flower vendor and I was brought back into Aunt Julia's room. If he had not visited her in over two weeks, then who had brought the fresh frangipanis? Why was my aunt so adamant that my mother not know about this man? I thought I should call Joe when I got home. But just then, I spotted a pay phone in the park and decided to call him right then and there, to get the matter over with.

"Hello? May I speak with Joe, please," I asked.

"Wait," a man's voice answered. "*Oy*, Joe! One of your chicks on the phone again," the man shouted, even though he seemed to have covered the receiver with one hand. I could hear men's laughter in the background. I was beginning to get a bad headache.

"This is Joe," a deep male voice from the other end of the line broke through the background noise. He sounded like a disk jockey, a young disk jockey.

"Hi, Joe, Aunt Julia asked me to call you," I said without preamble.

"Oh, how is she?" he asked evenly.

"Not very well," I answered candidly. "She is wondering when you might visit again."

"Well, it's kind of difficult right now," he began, "but tell her not to worry, as soon as I get a few things sorted out, I will visit her. And I will bring her the check," he said, as if an afterthought.

"The check?" I asked. I did not know there was money involved in this.

"Why, isn't that the reason she asked you to call me?" he inquired in a mean tone, which I did not like.

"Of course," I said. "Will this be in full or partial?" I shot back.

"In case she did not tell you, our agreement was that I will only repay twenty-five thou of the total amount, the rest was her investment," he pointed out helpfully. "I will repay the full amount we've agreed, of course," he said smoothly as if in a sales pitch.

"Okay, so when can she expect a visit?" I persisted.

"Next month probably," he replied. "Hey, I left her a five-thousand check the last time I saw her," he said sounding piqued.

"And when was this?" I inquired calmly.

"A couple of weeks ago," he answered.

"Well, goodbye then. She'll be expecting that check next month," I said. "I would appreciate it, of course, if you could bring it while she can still use it," I added. "In case you didn't know, she is seriously ill." I placed the receiver down without even hearing the response from the other end of the line.

I was so mad that I did not realize I was crying. I ignored the pointed stares of people walking by. I sat on a bench and wept quietly for Aunt Julia and her dreams. She will have her dreams, I swore to myself. I will make her dreams as real as possible, even if I had to invent the man in them.

I spent the night creating a different conversation with Joe for Aunt Julia's benefit. Yes, yes, he was busy. He really wanted to come but business was picking up and he still had his other job. Of course, he will come soon. He sends his greetings and frangipanis. Yes, his love, too. Yes, the frangipanis are signs of his eternal love. No mention of money.

I went to see Aunt Julia the next day. She was sitting up in bed with a couple of pillows propped behind her. She looked almost radiant. She could not stop chattering about Joe this and Joe that. They were going to get married, she confessed. She did not want my mother to know until the last minute because she was sure my mother would not agree. She asked me to bring her the frangipanis and she cheerfully arranged and rearranged the flowers in the vase. She was glad business was turning for the better, she continued. Joe should be able to quit his sales job soon. He was destined for better things, she added. Finally, she handed me back the vase and asked that I help her lie back down. Then she fell into a deep sleep.

From that time on, there was always a fresh vase of frangipanis in her room. She never saw who brought it and she never asked. But she always had a secret smile when she saw it. I guess she always presumed that Joe sent them. The nurses and I called those flowers Joe's frangipanis. And Aunt Julia had no reason to think otherwise.

The news I was expecting for a long time finally came one day. The doctor said it could happen that day or that night—soon. My mother called me from the hospital. I left the house immediately and hurried to the hospital. When I opened the door, I saw my family already there. It was as if the room was cloaked with a black curtain of grief. The smell of death was strong. I stood at the foot of Aunt Julia's bed. My mother was leaning towards her on the side of the bed.

"Well, he left this here while you were sleeping," I could hear my mother say softly. "He will be back soon, he just went out to get some donuts, Nang Julia."

Aunt Julia's eyes were closed but her hands were clasping a bunch of frangipanis, its sap a fresh stain on her bedclothes.

She looked at peace and ready for her one last trip.

"I'm so tired, I want to sleep," Aunt Julia whispered. "Tell Joe I'm sorry I could not wait for the donuts," she said as she attempted to smile. "Emily," she opened her eyes briefly and held her hand out to me. As I took it, she said, "Thank him for the frangipanis, will you?"

"I will," I said, in unison with my mother.

(2001)

Gémino H. Abad

Born 1939, Sta. Ana, Manila, Philippines

About the Author

Gémino H. Abad is a professor at the University of the Philippines. He has a number of awards and books of poetry, fiction, and criticism to his name, including a three-volume historical anthology of Filipino poetry in English.

Philippine Folklore

My story draws from Philippine folklore. The *agta* is a giant, black as midnight, who dwells in a tall tree, wears a hat, and smokes a pipe; he is helpful for so long as one does not offend him or take him for granted. The *santilmo* is a baleful spirit of the damned; for other people, it is St. Elmo's fire. In Bisayan folk belief, *gaba* is a curse that one incurs for evil or culpable neglect, so that inevitably one suffers a misfortune as punishment.

Houseboy

— Gémino H. Abad

Standing side by side, Lem and his brother Dan hold on to the truck's rickety railing, with Mama sitting amid the jumble of their household things in boxes and crates. Lem is short and frail-looking but secretly proud of the first faint hairs of manhood on his upper lip, while Dan is wiry and brims still with a child's carefree bouncing innocence. They laugh and thrill to their railing's perilous tilting as the truck wheezes through the hubbub of vehicles and stevedores at Pier 8. Mama hardly notices; she sits on a *baul* praying the rosary, her lips whispering the words over the mysteries. From time to time her eyes stray to the hired jeepney ahead, alight with decor like a Christmas tree, where Papa waves at them as he leads the way to their new apartment in Sampaloc. The jeepney's footboard displays a sign which reads "Kiss Me Tender," and Lem can just make out Tomasa, their housemaid, among the luggage and boxes. Facing the brothers on the truck, balancing himself against an old *aparador*, is Rufino, their houseboy, his mouth nervously twitching as he clutches the leash of their frightened pet dog, Petrel, whose stubby tail wags uncertainly.

The truck rumbles up Quezon Bridge across the Pasig River. "Look, Pino," Lem calls Rufino. In the dark undulating waters, an oil slick glimmers like the remains of a drowned rainbow. Suddenly, their eyes flood with light as they reach the top of the bridge and a panorama of the city heaves into view.

O, never have they seen such a show, tall buildings bright with neon lights! Everywhere they look, the lights write in big sparkling letters, one at a time as though spelling carefully each word, but sometimes, flashing whole phrases out of the dark, as if the city wishes to speak with them. Everywhere a fiesta of lights! There, a man appears with a long beard and points with a dazzling sceptre to a crystal dome pulsing with stars—and then, as man and dome blink out, a blaze of letters unscrolls a command: FOLLOW YOUR DREAM. And there, too! a woman traipsing on golden sandals, they can almost hear her laughing as she scatters flowers like rubies and pearls across the sky. No alphabet unfurls her mystery. The brothers consult each other on who she may be, what she may be telling the city, but cannot agree on her scripture. For Lem, the sky has lost its stars, and in their place, scrolls of *santilmo* run wildly about the city's roofs.

Rufino is aghast, shaking uncontrollably even as Petrel moans and snuggles against his feet. He leans hard on the *aparador*, his mouth agape, the sounds of his astonishment "*Ooy! oy, oy!*" tumbling, his eyes wildly dilating at every flash and glare of image and word in the electric dark. The brothers themselves can find no words to shape their marvel. Their eyes only fill with the new sights shimmering around them with strange promises. The truck lumbers past Quiapo Church down Quezon Boulevard. On either side the movie houses and department stores are ablaze with the pride of commerce and a kind of open sensuality which the brothers dimly sense as sin; and spilling over the sidewalks, cluttered with stalls and goods on the pavement, are crowds of people like apparitions in the electric flood. And as they look, now here, now there, the brothers long for sight of their familiar *tartanilla*, the sound of the *cochero's* clucking tongue, the rattle of his whip's handle against spokes of the wheel.

The dust and fumes of the roaring traffic bring them back to themselves as they drive past F.E.U. which they recognize from postcards that Papa had sent to Cebu. They speed down wide-laned España, coruscating with the same electrical sky-show, and suddenly, they are right at the very gate of a green apartment block on P. Noval, a cool depth of verdure bathed in light from a row of street lamps.

The brothers clamber down the truck and race to see their new home. The gate opens into a small enclosed space with a few potted plants, the front door gives on to a brightly-lit *sala* with gleaming white cement walls. They scurry up a staircase to the second floor where they find two bedrooms with green Venetian blinds, and a narrow corridor to the common toilet. And down again, they notice a *bodega* under the stair, and after the dining room and kitchen, a maid's room and an enclosed yard for laundry. *Oy*, what a great place! still smelling of fresh paint, clean and well-lit, so different from the leaky house they rented on F. del Rosario in Cebu.

The brothers join Mama who is supervising Rufino and Tomasa unpack their household things in the *sala*. They help pry open the crates and untie the cords around the cardboard boxes, anxious to collect their comics and marbles from one or the other unmarked box. "*Aguy!*" cries Tomasa, a line of blood quickly forming across the back of her hand that caught a protruding nail between the boards of a crate. Instantly, Rufino puts his mouth on her wound. "Pino!" Mama frowns. "Go, get the Mercurochrome there," pointing to a little black bag on the floor. The brothers laugh. "*Oy*, Pino, ha?" they tease as Mama applies the red liquid to Tomasa's hand.

Both Rufino and Tomasa are practically members of the family where their own childhood passed, and both, before Papa left with Tomasa for Manila to teach Spanish at F.E.U., have regaled the brothers at night with stories of spirits and animals from a dim unchronicled past. At times, waking up in the morning with a guilty sense of his aroused manhood, Lem would imagine Rufino and Tomasa as the first man and woman in their forest home, and then he would feel not a little envy toward Rufino.

Rufino came from Cagay, two days' journey into the hills from Papa's hometown of Barili. He is tall and lean, with thick unruly hair, and taut muscles run like mice under his skin, but his arms and legs are covered with dark splotches as though forest moss grows over his body. But most striking are Rufino's eyes which have a haunted look as if some wild animal spirit were always calling out to him. He seems averse to light; even now, as he and Tomasa lug their things up the stairs, his eyes are half-closed as if to weave about him the forest's sheltering dark.

Tomasa is seventeen, two years younger than Rufino. She has long dark hair which smells of some fragrant herb unknown to the brothers. Her breasts seem like fruit of the *chico* tree which Lem, trembling in his imagination's cave, traces under the bright flower prints of her blouse.

Sometimes, at F. del Rosario, while he and Dan hurriedly dress up for school, Tomasa would barge in to make up their bed, and he'd quickly turn to hide the sign of his morning's unbidden maleness. But Mama's story about her is tragic, how when she was barely six, she lost both her parents in a mudslide in Doldol, two hills farther inland from Cagay. Her uncle then brought her down to Barili to serve with Tia Bebang, Papa's unmarried sister, who attended to the parish priest, Papa's brother.

During the Occupation, when a *juez de cuchillo* was bruited about in Barili, Papa fled with his family to the hinterland. Even now, the foot-trails to Cagay and Doldol are tortuous and gorged with leeches that rain down on one from the overhanging branches. After the War, whenever Papa needed servants, Tia Bebang would send for a farmer's son or daughter in Cagay or Doldol where Papa is known as a fair, kind-hearted man.

The brothers' school days at F.E.U. pass very quickly because their hearts lie elsewhere. They are teased for their Bisayan accent during the first week or so, but soon the embarrassment lies buried in the camaraderie that flourishes from the common suffering in the classroom. Lem remembers desperately forming the words, "*Nagisi*, sir!" ("Sir, it's been torn!") as he holds up his half-sheet of quiz paper to Mr. Babay, their English teacher, and his classmates jeering, "Ay, Bisaya, Bisaya *gid!*" But it was simply an act of self-defense then because Mr. Babay is so strict and decorous, and being effeminate, given to pinching his students near the crotch whenever anyone misbehaved or dared answer with a wild guess. Why, it does not seem so long ago. . . their lesson is the anecdote and they read one, "The Mad Dog." Then Mr. Babay asks, "Why is the story an anecdote?" and everyone is silent. He proceeds to call each one, obviously delighting in the prospect of pinching so many bewildered delinquents; and so it happens, and without hope, from the first row to the next, each one's dumbfounded silence or head shake is promptly rewarded with a pinch somewhere near one's little cowering manhood. Kiko, a skinny boy, is next in the row of penitents, and as Mr. Babay turns to him, he squirms like a worm and quavers a last despairing answer, "Sir, because the dog is mad?" The class roars with laughter, and even Mr. Babay, breaking into a wide smile, takes pity and foregoes the pleasure of pinching the mad reader of the day's anecdote.

But Kiko soon becomes the brothers' best friend because, silent and morose, he seems somehow to share their alienation in their new surroundings—the din and bustle up three flights of stairs among rowdy classmates, the dusty harum-scarum of jostling pedestrians, vendors, and jeepneys outside the school gate. To Lem, Kiko seems like a shy animal which prefers the solitude of those forests that at times he finds himself roaming in his dreams with his pet dog Petrel. The brothers often share their *baon* with Kiko, and sometimes, when they have pooled their savings from their two-peso allowance for the week, those brightly colored comics of the Phantom and Nyoka and Captain Marvel with their delightful smell of fresh print. But Kiko never seems grateful nor even seeks their company. The brothers would look for him at recess and invariably find him alone playing with a few faded marbles under the *kamachile* tree alongside the school cafeteria.

Unless it is Friday, when the brothers have their Physical Education class at the gym, they are off from school at four in the afternoon. They usually walk home directly, at times with Kiko who, from a few remarks he has dropped, lives with an uncle much farther off near the railroad tracks. It isn't so much the mysterious peril of the city as Papa's rule that confines the brothers at home. As soon as Mama has served them their *merienda* of fried bananas or hot *dinoldog,* they would postpone their schoolwork to as late an hour as possible, and delve instead into their storybooks—the Swiss Family Robinson, the Knights of the Round Table, Zane Grey, the Classics Illustrated—or else, draw on their large sketch pads the heroes and cartoon characters of their reading frenzy. There is no radio at home; TV is still unknown. Sometimes, when the brothers tire, they would go and "direct a movie" in the *bodega.* The *bodega,* which at night serves as

Rufino's sleeping quarters, has a small attic under the stairs with a single weak electric bulb. They would climb there while Mama is busy preparing for supper, and put on a stack of old magazines an empty shoebox with a sheet of onion-skin paper across its wide mouth; lighting a candle behind this paper screen—the very thing that frightens Mama so!—one would manipulate carton figures of heroes and animals pasted on to little sticks, and the other watch the shadow play.

But in that attic is also Lem's most guarded secret; he would, as often as he could leave Dan to his own diversions, ensconce himself there between the *palo china* boxes, and read guiltily as much as he could of his first big novel, *Gone With the Wind*, and read over again marked passages which seem to secrete the mysterious passions of human beings.

Toward six, as the cool evening air begins to flow through the apartment like a breath from deep forests that Lem imagines surround the city, the brothers would impatiently await their father's arrival. They shall have by then rushed through their schoolwork at such speed as Mama, sometimes checking on them, would reprove them for. Almost always, a little before the hour, Papa would come in quietly, hang his old *bustipol* hat from a nail on the wall, smile affectionately at Mama, still bustling about the dining table, and nod his head toward the brothers reading comics on the sofa, for their orders to Rufino. "Which will it be tonight, sons?" a lift of his eyebrows would ask, "'what flavor?" There is a wide field of choice among soft drinks in the Chinese grocery down P. Novel—Bireley's, Clicquot Club, Mission, Coca-Cola, 7-Up, Sarsaparilla. Each night the brothers would sample a brand or flavor, or return to a favorite drink. This after-supper drinking ritual, to which the brothers look forward all day, has become since their first week in the city, the family's way of celebrating another day's quiet, uneventful end. Then Mama would be her most radiant self, beaming with happiness and pride over her home.

A sense that each day would pass always the same as yesterday fills Lem with a vague discontent. All those perilous quests, all riddles—shall he only read about them? The whole world seems content, and he imagines the mountains bearing patiently the forests on their back, and seas rolling ashore and withdrawing, endlessly, moaning around the land. And the days repeat themselves and lose their memory, and only seem full as when one eats without joy and the hunger turns into a sour emptiness in the pit of one's stomach. So it feels to Lem at night as he lies in bed, watching the lizards stalk the moths and other ghostly insects cavorting about the fluorescent light. Sometimes, deep into the night, the mournful hooting of a train pierces through the forest in his dream . . .

The brothers conspire to go out by themselves, explore their neighborhood, even perhaps go and see a real movie during Papa's siesta on a Saturday. Their classmates talk of the many movies that they have seen, and to avoid ridicule, Lem and Dan fall silent or pretend to follow their classmates' excited recounting of "The Crimson Pirate" or "The Broken Arrow." O, what adventures they would see on that wide screen in technicolor, what stories would come alive before their very eyes! They already know from Kiko that a few blocks down España is a movie house called Mercury. "What is now showing?" They check the movie page. A double program! and surely, a lot of cartoons in between. The first movie, "Bird of Paradise," promises a volcano's resplendent eruption, but the other, called "Apache Drums," is more exciting, for Lem is fascinated with the Indians, their wildlife lore, their ferocity and fearlessness, their great wanderings as a people over trackless lands full of peril and wonder. He has in fact found a public library in Lepanto where often on a Saturday he would read. Papa never allows them to go out by themselves after school, but has made an exception for the library, a short walking distance from P. Noval. Lem knows all the tribes, from the Arapahos to the Zunis, he has sketches of their weapons and wigwams and wampum beads, he has travelled many times in his mind with their war parties, their shamans, their buffaloes. So now, as Lem contemplates the movie page, those Apache drums sound again the Redman's rage and grief over those vast prairies where the Paleface creep in their covered wagons. The next Saturday now seems to Lem the highest good, the pinnacle of desire.

But how? Every evening as they wait for Papa and their soft drink ritual, neither brother can muster enough courage. It simply can't be put so directly, "Papa, Dan and I will go see a movie this Saturday." No, some scheme must be found. Perhaps, next Saturday, they need to do research in the library, or perhaps, Rufino can go with them and look for some school things in Goodwill Department Store, or some presents for a classmate's birthday. It would be lying! Perhaps then, they can confess it the following day in San Sebastian church, they would just have to be sorry, truly sorry, for having had to lie, and Papa will never know.

The brothers scheme each day without hope. At night, Lem imagines that a forest spirit will take the matter in hand, the same *agta* who, in Rufino's stories, sleeps at the bottom of mangrove swamps and rescues lost children from the wilderness. But there is grave danger with this *agta* who is ugly and deformed, matted with hair from head to foot; he is helpful only if the children can look on him without fear and offer something afterwards like a parting gift, a top perhaps that has survived many trials in the dust, or a slingshot that has brought down many birds, anything at all that they truly value as though it were a part of their own body. Otherwise, since he has a nasty temper and such monstrous strength that he could uproot trees with his bare hands, he tears and devours the hapless children. Ay, can they pass the test? Will he ask them for his name which Rufino mysteriously refuses to tell?

The brothers are helpless with the simple words that shape so clearly their wish; they already know what Papa will say. But then, one evening, as Papa and Mama chat in the *sala* and the brothers glumly sip their beverages, they learn that Papa would be flying to Cebu for a weekend congress of teachers of Spanish. Where before Lem's mind went in circles, each scheme always turning dark like a tree at night, Papa's trip suddenly lifts the cloud of gloom in the apartment—as though he and Dan, trapped in some dark wood, have burst upon a sunlit clearing! It has simply happened, a magical snap of the forest spirit's fingers, and the way is suddenly clear, for Mama is no problem. She may at first demur and sadly shake her head, especially since Papa would be away, but finally, if they press hard and suggest that Rufino accompany them to the movie, the brothers are sure she would drop her anxiety with a sigh. "O, *sige na*," she'd say, "take Pino, but be careful now, ha? don't run when you cross the street, don't ever try those germ-ful icedrops, et cetera!"

Saturday is still three days waiting, but the brothers are already excitedly rehearsing their scene with Mama. What adds a special flavor to their plot is Lem's latest discovery. "I asked Pino this morning," Lem tells Dan as they walk to school, "we were just feeding Petrel. 'Pino, have you ever seen a movie?' Pino shakes his head, he doesn't even know what it is! Then I say, 'Okay, we'll go to Mercury this Saturday,' and Pino gives me a blank look." The brothers laugh, and Lem feels a kind of superior pity toward Rufino.

One late afternoon, Lem leaves Dan to their drawing project for the World History class exhibit. He climbs to the attic in the *bodega* and is about to turn on its weak light on the ceiling when he hears the door below creak, as though a thief were intruding. A pale shaft of light shoots across the floor. It is Tomasa! She stands as though lost. Lem crouches as he looks over the attic's edge. What if she should climb up the ladder, searching perhaps for something that Mama needs in the kitchen? But she is standing very still like a tree, exactly as in legends a tree holds still when it is bearing fruit or when birds alight on its branches. What will Dan say if he should claim that now he understands why sometimes suddenly a tree seems to hold its breath, all its leaves hushed by an invisible power? But Lem's thought flickers out as, with a start, he sees Rufino slip in, gently closing the door behind him. In the dark, he takes Tomasa into his arms and kisses her on the mouth. They embrace for a long time in absolute silence, and sway as in a dance. It is all very still on a sudden in the *bodega* as though it were a forest just after a terrible storm and all its creatures were still hiding in fear. Lem can hardly breathe, he feels hard and faint with his rising manhood. Tomasa is moaning low like a wounded animal as she presses herself against Rufino. Then abruptly she pushes him away, touches his face as though to ask forgiveness, and quickly slips out. Rufino waits a little while, leaning his head against the wall, and then leaves Lem to the fever of his own heat in the dark.

Mercury Theatre is tumbledown and crowded, hot as a stove, stifling with cigarette smoke. Though the sign at the ticket booth reads, "Standing Room Only," the brothers buy their tickets and rush inside where the sweaty press and smell of human bodies feel like oppressive undergrowth in a muttering forest. They inch their way squeezing through yielding walls of flesh, and from time to time, look over the crowd's heads for fleeting glimpses of the movie. Soon Lem is able to see better, and notices a small figure snaking between jostling bodies, softly calling, "*Mani, mani! Yosi, bos, yosi!*" ("Peanuts, peanuts! Cigarettes, boss, cigarettes!") The boy-figure is vaguely familiar but Lem loses sight of him in the press of people ceaselessly bumping and shoving for a view. But then, as he looks again to his right over someone's shoulder, he recognizes Kiko. He is about to call when he trips over someone's foot, and loses him again. Kiko! A strange feeling of sadness overcomes Lem. He suddenly seems to understand Kiko's moroseness in school, and senses something amiss in his willful escapade.

After what seems a very long struggle in the dark, groping and pushing, during which time the brothers lose Rufino, Lem and Dan finally find themselves standing near a lighted sign which says "Men." It isn't a very good viewing post; each time the door swings open, a strong forlorn draft of urine assails their nostrils. But at least they now have a clear view of the movie, although they are hemmed by a crowd which keeps breaking for others to pass through.

War drums roll their wild terror, then suddenly cease. An ominous silence falls. With a blood-curdling war cry, an Apache brave bursts out from a high window in the church, and leaps at the colonists below, swinging his tomahawk. He is shot dead, but another painted brave lunges from another window, and still another, and arrows fly, and the women shriek. Pandemonium of smoke and fire and falling bodies. The war drums sound again, and the high windows are blank with fear. But then again the drums suddenly cease. Lem tenses, waits for the terrifying outbreak. The church's massive door is even now fast burning down . . . A sharp bugle call! The colonists look at one another in disbelief. The U.S. cavalry charges down a hill in a thunderous cloud of dust, and the Apaches scatter with desperate cries to their Sky Father. The weary survivors file out of the burning church to welcome the proud troopers.

The lights come on and people rise from their seats, and with a noise like a great wind through a forest, others rush to take their places, some clambering over the seats like antelopes. The crowd along the aisles mills and shoves in slow-motion stampede for the exits. Spotting a woman with a young girl preparing to leave, Lem inserts himself between jostling bodies and, in the narrow space along his row of seats, works slowly toward the woman over a tricky underbrush of feet and legs. A man from the opposite edge of the row bounces forward and takes the young girl's seat, roughly pulling her aside. He ignores the spate of obscenities from the girl's woman-companion and, holding the other empty seat down, nods at Lem with a twisted smile, an unshelled peanut in a corner of his mouth. Dan, who is behind two other boys scurrying after Lem, retreats toward their original post of odors. The man now seated beside Lem is short and dark and smells like rotten papaya. "Have some," he says, offering Lem boiled peanuts in a brown paper bag. Lem politely declines.

Soon the lights fade out, and the brothers are regaled with a run of Bugs Bunny and Mickey Mouse, followed by a newsreel on world events and sports in black and white. Lem worries about the time, but "Bird of Paradise" comes on. The brothers are all eyes for the brilliance of color and the sweep of seashore and mountain, and Lem remembers the beaches in Cebu. He is not able to catch all the English words, but the story is clear enough. The islanders are similar to the Indians but gentler in their ways and peaceable; perhaps, thought Lem, like Humabon's people when the Spaniards came. White people like the young hero seem to want to dwell with the natives; in fact, he falls in love with the chief's beautiful daughter and marries her. The young lovers kiss and make love in a small hut while the natives make merry outside with drums and dances. Lem watches with bated breath as though he were spying on Rufino and Tomasa. He feels his manhood rising. Then he senses with a start a hand on his thigh as if it only slipped from the man's arm-rest beside him, but it crawls, presses, grows warm. He glances at the man, and the man meets his look, and pouts. *Porbida!* Lem rises, spilling the man's bag of peanuts, and hastens toward the end of the row, and the spectators against whose knees he brushed, mutter and complain. Dan throws him a questioning look.

"Let's go, Dan," he urges, his voice trembling, "it's getting late."

"Oh, no," Dan demurs, "it isn't over yet."

"But we promised Mama, before six."

"Ay, just a little longer," Dan pleads.

"No, Dan," he shoves his brother, "let's go look for Pino."

Outside Mercury, the city is already phosphorescent with neon lights. Rufino hurries alongside the brothers, but no longer seems in awe of the electric glittering that enwraps the stores and buildings. "Were you scared, Pino?" Dan keeps asking, but Rufino only shakes his head as they jog, swerving now here, now there, to get ahead of slower pedestrians. It is well past six! The honking of jeepneys and cries of hawkers seem to Lem a distant hubbub. He feels lost as though he were moving in another time. His thoughts swirl about, and no words can speak comfort to them. That stray hand, as he watched on screen the lover's dark bride and felt his own blaze, now cuts his soul with strange humiliation, he can hear himself crying secretly as though he were covered with earth's humus. Then the thought of Rufino and Tomasa together fills him with aching desolation as if he had deeply eaten of a rare fruit and the next moment, the tree that bore it had been cut down.

"Papa will be home tonight, boys!" says Mama, her face lighting up with the certainty of it. The flight from Cebu the day before had been cancelled because typhoon Elang threatened the Visayas. Lem and Dan are checking their schoolbags in the *sala*. It is early evening and a hard rain is falling, its steady murmur coming through the walls like the hidden sea in the conch shell. Lem has been feeling low all day, avoiding Kiko in school as though, somehow, he had hurt him by seeing how poor he was. *Ay*, what strange torment, all thought in tatters. And now, with Papa coming, he feels an inner weariness that makes him want to cry where no one will see. Surely, too, Mama will sooner than later come around to telling Papa. Their escapade is past anger, but Papa's silence may become more unbearable than physical punishment.

But Papa is long coming; perhaps, says Mama, traffic is at a standstill in flooded streets; perhaps even, Elang has veered toward Cebu and no flight again is allowed. They wait in the *sala* as the hour drags, and the brothers listlessly read on the sofa. The table has long been set with Mama's special chicken *perdiz*. As the wall clock whirrs and tolls seven, Mama remembers their ritual and calls Rufino. "Hurry, Pino," she urges, "get our soft drinks before Cheng closes shop."

Mama now wears her anxiety like a mourning veil. Her bottle of Clicquot Club only sweats icy droplets on her crotchet work on the side table. The brothers too find their beverages stale. Mama closes her eyes and her lips seem to be moving in prayer. As Lem steals a glance at her, a vague sense that he has wronged her tears his soul. A hard knocking shakes the wall! The brothers simultaneously jump toward the door. The rains lash at them as they open, and a stranger, a tall American in an orange raincoat, accompanied by a policeman, asks, "Is your mother home?"

Mama suddenly cries out beside them in the rain's scattering spray. "Oh! has something happened? *Ay, Hesus, Ginoo*! I knew, I knew—something terrible was coming!" The brothers gently shove her inside. The strangers follow, making a pool of water as they stand and wait for Mama to calm down.

Then the American, having introduced himself, "Adams, ma'am," recounts what had happened, the policeman silently looking on. Rufino stands by the door to the *bodega*, his eyes fixed on Adams as though he were his quarry; Tomasa sidles up to him, and Lem notices how for a trembling instant her hand reaches out to caress the back of Rufino's neck. Mama is sobbing on her chair, and the brothers stand by her and gently rub her shoulder and press her hand as they listen to Mr. Adams. He is driving in the heavy downpour down España on the wrong lane; it is too late to stop when he catches sight of Papa crossing the street. *Ay, Hesus*! cries Mama. He is very sorry, sorry beyond words, and shakes his head; he has just arrived from New York, and has only borrowed a business partner's car. He is on his way back to Manila Hotel, visibility is very poor, the driving rains lash and whip the flooding streets. Lem sees in a flash Papa being flung to the pavement. But it isn't fatal, no! Papa is still alive. Lem sees his body in the swirling floodwaters along the curb, and Adams and the policeman lift the unconscious body to the police car.

They rush to U.S.T. hospital, Lem hears the siren wailing, and they wait for the attending physician and the hour ticks infinitely slowly. Papa's wallet identifies him and gives his address but no telephone number. Then the doctor comes, Papa is in pain but safe, he has a fractured rib, and the doctor says the patient should be able to go home in a week's time.

Lem dreads Papa's homecoming. Surely he must already know, although in the hospital he is gentle toward them—know not only about their movie-going but also about Rufino and Tomasa. Lem recalls vividly the shock of Mama's discovery.

On the third night after the accident, he and Mama retrace their steps home from the U.S.T. gate because it suddenly occurs to Mama that she has not turned off the gas stove and Tomasa may just be too busy ironing to notice. Lem finds their door open and Mama is angry. "Tomasa!" she calls, but no one seems at home. Lem is suddenly uneasy with a vague foreknowledge. "Pino! where are you?" Mama calls up the stairs. The house seems deathly still like a storm-struck tree. But Tomasa suddenly comes out of the *bodega* with a terrified look on her face. Her hands hang like dead branches by her side, she is looking down at her bare feet. She turns her face from Mama. "What were you doing there?" pursues Mama in a rage, and pushing her aside, goes inside with Lem and screams at the sight of Rufino shivering in a corner as though he were cold. "*Ginoo!*" she screams again and shoves Lem out into the light. Tomasa runs sobbing to the kitchen. Mama sinks on the sofa and seems ready to cry, and then collects herself, saying, in a trembling voice, "Lem, you're much older, you must not tell Dan about this." She straightens up and goes to the kitchen, and Lem hears her calling Tomasa without anger. He feels a monstrous darkness sweep through the house. He waits for Rufino to come out of hiding but Mama has returned with a small basket of fruits, and pulls him to the door, and they go out and hurry back to the hospital.

On Papa's first evening at home, Mr. Adams drops in with a sandalwood box of rare Havana cigars. He has never missed a day of visiting with Papa in the hospital, with Babe Ruth chocolate bars and rubbery licorice sticks for the brothers. Papa is very polite with him but their talk lags as the brothers pretend to read in the dining room. Lem is sure Mr. Adams would soon stop visiting.

After he leaves, Papa calls Mama to the *sala* and beckons the brothers to come too. "Well," he says, looking at them tenderly, "what drinks shall we try tonight?" Lem suddenly feels like crying; only, Dan is by who looks quite abashed. Then Papa calls Rufino and the brothers are glad for the diversion of the ritual. "We'll go with Pino," says Dan suddenly. "No, Dan, you stay," says Papa, "I have something to tell Mama, and you and Lem should hear it." Rufino impassively takes each one's orders and as he leaves, Lem sees his shadow flung upon the wall. He almost cries out and Mama gives him a frightened look. For a fleeting instant to his mind's eye, it isn't Rufino or his shadow crossing the room but a dark spirit from the swamp asking for his name! Mama taps Lem's hand, saying, "Your Papa already knows, but he isn't angry, he only regrets he hasn't thought of the danger, the temptation . . . and the *gaba*." Papa only looks on, smoking his first Havana from Mr. Adams, and seems to be quietly considering the words to speak. Then, as though he were speaking only to Mama, he says, "It is time for Rufino and Tomasa to go back to Cebu." Mama nods her assent with a grave expression. "The *Don Julio* leaves this Friday." Lem sees in Dan's face his share in the lovers' guilt. For Lem has told Dan about his secret, only carefully omitting the details which seem shameful. He senses his forgiveness from Papa's gentleness with them, but a strange desolation of spirit sweeps through him. *Ay*, Rufino and Tomasa banished!

For the next few days, Rufino and Tomasa seem distant to Lem like strangers. He can hardly bear their silence, they move as if bound. Or as if they have lost their names and no one could call. Like two shadows that take flesh and then vanish, for a moment human, and the next moment, are mute presences of beings that inhabit the forest. Lem wishes it were already Friday, and they were gone!

After school, the brothers come home to a gloomy silence in the house. It is Friday. The only bright news for Mama is Dan's third prize for his drawing of Henry VIII in the World History project. After kissing Dan, Mama says to Lem, "I've been missing Petrel." Lem heads straight for the kitchen and out to the laundry yard where some clothes are still dripping on the hard, bare ground. "He must just have slipped out," says Lem, "Or even jumped over that wall." Dan points to their next-door neighbor's wall. "I've seen him jump, going after a cat."

"He has lately been quite restless," says Mama, "and howls at night as though he were seeing ghosts."

"Oy! are there really ghosts, Mama?" Dan teases.

She does not take the bait and turns to Lem. "What can be the matter with Petrel do you think, Lem?"

Lem is silent.

"Ask me, Ma," says Dan, "I've an idea."

"What? Is the dog just ailing?"

"No, Mama," says Dan in earnest, "he misses Pino and perhaps still sees his shadow."

Lem keeps his own thought to himself. He sees Petrel, a forlorn speck of brown among jostling crowds, roaming in the city's warm, phosphorescent dusk.

(1996)

We hammer the doors of silence,
bruising with words we could not speak.

— Merlie Alunan

Alfred A. Yuson

Born 1945, Manila, Philippines

About the Author

Alfred A. Yuson, a.k.a. Krip, has authored four poetry collections, two novels, three essay compilations, two children's stories, and a short fiction collection. He also edited the coffee table anthology *FIL-AM: The Filipino American Experience*.

He has gained various literary distinctions, including a SEAWrite (Southeast Asian Writers) Award given by Thai royalty in Bangkok in 1992. He has also won First Prizes in the *Asiaweek*, *Philippines Free Press*, and *National Midweek* magazines' short story competitions, the Cultural Center of the Philippines poetry contest, and the Grand Prize for the English Novel in the Carlos Palanca Memorial awards. His second novel, *Voyeurs & Savages*, won a Centennial Literary Prize in 1998.

He is currently Chairman of UMPIL (Writers Union of the Philippines), and is a founding member of the Philippine Literary Arts Council, Creative Writing Foundation, Inc. and Manila Critics Circle. In 1999 he held the Henry Lee Irwin Professorial Chair in Literature at the Ateneo de Manila University where he teaches. Yuson contributes a weekly culture column to *The Philippine Star.*

EDSA Revolution

In 1972, Philippine President Ferdinand Marcos imposed martial law in the Philippines and embarked on a dictatorship that ended in 1986. The repressive Marcos government brought about a proliferation of rebels, some of whom fled to the hills to join the more radical rebels. On February 22, 1986, Filipinos took to the streets to wage their peaceful revolution. Called "People Power" this display of prayerful yet determined protest toppled down the Marcos dictatorship. In the face of such quiet but determined defiance, Ferdinand Marcos fled the Philippines and Cory Aquino became president.

Voice in the Hills

— **Alfred A. Yuson**

That day the men came down openly from the hills, the barrio had risen early for Meniang's wedding. Teodoro the groom had trudged in from San Ildefonso before daybreak. He was accompanied by a dozen of his kinfolk. The rest of his party would come later in the morning, he said to Ka Ambo whose small hut would serve as their waiting station. A bamboo arch had been constructed before Ka Ambo's hut, and Teodoro and his companions now helped put it in place by the old mango tree close to where the dirt road curved down past the ricefields and led away from Barrio Bayabas.

Bingo lay by the edge of a haystack surveying the proceedings. He hadn't slept much through the night. Rudy had kept him up with stories of a bride's first night, and they talked and laughed all they wanted to because his Mamang was deaf anyway and his older sister Nelfa was spending the night with her friend Meniang.

Rudy had taken off at cockcrow so he could put in some work in their poultry yard before the day's festivities began. And Bingo had hurried to where the groom was expected at sunrise, curious as to how this Teodoro would look like after hearing all the giggly chatter the past weeks between Meniang and Nelfa.

They had mentioned how Teodoro fished off the coastal town of San Ildefonso, four valleys away, or half-a-day's walk. Looking now at the groom, Bingo felt disappointed over his lack of golden hair. He had heard of how the sea turned fishermen's hair a reddish gold. But Teodoro displayed nothing that would distinguish him as someone who took a boat out to sea for a living. He wasn't even as dark as most of the folk of Barrio Bayabas. Perhaps he was a lazy fisherman, Bingo thought. He had heard too of how they could sleep away whole afternoons. And how does hair turn gold that way?

Ka Ambo was pushing Teodoro up the short bamboo ladder that led to his one-room hut, saying that the groom should now have some sleep or his knees may give way before Meniang's hour of happiness and the folk of Barrio Bayabas might send him back alone to San Ildefonso, and remember, we still have to drink river after river of coco wine after the ceremony, so stop showing us how helpful you can be, Ka Ambo was saying to Teodoro as he pushed the groom up into the hut, and the menfolk around were laughing including the kinfolk from San Ildefonso.

Bingo yawned and settled deeper into the drying rice stalks. He stared absently at the blue sky of a clear December, then fluttered his eyes once, twice, and slid into a light sleep.

When he awoke he knew it was due to some sudden stillness from among human voices, except for an unfamiliar one that droned on for a spell without really seeming to be talking to anyone. Bingo leaned forward and saw how most of the barrio folk had now gathered quietly before the bamboo arch by the great mango, and how the stranger stood before Teodoro and Meniang who had their heads bowed, and then he heard their voices, short and weak, and a tittering among the crowd and the stranger's voice again and suddenly the crowd began to move forward and there was joyous shouts and he could see his sister Nelfa in a tight sobbing embrace with the bride and Teodoro being patted on the back by everyone.

Bingo tried to see if Rudy was already in the crowd, but he felt hungry and told himself he should now go and join the feasting. It was as he got to his feet that he espied the tiny column of men trudging down the foothills, and another already beginning to cross the small paddy-field valley towards Bayabas.

Bingo tried to count how many men were in those two long lines snaking their way across the paddies. About thirty, he thought. Each one carried a longarm, and even in the distance they looked fresh and more smartly dressed than when they had come to the barrio in smaller groups some times past. The uninvited guests, but gentle guests just the same, Bingo repeated in his head, or so Ka Ambo had said and all the other folk had then agreed.

As he watched the men from the hills make their way slowly across the paddyfield valley, Bingo savored the moment's secret he alone knew, that the wedding feast would have to be shared with the uninvited guests.

"Ceasefire, ceasefire!" Rudy had chanted endlessly a week ago, and his sister Nelfa suddenly wore a crease on her brow, until Capt. Ocampo explained to them what it meant, that there would be no fighting with the rebels for the Christmas season, and how it would mean that he could spend more time with them in Barrio Bayabas, perhaps even go with them to the river where Bingo had said there was a diving rock. He'd teach Bingo how to make what he called a scientific dive, and how to cross the river back and forth in a scientific swim.

Capt. Ocampo was always talking about things scientific, and Nelfa his sister seemed to listen patiently to him all the time. She didn't seem to like him much, but she always listened to his stories of Mindanao and Manila and perhaps it was because he brought her some imported soap and chocolates and once a yellow blouse which she now wore for her friend's wedding, perhaps that was why she gave him so much of her time whenever he came to the barrio with the other soldiers, Bingo thought.

"Ceasefire! Ceasefire!" It was Rudy chanting loudly as he approached the wedding feast by the bamboo arch. Bingo saw Rudy reach the crowd and say something that made the men scurry forward until some of them broke off and began to head his way. Bingo knew his secret was no more. Rudy had spotted the men from the hills too, the rebels as Capt. Ocampo called them, and had told the rest of Barrio Bayabas.

The suckling pig was good, Bingo thought, even as he eyed the men from the hills now seated around sharing in the roast and looking like they had indeed been invited, so crisp and fresh were their shirts and pants, their longarms glistening. He recognized one of the men as Ka Romy, who had courted his sister some years back, and who was said to have slipped into the barrio a few times in the past since he turned "rebel," although Bingo had not seen the fellow himself.

Ka Romy seemed to have sensed Bingo staring at him. The man walked forward with his longarm hung over his shoulder. He smiled intimately at Bingo as he approached.

"You've grown," the man said.

Bingo nodded shyly and brought another piece of the roast suckling into his mouth, forgetting to dip it into the liver sauce.

"You remember me?

Bingo nodded again, his eyes growing large at the longarm slung over the man's shoulder. He offered his plastic bowl of roast tentatively.

"Don't you care to eat, Ka Romy?

"It can wait. My, even your voice has broken. Have they circumcised you yet?"

"No, sir," Bingo muttered, blushing.

"What are they waiting for?"

"For the herb doctor to come in the summer, Ka Romy."

The man swung his longarm down and lay it on he ground. He sat in the shade beside Bingo and took off his shirt. The muscles of his arm rippled as he stretched out to hang the shirt from the branch.

"You know, Bingo, it doesn't have to be done in the summer. We have someone with us who's an expert, if you want it done and healed before Christmas."

Bingo looked around wildly for Rudy wondering what his friend would have to say of the offer. Perhaps they could have it done together. That way he would not feel so disconsolate walking about awkwardly for days.

"I'm surprised you still haven't become a man," Ka Romy kept on. "When I was a boy we used to come here to your barrio just to gather the guava leaves, and at that time the boys around here used to laugh at us for having it done so late."

"The herb doctor didn't come around last summer, sir."

"That's because he's joined us," Ka Romy laughed. "He's been with us in the mountains. He's not with us today because he's on assignment elsewhere. But as I said, we have someone else who's an expert."

Bingo could only nod, staring enviously at the man's biceps and occasionally lowering his eyes towards the longarm. It didn't look as menacing lying like that on the ground by their feet.

"M-16," said Ka Romy.

"Sir?"

"That's what you call this, an M-16. One burst and I can send a lot of coconuts down from a tree. If you want to try it sometime, I'll let you. But only if you have yourself circumcised. You have to become a man soon. Your barrio needs more men. The mountains too need more men."

"You'll really let me try the rifle, sir?" Again Bingo looked around for Rudy. Where was he? He would know how to handle this offer.

"The M-16? Sure. How old are you?

"Fourteen, sir."

"Man enough for it then. But you have to be man enough below the waist too, right?" Ka Romy laughed, but there was something to his laughter that appealed to Bingo, it sounded so full yet so friendly, without contempt. He was still smiling openly when he asked Bingo, "Isn't your sister supposed to be here?"

Bingo realized that he hadn't seen her on his way to the tables where the food had been spread out. He looked around and immediately spotted the newlyweds, but Nelfa was nowhere to be seen. There was Rudy though, stripping off what was left of the suckling pig's crispy skin. Bingo waved, but Rudy never looked in his direction.

"I don't know, sir. She was here a while ago."

"We'll be around for a few days," Ka Romy said nonchalantly. "It's ceasefire, you know. Do you understand what that means?"

"No more shooting, sir, that's what I heard."

"No more shooting, yes. Except at coconuts, you and I. Perhaps the soldiers won't mind. What do you think, Bingo?"

It was the first time someone older had asked him for his opinion, Bingo thought. He looked open-mouthed at Ka Romy, who was now slowly settling his dark muscular body on the ground. Bingo thought better than to answer. Ka Romy didn't seem as if he would mind, his eyes were closed now, and his face seemed so much more at peace, at rest, than those of all the other men who had come down openly from the hills.

Bingo stared at the M-16 lying at his feet. He wondered if he would ever really find the chance to fire it. Instantly he became sure he would, for the man who now lay on the ground before him would be true to his word. Ka Romy had sounded so confident giving it, so that Bingo knew in his heart of hearts that his chance would come.

Nelfa wouldn't answer him when he asked her why she had disappeared from the wedding feast. She had changed into a simple loose dress, and Bingo noticed the yellow blouse she had worn earlier lying crumpled on the bamboo flooring outside her small room.

"I brought some *lechon* for you, Mamang. We could have gotten more of the other food if Nelfa had stayed. I don't know why she left her friends' own wedding."

With an appreciative nod, Mamang acknowledged the banana leaf wrap Bingo lay on the table before her. She was a hefty woman in her forties, given to silences. Bingo and Nelfa knew she hadn't heard what Bingo had said. She was totally deaf. Her occasional voice sounded much like a bird's but all she ever had to say to them was to sweep the yard, burn the leaves, and see that there was enough water in the jars. In her silence she worked the fields industriously, making sure she earned more rice than necessary and bartering the rest for vegetables and some chicken meat.

Bingo tended the tubers, gathered bananas and other fruits, and helped some of the men catch a few fish in the river. Nelfa worked for a handicraft lady, weaving baskets and trays for some cash and a regular supply of canned sardines and meat loaf.

Mamang used to prattle on birdlike about how her well-off sister would come back someday, perhaps from the States, or from somewhere in Manila, and how she would take both of them to the city for more schooling. Bingo always hoped that Mamang's sister would turn out to be their mother, for he wasn't too sure if Mamang had indeed borne them, and no one in the barrio seemed interested in finding out from her either.

Now she opened the banana leaf wrap and gazed happily at the leftover *lechon*. Her voice sounded like a bird's. "Do we still have vinegar?"

Bingo went to fetch it instead of replying. He placed the bottle before her. Suddenly he felt like telling her that he thought he should become a man soon, so he motioned towards his shorts and made quick cutting gestures in front of him.

Mamang laughed her birdlike laugh, tossed herself back and spread her arms out, and Bingo knew she was saying she wished she knew how.

The men with longarms are down from the hills, mimed Bingo, and the man who knew Nelfa said there was someone with them who could do it. Then he would get to fire Nelfa's friend's gun, fire at the coconuts and cause them to fall, for Capt. Ocampo and his men wouldn't mind because there was to be no shooting between the soldiers and the rebels this Christmas but that coconut trees were not covered by the—"Ceasefire!" shouted Bingo at Mamang. "Ceasefire! Merry Christmas! Ceasefire!"

"What are you talking about?" cried Nelfa as she rushed out of her small room.

Bingo knew she had seen him through all his motions to Mamang and had understood everything, she was just crying out as loudly as he had because she was angry about something.

"Ka Romy was there, he was asking about you," he told his sister.

Nelfa looked at Mamang as if to make sure she had not heard, or understood. When she looked back at Bingo her anger was gone. "So he asked about me. I haven't seen him for a long time. Are they staying?"

"Yes, because there'll be no shooting."

"What makes you so sure?"

"That's what everyone has said, that's what Ka Romy said, he said he'd teach me to fire his M-16, but that I should first have myself . . . " Bingo trailed off in embarrassment.

Nelfa smiled. "You fire that gun of his and the soldiers will come to get you, and I won't ask the Captain to save you from walking all the way to town with them so that your little *tu-tu* would grow as big and as red as a tomato by the time you get to their jail."

Bingo couldn't help but laugh as he blushed. Nelfa herself was pleased with her joke, and they hadn't for a long time laughed like this together until tears formed in their eyes. And Mamang too was laughing as Nelfa acted out her threat, taking over from where Bingo had shot at the coconuts and off he's hauled away by the soldiers to the distant cell so that the forced walk causes Bingo's freshly cut little *tu-tu* to swell painfully. She rushed to pick up a red tomato from the kitchen and shoved it towards Mamang's face, and then at Bingo's, and they were all laughing so hard that Bingo fled from the joke and Nelfa hurled the tomato past his head as he ran down the bamboo steps nearly doubling up with laughter.

"Call me Buddy," said the Captain. "Your sister calls me Buddy. Here, here's a T-shirt for you. You see, it's got the President's face, she's smiling so nicely. Here, take it."

Bingo quickly wiped his dirt-stained fingers on the seat of his pants and reached for the orange-colored T-shirt. He had been digging for the month's yams when Capt. Ocampo had walked into their small yard with two of his men. Bingo felt sorry that he had not been too careful in receiving the present. He had smudged a part of it right above the president's smiling face, where the words PEOPLE POWER proclaimed themselves in a bold black arch.

Nelfa appeared in the open doorway. She was wearing the yellow blouse the Captain had given her, with a simple white skirt that reached all the way to her ankles, making her look like one of the barrio's married women, Bingo thought, except that she was slim and had a fetching coyness that still marked her as a barrio-lass men from valleys away would come to visit. Nelfa was smiling her faint smile that seemed to Bingo like a perfected imitation of Mamang's own little birdlike smile, so tight and thin and alert.

The Captain met her as she went down the bamboo steps. No sooner had she reached the ground in her red rubber slippers when the Captain led her off silently to the small grove of guava trees by the edge of the paddyfield. Nelfa walked so close beside him that even if she were a step or two behind, they appeared as if they were walking off abreast.

The two soldiers ambled off to the dried-up well beside the hut, propped their longarms down against the old adobe blocks and settled themselves on the ground where there was shade.

The water jars were in that spot the soldiers had chosen, so Bingo thought twice before proceeding up the hut and to the kitchen where he got a tincupful of water from the clay pot and quickly washed his hands of the tubers' grime. He wiped his hands hurriedly on the seat of his pants and picked up the Cory T-shirt and this time held it aloft to inspect, noting the smudge, working it off with a half-wet thumb and holding it up again before him like a flag and it was so brightly orange that he knew Rudy would spot him a good distance from their meeting place by the granary and he'd come closer and brighter in orange with Cory's wonderful smile on his chest.

Mamang was snoring her birdlike snore, her breasts heaving up from the frayed brown mat. Soft shafts of light fell on her feet through the slats on the palm-weave wall, and when Bingo tilted his head he could see her as if standing on light, while her snore persisted birdlike.

Out the window he could glimpse Nelfa and the Captain, Buddy, that's what he had said to call him, by the guava trees standing close to each other. Bingo felt like bathing but the soldiers were resting near the water jugs. He went back to the clay pot and saw that there were just a few cupfuls of water left. He took off his shirt, splashed his body with the water and wiped himself dry. Then he put on the new one with Cory's face and her nice smile and PEOPLE POWER arching above her and ran down the bamboo steps and towards the dirt road to see where his friend Rudy was.

They had taken a swim in the river and were drying themselves on the rocks when Rudy told him that the next wedding the barrio would have would likely be between his sister Nelfa and Capt. Ocampo, the whole barrio knew that, and said too that she'd probably just go off with him without even marrying but just go and live with the Captain in the camp several towns away, that was what the barrio folk kept talking about. Bingo kept silent as Rudy told him all this, although he didn't feel surprised about what his friend had said but about how he had said it.

"So you're going to get more T-shirts from the soldiers," Rudy was saying with a sneer.

Bingo looked at his new orange T-shirt lying neatly on a rock beside them.

"You'll probably get a yellow one too with Cory's face on it, and then a red one and a green one and a blue one, all the soldiers in that camp will give you one because everyone knows any girl who lives in the camp with the soldiers will have to marry them all, you know, not really marry them but treat each one like a husband. That's what Nelfa will do. So her brother will get a lot of T-shirts."

Bingo stopped skipping little flat pebbles on the river's surface. He knit his brows as he stared glumly at Rudy, failing to comprehend why his friend was saying all these unlikely things.

"That's not true," he said weakly. "You know that's not true."

Rudy stood up and picked a large rock and tossed it into the river. "Oh yeah? Ask the soldiers. Ask the Captain. You think you're so smart just because you have a new T-shirt."

Bingo felt anger rising within him, but tried to stave it off. "You can have it if you want it," he suddenly shouted at his friend.

Rudy picked up the orange T-shirt. "This?" he asked mockingly. "Why would I want to wear a woman's face on my chest? If you don't want it, then the river can have it."

He bundled up the T-shirt and tossed it into the shallows. Bingo rushed after it, splashing his way into the water. Picking up the T-shirt, he turned to confront his friend, but Rudy was now running as fast as he could up the path that led to the paddyfields.

Bingo looked sadly down at the wet T-shirt in his hand and made a halfhearted effort to wring it dry. If he had laughed, Bingo thought to himself, if that Rudy had dared laugh as he ran off, then I would have gone after him and given him a blow. Sadness and anger stirred together inside him as he slapped the T-shirt down on a rock. Tears were beginning to well in his eyes when Ka Romy appeared quietly before him.

"We all have problems, don't we? Us little people, our problems never end. That's why we try to do something about it. That's why sometimes we have to do it through force of arms."

He lay the M-16 gently down on the ground close to Bingo, then pulled out a menacing-looking knife which he began to whet against a smooth rock.

Bingo fought back his tears and looked at the muscular young man before him. The knife glinted in Ka Romy's hands as he pushed and slapped it against the flat rock. If he had a knife like that, Bingo thought, not Rudy, not anyone, would dare throw anything of his down the river. He looked at the M-16 on the ground, and wanted so badly to touch it.

"I am ready," he said softly to Ka Romy.

The muscular young man looked up at him with a gentle smile. "Ready for what?"

"You said you had someone with you who could . . . who could make me a man. I want to learn how to use the gun. You promised."

"There are many steps to become a man," said Ka Romy. "But I'm glad to know that you're willing to take the first one."

"Where is your friend who can do it, circumcise me?"

"I am right here," replied Ka Romy, "and this is the knife that has done it to hundreds of little boys like you who've wanted to turn into men."

Ka Romy stood up and walked off. Bingo got to his feet too, wondering whether he was supposed to follow. But no, they couldn't just go and leave the M-16 lying around like that, he thought. He'd heard of how it took many cavans of rice to trade for one. Now he heard some hacking sounds from behind some bushes, and presently Ka Romy was back with a forked branch and a sprig of guava leaves.

Bingo knew the time had come to be brave. He cast off all shyness before the man with the knife and pulled down his trousers. Ka Romy held the leaves out.

"Here," he said, "chew on these, then spit on the wound."

Bingo thrust the leaves into his mouth and began chewing on them furiously, even as he felt Ka Romy stretch him out over the forked branch, and the cold bite of the knife testing his tenderness. And the courage welled up in him so that with the slash of blade against his skin he felt the river roar inside him and the sky turn in shame until the pain rose with such fury that he remembered all the men's tales and spat the guava juice onto his wound and stifled a cry as he ran naked and remembering and flung himself still without a cry into the river.

It was nearing dark when Ka Romy helped steady him up and they started to walk back to Barrio Bayabas. He had put his trousers back on, and now tried to walk as slowly as possible to avoid chafing the wound. Each step was tortuous, but Ka Romy guided him on patiently, and thankfully without bothering to make small talk.

Once in a while Bingo tightened his grip on the orange T-shirt in his hand, which Ka Romy had used to wipe him clean, and it was now bloodied with the magnificence of his wound, and he thought of Mamang and how she would squeal birdlike when she saw him stagger home a wounded little man, and how Nelfa would smile in her cold coy way as if she knew everything there was to know about such things, even about how it was to become a man.

He had done it before Rudy had, he was first, he prided himself too with each tortured step. Now he can tell the story. Now he can slap down the bloodied orange T-shirt on Rudy's face and force him to wear it, blood, grime, river water and all . . . And he'd show him his wound of manhood and tell him how glorious the pain had been. And how now that they neared the barrio Ka Romy stopped upon sight of the first grove of coconut trees and slipped in something with a metallic clack into the M-16 and fired a loud rapid burst that nearly shattered his ears and he forgot about the pain seeing the coconuts falling as fast thuds on the ground and the fronds jumping and breaking in mid-air before they crashed softly with their long thrashing sounds. And he'll tell Rudy how Ka Romy had given him the M-16 and placed his finger on the trigger and helped him steady it up as he pointed the gun at another tree then squeezed and found himself fighting the sweep of its force and how the burst of fire erased his pain completely, so that he could hear the thud of coconut or crash of frond there was nothing else ringing in his ears but the scream of how it was to be a man.

For days he stayed home and tended to his thoughts. The nights were becoming cooler as Christmas approached, and Nelfa was hardly ever home, she worked till late at night on star lanterns for the season, she told Mamang. But some nights he saw her walking back with the Captain, and they would stop a while by the guava trees before she'd hurriedly go up the hut and he'd slip back into the dark.

There were afternoons too when Ka Romy would come and talk to him after failing to see Nelfa, and he'd teach him how to spin the knife into a banana stalk, but he had said they couldn't play around with the M-16 again for there was no telling when he'd need the bullets for the soldiers, Christmas or no Christmas, Ka Romy the rebel had said.

Bingo wondered if Ka Romy knew that Nelfa had a captain of the soldiers for a friend. One time Mamang came home early from the fields and she recognized Ka Romy and shrieked at him birdlike so that to Bingo's surprise he quickly carried off his M-16 and the knife and disappeared down the road before Mamang could continue crying out.

Bingo had forgotten the last time he had seen Mamang quite as angry. But he decided against asking Nelfa about it, although he worried that Ka Romy would not come around again, he'd miss the stories about life in the hills and the songs of revolution Ka Romy said they sang, and the feel of the knife in his hands.

Ka Romy came back, however. And it was all Bingo could do to keep himself from jumping for joy when Ka Romy said he was leaving the knife so that Bingo could train himself with it as much as he wanted to.

Rudy came unexpectedly that same afternoon. Surprised as he was, Bingo quickly asked him if he wanted to be a man too. Rudy said he didn't understand and Bingo pulled down his trousers and proudly showed Rudy the reason he had stayed home all this time and Rudy's mouth fell.

"I was responsible for that," said Ka Romy, smiling. "It will take very little courage on your part,"

"No, no," stammered Rudy. "My father will whip me if I have it done without his word."

Bingo snickered and made as if he'd spin the knife into some imaginary target. Ka Romy smiled and slung the M-16 firmly on his shoulder. "Take care of the knife then," he said to Bingo, "until your friend here takes courage from his father's word."

Ka Romy walked off and Bingo stared sullenly at Rudy. He didn't feel like telling his former friend any of the stories he had run in his mind since that day in the river.

Rudy tried to coax him out of his silence, saying that he had waited several times at their meeting place by the granary, and that he felt sorry about what he had said and done that last time in the river. Bingo kept quiet, toying with the knife, shaving off some slivers of bamboo from the steps.

Rudy said there had almost been some shooting the day before, some soldiers had gotten drunk and wanted to look for some rebels they knew were in the barrio, but that Ka Ambo had fetched Nelfa from the handicraft lady's place and she had in turn called for Capt. Ocampo to pacify his men.

And your sister threw up right there on the road when Capt. Ocampo came to assure her and Ka Ambo that everything was alright, Rudy was saying, she threw up suddenly and seemed ready to faint that they had to lay her down to rest for a while. And she had gotten up and insisted on walking home alone, and Capt. Ocampo couldn't stop her, he just stood there on the middle of the road with Ka Ambo, scratching his head and looking glumly at Nelfa's little puddle of vomit on the dust. And I saw it all, you know, Rudy was saying, and when Bingo hardly even looked at him, Rudy went on, and you know what I think your sister is carrying a child and it must be the Captain's unless, well, it could also be Ka Ambo's ha ha ha . . .

Bingo hurled himself forward and struck Rudy flush on the mouth. His friend fell backward, stunned. Rudy brought his hand up to stem the bleeding, and in an instant was up on his feet, but Bingo slashed at the air between them with the knife, and Rudy saw the look on Bingo's face and recognized the absence of anger, so that he turned and ran without a look behind his back.

That night Mamang slept soundly, without a bird ever rising roughly from her throat. Bingo picked himself up quickly from the floor when he heard the scurrying of many feet past their hut. He peered out into the moonlight night and saw the men with longarms move quickly up the road. They hardly spoke to one another, but occasionally one of the men would urge a faster pace as they filed past towards the edge of the barrio.

In the hut's stillness Bingo knew that Nelfa was also watching the men from her window. It didn't alarm him either when he heard a familiar voice whisper from the shadows, calling out softly for his sister. It was Ka Romy, and for once his voice bore some loss of assurance.

Bingo heard Nelfa move quickly out of their hut to meet him. The pair of shadows disappeared swiftly behind the guava trees. Bingo peered out of their doorway but didn't dare go down the steps. He could hear them arguing in the dark, while the rest of the landscape breathed silently in the weakened light of the moon.

I cannot go with you to the hills, Nelfa was saying, and you refuse to take me away elsewhere. But the child is mine, Ka Romy said, and if you do not come with me then I'll come back for the child, and you can go off with your Captain if you want. I am too big now, Nelfa said, you cannot expect me to share in that kind of life with you in the hills, running off here and there, living the lives of fugitives, no, no, I cannot. Don't come back, Romy, don't come back.

Suddenly Nelfa burst out of the shadows with Ka Romy in desperate pursuit. A single shot rang out, and he crumpled quickly to the ground. Bingo saw more flashes of gunfire as heavy boots descended all around the hut. He saw Capt. Ocampo firing at the crumpled figure of Ka Romy, whose body twitched wickedly on the ground then finally lay still, while Nelfa had frozen in her flight and no sound but a soft birdlike cry came from her mouth as she looked in pain at the Captain emptying his gun on the still figure on the ground.

Bingo whirled back and plunged into the corner of the hut. There the knife lay beside his mat. Mamang slept soundly some distance away. Bingo wanted to wake her, cry out to her, make her heave to his growing pain. But all he did was to scoop up the knife and charge outdoors into the spearing glare of flashlights.

"Don't shoot! Don't shoot him!" cried Capt. Ocampo. "Bingo, get back in!"

His sister remained frozen where she was, her face in silent anguish, her fingers gripping the sides of her loose dress. The soldiers pointed their longarms and flashlights at him, and he felt trapped in the awful loss of voice and the tightening of space around him. With a quick leap he was at Ka Romy's side, wrenching off the M-16 from a fallen shoulder and scampering away as fast as he could past the guava trees and across the paddyfield.

"Nobody fires!" He could hear Capt. Ocampo shouting at the top of his voice, and footsteps racing behind him. "Bingo, stop! Bingo! This is Buddy! Don't be foolish, Bingo!"

And Bingo thought he heard a birdlike cry come soaring out of the hut he was leaving behind, louder than the beating in his chest as his bare feet pounded on the caked mud of the paddyfield, drowning out the Captain's cries and footsteps as he ran on heedlessly towards the hills. There was where he knew a voice waited to assure him that his knife and his gun would soon learn to speak such terrible silences.

(1987)

Vince Gotera

Born 1952, San Francisco, California; lived in Manila for some time as a child

Photo: Mary Ann Blue Gotera

Vince Gotera with son Gabe, 4 years old

About the Author

Vince Gotera is the editor of the *North American Review*, the oldest literary magazine in the United States. His books include *Dragonfly* (Pecan Grove Press, 1994), a collection of poems, and *Radical Visions: Poetry by Vietnam Veterans* (University of Georgia Press, 1994), a literary study. Another poetry book, *Fighting Kite* (Pecan Grove Press), is forthcoming. His poems, stories, and essays have appeared in such magazines as *Kenyon Review* and *Ploughshares* as well as anthologies like *Bold Words: A Century of Asian American Writing*. Vince is a professor of creative writing and literature at the University of Northern Iowa. He and his wife Mary Ann live in Cedar Falls, Iowa with their four children. He also has an older son who is a graphic designer in San Francisco. Vince loves all shades of blue and has been known to thunk a bass guitar from time to time.

Growing Up in America in the 1960s

"Manny's Climb" mines its emotional power from the experiences of young Filipino Americans growing up in America in the 1960s, a time when the racial sensitivities of the U.S. were attuned to only two colors: black and white. It was difficult then to be teenage and brown, yellow, or red. I recall distinctly how I and my Filipino American friends and peers slipped on whiteness (Derby jackets and Ben Davis baggy pants) as well as blackness (pimp socks, dashikis, knit shirt-jackets) but not so much "flip-ness"—*Barong Tagalog*, the *terno*—even though we would wear these to the many "Fil-Am" social events our parents would drag us to. I was probably nineteen or older before I began to really accept being Filipino, and older yet when I could see those experiences more lucidly, as I hope they are depicted in this story.

Manny's Climb

— Vince Gotera

"He looks just like a damn spider in a web!" It must have been Piggy Figone who said that. "A Flip spider!" We had all laughed—me, the Three Rons, Crazy Greg, and a couple other kids—as we watched Manny climb the transmitter tower. Hanging by the tips of his fingers. Even now, more than twenty-five years later, I can still imagine what he must have felt like; just the week before Manny's climb, the Three Rons had made *me* scale that tower. I can still remember how it felt: the wind parting your hair like a cold hand, the tower creaking as it swayed, like the rivets were gonna pop off one by one as if you were Wile E. Coyote in a *Roadrunner* cartoon, and the sky all around you a deep blue fishbowl. Manny just kept inching, shinnying up. Filipino spider, indeed.

I'll never forget the day Manny—Emmanuel was his full given name—transferred to St. Alfred's in the sixth grade. Third week of school, a bright Indian-summer morning with just a hint of crispness in the air. A new kid was in the schoolyard, where we were all waiting for Sister Mary Michael, the principal, to come out and ring that huge handbell of hers, telling us to line up. "My name is Manny Mendoza," he was saying to one kid after another, "D'ya want me to eat this paper?" He would then hold up a piece of paper, shredded on one end, where it had been torn from one of those pocket-size spiral-bound notebooks. Of course, each one of us, when asked that question, said "Yeah!" What else could a self-respecting, red-blooded, American eleven-year-old say? Boy, did he gather a crowd of kids as he chewed up and swallowed piece after piece of paper. Kids were beginning to cheer, to egg him on, "Manny! Manny! Manny!" In fact, just as Sister Michael came out on the school steps with her bell, Manny's pad ran out, and he tore a chunk out of his brown lunch bag with his teeth.

Well, I didn't know what to think about this new kid. For five years, I had been the only Filipino kid in the class, and now Manny made two. But, jeez, what a clown! Did I want to be associated with this guy? One thing about Manny, though, he knew how to dress. His St. Alfred School uniform—white shirt, brown "salt-and-pepper" corduroy pants, brown cardigan—was always impeccably cut. The rest of us always seemed rumpled and baggy in our uniforms next to Manny. His pants had been altered, form-fitted to a sixteenth of an inch outside what the nuns might deem too tight. And his pants—I tell you, this is hard to do with cords—his pants were always starch-ironed with folds like razor blades. His sweaters always had a blousy look, kind of like "poet shirts" in lingerie catalogs, billowing out slightly in the sleeves before the gather of the cuff, a whisper of fullness at the waist before the cummerbund-like tightness hugging the hips. His white short-sleeve shirts, too, were always professionally starched. By 3:30 in the afternoon, we would be limp as wilted cabbage, but Manny's collars would still be crisp as cardboard. And he wore imported Italian half-boots! The rest of us wore Kinney's wingtips, but his boots were what we could call, in a year or so, "Beatle boots"—coming to a chic, sleek, and trendy point at the toe. Man, that Manny was sharp!

Don't get me wrong, now, Manny was no sissy. He may have dressed like a dandy, but he was no slouch on the basketball court. Every day at lunch, the Three Rons would rule. That was Ron Johnson, a tall black kid who played center on our fourth-grade team; Ron Morse, a freckled and carrot-topped Irish boy with a short-man complex, who would fight anybody that looked at him the wrong way; and Geronimo Lee Wong, a sullen half-Chinese, half-Apache kid who had beaten up white Ron the second week of school in second grade to earn his slot. It occurs to me now that the Three Rons were like some kind of demographic slice of early 1960s San Francisco. Anyway, the Three Rons were the apex of the boys' social pyramid, and some of the girls rather liked the Rons' dashing ways, at least until Manny showed up with his Italian half-boots. So Manny had to prove himself that first day. Well, no, it couldn't have been the first day, because Manny was sent home right after lunch with a stomachache. In fact, he had thrown his lunch away (what there was left of the paper bag), 'cause he just couldn't bring himself to eat anything. But anyway, Manny showed himself over the next few days to be a pretty decent point guard. He could dribble real fancy—between scissoring legs, pizzicato behind the back—and he could sink two out of three jump shots from the top of the key. Until now, though, I can't figure out how he kept those Italian half-boots shined throughout the day, but he always did.

Back at the tower, all I could see of Manny's boots were his soles, and they were just as worn as the bottoms of anybody else's shoes. In fact, it seemed like there was the beginning of a hole in the left sole, but he must have been thirty feet above us, so who knows? In any case, the pointed toes were coming in real handy as Manny slipped them into one acutely angled foothold after another, as diagonal braces crisscrossed in front of and around him. As I looked at him against the backdrop of drifting clouds, the tower seemed to ripple and shimmer, sway slightly like the tower of Pisa must, I imagined. Jeez, that was one climb I would never want to do again.

When white Ron, in the sixth grade, noticed that the rest of us were growing taller around him, and that he was fading back in the growth curve, becoming a runt, one might say though still no one dared to say it to his face, he and black Ron devised a series of tests by which the rest of us boys could prove our manhood. One was to jump off the top of Chinese Ron's stoop to the sidewalk. Now this wasn't a straight-down drop, some ten feet or so. That wouldn't have been sporting enough. No, you had to sail at a forty-five degree angle across the gravitational pull of the earth, about fifteen feet over the steps. And there wasn't much room at the top of the steps for a running start. You just had to stand there and take off, hoping your knees could take the shock when—and if—you hit the sidewalk and not the last step. I guess it was fortunate no one got more than a skinned knee or torn pants. There were twenty-one steps, I remember distinctly, and that split second while you were in the air seemed like forever. Then you would hit rock bottom. Piggy was the best at that free fall. Piggy wasn't fat; he just had a little upturned nose and with a name like Figone, well, his nickname was a natural. Manny survived that test too, though he did scuff his right boot.

Another stunt black Ron devised was walking around and over the N Judah tunnel entrance. The N Judah was a streetcar line that went underground for a mile and a half, or thereabouts, and then surfaced to continue its way downtown. For a while, we had been jumping on the back of the streetcars, riding on the outside and making funny faces at the backs of passengers' heads. One time, Chinese Ron and Crazy Greg even rode the N Judah—again, on the outside, hanging on to the back window ledge—all the way through the tunnel. After they rode back, Crazy Greg—his full name was Gregory Romanoff, a good Russian boy—Greg was jumping around like Daffy Duck, he was so jazzed. Now that tunnel ride's something I *just* could not do. Black Ron couldn't do it either, so he proposed the tunnel walk.

The tunnel entrance was flanked by two sidewalks which climbed the hill above the tunnel; at the top, the sidewalks met and continued up. Next to the sidewalks was a four-foot-high concrete banister, maybe a foot or so wide with a fairly gentle incline, while at the top, where the sidewalks converged, a level segment, about forty feet across, formed the upper rim of the concrete wall that edged the tunnel archway. Black Ron's idea was to walk on the banister, an uphill climb of maybe a hundred feet, then across the straight edge above—a real tightrope act, since you'd look down past your feet at the rails glinting below, with an occasional rumbling streetcar to shake you up, literally as well as figuratively—and finally downhill on the other side. White Ron and I, both small and fleet of foot, were the best at this stunt. Manny passed this test too; in fact, he stood on one leg in the middle of the level crossing, and mimicked a statue of Mercury perched on one winged foot. "Look at me, you guys! No hands!"

Manny was getting close to the top of the tower, now. He had been climbing for a solid seven minutes. With a couple of shaky transitions, I must say. I particularly remember that loose strut he encountered some ten feet earlier. Well, not exactly loose, since the rivets on either end were still holding. The strut would nevertheless quiver and rattle if you touched it, and you sure didn't dare put your weight on it. When I had climbed the tower the week before, I had looked down as I passed that strut, wanting to make sure I didn't put a foot on it. The view was magnificent. The Three Rons and the other kids were distant as ants. Crazy Greg's mouth gaped open. With sheer bravado born of adrenaline, I had leaned out over the abyss and yelled, "Hey, Crazy! You catching flies?" Boy, what a rush! The sun shining, reflections glinting off the occasional shiny surfaces on the tower. Down below, on the other side of the tower from the kids, was Sutro Lake, also flashing reflections like you wouldn't believe. Well, not exactly a lake, more like a pond, really. It was beautiful.

Piggy and I went over to Manny's house one afternoon, after school. He had invited us to have cookies or something. His parents weren't home, but that was pretty common among us kids, all latchkey types. Manny lived in a typical San Francisco flat, a little dingy and dark, with most of the shades pulled down. All sorts of Filipino bric-a-brac all around: on the dining room wall hung a giant wooden fork and spoon, carved fancifully on the handles; also a black shield like an interstate sign, with miniature Moro swords and knives arrayed on it like inlaid stripes; in the corner of the living room, a hanging lamp festooned with a mobile of circular capiz-shell slices; and other touristy knick-knacks.

"Jesus H. Christ," Piggy laughed, "we're in the Philippines now."

"I can't help what family I was born into," Manny muttered, his eyes glowering as he turned on the tube. So anyway, Piggy and Manny and I were sitting in the living room munching down on ginger snaps and watching Rocky and Bullwinkle, when Piggy's hand darted up into the air in front of his face. He had caught a fly. Not much to brag about, 'cause that fly had clearly been in the house for a couple of days, and it was starting to slow down. Not yet at that stage where the fly becomes delirious and begins bumping into your face, but certainly not at the peak of condition either. After Piggy let the fly go, I reached out and grabbed it too.

"Hey, watch this," I said, leading the way into the kitchen. Still holding the fly buzzing around inside my right fist, I asked Manny for a glass of water. He set it down on the counter, and I lowered my right hand into the water and let the fly go. "What do you think? Will he drown?"

"Sure," Piggy snorted, "he's a *Flip*, that fly!"

Manny's lips were pressed into a firm straight line. The fly lay at the bottom of the glass, motionless, for quite a long time, maybe a minute, as we watched intently. And then I poured the water slowly into the sink.

"Now watch," I whispered. In the empty glass, the fly lay there for a moment and then seemed to shrug feebly. After a few seconds, he was on his feet, though a little shaky. In another half-minute, he had recovered enough to sail into the air, buzzing as well as ever before.

"That's nothing," Manny said. He then snagged the fly in his palm, got it between finger and thumb. I remember how mad it was, buzzing and wriggling its legs. Then Manny popped it into his mouth and swallowed noisily. "There you go, Piggy," he said. "So much for your Filipino fly. I hate *everything* about the goddamn Philippines." It was only at that moment that I realized how much Manny and I were in competition.

Manny was almost at the top of the tower now. He just had to reach his left arm upward and he would touch the base of the transmitter itself. That's as far as any one of us had ever gone. Just a momentary touch, to say you too had been there, had planted your flag in the North Pole, then back down to terra firma. Of course Manny went further. Pretty soon he was standing on the transmitter base, swinging from the antenna itself like King Kong on top of the Empire State Building. "I'll be damned," black Ron said. "I thought that antenna would give you one hell of a shock." We all stood there with our mouths hanging open, like lightning was going to strike Manny any moment.

And then Manny turned to face the lake. He was just a silhouette up there, a figure cut sharply from the blue background of sky. Manny dove, kicking his legs to clear the chain-link fence around the bottom of the tower. In the air, Manny spread his arms like bird's wings. "Holy Mary," white Ron whispered, "Mother of God." In my head going on thirty years, in all our heads, I'm sure, though we never talked about it, Manny was dazzling as an eagle flashing in the heavens. None of us could tell at that moment if he was going to make it into the lake. I turned away, the image of Manny spread out against the sky indelibly burning in my brain.

(2000)

Oscar Peñaranda

Born 1944, Leyte, Philippines; immigrated to Canada in 1956

About the Author

Oscar Peñaranda has been writing since he was fourteen years old or so. He attended San Francisco State University where he got a B.A. in Literature (1967) and a M.A. in Creative Writing (1974). He has been a teacher for about thirty-one years, twelve years in San Francisco State University, ten years in Everett Middle School (San Francisco) and nine years at James Logan high school in Union City, California, where he continues to teach. He has been teaching Tagalog and Filipino Heritage Studies at this high school. For establishing these two classes in the California school system, he received an award and California State Recognition. He was the first president and founder of the San Francisco chapter of the Filipino National Historical Society in 1988. His works include short stories, plays, poetry, essays, novels (in progress), TV and film scripts. He also helps coordinate Filipino American events in the Bay Area.

Filipinos in California Farmlands

Between 1900 and 1930, 100,000 Filipinos left the Philippines to work in Hawaii and the United States mainland. The majority worked in the sugar cane and pineapple fields of Hawaii, the farms of California, the canneries of Alaska and the Pacific Northwest, and in various menial positions in metropolitan cities of America.

Many Filipinos in the U.S. through various connections knew someone who worked in the vast expanse of farmlands in California, especially before 1965. For young students this meant a little pocket money, especially for items that their parents disapproved of as a waste of money, like contact lenses, for example. These part-time summer workers should be distinguished from the real farm workers of California who worked the farms as a living. But of course if one is observant, one does not have to be a permanent farm laborer to appreciate their struggles and experiences. Here is one story from a youthful, part-time farm worker.

Day of the Butterfly

— Oscar Peñaranda

I was not there at all. I was sick from eating too many peanut butter sandwiches and had to stay behind in camp that day in the summer of '62.

It was the sort of story that I've been told constantly by participants, but in different stages of their lives, at different intervals. They told it to me so many times, yet I know so little of it. Maybe you can tell me. As I've mentioned I just heard it from the participants at different times in their lives afterwards, in The City, on separate occasions, sometimes from two or three of them together, at other times, individually; and though all of them told it more than once, never have they told it all together at one time in one sitting. It was the sort of story that you keep hearing parts of and at times in differing versions, so that it could not be completely forgotten. Scenes and times would change but the story would remain eternal, yet elusive. So you can see the pains I had to take to tell the whole thing coherently when pressured by the old crowd for that particular story during some once-in-a-blue-moon Get-Together. I had to piece things together, use liberties to fill in gaps, iron out seeming contradictions, and restrain the implausible, to make palatable, to make sense out of the whole fiasco that was the roadside showdown on freeway Interstate 80, about 40 miles northeast of San Francisco where we were all from. And even then it was still open for several interpretations. Though I heard about the incident in relative solitude, I was always forced to tell it in company. Sometimes I felt like a priest talking at the pulpit about his parishioners' confessions.

We were all from San Francisco, but in the summer months, all worked in various fields and orchards of California. My older brother Antonio and his schoolmate from U.S.F. Bong was there, and Batok, the Elvis Presley of the group, and Clarence, the smallest and the one who really started the whole thing and the one who got married first, and then went to Nam. He never really did explain why he did both. And when he got to Vietnam, they said he volunteered to be point-man.

And then there was one more with them that day. There were five of them, they had all said, but none of them could remember the fifth man. When they told the story and when they came upon the tally of the participants they all quickly said five. But upon request, they could only name four, the same four, and it would take for the whole story to be told before they would even remember there was a fifth man. It'll come to me later, was a common phrase.

Batok had definitely the most luscious hair among them. He would take hours of facial pantomime with the mirror, touching different parts of his hair. The word *batok* is that flat area in the back of one's head between the ears. There is something very vulnerable and humiliating about that part of a person's anatomy (especially when one gets hit there, and therefore connotations of that word were often not too uplifting for one's ego).

They called him Batok because once when Clarence was giving him the finishing touches of a haircut, Batok complained that the neckline was slightly crooked. "How about straightening this out, boy," he said, chewing his gum. In those days in San Francisco, in every *barkada* (circle of friends), one or two could cut hair fairly decently.

Clarence and I were the two barbers of our *barkada*. In fact I was somewhat his pupil and he my mentor in haircuts. Undoubtedly and ubiquitously, Clarence was the best barber even among other *barkadas* that we knew. But that day, the gift of the gods was just not with him. He must have, as the old ones liked to tease, forgotten to wash his hands after he took a shit.

"You ain't no good no more. Washed up. *La-us*!" Batok chewed his gum bobbing up and down, neck twisted, his eye straining to get a better look at that crooked line in the mirror.

"Here," Clarence finally admitted. "Sit down. That ain't nothing. I'll fix that. That's only hair. It's your face you should worry about," he added, "my preng."

"Puck you . . . my preng."

But Clarence seemed to have straightened it out anyway. Yet upon closer inspection, Batok noticed that the other side of the neckline was lower now. Clarence had raised the right side too high.

"Hey, man. How much booze have you had? The other side is messed up now."

Clarence put down his beer and really got to work. But it was too late. By the time he took another good long look at the back of Batok's head, his neckline had crawled up above one of his ears, a good part of scalp on the back of his head, his *batok*, was already quite exposed. And especially for a person whose only source of pride and self esteem was his hair, it was disastrous, and from then on, he was called Batok. He was not really a bad looking individual. It was just that his looks were unusual not because of his brown skin and broad nose and other outer features, but because of a boyish fire of lustful madness that lightly gleamed occasionally from his big restless lips. *Malibog* is the Filipino word that comes to mind. He was rather stocky, broad-shouldered, and had somewhat of a voice, unschooled, of course, and that voice he bent out of shape every time he up-tempoed it to sound like Elvis Presley's grunts and groans, his Elvis Presley hair gradually but precisely falling in bunches on his Elvis Presley brow.

The family of Bong used to visit from The City about twice a month and everyone would anticipate more than Bong himself because he had a sister whose name was Maganda. They would bring Bong some Filipino food and a little left over for some of us who might want, too. Batok would run around crazy looking for a tree to lean on while plucking his guitar pretending he didn't notice her face glowing in the car that had just pulled in. "Oh, hi, Maganda. Was that you guys that just pulled in?" It was an idyllic scene indeed. Save for the fact that the keenest of observers might have noticed that Batok was left-handed, and being left-handed had to strum his romantic guitar from the bottom up, with his thumb jerking upwards in each stroke and his mouth going slightly askew as a result of it. And then he would sing. And his voice would float in the evening like a velvet veil. Batok had a beautiful crooner's voice with so much passion that it carried far into the evenings of camp life.

They had just finished high school then, though Antonio and Bong were already in college. But it was summer. It was in the dead heat of summer, in the Suisun Valley of California, just northeast of San Francisco. The young men who had been working in the fields just had a day off, after more than three and a half weeks straight of picking apricots. Apricot is the most brittle of trees! A puff of casual summer wind I have seen split a tree like lightning would. All it took was air, a gust, a puff. They had hitchhiked to town, bought some groceries to save on food expenses, (actually some stole some groceries), and were now walking back along the freeway Interstate 80, hitchhiking. Five brown, young men, Filipinos, walking with packages and bags and hitchhiking along the freeway between Vacaville and Vallejo. This was 1962. The Summer of '62.

They had just gotten off their first ride, a brand new '62 Dodge Pickup. The driver was a nice white Okie farmer who had some stories himself for he never stopped talking. Bong said he was one of those country-philosopher-type Okie. He had told them about five riddles, still the most difficult ones he's heard, then dropped them off without telling them one answer. "Okay, while you're thinking of that one, lemme tell you this one. Maybe this will be more to your liking." Then he would rattle off another, each one more fascinating than the one before, Bong recalled, his rabbit nose slightly twitching. The Okie kept saying, after a laugh, sometimes the essential is absent, and sometimes absence is essential. Puzzles and riddles and ridiculous statements of such sorts got to Bong. He was smart in a lot of useless things like that. He would touch his earlobe then smooth his lower face with his hand. He was the only one that really bothered to solve (or even remembered) all those problems. In fact, he was pondering over them the night the cook busted in on them with a shotgun looking for his light bulb.

But this day, this walk along the highway, was their first day-off in three-and-a-half weeks, and though they would have to work again all day the next day, they could take it relatively easy because the seasons were shifting from apricots to pears (or was it from pears to peaches?) And in many camps if one worked by the box (contract), you could take some time off, depending on what you prized more at the moment, your rest or your pocket.

Working by the box meant you've chosen (or were chosen) to work for an employer who pays so much money for every box you pick (plus bonuses, of course, if you're a good boy) of the fruits of California summers: cherry, apricot, pears, peaches, nectarines, strawberry, grapes, and more. The dying pear season was gliding quickly into peaches. I remember the burr-like fuzz that got so many people sneezing, and the smell of peach blossoms clinging to the still air and warm starry nights. Engulfing the brittle and now fruitless apricot branches, the lavender sky glowed in the twilight like a god pinching homesickness from those far away from home, and a mixture of fragrances; blossoms, soil and fruits hung heavy in the soft evenings after a hard day's work.

The counterpart of, or the other alternative to, working by the box was to work by the hour. Here they paid you for your time regardless of the amount of boxes you've picked. The foreman and peer pressure, of course, kept one moving pretty fast. Consequently, the politics of survival became so that the workers with less responsibilities (that usually meant those without a family), or the worker who had a rebellious nature, or the worker who tries to redress injustices, as well as the plain lazy in nature, for obvious reasons, chose by the hour, and had their own interpretations of the trick to being good is not to be too good, as the veterans would say. Those who were new to farm work usually worked by the hour. They would not get hired by contract. They weren't fast enough and lacked the experience in handling the tender fruits. Some had the speed and the experience, but were content to get paid by the hour so they didn't have to work like burros, as the Chicanos would say. They were mostly single men who could afford to feel like this. They fooled around a lot and used their experience and knowledge (of camp life) not only to survive, but to get over. Before one can make it at something, they claimed, one has to make it first. They would pack the inferior quality fruits for the company but cover them with layers of first-rate picks. The hundred-per-cent-quality fruits they would steal and secretly give to visiting relatives and friends, some of whom in turn would, when they got to town, sell them to someone else.

So into the orchards of the Suisun Valley we started work early in the still-cold mornings before dawn, and we clambered onwards with ladder and container in arms marching into the coming day. There was always that daily conflict in deciding whether to bring a jacket or not. For though one will be comforted from the cold and damp of false dawn, shortly after light break that sun would be beating down mercilessly on your neck and you'd be burdened the rest of the hell-hot day by lugging your jacket everywhere and eventually forgetting it somewhere under some fruit-laden tree. In the long days of summer the sun would hang around well past 9:30 in the evening like a nervous guest preparing to make his leave. The worst nightmare of course was if one should get caught wanting to take a dump when one was out there in the fields because there were no outhouses or anything like that. One worker was forced to take a dump out there because he couldn't hold it any more and he wiped his ass using poison oak. Oh, he was in pain!

Anyway, the Okie farmer let them off at a fork on the road and they were now walking with groceries in hand somewhere between Vacaville and Vallejo. They had decided to cook their own meals and not pay for those provided for them by the company. They would save more money (for gambling, of course) and not get constantly and mysteriously overcharged by the company store. Besides, the cook, a tall, lanky Filipino, but with a gut, was a token company man, a poor loser in gambling, a bully, a braggart, a coconut, an Uncle Tom, and just an all-around asshole. They had asked him for some light bulbs for their bunkhouse before (the cook was also the utilities supplier), and he had derogatively refused, making some snide remark about how real-Filipinos are not afraid of the dark, anyway and telling the boys to buy their own, even though such items were supposed to be supplied by the company. The cook did this, they figured, because they had beaten him so badly in their last poker game that his rage was bordering on suspecting the youths, the young eggs, of playing partners without declaration, a conspiracy-by-camaraderie, so to speak, a practice considered quite unethical and unfair in poker. The cook basically accused the boys of cheating.

Clarence, one participant in the showdown and who had the youngest-looking face, relished this particular section of the anecdote, even though it had very little to do with the showdown itself. Over and over he told about how someone had snuck into the cook's room the evening after the showdown and had taken one light bulb, and for several hours, things were back to normal in their bunkhouse, when suddenly, in the middle of their card game, while all were huddled under that one bulb, while Bong was deliberating on the Okie's riddles between inside straights and unfilled flushes, the door flung open, and by the time anyone had time to react, the cook, with a shotgun in hand resting on his belly, had spoken almost wearily, "All right. Who took my light bulb?" And to this day no one had admitted to it. Clarence said they had duped Batok into doing it, telling him that they had seen Elvis Presley do it once in a movie. Batok had admitted he had agreed, but that was just to pacify the taunters, he had said in Filipino, for he had, as usual, lost his nerve at the last moment.

But according to Batok, the cook was not all that much of an asshole. He claimed that Clarence always teased the cook behind his back, that's why the cook had a minor grudge against him, and well, that's just the way Clarence was. He could not keep from publicizing some of his feelings. He always brought his own brand of perversity along with him and when he came upon things already perverse, why all the more he laughed at it. For laugh he must. And laugh now, because soon he would be "Going to the Chapel," as the Dixie Cups swayingly sang sweet "I really love you," and so on and so on.

My brother Antonio denied that he had anything to do with the theft. In fact, he claimed he was the one who broke up the melee, just as he had done the time he broke up or tried to break up the skirmish in the mid-day sun just hours before, the showdown, as it eventually came to be known since then.

From the incidents of that same day, Antonio's nickname would be the peacemaker with a grin. But all had denied the theft of the light bulb then, and the more vehemently they would deny it as the years rolled on.

Clarence at the time loved to tell humorous stories and play practical jokes on everybody. He was about to get married and everyone knew he was nervous about it and scared, and he was trying to coolly deflect it by making people laugh so he can make himself laugh. It was also around the same time that Vietnam was getting hot and the draft was in full-swing and Clarence (along with many others) was thinking of the not-too-pleasant-a-prospect of going to a fucking war, not because of the fucking war itself, but because he would rather be fucking his wife-to-be. The Service would drive him away from his girl and, being a fairly astute gambler, he knew his luck and it was not good.

It would not stand the test of the times. The girl maybe, or him, but not his luck. One thing about Clarence, he hardly blamed people for anything. He always blamed his luck. "The odds don't look good, kid," he was telling me in my room in the Mission District of The City one day. He looked like he'd been up a good part of the night. There was not much, but there was a faint smell of liquor. I was still of course living with my parents at the time and I don't remember anybody ever coming through our front door messed up. I guess that was one of the reasons for the back door.

"Slim to none, I'd say. Stakes don't look too good, either," I reminded him.

"You got that right." He also said that if he stayed he would have to tangle with both Uncle Sam and Raul. Raul was his wife-to-be's not-quite-ex-boyfriend, who always had a *bolo* hidden in his back when he went to dances.

"But it's not going to hold up, man." He was talking about his luck again; and later, running out of explanations, dismissed this dilemma as staying pat on a ten in lobule poker.

"I know," I said. I have stayed pat on a few ten's myself and what one remembers is not so much the loss or the win, but the long, drawn-out discomfort of fear and resignation, your fate completely left to the mercy of chance, for you had to wait on everybody s turn to have their chance on drawing a better hand than yours because you stayed with your hand that was dealt to you; you didn't want to replace your cards with others, thinking that you might get an even worse hand. So you stayed at a relatively just-above-mediocre hand.

Clarence was staring blankly at my bedroom window. (It was also my brother Antonio's bedroom, but he was not there at this particular time). "It was like the time when we were hitchhiking Interstate 80 and we somehow got in a beef with these nine white guys on the side of the road." And he recounted the tale for the first time. "Nine of them, man!" he emphasized again. There was a twinkle all of a sudden in his eye. "Football players, they looked like, you know, no-necks." Then he slowed down his talking and sat down at the end of the bed looking out the window. "Odds weren't too good then, either fucking and fighting, they're always bad bets . . . " In some perverted yet natural way, Clarence had a wisdom all his own. "You weren't there, kid. Let's see who was there . . . " And then, winding up for the story, he started to rub his chin. For a while, immersed in the telling, he would forget his card game with fate.

It was in the dead heat of summer, he said, and they had just been dropped off at a fork on the road, so they continued thumbing toward camp toward Green Valley Road in Suisun where their orchards were. In town they had stolen about forty dollars worth of groceries and other sundries and had bought about twenty dollars worth. They had gone to the store in the hundred-and-ten-degree heat with trench coats and jackets, Clarence recalled with a chuckle. But when they got to camp later (after the showdown) and emptied out their pockets onto the table, they rolled out three bottles of ketchup, two bottles of chili peppers, two can openers, a toe-nail clipper, six jars of pomade, coffee and creamers, sugar cubes, assorted candy bars, and not one light bulb. Someone had to go and get that. The planning in their thievery definitely needed better coordination next time.

Back out on the road, Clarence went on, they had been hitchhiking for some time. They were getting restless of each other's company, for some could banter better and intimidate more than others. A black Cadillac with about four or five young people in it sped by and its passengers were laughing and yelling, saying something as they passed, and then quickly started to shrink from view.

"Did you hear that?" Clarence had said to Batok. "Someone in the car called you a motherfucker!"—and started snickering.

"What?" Batok, seemingly in deep thought, was totally surprised.

"Sure, man. And look! He's giving you the finger now."

True, there were arms being wildly waved, but the car was dwindling so fast down the road that Batok had to ask again. "You sure about that, man?"

"There, there, look!" Clarence had shouted right at Batok's face.

Perhaps indignantly, perhaps in self-defense, perhaps in total or partial confusion, perhaps intensity is just contagious, but Batok suddenly shouted also. "Puck you, too!" his middle finger bold and defiant, solidly thrust upwards toward the speeding Cadillac climbing up into a hill and out of view. "Madapaka," and trailing into a mumble, "ones op dis day . . . "

"You weren't there, kid. Let's see . . . who was there?" Clarence kept trying to remember, pressing a finger to his lips, still looking out the window, through lime-green and red-wine still trees, between rooftops and treetops and covered chimney tops into the dis-symmetry of a skyline made up of steeples, spires, telephone wires, antennas and way, way out toward the iron skeletons of shipyards in Hunter's Point, way out into the Bay against the eastern Berkeley and Oakland Hills and jutting out from the right corner of the horizon, the lights from Candlestick Park glimmered in the fragile gauze of falling twilight where the hometown Giants were battling out a nightcap with the despicable Dodgers from the Southland.

"You should have been there, kid. You missed out." And he would laugh again. "Well, anyway, as I was saying about this Batok and his Cadillac . . . " and he would continue his story.

"Puck you, too, Madapaka!" Batok had shouted at the speeding Cadillac.

Casually he had shifted the grocery bags that he was carrying into Clarence's arms who in turn had grabbed them without thinking; the better for Batok to say, "Here, eat dis!" with his two obscene and stiff middle fingers. "Puck you! Puck you!"

Batok, and soon all of them, found themselves saying with increasing intensity and ritual, like chanting. Then Batok took back his bag of groceries from Clarence.

Bong said it seemed that their seething violence made the Cadillac shrink as it slipped away onto the freeway. Bong told me this, however, on another occasion. Another occasion but actually the same occasion. He too was looking out the same window some years later. What was on the radio was the same. The same San Francisco Giants were playing against the same despicable Los Angeles Dodgers. Bong said (of the showdown) that it was the rage of the brown man rising. He really never overlooked the larger picture. "It was a rage of centuries," he claimed. Then he became philosophical again. "Some uncontrollable, nameless, nebulous and amorphous indignation started getting monstrous inside them, first building up individually, then gathering itself into a ball collectively." As the varied fruits of the seasons were shifting so the seasons inside them were changing, it seemed, but no one knew about or understood the changes. They were beset with large questions that they did not want to ask, let alone answer. Sometimes one felt that some people always have the answers and others only the questions. He definitely knew which group he belonged to that time. It was a part of their lives in which something had to give, burst, given the right moment. The incident on Interstate 80 just triggered it. This was also that time of the year when the three or four major sports of the country, football, basketball, baseball, and hockey, too, were equally capturing the sports media, and everybody had a tendency to express their opinions on something, so philosophizing was just an indirect result of this multi-season time of year, and people tended to be more schizoid.

Bong told me a lot that late afternoon. I had taken over the rent since my folks went back home to the Philippines to visit and he had passed by.

He said he was the one who christened my brother Antonio, peacemaker. . . with a grin from that anecdote at the highway. Although he was telling me about the showdown, I could tell at the time that his mind was someplace else, as though he were using the telling of the story as a comfortable distraction.

Bong was looking out that same window that Clarence was looking out of about a year back, though this time Bong had just recently found out about his mother. His mother died when she gave birth to him. He suspected it all along, he was saying, but he had to find out for himself, so one day he visited his mother's grave in Holy Cross Cemetery for the first time. And sure enough, there it was. The date of his birth and the date of her death were the same.

When he was growing up, there were more than a few times that he overheard people asking his Dad and his relatives and then pointing him out among the rest with or without gestures and saying or asking " . . . is that the one?" And "yes . . . he's the one . . ."

"Strike 'em out, Juan!" Like the atmosphere of the time when Clarence was last here, it was baseball season, multi-season really, and suddenly Bong was talking to the radio. Bong was one of those people who could devote equal attention and intensity to many things at once. That was what he was good at. The baseball game on the radio, the showdown story, and the present conversation, all these he juggled fairly well.

Me, I was good for nothing. Out in the fields, I couldn't even pick right, nor fast, and I was one of the youngest. I was the rookie and I was a victim of a rookie mistake that year in camp. I over-ate. And because I wanted to save up money for some contact lenses so I could not only look cool but play basketball without the distraction of glasses, I ate only one thing. Peanut butter sandwiches. I thought that as long as you're full, you're OK. I got sick. I started seeing spots, double vision, blackouts, a whole range of symptoms, till finally my head and stomach revolted simultaneously. So the next day, I stayed home while everyone went to town to celebrate their first day off in three and a half weeks. That was the day of the showdown.

After the brief tense moment of the Cadillac speeding by arrogantly while the boys were humiliatingly hitchhiking in the dead heat of summer, and the finger posturing and loud cursing had ceased, the boys became curiously quiet. There was no conversation or communication of any kind. They were all immersed in their own thoughts. So they did not notice the Cadillac, the same black Cadillac, coming down the freeway again, slowing down, edging onto the shoulders of the road, and coming dead smack toward the Filipino boys. The black Cadillac had come back and this time the car was really packed. When it finally stopped right by the roadside where the boys were walking, and they started coming out of the car, nine of them could be counted. All football player type. No necks. Big, white, and ugly.

"That's the motherfucker that gave me the finger." A big blond boy stepped out of the car pointing straight at Batok and kept on moving towards him, not hurriedly but steadily. There were a group of people there but the focus of attention was definitely on this particular white boy. He was one of the biggest in the pack. This could very well be why Batok replied, "No, man. It wasn't me."

Clarence almost imperceptibly tried to take the groceries from Batok's arms. "Go get him, man. You can take em."

That's easy for you to say . . . he said in Filipino, and held the groceries a little tighter.

"Don't worry. We'll help you out," Clarence assured him. And tried to yank the bags from Batok.

Batok slid his whole body towards Clarence this time. "There's eight of them," he told Clarence in Filipino.

"Nine," Clarence retorted in English.

"Yeah, that's the little motherfucker right there." The blond boy got within striking distance of Batok.

Batok tried to stay firm in his denial. "No, man," he said shaking his head slowly but not taking his eyes off the blond boy who had no neck, a lineman in a football team, no doubt.

"Yeah, you! You gave us the finger, right?"

Batok was at a loss for words in both languages. He was in a fix and he knew it. He made some sounds but he said nothing. At least, nothing comprehensible to anyone else.

The big blond boy seemed to be thinking. He thought for a long excruciating while. Then he said, "All right. Let's forget it." He looked around and motioned to the rest of his friends "Let's get going." They were pretty much all in their car, just a few of the football players were left outside, some even having a pretty friendly conversation with Bong, and Batok actually shook hands with the big blond dude. As the *Puti* (white) turned around to enter the Cadillac, Clarence said quite firmly, "Just don't think we're afraid of you." That's when Clarence got hit. By the time Clarence got off the ground and turned around straight, there was a mob of big white dudes around him.

Antonio picked up a big boulder, held it up in the sky just like Moses and started saying, of all things, "Peace! That's enough! Peace! We're all brothers, goddammit," then hurled the rock towards two or three of the football players huddled around Clarence, who in turn, kept looking for Batok.

"I kept looking for him 'cause I wanted to know why he hit me," Clarence told later on.

"I didn't hit you, stupid. I kept telling you. That white guy in front of you did. His arm was so long that by the time his swing got to you, it had gone around your ear and into the back of your head." Batok kept trying to explain to Clarence.

It probably shocked the rabble into silence, just like in the movies, because surprisingly, there was peace. They looked up at Antonio on some mound, like Moses who had just hurled the tablets of the Ten Commandments. Scurrying into a more open area, Clarence ran into Batok, who unluckily was in a worse predicament. The same big white guy had Batok backing up into a roadside cliff.

"That's the motherfucker that gave me the finger. This one." He picked up his line of contention from before. He was pointing straight at Batok again, who had quite a load of groceries. Clarence offered to relieve him of it by extending his arms to take it. No response, however, from Batok. Clarence started to pull on his arm, but Batok resisted. He wanted to keep the groceries so he could have an excuse not to fight and maybe the big ox would go on to the next victim. But this was far from random. "There he is. That's the one. Lemme at 'em."

"He wants you," Clarence resignedly told Batok, lightly taking again the bag of groceries from Batok. Immediately, the white guy lunged at Batok who somehow moved to the side unhurt. The two Filipino boys looked at each other, and with his left hand held up, Batok suddenly screamed "Dat's enough!" His right hand hung loosely near his pants pocket. The white boy had just gotten up anew and was ready to lunge again when Batok repeated, "Don't come any closer . . . please."

But the white boy lunged again. But this time when he lunged, it looked like he stopped in mid-air like a frozen shot in the movies. Because when he landed on the ground he was back-pedaling. He had met the point of a butterfly blade in mid-air.

The butterfly knife has nothing to do with butterflies. It is the English-speaking world's name for that type of knife. It is called *balisong* in Filipino. Batok told one time of how he remembers first seeing a butterfly come out of its cocoon. He said when he saw that butterfly coming out of its cocoon, he thought cruelly, that larvae must have had some rage in the process of metamorphosis, for stretching too much, thus abusing, reality and substance, and eventually participating in its own murder into another state of being, the butterfly, the chrysalis. Should not then larvae, the worm, look at a butterfly as an adversary? The only way for a caterpillar to become a butterfly is to first survive, stay alive. I'd sure hate not to see or live a day being a butterfly after spending all that icky, itchy time of being a worm, Batok said. Their cocoons too were bursting upward and onward and spinning every which way like the way his '62 Impala spun around the red light by the curb of the park's edge by Fulton and 25th Avenue almost every frustrated evening after a party in the City.

This was the butterfly knife that the white boy suddenly came face to face with in mid-air. Batok himself was surprised when he pulled it out so smoothly with his left hand, because in camp he always messed up clearing the hinged part of the handle by the front pocket overlay, and finally taking too long to open the *balisong*, the butterfly knife. Batok's hands were more practiced with the microphone, like Clarence's were for the barber's shears. Scissors and knives, though from the same family, were not siblings. But this time, all in one motion came the opening of the knife as it was being pulled out of the pocket, then the close-open close-open action of the palm, the clip-clap of the blade and the ivory handle, and the closing grip on the flying half of the knife itself, then the thrust, all in one motion. Batok was magnificent.

The white boy stopped in mid-air about a hand's length from the blade point and when he landed he was a good arm's length. "Hey, man. None of that shit. C'mon." Batok did not know whether he detected a pleading tone but the white boy's mouth started to resemble that of a duck's. If he were Filipino, one might have said he was pointing with his mouth. "Ppput that down . . ." But Batok was quiet. He circled around him so that now it was the white boy nearing the edge of the cliff and he spoke again. "Hey, c'mon, man. Put that thing down. Let's fight square. No knives."

Batok only shook his head looking straight at him and said, "No . . . no . . . no."

"Do you know Dominic? He's Filipino. He's a good friend of ours."

"Neber heard ob him. You think we're the only Flips in San Francisco?"

When Batok and Clarence and Antonio and Bong collected themselves they found they were only staring at each other. There was only the white boy that Batok had cornered by the cliff that was to be seen. The eight of them had all scurried and disappeared from view, their Cadillac engine still running.

"I want you . . . I'm goona get you . . ." Batok's eyes bulged in excitement just like they looked when he sang "Remember When/To my surfrise" by the Platters. Batok seemed more like he was talking to himself when he almost whispered, "One op dis day . . . and dat day is here."

When the lone white guy also realized the disappearance of his companions, he said to Batok, "Listen . . . There's a party. Tonight. And next week, too. We'll give you a ride to your camp. Where are you headed?"

"Green Valley Road. All the way to the orchards," was Batok's quick reply. "You got the keys to this thing? It's still breathing."

"Yeah, of course. It's running, ain't it?"

Antonio interfered. He didn't want to let it get hot again. "Well, let's go," he offered.

"Can we wait till at least one of my friends comes back?"

"Sure, why not?" Clarence interjected. "Hey, white boys! Where are you? You can come out now. It's over!" He was calling people as if it were the aftermath of a hide-and-seek game. Sure enough, the *Putis* started coming back in out of nowhere. They emerged out of freeway underramps, mounds of dried tall weeds, behind trees, and out of low bushes. Some still had dried grass stuck to their naked tops.

"It's OK." The big white boy that confronted Batok explained curtly to the rest of the white boys. "It's OK. He's OK. They're OK. They're coming to the party tonight. And maybe next week. You all stay here for now. I'll bring 'em to their camp just down the Highway. Green Valley Road. Be back in about an hour." He turned to the Filipinos and asked. "Can I bring Red with me?" He pointed out a red-headed boy among the approaching white boys. He's my brother."

"Sure. It's your car. The more the merrier," Clarence answered.

"Stay under this tree here." The white boy told the rest. "We'll be right back. There ain't no room for all of us."

Bong went to dig into some grocery bags and said to the remaining white boys, "Here. Get some drinks from here, while it's still kinda cold. And there's some sardines and pork and beans there, I think." And he left them a bagful of food.

All the Filipinos went inside the Cadillac. The blond drove and the redhead sat in the back. They saw the remaining seven white boys mill around the shade of the big walnut tree by the highway and when the car dipped down into the valley, they disappeared. Inside the car on the way to the camp there was silence in the beginning. After a few tense moments of feeling each other's vibes, they got to be talking like old friends with the redhead inviting them again to a party next weekend in Benecia, a town not far off.

Years later, after everyone had returned from the service, we all got together again, and this is how I got to telling this story. They insisted. I told this story to some people before but I hardly tell it to anyone anymore. Like I said I wasn't really there, and when people find out you weren't really there they tend to think that you are not telling the truth (as if people who were there always tell the truth), even though it was upon their insistence in the first place that you relate the damn thing. We haven't really kept in touch at all. Most got married, got themselves houses, and moved away. Some got divorced and moved away. Some planned to stay because they couldn't move away. Some of the people who stayed, stayed away from each other. Some moved away because they couldn't stay. The last time I heard from Clarence was about three years ago. He phoned one night when it was raining hard. He sounded just as excited as the weather. He was inviting me to come to an Amway party or meeting of some sort, of which he was an aspiring director, and that he was going to go back to the Philippines and make millions. My own brother Antonio has been living in Hawaii for about a dozen years. Batok had gone to Las Vegas after a term in jail and disappeared without a trace. Bong went to Alaska one summer and never came back.

"There was a fifth person in that incident. Who was that sonnofabitch . . . ? Are you sure it wasn't you?" This question was always asked at the end of each telling by all the participants, and there would be a litany of curses attributed to that person whom they couldn't remember. "For the life of me I can't think of him now, not just his name. I can't think of any images of him, nor his part in the story . . . It'll come to me later . . . I could have sworn there were five of us . . . Are you sure it wasn't you?"

Before, I was. Now, I'm not too sure.

(2000)

Brian Ascalon Roley

Born 1966, Los Angeles, California

About the Author

Brian Ascalon Roley is the author of *American Son*, a novel, published by W. W. Norton (2001). It was a *New York Times* 2001 Notable Book of the Year, a *Los Angeles Times* Best Book of 2001, a Salon Best Book selection, and a Kiriyama Pacific Rim Book Prize Finalist. His fiction and non-fiction have also appeared in the *San Francisco Chronicle*, the *Georgia Review*, and *Epoch Magazine*. He is the recipient of the Arthur Lynn Andrews Prize in fiction given by Cornell University. He holds an M.F.A. from Cornell and a Juris Doctor from U.C.L.A. A biracial Filipino American, he lives in San Francisco with his wife, Gwen, and their baby, Brendan. His website is http://www.brianascalonroley.com.

Filipinos in America

People are amazed when I inform them that Filipinos are one of the two largest Asian ethnic groups in America, along with the Chinese. Where I live now, in California, there are about one million of both, and though the Chinese are very visible—their shops and markets have flooded over from Chinatown to take over Little Italy, and now the huge Richmond and Sunset neighborhoods too—by contrast, Filipinos are rarely noticed. Few Americans know that the Philippines used to be a U.S. colony; I was never taught about our common history in high school, though we spent two weeks on British Colonialism in India.

This "Epilogue" was originally the tail end of my novel, *American Son*, about two Hapa (biracial) Filipino American brothers and their shy mother. They have identity crises, wishing to be at turns White or Mexican; my notion followed from the idea that being invisible, they felt compelled to look elsewhere for a way of presenting themselves to other Americans, and also that their mother was colonialized, ashamed of being Filipina. The early reviewers noticed none of this, I suspect because they did not realize the Philippines was a U.S. colony, but the response has built over time, and with the recent U.S. involvement in the Philippines perhaps that ignorance will change. I would not count on it, however, as I have yet to see one U.S. news report on the war on terrorism there which has mentioned our common past.

American Son Epilogue

— **Brian Ascalon Roley**

It has been four months since my brother Tomas and I beat up that Jewish boy, Ben Feinstein, with a tire iron. I can remember the look on his face as he peered up at us, so trustful and boyish, thinking we were his friends, and then the surprise that came over his expression as he saw my older brother descending upon him, fists ready, temples tensing, forearms taut beneath a dense tangle of Mexican gangster tattoos. And then the feel of Ben slipping from my grip and falling, like a sack of rice, onto the dusty ground. I also recall the satisfying feeling of the heavy tire iron in my grip as I slammed it into Ben's back and legs, making a sound like a baseball bat slapping into raw meat.

I hated this white kid whose film-producer mother had humiliated our own Filipino mother in front of our school, Saint Dominic's, scolded Mom as if she were some lowly housekeeper, an insignificant ant, in front of all my classmates and their parents and our teachers. And nobody did anything to defend Mom from this woman's hard words. Not the teachers. Not the priest. All my mother had done was accidentally bump her Land Cruiser, and this woman shouted her down, called her stupid, as Mom blinked shyly up at her—looking confused and nervous and sorry. And I hated that blond woman in her expensive yoga tights, her Starbucks Latte in hand. And I wanted to get at her, and so it felt good to hurt her son on the very front yard of her fancy, Santa Monica Canyon glinting modern steel-and-glass house.

If you tell anybody about this, we will come by and beat up your mother, my brother told Ben as the boy looked at us, frightened, blue eyes pleading. Blood smeared his cheek.

The beating was, of course, as surprising to myself as it had been to Ben. My gangster brother had brought me there unawares. But I was willing.

As Tomas drove us away, having left Ben bleeding on the grass, we sped through the narrow canyon roads, past expensive houses and young starlets walking their big shaggy dogs, beneath curtains of dripping eucalyptus trees—and I felt sick. Sick as on a fishing boat. I had never hurt anybody before—had always been the shy, quiet brother—but now Tomas turned to look at me, and he seemed pleased.

That was four months ago, a day before I was expelled from Saint Dominic's, and two days before my brother was arrested and released on bail, pending a court hearing. I was not charged; I'll soon get to explaining why.

I live with my white father's sister, Aunt Jessica, now. My father left us a long time ago, but his sister has taken Mom under her wing, and refuses to speak with him anymore. Aunt Jessica is trained as a lawyer, runs a lingerie boutique on trendy Montana Avenue—the new Rodeo Drive of the Westside—and sells expensive underwear and nightwear to rich people and celebrities.

I sleep in her guestroom, which she has redecorated for me with white bookshelves filled with the biographies of good, productive men, role models to emulate. Last night I was up late figuring out what to say to Father Ryan, the admissions official at Saint Dominic's High School where I was expelled, and who my aunt and mother now want me to convince to take me back in. Though Aunt Jessica finally made me finish practicing and go to bed— around one o'clock—I lay awake all night, too restless to sleep. In my mind I went over all the things Father Ryan might ask me, and what I might say to sway him. Aunt Jessica had already bought me a pair of chinos that fit right, and an Oxford shirt with a buttoned collar, and a blue blazer from the Weathervane. She showed me how to line up the belt buckle with my pants zipper and how to knot a tie, which she did by standing behind me as I faced a mirror; her breath felt warm in my ear.

She'd had a writer friend of hers over for dinner to help come up with something to say—Brandon, an old guy with a white ponytail who looked real trembly despite his age. It worried me the way he would avert his eyes whenever she asked him a question, and how his jaw would tremble when he gave an answer. At first it had been encouraging to see that a successful adult could be shy. But then it started to worry me that you can get to that age and still lack confidence. Could I still be that way when I have snowy hair, my hands parched and wrinkling? At one point Brandon even awkwardly dropped the breadbasket on his lap and the Italian rosemary bread tumbled out onto the floor. I was embarrassed for him and looked away. It seemed weird that Aunt Jessica should ask him to help me, since I couldn't imagine him being good in any interview. But after dinner he got out a notebook. He seemed confident now. He said he'd have to know why I got kicked out of school in order to come up with something to say to get me back in, and I sensed Aunt Jessica move in her chair uncomfortably—which surprised me, since I haven't seen my put-together aunt nervous before. She must have worried what Brandon—who was appearing gentle to me now, rather than creepy—would think of what Tomas and I did that day. It gave me hope that she cared what a shy man thought.

It has been four months now since I moved here. Living with Aunt Jessica hasn't been as bad as I thought it would. She isn't angry with me anymore; she bought me all these new clothes, and I'm even getting used to the trendy Montana Avenue neighborhood. You don't find people standing around their yards gardening, or hanging out on the porch, but you see plenty of them walking around—though they walk fast and seem to be going somewhere. I think many of these people just park on our street so they can walk to the shops, and you also get all these skinny people carrying colorful yoga mats rolled up under their arms, making their way up to the yoga place. You can walk around safely at night, and they have places you can get something to eat or buy an iced tea and do your homework.

I first came here because Tomas has enemies, and with him in jail (Aunt Jessica was refusing to pay his bail), our home wouldn't be safe without him. Mom comes over here a lot after work—for dinner—and sometimes sleeps over on an air mattress in Aunt Jessica's study, though I still try to get Mom to use my bed. It's nice to have her over, and she likes it too, though sometimes she seems a bit distracted and funny the way she will quietly putter around the house. She is always cleaning things and doing Aunt Jessica's laundry and suddenly one day I realized that she was worried I was a burden on Aunt Jessica. That made me feel a bit funny about being here, too. Mom mostly is cheerful with Aunt Jessica and talkative over dinner. But sometimes I can sense her in those strange moods when she is quiet and lost in her thoughts, even uncomfortable with my father's sister—especially since Tomas came home from prison.

When he first came home Mom wanted me to return too, but Aunt Jessica said Tomas was a bad influence on me and suggested I stay with her for a while. She pointed out that while Mom is gone all day and has a commute, Aunt Jessica lives only three blocks from her lingerie store, allowing her to come home to eat lunch with me; she also spends many afternoons here doing her accounting and bookwork. (And it's true that Aunt Jessica helps with my homework; she even set up an office for me.)

As she told Mom all this, Mom nodded too automatically, as if she were trying to hide her true hurt feelings, and I knew that Mom was uncomfortable and nervous and not necessarily agreeing with my aunt. She was clearly afraid of disagreeing with her, though.

After Aunt Jessica finished, my mother sat quietly for a long time.

Well think about it, Dina, my aunt finally said.

Mom looked carefully at the houseplants hanging above the kitchen window; she didn't seem able to look my aunt in the eye.

You say you come over for lunch everyday?

Yes.

I see.

Aunt Jessica didn't say anything but looked at Mom patiently with an understanding look, her fingers supporting her chin.

And you help him with homework?

Every night.

I try to help with homework when I can.

Of course you do, Aunt Jessica nodded.

I am not so good with the math. But I can help with English pretty well. The American nuns were very strict.

I know they were, Dina. Your English is better than mine.

Mom dismissively waved her hand, but the gesture was halfhearted and seemed to fade before it was finished, as she stared distractedly at the plant. But it is only formal, she said. Like my mother's Spanish. People may have spoken like that a hundred years ago in Castile, but nobody speaks like that anymore in Spain.

Among some people correct English is important, Aunt Jessica said.

Mom kept looking at the plant, and the silvery overcast light shone on her face. I wondered if she was going to cry, but her eyes didn't water.

Aunt Jessica seemed concerned and leaned further forward. I expected her to tell my mother that I should go home with Mom after all, but she didn't. I think more people should speak properly, Dina, she said. Gabriel is very well spoken for a boy his age. She placed a hand on Mom's wrist and Mom didn't move. Dina, I only meant that you are so busy whereas I have certain opportunities. I'm lucky enough to be around Gabe more than you could, and to give him supervision.

Of course, Mom said.

And of course my neighborhood is safe.

Mom nodded.

He should stay here with you, my mother finally said.

Well, I think you should think about it, Dina.

Mom was looking down at the table, shaking her head.

No. No. You are right.

Are you sure? Aunt Jessica said, and though she asked it like a question, in some strange way—I don't know how—I knew that she expected Mom to say yes, and my mother did.

Since that conversation Mom hasn't seemed quite as comfortable around Aunt Jessica's condo—though if anything she comes here more often—and I worry about her. I've been visiting home a lot, especially on weekends, and try to bring homework to do there in her presence and ask her questions on all my subjects, even math, and even if I really know the answer. Recently I haven't been able to visit her as often, though, because Aunt Jessica's boutique has gotten busy with Christmas shoppers.

When my mother's brothers found out what happened, she had to beg that I not be sent to live in Manila with Tito Betino, to go to school there. Mom would have me tell them what I'd told her, the lies I'd told her where I'd denied I ever beat up Ben, and my titos would quietly listen for the sake of my gullible mother. They didn't believe me, but they felt too embarrassed to call me a liar in front of her, though they continued to insist that I come to Manila. In the end, when they found out I would remain with Aunt Jessica, that seemed to assuage them—they could see that my Germanic aunt was a firm woman. So we could wait and see.

Sometimes I wonder why my mother agreed with Aunt Jessica's suggestion that I stay here in the condo. It must be hard for a mother to part with her son. Maybe she was recalling the day of Tomas's third court hearing. By this time the Filipino parking attendant had figured out that Mom was Filipino, and he let us park for free, and we hurried across the hot parking lot; the sun heated my hair, and I tried to keep Mom protected in my shadow. We passed the dry fountain—bare concrete, waterless for so long it wasn't even stained—and just the sight of it made my mouth parch. Inside, Mom was ahead of me when we came to the door of the waiting hall where we normally waited alone outside the courtroom.

I hurried to open the double doors for Mom. She started to enter, but suddenly clenched my arm, stopping me in the doorway. I looked up. The hall was almost empty—for a second I thought it was—but then I noticed at the far end, thirty feet away, Ben sitting in a wheelchair. He had a mineral water bottle cradled across his lap, and his mother stood with a hand lightly resting on the handle behind him, though she faced him and hadn't seen us yet. She wore a suit skirt and jacket and was talking to Ben. He had white bandages wrapped around his forehead, and some kind of a metal brace attached over his left leg around his jeans. You could see the bulky hinge at his knee. Mom stared at him. Then Ben noticed us, seeming to peer out from his puffy orange jacket, and Mom jerked her gaze away—her mortified eyes catching my own only for a second—her fingernails clutching into my arm. When his mother looked at us—at Mom, really—

Mom took my elbow again and quickly sat us down. For a long time afterwards, she stared forward at the empty wall.

Mom arrives at the condo midmorning, to pick me up for Father Ryan's interview. Aunt Jessica fixes my tie and coaches me on how to behave and can't resist giving Mom advice too, before wishing us good luck and seeing us off.

Mom drives, appearing nervous, twists her hair with her finger, and runs it along the coarse black strand above her glasses. They are the same embarrassing purple ones I normally hate, but now they don't bother me—maybe because my classmates aren't around. When I think of the time I pretended she wasn't my mother, and how much that hurt her, I tense and heat up and hate myself. She finds a parking space near the old-fashioned, Spanish-mission-style church.

We have extra time, Gabe, she says. Do you want to go inside and pray?

In the past, before I moved into Aunt Jessica's condo, Mom wouldn't have bothered to ask, but would just have told me we were going inside. Now she looks at me shyly (her confidence gone even with me), shading her eyes with her thin brown hand.

Sure, I say.

We could pray for you to get back into school.

Okay. Whatever you want to do.

If you ask these things sincerely, Gabe, God will give you what you want.

I could tell her that I doubt God would have time for a little person like me, but I don't; it's not just that I don't want her to think I don't believe God would do this for me, I also wouldn't want to put the idea in her head that God wouldn't do things to make her life better either. She is, after all, a small person too.

Instead I say, *Sure*, and we enter the cool church.

As we kneel in the front pew, the incense-rich air flowing deep in my nostrils, my mind drifts.

The last time I was at Saint Dominic's—the last time I saw Father Ryan—was the day after Tomas and I went over to Ben Feinstein's house.

When Father Ryan called me up to his office I'd had an idea it was about Ben's beating, but I had no idea he'd called Mom over, and I was surprised to see her sitting in his office, facing his desk. My heart pounded. Her chair looked uncomfortably small for her, made for students. I avoided her eyes, but a glance told me she didn't believe I had been involved, and was hoping I would give an alibi.

Gabe, take a chair, Father Ryan said.

He tapped his reading glasses lower on his nose, and peered at me over the gold rims.

Gabe.

Yes sir?

Your mother and I have a few questions for you.

He turned towards her and she seemed surprised at hearing her name and sat straighter. She still didn't want to look at me, but felt like that was what the Father expected, so she glanced at me, her eyes quick and nervous.

He coughed. Look. Gabe. Let me be pointed with you. Were you with your brother last night?

No.

Not for any part of last night?

No.

Well, that's interesting, he said. Because your mother said you returned with your brother in his car yesterday evening.

Mom shifted and I thought she must have known I was lying and felt angry with me; but then I sensed that she was moving nervously and her head was strangely bowed forward: suddenly I realized she was ashamed with me that she had said this to Father Ryan and gotten me in trouble. It seemed strange that she should feel this way.

It's not a car.

What?

My brother owns a truck, I said. It's not a car.

Father Ryan looked annoyed.

That doesn't matter. Listen. Gabe. You're going to have to level with me. Mrs. Feinstein called up last night. She has stories. Ben has stories. She found a receipt with your brother's credit card number on her driveway. It seems to have fallen out of his car.

I refused to say anything. But my guilt must have been obvious, and my mother bowed her head.

After he expelled me, Mom and I emerged on the blacktop parking lot, the heat that rose off it smelling like hot tar.

She asked if we could pray and strangely she didn't seem angry—almost timid—and I said *yes* and we went into the church. The cool damp scent of rosemary and sandalwood brushed like a breeze against my face and the pews were empty except for a few kids waiting to make their first confessions at the far wall, kneeling and being watched by some plain-clothed nuns. We knelt in the front pew. Mom didn't tell me what she wanted us to pray for, but I knew she was praying for Tomas and me. Maybe that we wouldn't go to jail, or that I would get back into Saint Dominic's. It seemed like she wanted me to pray for these things but it seemed odd to pray for myself—so I didn't—I just prayed for my brother. It was strange to pray for him. A gangster. A bully. A cruel older brother. It was also strange to sit here in this church—our church—welcomed to pray and feeling obligated to pray, after I had just been kicked out of school. I felt guilty. But I tried to make it real with my eyes shut and to concentrate and not think or to wander in my thoughts or worry or even to feel bored, because I was sure she would be able to feel me thinking. Even with my eyes shut.

And then I forgot that she was there or that I was praying and it was only after she tapped my shoulder that I realized how peaceful and without self-consciousness I had been. Outside I blinked and squinted and we found a stone bench carved out of the eastern wall, facing a statue of the Virgin Mary. She was white and concrete and stood in a dry fountain and there were black water stains along her robes and some stains that looked like tears on her face. They had planted roses in the fountain, but these were dried out from the drought—which seemed sad—and the grass around her was brittle and beige-colored. My Lola had loved this virgin, and before she died we used to sit here often while she prayed the rosary, as I squirmed, bored.

Finally Mom turned to me. Gabe.

Yes?

I am going to ask you a question. Please be honest.

Sure, I said, facing the Virgin.

Please.

I faced Mom. My throat clenched and swelled. Okay, I said.

Do you think your brother will go to jail?

Shockingly I realized she believed I hadn't been involved, even after my incriminating silence in Father Ryan's office.

No, I said.

Why don't you think so, Gabe?

Because Tomas didn't do anything, I lied to give her the impression I'd beaten Ben alone, to save her at least half her grief.

He didn't?

No.

And you're telling the truth?

Yeah.

She looked relieved and faced the Virgin again. The worry vanished from her face and I even thought I saw a smile in her eyes. Suddenly I realized she had not only believed my brother wasn't involved, but had mistaken me to have said I wasn't guilty either. It was strange to think she could be so deluded. I couldn't believe it. I'd wanted to spare her feelings, but I felt sick with myself now, and looked at my feet.

That Father Ryan! she shook her head. He thinks he knows everything. And after I invited him to all those family parties—like a member of our family! Like a godfather to you and your brother!

She expected an answer, so I quietly nodded. I looked at the Virgin and didn't contradict her.

Is something the matter, Gabe? she said reaching out and touching my cheek.

I shook my head and felt her warm knuckle brushing my face.

Oh, Gabe, don't worry so much. They will see. We will show them nothing happened. Then he will beg for apologies.

I just nodded—with her hand there—and didn't make a move to move it, and didn't want to.

That my mother could be so self-deluded about Tomas and me, still causes me sadness. Later Tomas lied to the police and said he had beaten Ben up alone, to spare Mom's feelings, but saving me also.

Now it's three months later, we are kneeling in the front pews, and Mother prays for Father Ryan to take me back in to Saint Dominic's, and my brother not to go back to jail. I pray to know what I should pray for.

Then I imagine the chapel in the Philippines, on our farm, where they have cobwebs in the rafters and dolls of the saints that poor tenants place on tables. Instead of putting candles below the Virgin's feet that you can light for money, they strung up light bulbs—the big colorful kinds, like tacky Christmas lights old people use, bright red, green, yellow, and blue. They have lots of Virgins there, many more than you find in America, and these statutes often have names. I start wondering why they would have different names if they are all supposed to be Jesus' mother, Mary. Maybe they aren't all Mary, or maybe she is different to different people. It doesn't make sense and nobody here tells you about that sort of thing.

We exit into the same courtyard—the courtyard of the Virgin—and Mary (or whoever she is) still stands there, ankle-deep in dead leaves that fill the dry fountain, black water stains streaked sadly down her plaster robe and sculpted face. We have some time still so we sit down on the same bench we sat on three months ago.

Don't be nervous, Gabe, Mom says to me, Father Ryan likes you.

I'm not nervous.

You aren't?

No.

She doesn't seem to believe me, but for some reason my words seem to reassure her anyway and she ponders the Virgin again. Then she turns back to me, smiling, and sets her hand affectionately on my cheek, her skin slightly damp with perspiration.

A moment passes. Then we hear some voices that echo between the stone courtyard buildings, and her hand comes away as we look up and see some students approaching. They are just a year older than me—a rowdy group—and I feel the old embarrassment rising within me, and try to force it to go away. I meet the boys' eyes. As they pass I do not look away and even greet them, hoping she'll notice this. But she looks worried that they might have seen her hand on my check, embarrassing me. It seems strange—this notion—that a person should be embarrassed of being touched by their own mother.

Two months ago, after we saw Ben crippled in his wheelchair, Mom had stared at the wall and didn't look at me. I thought she might be angry with me, though when I finally got up the nerve to glance in her direction, what I was surprised to notice on her face was a look of sadness. But now, in the courtyard of the Virgin, we stand to walk; the echoing voices and footfalls of more teenagers are approaching now. Though she is quiet and keeps a few steps apart from me—conscious of the other American school children—I move closer and take her arm. She seems surprised and nervous.

(2001)

Alberto Florentino

Born 1931, Sta. Rosa, Nueva Ecija, Philippines; immigrated to the U.S. in 1983

Photo: Rene Ner

About the Author

Alberto Florentino attended the University of the East (1948-1956), the University of the Philippines (1956-1958) and Far Eastern University (1959-1961). A writer-playwright, editor and publisher, Florentino's contribution to Filipino and Filipino American literature are far-reaching. His published books include *The World Is an Apple and Other Prize Plays* (1959), *The Portable Florentino: 7 Representative Plays for Stage and Television in English and Filipino* (1954-1998), and *Panahon ng Digma: Tatlong Maikling Dula (Three Short Plays)*. He has received numerous awards including the prestigious Ten Outstanding Young Men Award (TOYM) for Theater (1960), *Patnubay ng Kalinangan* (*Araw ng Maynila*, 400th anniversary of the founding of Manila) and several Carlos Palanca Memorial Awards.

Mexican Influence in the Philippines

Because the Philippines was a colony of Spain for over three hundred years, it is a Catholic country. Throughout the Philippines, huge stone churches, remnants of colonial times, can still be seen. Heavily influenced by Mexico because of the Manila-Acapulco trade, the foundation of a Filipino town was patterned after the Mexican mission complex. It included the construction of a huge church and convent. These colonial stone churches resemble colonial churches in South America.

In olden days it was the practice for convents to have a "turning cradle" so unwed mothers could have a place to surrender their children and know that the babies would be cared for by the nuns. Florentino's story features this ancient "turning cradle."

The term "Indian-Giver" refers to one who gives a gift, but then takes it back.

Indian-Giver

— Alberto Florentino

"God is subtle."
—For Ponette

1 - THE "RECALL"

AT THE FUNERAL RITES Annette's sharp ears, in spite of her sniffles, caught some of Fr. Penzio's soothing words of comfort for those left behind:

"Seven days ago God gave Annette—and her loving family—a sister, who, after God's gift of short life that lasted but one week, left us so soon, to be by God's side . . . What God gives us, God sometimes takes away . . . for reasons we may not fathom . . . God works in mysterious ways . . ."

What Annette remembered most was:

"What God gives, God sometimes takes away . . .

The day after the funeral the phrase took form in her mind: "Indian-giver . . . Indian-giver . . ."

Then she started to speak it, but softly, like a prayer: "Indian-giver . . . Indian-giver . . ."

Soon she started repeating the words every second, and louder each time: "Indian-giver . . . Indian-giver . . ."

Towards noon she was reciting it like a litany, loud enough for everyone to hear: "Indian-giver . . . Indian-giver . . ."

Until, by the week-end, it became a mantra reverberating in everybody's mind: "Indian-giver . . . Indian-giver . . ."

Annette's family and friends started worrying because she would not even pause to eat or drink . . . or to go to the bathroom . . . or to her church or her kinder-school . . . but stayed in bed murmuring: "Indian-giver . . . Indian-giver . . ."

The story about Annette . . . refusing to leave her bed . . . reciting "Indian-giver . . . Indian-giver . . ." the whole day . . . and refusing to do anything . . . or go anywhere—soon reached the local papers.

Reporters and photographers tried to get an interview or even just a sound-bite from her, but all they heard from Annette was: "Indian-giver . . . Indian-giver . . ."

Then Annette's story reached the national papers and was splashed on the front pages. Soon the media came in droves. The paparazzi, the TV channel trucks, the satellite dishes, the helicopters, the anchors . . .

Even Barbara Walters, the best anchor in the world, came to interview her in her own inimitable style. But in the end Barbara left in shame because Annette would only say: "Indian-giver . . . Indian-giver . . ."

Doctors and nurses came to Annette and took turns helping her, hovering about her, devising ways to make her eat—since she refused to take in anything except water.

However, they were able to feed her, intravenously, dextrose and fluid nutrients, but only late at night when, sleepy and exhausted, her lips would fall silent. But only until she woke up the next morning with her first words of the day: "Indian-giver . . . Indian-giver . . ."

Even the Cardinal, bishops, priests, nuns, and acolytes came to soothe her, gave her comfort.

The Cardinal suggested that she might want to pray to Mother Mary or Lord Jesus or God Almighty Himself. But all Annette said was: "Indian-giver . . . Indian-giver . . ."

The nuns begged Annette to eat and drink, and to rest and sleep. The doctors and nurses begged her to visit the bathroom.

But all they heard from Annette was: "Indian-giver . . . Indian-giver . . ."

Then it seemed the whole world knew about Annette, the little girl who, for many weeks now, had repeated every few seconds only the words: "Indian-giver . . . Indian-giver . . ."

Even the Ambassador from India flew in to offer condolences for Annette's lost sister. The diplomat tried to tell Annette—very diplomatically, of course—that what she was muttering may not be necessarily true of all 900 million Indians in India—or even all American "Indians" if she had actually meant them—but the diplomat got no answer.

So, chastened, the Indian Ambassador gave up and left, his head ringing with the only words she spoke during the one-way conversation: "Indian-giver . . . Indian-giver."

Then the most traveled Pope in history made a special trip to this little innocent girl who apparently wanted to talk with God but didn't know how—and who else but the Pope could best speak on her behalf?

The Holy Pope came, sat down beside her bed (he being too old now), touched her head and blessed her first. He spoke to her and tried to get her to speak her mind. But all that the Holy Pope heard her speak was: "Indian-giver . . . Indian-giver . . ."

The people were quite sure that if Mother Teresa had come, the "Living Saint" could have calmed her down and offered to get down on her knees with her and ask God for whatever she wanted to ask from Him.

But, of course, as everyone knew, Mother Teresa had left our world and gone away and was now unable to intercede on Annette's behalf here on earth.

Then, once, when Annette saw a visiting Mother Superior, she paused from reciting those words and asked her if she knew where Mother Teresa was. The Mother Superior bent over Annette and whispered something into her ears.

Annette cried out: "Oh, no!" then wept . . . then resumed muttering: "Indian-giver . . . Indian-giver . . ."

Princess Diana herself, if she had heard of this little girl, would have flown over—on the Concorde, no less—to be by Annette's side. But, alas! like Mother Teresa, Princess Di herself had also gone.

Wisely, no one mentioned a word to Annette about the beloved princess and she never asked.

People thought the two people Annette would have wanted to come had left and gone to that special place where the two of them would have surely met and could have prayed together and asked God for a little gift for this disconsolate little girl: a little miracle in a world where it has become rare!

One Sunday morning some of Annette's friends, who had been taking turns attending to her needs after school, were walking to church to attend the morning Mass.

Passing by the convent, one of the girls heard what seemed to her like a baby's cry coming from the direction of the convent door.

The little friend broke from the group and tarried behind until she was all alone on the street; then, unseen by anybody, she walked to the convent door. The convent door was closed but she pressed her ear to it and listened . . .

2 - THE "TURN"

THERE WAS IN THIS TOWN a church and convent which were more than 100 years old. The convent had a rotating shell attached to the front door—called the "turn"—so that anything placed on it from the outside, with a light push, was suddenly safely inside the convent.

For as far back as the townspeople and their children could remember, the convent door with the rotating shell—the "turn"—had always been used to convey gifts and donations—flowers, cakes, pies, prayer cards, cookies, toys, new or hand-me-down dresses—for the priests and the nuns, for their own use or to give away to those in need.

Hundreds of years ago—the grandmothers explained to their grandchildren who grew up seeing the convent door with the rotating shell—the "turn"—and had plagued their elders with endless questions.

The children, who themselves later became mothers and grandmothers, were plagued with the same questions about the "turn" from their own young.

And this was how the story was told and remembered:

That when a young girl, wed or unwed, became a mother herself, wittingly or otherwise, and for one reason or other wanted to "donate" her baby for adoption without the people knowing the donor, the young mother placed her infant—just born and newly torn from her body, still pale and pink, with not a stitch of clothing nor a blanket, with only a blood-soaked towel binding her tightly, the hurriedly cut umbilical cord coated with blood clots—placed the infant on the rotating shell—the "turn"—and gently pushed it in; and once the baby was safe inside the convent, the distraught mother, weeping, having fervently kissed the baby goodbye, without looking back, fled in the night (or in the wee hours of next morning), the whole scene unseen by any body or soul, such that the young mother would forever remain anonymous.

This could have been an apocryphal story as the convent door had not been used in this manner as far as any living person had known, not in a very long long time, and the people who heard this in whispers knew not whether to feel happy—or sad—about this "turn" long unused.

3 - THE "GIFT"

ANNETTE'S FRIEND excitedly ran from the convent straight to Annette's home. Once inside, she walked to Annette, lying in her bed, murmuring: "Indian-giver . . . Indian-giver"—and whispered something into her ear . . .

Without breaking her murmurs, Annette gathered her strength, stood up weakly and—held up by a nurse and a nun—followed her friend to the convent. In no time at all, a procession of people had formed behind them as far back as anyone could see.

All the people following Annette—the friend, the nurse and the nun holding Annette up, and a crowd of townspeople—arrived in front of the convent. The crowd stopped at a respectful distance. Held up by the nurse and the nun, Annette weakly stepped forward up the steps to the convent door—with the "turn." There she paused, made a sign of the cross, then peered inside the partly opened door . . .

Suddenly, hearing what her friend had earlier heard, Annette stopped in the middle of her litany: "Indian-giver . . . Indian-giv—" and turned to the crowd behind her. Those who were nearest to Annette heard what the rest would hear from the other side of the door—a baby's cry!

The crowd then heard Annette say, this time loud enough for all the people gathered to hear: "Thank you, God . . . God, thank you . . ." Then everyone saw what they had missed since the funeral: a smile breaking like a sun on her face.

4 - "THE GOOD NEWS"

THE GOOD NEWS was spread in print and photographs, was read or watched and heard all over the world, in black and white and in color, on the pages of the papers and magazines, on television, radio and on cable. The coverage mostly showed . . .

First, the baby in her bassinet . . .

A close-up of Annette with her sister, always asleep . . .

Annette's family and neighbors and friends in school . . .

The convent door with the rotating shell—the "turn"—as everyone now calls it . . .

The church and convent, both now attracting out-of-town tourists . . .

The church grounds and the gardens in bloom . . .

The best and happiest parts of the town and its now happy townspeople . . .

But specially the bassinet, now full of bouquets and gifts for the baby who had come back!

6 - AN "APOCRYPHAL" STORY

MANY YEARS LATER the townspeople said that on that day of days an unwed teenager, merely a child herself, gave birth to her child, alone and unattended by nurse or midwife, and later gave up her day-old baby by leaving her on the convent's revolving shell—the "turn"—thus offering an unseasonable gift to whoever could give the baby the life and love she couldn't give.

(Surely, she must have left the next day for parts unknown.)

These same people were later heard to say that the five-year-old Annette didn't really get her sister back but got another baby, another baby girl.

Annette, once she knew and saw the girl after the priests and nurses had prepared her, had assumed it was her sister returned to her in answer to the only improvised prayers she could come up with.

The town's elders, led by the priest, the mayor, the parents, the family physician, the town doctor, and many others, met that same day in the convent behind closed doors.

When they came out they were all smiles, the mayor and the parents carrying a bassinet with the baby in it, and headed for Annette's house where the five-year-old sister waited beside the empty crib in her bedroom.

People who were not privy to what happened in the meeting started talking: The five-year-old Annette, they whispered, was then too young to know or was spared the truth—besides, don't day-old babies—like day-old chicks—all look alike?

None of the parties present at the convent meeting said anything—not to the press, not to each other, and not to the townspeople; and the talk soon died down.

More people believed it was a gift from Above, a little miracle for a little five-year-old, wrought together by family and neighbors and friends—and strangers! some of them the "Powers-That-Be," some from "High Places"—and who is there to say that after one hundred years one such young mother could not have come from somewhere, from nowhere, to deliver her first child and give her up on the same day, or that same night, a baby girl that would end up on the long-unused rotating shell—the "turn"—on the door of a hundred-year old convent—a baby who would end up in the empty crib beside Annette's bed, and who would grow up looking more and more like Annette—which, taken all together with all that happened on that day of days, true or not—are a miracle enough.

(2002)

Joel Barraquiel Tan

Born 1968, Manila, Philippines; immigrated to the U.S. in 1976

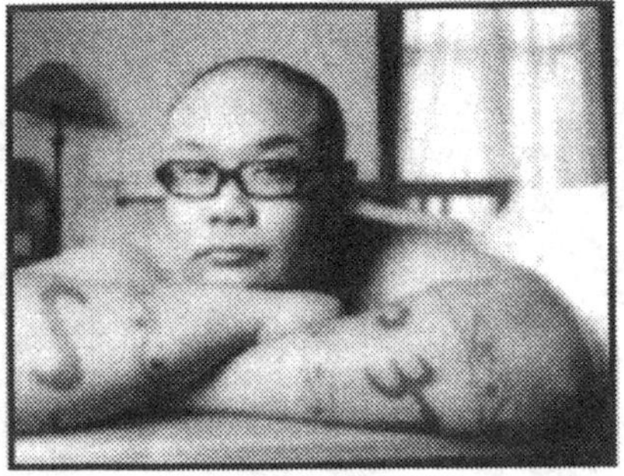

About the Author

Joel Barraquiel Tan has a B.A. (Ethnic Studies, 2002) from U.C. Berkeley and is currently completing his M.F.A. in Creative Writing at Antioch University. A writer, playwright, and activist, he is the author of a collection of poems entitled, *Monster* and the editor of *Queer Pilipino, Asian, and Pacific Islander Porn* (Cleis Press, 1998). Joel's essays, poems, and fiction have been published in: *Q&A: Queer in Asian America, Asian American Sexualities, On a Bed of Rice: An Asian American Erotic Feast, Eros Pinoy, Flippin': Filipinos on America*, and others. Joel is also a well-respected AIDS activist and has advocated for communities of color in various capacities for the past fourteen years. Joel is a co-founder of Los Angeles' Asian Pacific AIDS Intervention Team. Joel currently lives in Southern California with his partner.

Filipino Mother

Most Filipino sons regard their mothers as saints. Among my circle of friends, Mama (or Ms. Toni) was considered the patron saint of queers. She protected her flock and guided them through the challenges of being gay in a homophobic world. "San Prancisco" is a tribute to "St. Toni" and an account of growing up Filipino, gay, and immigrant in the U.S. during the '80s. Mama had raised me to always be proud, to never forget who I am and where I came from. Mama would say, "*You are my son and you are a Filipino. You have nothing to be afraid or ashamed of.*" Mama echoed these sentiments of pride during an interview for Alice Hom's article on gay parents, "*Even if I think that because I raised him alone as a mother, even if he came out to be gay, he was raised as a good person. I'm still lucky that he came out to be like that.*"

When I was young, I thought that leaving my mother's home would mark my independence and that I would find "gay liberation" by moving to San Francisco. I now realize that one can only be truly liberated by unconditional love and acceptance. How lucky I was to have had a mother who was both a fierce protector and an invaluable friend. Mama would always say, "You are going to miss me when I'm gone. You will climb the highest mountain, shouting to the world how good Mama was and how lucky you are, you spoiled boy. You'll see!"

Mama, how right you were. I've only begun to shout.

San Prancisco

— Joel Barraquiel Tan

Coming Out

I was sixteen when I told Mama. She was rubbing off old nail polish from her toes when I took a deep breath and declared that I was gay and there was nothing she could do about it. Without looking up she asked, "Are you happy being a-gay?" I said that I was indeed. "Okay! Good . . ." wiggling her toes, she asked, " . . . Brick Rose or Chocolate Fantasy?"

I had none of the screaming, the crying, or the hysterics I had prepared myself for. In time, I grew to resent Mama's blasé reaction. As I met other gays and lesbians, I realized that Mama had deprived me of my requisite "coming out" story. I wasn't subjected to shock treatments or the ghastly counsel of a priest. I wasn't kicked out of the military for diddling my fellow privates. I never even had the thrill of leaving my homophobic but otherwise quaint hamlet in search of big city glamour and a boyfriend named Chazz. Nothing. I was forced to make up my tragic un-closeting.

"It wasn't easy growing up gay in a religious rodeo family. At sixteen, Pa discovered my erotic collage of Eric Estrada next to an empty tub of Noxzema. I was sent off to the Holy Jesus Ex-gay Ministry Camp but I ran away to Hollywood where I wasted three loveless—but highly sexually charged—years with one David Geffen. After leaving D. G. and the empty but glamorous life of runway modeling, I turned to a full-time career as a celebrity spokesperson for Gay rights. Tell me, what was coming out like for you?"

Mama wasn't about to come unhinged by my coming out; she'd defied convention all her life. Mama, according to Philippine standards of traditional femininity, was a disgrace. She was no pearl of the Orient nor had she ever aspired to be. She hated cooking and skirts. She rarely wore make-up and didn't respect men enough to surrender her will to one. She did that once and learned her lesson. Mama came from a long line of thick, sturdy women who ate heartily, laughed too loud, and cussed with great gusto. Trying to picture Mama acting coy and demure was like trying to picture her power walking in stilettos.

I was only eight when we were forced to flee Manila. Local officials, Marcos sympathizers, didn't take kindly to the fact that Mama was holding guns in our basement for the resistance. Risking her life for her nation was one thing but risking my life was another matter altogether. Unlike the rest of our family who enjoyed the cushy stateside life of TV dinners and amusement park vacations, Mama thought of our new life in North Hollywood as exile, as displacement. Those early years were difficult and lonely. I can never forget Mama's sobbing thinly disguised by the sound of water running from the bathroom tap. Was she crying over my father who moved to Canada to marry another woman? Was it the revolution that never happened? Was she just exhausted from working two full-time jobs? And as children often do, I thought that I might have been responsible for her tears. Regardless of what caused her sadness, Mama almost always cried alone. I'd only witnessed her cry twice: when the Marcoses were forced to flee Malacañang Palace and when she caught me lifting a dollar bill from her wallet.

Mama never treated me like a child—she didn't have the patience for it. She was never one to entertain notions of Santa Claus, tooth fairies, or any gilded representations of the world around us. While other kids were watching Disney movies and teen dramas about summer camp I was catching weekend matinees of "Cruising" and "Reds." I shared my mother's love for Gibran and her weakness for Judith Krantz novels. I was even allowed to stay up late on Thursday nights for our favorite nighttime soap, "Prisoner Cell Block H"—a violent and lusty Australian drama set in a women's penitentiary. Mama took me to my first concert—Donna Summer's legendary "Bad Girls" tour. Communism, leather queens, poetry, trashy novels, jail drama, and disco divas. I guess it wouldn't take a licensed cosmetologist to figure out how I ended up a-gay.

San Francisco Dreaming

In my teens, I dreamt about San Francisco. West Hollywood, while certainly a gay epicenter, only offered a chintzy three blocks of gay liberation. San Francisco, on the other hand, was seven square miles of gay, gay, gay.

I dreamed about waking up in my Castro penthouse, to the chirping calls of lesbian bluebirds perched on a lavender windowsill. I'd linger in bed for a bit, nestled in the hairy muscled arms of my gorgeous Sicilian boyfriend, Chip. After crimping my hair and flossing, I'd be ready to begin my gay positive day. Bullet, the doorman, would tip his hat and offer a cheery, "It's a gay, gay day, isn't it, Mr. Mayor?" I'd smile and wink before getting into my waiting limo. Nestled comfortably inside the creamy leather interior of the Rolls, I would look out at the utopian expanse of my city and thank goddess for being blessed with such fortune and flawless skin.

I celebrated my eighteenth birthday by making my first trip to San Francisco for the first time. I came ready with a fake I.D., my first charge card, and a mission to find a new life with a genuine San Francisco gay boyfriend. I stayed with María, my newly eloped chum who had recently dropped out of U.C. Santa Cruz. María's Pacific Palisades parents disowned her for marrying "trailer trash." María married Jeb, a forty-five year old mechanic with red hair and a face and body reminiscent of fur togas and cave paintings. I fell in love with Jeb the first time I laid eyes on him.

"Back off, you bleedin' cow," María warned, lighting two thin More Menthols and handing me the one with the half-lit cherry. María had recently taken on an English cockney accent. She had just formed an all-girl punk band, The Menses U.K. and she thought that an accent might help them get gigs.

"Yum. I hope I look that good when I'm forty-five. Tell me Eliza Doolittle, how's life as a child bride?" We sat on their stoop, admiring Jeb's bountiful thighs jutting out of a vintage Firebird.

"Full. Filling!" María opened her eyes wide and pointed to the sizable mound of the front of her husband's jeans. I was sick with envy. María had somehow managed to score the gay life I wanted for myself: a cute flat in the Castro, a promising retail career at the Gap, a literary agent interested in her angst-filled collection of poetry, a shot at punk fame, and a mechanic husband with size 13 feet. María went on and on about how much L.A. sucked and how her parents can kiss her ass and how she planned on living the rest of her natural life in the city by the bay.

"María, I'm gonna move up here and start my life," I declared.

"Wot? Why? And leave yer mum? Forge' it. Stay in Los Angeleez. If my mummy wuz as cool as yours . . . Yeesh, you're bloody daft!" María was among Mama's devoted minions. In addition to providing counsel and comfort to every homosexual I knew, Mama also case-managed my deeply troubled female buddies: young women who chain-smoked, cussed excessively and cranked out angry love songs on their twelve-string guitars. Before graduation, long before she turned cockney, María spent inordinate amounts of time at our apartment swapping dirty jokes and menthols with Mama. Mama affectionately referred to María as the son she never had. They had amazing chemistry—a bond one might imagine between two frat boys sharing a twelve-pack and a hooker on Super Bowl Sunday. Before I left, Mama had given me a care package for María: a volume of Jose Garcia Villa's surrealist poetry, a four-pack of pine-tree car fresheners, a carton of cigarettes, and a thirty-minute cassette of Mama complaining about increasing property taxes and how her blood-sugar medication made her dizzy all the time.

I said, "You don't understand, Mari. I need to move somewhere where I can be me. Where I can be gay."

She just sighed and shook her head slowly, "What you got planned on your first night in the big city, love?"

The Castro. Gay Mecca. I imagined myself milling about at the bars, throwing back exotic concoctions of Amaretto and Drambuie, and bubbling over with witty quips. I'd introduce myself as Dallas or some other exotic creature. And when asked to dance . . .

"Who me? Dance? Ha ha (*said with flirty undertone, hand at the hollow of my neck*). Really, I'm quite captivated by the thrill of a warm night and my Mai Tai. Perhaps the next dance? (*slip him a look that lets him know you're interested but not easy*)."

Walking down the steep slope of Divisadero, I was greeted by the Friday night lights of the gay strip. "The Castro," the neon sign read. 'This was it.' I thought. This is where my life begins. It was ten o'clock and my first stop was "A Different Light"—**the** gay bookstore. I walked in to find the store empty except for the cashier—a gaunt, bored looking black man with short dreads wearing a shirt with "Shut-up Bitch!" emblazoned in huge red letters. He didn't bother looking up from his book as I approached.

"Howdy-ho!" I chirped enthusiastically.

He looked around, announcing to an invisible clientele, "A Different Light Bookstore will be closing in ten minutes. Please bring your purchases to the cashier immediately." His hostility certainly provided a sound explanation for the empty store. I chose to ignore him. I wasn't about to let this sourpuss ruin my gay holiday! I was perusing through a History/Activism shelf when I felt someone behind me. I turned to find the dreaded "Shut-up Bitch" guy giving me the once-over. He was leaning on an aluminum cane. I noticed a bluish purple lesion on his left cheek peeking out under a thick layer of face powder.

"You're not from here," he said.

"No, I'm not," I replied.

"Thought so," he chuckled and headed back to the front counter. I followed him.

"Excuse me! Hello? Why are you so rude?"

"Rude? This isn't rude, Miss One. I ain't got the time to be rude. Rude would be if I told you that this ain't the place for you!"

I was livid. Who was this man to tell me that I didn't belong here? I banged my fist on the counter. "What makes you so sure I don't belong here?"

"Go away, kid." He sighed. He went back to reading his book.

I stomped out of the store and found myself walking in a light drizzle that quickly turned into a steady rain. I ducked into a donut store where I took comfort in a cup of cocoa and a chocolate twist. There were a number of men in the shop—none of whom fit what I expected of the enchanting Castro life. A couple faced each other over a game of chess. The heavier of the two donned a pair of oversized shades; he appeared to be blind. His opponent, a rail-thin man in overalls with oxygen tubes plugging both nostrils called out the movements of the board in a loud voice. A small green oxygen tank with a radio taped to the front was parked next to their table. Next to me sat a dour middle-aged transvestite who was freshening up her Betty Boop lipstick and adjusting her jet-black pageboy wig. When I took the seat next to her, she drew back nervously and tucked her gold-glittered purse under her arm, away from my reach. On the other side of the glass window, I noticed a young man plagued with acne wearing a sleeveless Led Zeppelin shirt, wet and shivering. His blue hair was cut into a raggedy Mohawk and spiderwebs and crosses were randomly etched into his thin pale arms. Pimpleboy caught me staring and made his way inside. He slid in next to me on the plastic bench, extended his hand and introduced himself as Viper. Viper reeked of nicotine and old sweat. He was sitting close enough that I felt his hot breath on my neck. His hands were long and slender with black dirt jammed underneath his nails. I accepted his hand cautiously and nodded as if greeting a space alien on a peace mission. Viper lifted my cup of cocoa to his lips and reached for my chocolate twist. He slurped and chewed until there was nothing left. "You Japanese or what?" He placed his chocolate stained hand on my thigh. "Japanese guys are fucking choice!" To punctuate his love for Japanese men, he dropped to his knees and started a mean strum on his air guitar.

"Filipino. I'm not Japanese."

"Oh. Bummer . . . okay." Viper said dejectedly. He then opened his mouth wide and showed me his teeth. His breath smelled like moldy sheets with an underscore of anise. His teeth had been filed into sharp fangs. "I'm a modern day vampire. Half-man, half-viper," he growled. He then went on at lightning speed about God-knows-what, occasionally banging his head on the yellow plastic table top or hopping about like a bunny to make a point. I had no idea what was wrong with him so I simply got up and walked out. I didn't realize that Viper was following me until I felt a hand cup my behind.

"Big can. Viper likes a big can," he whispered. Now, I've seen plenty of prison movies. And that would be just like my luck—to attract a prison boyfriend who'd gladly trade my "services" to other cons for a Twix bar or fat line of Ajax.

"That's mighty sweet of you to say, Viper." I removed his hand from my butt. I started to walk away again and Viper followed behind demanding that I kiss him. I calmly explained that I was a Shaolin monk vowed to chastity. Viper started yelling at me, calling me a "godforsaken lying sack of chicken heads." I broke into a run with Viper trailing close behind. I turned the corner and ran into a line of men waiting to get into the "Midnight Sun." Viper spotted the doorman and backed away quickly.

The doorman, a muscular brute with sassy blonde highlights and an orange tan braved the cold wearing only a pink mesh tank top and green nylon running shorts. Perched high atop his black leather stool, Frosty the doorman was laughing it up with the customers near the front of the line. Now this was more like it. Laughs. Camarederie. Gay Brotherhood. In line ahead of me stood two men. The shorter one, a black man, wore his hair in a fashionable jheri curl. He was sporting a dapper mustard-colored sweater and slacks ensemble, his fingers, a glittering display of gold nuggets and gems. His tall friend, a Samoan with a long ponytail and thinly plucked eyebrows, was dressed in the same exact outfit—except his color scheme was grape. They too, were deep into their conversation, laughing and gossiping about their friends who they referred to as this bitch or that heifer. After a few minutes, the couple ahead of me was finally at the front of the line.

"Bobby? Is that you, girl?" the doorman called to the man behind me. Indeed it was and after a few pleasant exchanges, the doorman allowed his buddy to enter. A few minutes later, another man came up and hugged the doorman from behind. The hugger was quickly granted entrance after twisting the doorman's nipples and grinding him from behind. It was cold outside and I briefly considered twisting the doorman's nipples myself. The three of us waited. And waited. Until another man fell in line behind me. This time, the doorman didn't seem to know him but he was summoned forth and allowed entry. And there we were, still outside, and still waiting. "Excuse me," the Samoan asked the doorman, "how long do you think it might be because I have to tinkle."

"This isn't a public restroom. There's a two-drink minimum too, you know? And we'll need three pieces of ID," the doorman said curtly.

"Three pieces of ID? Immana tell you what . . . " the smaller one shoved his face inches away from the doorman. The taller one pulled him back and smiled nervously.

"Don't mind her. Miss Girl just needs a cocktail. Do you think that you can let us in now?" the taller one asked again speaking in the gentlest of tones. The doorman was standing by now with his arms crossed.

"You three are trouble. The Midnight Sun doesn't need trouble. So, just move along before I call the cops. Go on. Scat. Take your asses back to Oakland," the doorman spat.

The taller one managed to catch the smaller one in mid-air as he lunged for the doorman's throat. The doorman grabbed his walkie-talkie and asked for the cops immediately. The taller one dragged his smaller friend down the street. "I got your Oakland," the smaller one screamed, "I got your fuckin' Oakland, you fuckin' cracker!"

In the cheeriest of tones I explained, "Uh-sir, I'm not with them."

"You're with them, alright," the doorman insisted cracking his knuckles as if he were getting ready for a boxing match. "Scat," he hissed. Once again, I considered twisting the doorman's nipples and tearing them right off his chest but instead I walked away before the fucking chimpanzee could see that he'd made me angry enough to cry. When I was at the top of the block, I yelled, "You're a godforsaken fucking chickenhead!"

I hailed a cab and returned to María and Jeb's. When it came time to pay my fare, I found that the Viper had lifted my wallet. A sleepy Jeb opened the door and paid the driver. I immediately called Mama and told her what had just happened. The only thing she said was, "Come home, hijo. Come home." I couldn't sleep that night. The echo of the store clerk's words haunted me. *This ain't the place for you. This ain't the place for you.*

The next morning, I took the first flight back to Los Angeles.

The Portrait of the Artist as a Young Gay Man

I had been living in Berkeley for less than a year when I ran into my godmother, Ninang Peachie, at a family reunion.

"How is San Prancisco, Joel?" Ninang Peachie asked.

"I don't live in San Francisco, Ninang. I live in Berkeley . . " I made a peace sign and smoked an imaginary joint to emphasize my point and repeated, "Berkeley, you know . . . la la la . . . BERKELEY."

Ninang Peachie looked at me as if she had suddenly happened upon an exotic species of gerbil. Shaking her head, she continued, "That golden bridge is beeg! Why dey call it Golden when it's RED! Ay, so stooopid! The weader der is berry nice in summer. Hot hot here in LA, *'sus!*"

"I don't live in San Francisco," I whined. Too late. Ninang Peachie was well on her way to the mahjong tables. I finally figured out that "San

Prancisco" was my family's way of acknowledging that I was "a-gay." The way someone would be a-schizophrenic, a-proctologist or a-tsetse fly.

"You know Bambam? Mrs. Delacruzamaravillasison's eldest-da doctor wid da nice perm? He is a-gay! Aaaay, dios ko!"

While Mama never gave me a moment's grief about being gay, the rest of the family was another story. "*Paciencia* hijo, the elders are from another time, another culture." she explained. In the Philippines, the-gays or "*baklas*" were flamboyant, dressed in women's clothes and battled ferociously in the lip-synch events at the Barrio Fiestas. In the Philippines, being a-gay meant taking on the characteristics, dress, identity, and equally, the burdens of women. Faced with limited social mobility, a-gay in the Philippines faced one of two futures: beauty school or priesthood. In this regard, I'm grateful that we moved to the States. Neither bikini waxing nor exorcisms have ever interested me in the least.

I was only six when I met my first *bakla*; his name was Esperanza and he was Mama's manicurist. Espie came to the house every other Sunday to care for Mama's nails. Rumor had it that Espie was the fallen heir of Sampaguita Studio's Romero clan. Ninang Peachie also came over to get her nails done and to catch up on the latest gossip. Espie was also the first blonde I ever met. Espie wore his hair in a high tight bun and sported purple tinted glasses with diamond-capped screws. Espie, like Ninang Peachie, complained incessantly about his boyfriends.

"Espie. *Malas lang.* What bad luck we have with men! What does a girl have to do?"

"Ay, Madama Peachie, a girl has to do whatever she has to do. Me? I'm saving up for my operation and after the chop-chop . . ." she sang the bridal march, ". . . Here comes the bride all dressed in white . . . "

"Espie," Ninang Peachie warned, ". . . the boy," shooing me away with freshly painted nails. Later, I asked Mama about Espie's chop-chop. Mama explained that Espie was born in the wrong body. She was going to have an operation so that she could turn her *bototoy* into a *pukengkeng*. "Will it hurt?" I asked, worried for our Espie.

"Yes, but the doctor will put Espie to sleep first. Before he uses his knife . . ." Mama explained.

"How come Espie has to get cut with a knife?"

"Ay, because God makes a lot of mistakes." Mama explained.

Mama neither denied nor confirmed whether or not I was a-gay to our family. Instead, she told them that I was an "artist." Ninang did everything she could to dissuade me from the "artist's lifestyle." She believed that my proclivity for "art" was merely a phase. She proposed deep-sea welding as a lucrative career option. She was convinced that once I got my hands on an underwater torch, the truth would come to me like a revelation. "Apter all, hijo," she said, " . . .Lipe can be bery hard and lonely por da artists." Ninang meant well despite her relentless campaign to find me a nice girlfriend and a job that involved heavy machinery. Ninang Peachie was everything Mama wasn't. At 4'9", Ninang Peachie frosted her hair and flitted about in assorted backless ensembles. Ninang spent her free time poring over Avon catalogues, attending mass, or complaining about her boyfriend *du jour*. She was always on the lookout for a husband and Mama had long given up warning her against the hazards of matrimony. Mama swore me to secrecy and confided that despite all her talk about men and jewelry, Ninang was still a virgin. At the core of her glamour and flamboyance was an obedient Catholic girl. Ninang's boyfriends weren't willing to wait until their wedding night. My life as an "artist" wasn't easy but neither was an aging bachelorette's.

We were both petrified of the same lonely future.

Patron Saint of the Gays

My gay friends adored Mama. It was like having Diana Ross or Cher for a mother. At our kitchen table, my friends would flock around her like disciples as she dispensed her own brand of cranky wisdom:

"Your problem is dat you look soooo cheep. Wilson, stop wearing dose short tight sherts that show opp your belly button, ha! No one will take you seriously."

"Cory, don't matter ip your parents kick you out. You hab to learn to porgive them, show compassion, be generous at dem because dey are stoopid! stoopid! stoopid! You can stay with us as long as you like."

"Ay please, Billy! Pager number? Why trust a boy that only gibes you a pager number? He has a boypriend already or he is a drug pusher."

"James, I am sorry dat your Mommy die. I'll be your Mama now, ha? Okay, hijo? Now, go help your brodder Joel clean da house. You bacuum da carpet now."

At twenty-two, Father called. I hadn't heard from him in ten years. He never once acknowledged that he'd moved without leaving a forwarding address or number. Father had just opened a new embroidery factory in the Los Angeles area. Father wanted to groom me to run his L.A. operations. Mama knew Father was up to no-good but she left the decision to me. I wanted to refuse his offer; I wanted to hate him. I didn't want to forgive him for abandoning us but I was also desperate to connect with him. Father's factory was a sweatshop. He hired undocumented Filipino immigrants and paid them less than minimum wage. On rush orders, his workers pulled fourteen hour, seven-day shifts. In short, I was being groomed as an overseer. He promised that a world of material bliss lay ahead of me in exchange for my filial loyalty.

"Joel, do you have something you want to tell Daddy?" he asked suspiciously as he was poring over the daily financial reports. My job was to double-check the account entries and summarize the findings. "Who is dat boy who pick you up eberyday?" Father flipped a page slowly.

"Oh, Manolo?"

"I don't like him. He's always wearing shorts, tight tight. Is he a . . . ? Is Manolo a . . . ?"

"Puerto Rican? Yes, Father. Manolo is a Puerto Rican," I confirmed.

"You tink Daddy is stoopid? You tink Daddy was only born tomorrow?" Father slammed the stack of papers on the desk and stood up, his hands balled against his waist. At 5'4", he was hardly menacing but his face had turned an alarming shade of red.

"Yes, Father. Manny is a-gay. And I am a-gay. And we are gay together," I said defiantly standing up. At 6'1" and 230 lbs., my shadow swallowed my father's tiny form.

"Deesgusting! You are a-gay together?" he spat.

"Every night except Thursdays. He's at basketball practice until late." This was the final straw. Father started a mad rant about psychiatric help, religion, and more football to save me from my perverted life. He threatened to tell my mother. He picked up the receiver as if it were a weapon. I laughed and informed him that she already knew. He called me a liar. Then, Father accused Mama of overprotecting me, of making me gay. "Nothing is going to change the fact that I'm gay. Call her. Call a shrink, a priest . . . Howard Cossell. But I'm not the one who's crazy, it's you, to think football can cure me from buttfucking!" The combination of the words "butt" and "fucking" sent him into a maniacal spin; he raised his hand to strike. I caught his small wrist and pushed him back into his executive leather chair. On my way out, I grabbed my framed picture of Manolo and an entire case of erasable pens. The last thing I heard was Father shouting, "*Demonio*!" and the sound of dialing.

I came home to find Mama in a fit of hysterical laughter. I knew then that Father had made good on his threat to report me to Mama. She kept pointing to the telephone and twirling her finger around her ear—the universal sign for "loopy." She was shocked to hear from Father at first. She almost hung up on him but he said he was concerned about "Her son." Father asked her if she knew that I was a-gay. Mama told him that, indeed, she did know. She added that she was the patron saint of the gays and if he had a problem with it, he could take it up with her boss. She found it funnier and funnier each time she told it. "Yes," her arms stretched out like a messiah, "I am dee patron saint of the gays. I am your heabenly guardian-protector almighty." I knelt before her and yelled, "HALLELUJAH! AMEN! AMEN!" We couldn't stop laughing for days.

The Thrilla of Manila

After graduating from high school, I went to work in the field of HIV/AIDS prevention and dedicated my life to social-justice work for Gays and Lesbians. Mama supported my activism and often participated by making donations or attending events. In 1993, the Los Angeles Gay and Lesbian Center and *Genre Magazine* presented me the Gay Role Model Community Award. Mama organized a sizable entourage of family and friends to cheer me on. When I accepted the award, I saw Mama through the spotlight, standing and boasting, "My son! That boy is my son!"

That same year I won the award, Jean, my co-worker, set out to form the first Asian American PFLAG—Parents and Friends of Lesbians and Gays. Jean thought it was a good idea to invite Mama. I disagreed. "Jean, you know Mama. She's all piss and vinegar. Besides, Mama's now wearing her hair in an afro. That will scare the other parents." After some intense begging and a lunch bribe, I agreed to ask Mama.

"No! I don't need support. Dat is so stoopid. Why do the payrents need support? Beecowse their children are the-gays?"

"Mama, you're supposed to be like a role model. Pleeeeeasssee!" I begged. She eventually gave in and we attended the first meeting of the newly formed Asian PFLAG. We gathered in Jean's home and after a tense round of cold dim sum and small talk, Jean called the meeting to order.

"Can we check in?" Jean suggested in a gentle, inviting voice—an artful demonstration of her extensive experience in group facilitation.

Mrs. Takahashi, Cory's mom, who sat next to me, began to cry. Cory's father stiffened up and shushed his wife. Darla's mom started sniffling with, "I can't even face my family. What will I tell Baba. That he should never expect to hold a grandchild?"

Baby's father jumped in, "She always had boyprends. Baby was da prom queen. Now she acts and dresses like a man! Dees is keeling me and her mommy!"

"It's me. I did something. I smothered him," cried Rico's mother.

"My son is living in sin. Dat is why he has da AIDS. It's a sin against God he li'dat!" Mr. Takahashi glared at his son as he said those hateful words. Cory bowed his head in shame. Mrs. Takahashi blubbered uncontrollably. Jean, in an attempt to maintain control, asked everyone to take a deep breath. She instructed everyone to breathe in, calm their thoughts, and focus. While everyone inhaled and exhaled, I turned to look at Mama. She was running her pick dangerously slow through her afro puff. Mama was breathing alright—fire was shooting out of her nostrils! To make matters worse, Jean looked at Mama and continued with, "Would you like to share?"

"Okay," Mama said in a tone, low and dangerous. I placed a hand on her shoulder to calm her. She shrugged my hand off and continued. "How do I peel? I peel sick. Shame shame on all of you." She pointed at the circle of parents. "Dees ees patetic! Why do you need support? It is your children who has a hard lipe. And all you can tink about is yourselp? Your job is to lobe your childrens and dat is all. Dey didn't ask to be born. And you!" she barked at the frenzied Mrs. Takahashi, "Cry! Cry! Cry! Shut up your mouth!"

"Mrs. Tan!" Mr. Takahashi yelled, jumping up to his feet.

Mama also stood, meeting his gaze. I hadn't seen a stare down like that since the Ali/Frazier match in Manila. "And who told you that I am Mrs. Tan? My son's last name might be Tan but I am Miss Guerra! I am not pinished so sit down and shut up your mouth. Your son has de AIDS and you are mad at him? Teenk how stoopid you are." Mama then addressed Cory who was crying and smiling at the same time and said, "You are a good priend to my son, Cory. You are a good boy. Joel, let's go." And just like that, we left.

I was laughing as we got into the car, "Mama, you showed them. You told them just like you told Father!"

"Shut up your mouth! Shet you! How dare you bring me to dat!" She hissed and folded her arms, sitting in stony silence all the way home.

San Francisco Has Nice Weather

2001. I was in Los Angeles for my cousin's engagement party—around the time of Mama's seven-year death anniversary. I ran into Ninang Peachie at the reception. She arrived late as usual carrying a gift box decorated to look like a wedding cake. In her early sixties, Ninang had managed to preserve her glamour. Her auburn hair was cut into a sassy bob. Her knock-off backless Tom Ford complimented her tiny waist and small frame. She was aglitter with rhinestones and gold-plated jewelry. She gave me a kiss on the cheek and took my hand.

"Hijo. Seben years already." It was Ninang Peachie who had discovered Mama's lifeless body. Ninang Peachie came to the house early one morning to drop off Mama's order of Avon nail polish. The paramedics found Ninang Peachie, sobbing violently and screaming next to my mother's corpse. Ninang Peachie couldn't speak for a week after Mama's death. Cardiac arrest exacerbated by her diabetes, the coroner explained.

Father showed up at her funeral. My aunts hissed as he walked past them. Father handed me an envelope and whispered that it wasn't much. "Business has been slow," he said. María sat next to me, huddled in tears. I thanked Father for coming, handed him back his envelope and politely asked him to leave. Through her tears María protested, "What's wrong with you, dum-dum? Take his fucking money!"

Two years following Mama's death, I buried four of my closest friends. Six months after Mama died, Cory killed himself rather than endure the slow torture of his AIDS-related brain cancer. Mr. Takahashi immediately flew Cory's body back to Manoa depriving us, his gay friends, of a proper farewell. Six months after Cory, I held Wilson close as he expelled his final breath. A week later, Billy slipped into a coma and died soon after. On the eve of my mother's second death anniversary, I delivered my best friend James' eulogy. If heaven indeed existed, Mama would surely be at the gates to receive my friends. Shortly after I buried James, I informed the family that I was moving to the Bay Area. I wanted to start fresh and make another life for myself. Although difficult at first, I managed to forge a new existence without Mama, my friends, and the familiar comforts of Los Angeles.

Initially, I'd planned on finding a place in San Francisco but the once wild gay mecca had been transformed into a commune for the bratty twenty-something millionaires of the dot-com revolution. Gay men had either joined their ranks or sold their Victorians for previously unimaginable sums and scattered to the suburbs of Fremont, Pleasanton, and Orinda. Gay liberation, if it had ever existed, succumbed to the inevitability of big money and cell phones. Without much deliberation, I dismissed my teenage dreams of a Castro penthouse, lesbian bluebirds, and a gorgeous boyfriend named Chip. I realized that Mama was the San Francisco I'd dreamed of as a kid. She was gay liberation. She was sexual expression. She was civil rights. She gave me the love and support that I imagined I'd find in the crowded gay bars and street parades.

I headed across the bay to Berkeley—a quaint university town of aging hippies and Nobel peace prize winners. Unlike Los Angeles' isolating culture of endless freeways and empty sidewalks, Berkeley's cozy neighborhoods, with their tree-lined streets, bookstores, and charming coffeehouses were clean of grief. There were fewer places to be haunted in my new home.

"Seven years. Long long time," she said softly, reaching up to slip a five-dollar bill in my shirt pocket.

"Long time," I agreed.

"Your mommy is watching ober you. Like an angel. She is wid da Lord now." Ninang wrapped her tiny arms around me and looked to the heavens. "Joel, you are a good boy. A berry good artist and your mommy, she likes San Prancisco bery bery much. Nice weader."

(2002)

FRIENDSHIP

There was so much laughter to push away the hours.

— Estrella Alfon

Wanggo Gallaga

Born 1979, Bacolod, Negros Occidental, Philippines

About the Author

Even though Wanggo Gallaga was born in the Southern Philippines, he was raised in Manila and considers himself a child of Manila. He finds a connection with the city, its people, its culture and everything else about it. Fascinated by all its facets, he wishes to capture these in his writing.

He has a B.A. in Literature from De La Salle University (2000). Gallaga was also a fellow of the first Creative Writing Workshop of the University of Santo Tomas. He worked as account executive and copy writer for an advertising agency, Blue Bottle, Inc. Gallaga has taught Philippine Literature and Art Appreciation at De La Salle University, and he was also coordinator of the Students Publications Office there. He is currently a freelance writer.

His poetry has been published in *The Philippine Free Press*, and the poetry anthologies *Eros Pinoy* (Anvil, 2001) and *Love Gathers All* (Anvil, 2002). This is his first short story to be published outside of school folios.

Metro Manila Malls

For most Filipino young adults, appearances are everything. We have around eight to nine malls littered all over Metro Manila, but if you want to be considered classy and sophisticated, there are only two options: the Glorietta/Ayala Mall or Powerplant. Both can be found at the high-end commercialized district of Makati. Only the wealthy can shop there, everything is expensive. But it is also the place to be for any Filipino teen during the day. I've noticed most teens just want to be seen, not just by anybody, but by people who "count" and that is why they find themselves in either of these two malls. But these malls also have very nice shops, good theatres and a very modern ambiance, which can always attract a young crowd after class or work. So when you are in the area, take out your cell phone and text your friends to find out who can meet you for coffee and talk about the day. When you are still trying to find out who you are, I guess, it is always a good idea to surround yourself with things you aspire to be—modern, hip and high-end.

The Purpose of Malls

— Wanggo Gallaga

"Glo?"

"Sol? Are you crying?"

"Please come here. I am at G4."

"Are you okay?"

"Larry left me. He just left me."

"Oh my God! Okay, I'll be there right away. Oh my God! What happened *ba?*"

"I feel horrible. Come quickly."

Sollen switched off her phone and put it down on the table. She had been with Larry for almost seven months. Flashing through her mind were all the gifts she gave him, all the movies they watched together, all the times they went out alone and, finally, like a slap in the face, his lips mouthing the words: "I can't take this anymore. It's over." She felt weak and devastated.

She picked up the plastic cup of her caramel frappuccino and was about to take a sip from the straw when she saw Dimitri through the large glass windows of Starbucks. Dimitri was alone. He was well-dressed in slacks and a collared button-down shirt. This wasn't some quick stop to get coffee, he had time to spare. She immediately picked up her phone and called him.

"Sol?"

"Dimi! Larry left me!"

"What? He left you? Huh? What?"

"He left me. I'm just outside. Come here when you are done ordering. Please?"

"Of course. *Sandali lang*—just a second."

She put down her phone and took the plastic cup and drank from the straw. Every once in a while, she would sniffle or let out a whimper. She put down her cup and rifled through her little handbag. She took out her pack of West Ice cigarettes, took one out and lit it. She leaned back on her chair and waited for Dimitri to come out and join her.

Dimitri walked out of the glass door holding his cup made of laminated paper containing his café latte. When he found her, he walked up to her quickly, sat down on a free chair and leaned forward. "You okay?" he asked.

Sollen began crying. He gave her a hug and they remained in the same position for almost five minutes. Every once in a while, Dimitri told her that everything was going to be okay; would say that it was fine, to let everything out. Occasionally, he would rub her back with his hands, trying to comfort her. Sollen took a deep breath and let go. "He just left me, Dimi. He just left," Sollen said, very weakly. She took a deep puff of her cigarette and then blew the smoke out. She looked down on the table. "We just watched *The Lord of the Rings*—it was pretty good, but *masyadong mahaba*, I got tired sitting down for so long—and then we came here to have some coffee and a smoke."

Tears began falling down her face. "Then we started fighting because I told him I didn't want to hang-out with *sina* Paul and Jenny anymore," she continued, leaning back into the chair and taking another puff from her cigarette. "He got mad. What's wrong with that? I just told the truth."

Dimitri took out a pack of Winston Lights. He picked out a cigarette and lighted it. He took two puffs and looked at her straight in the eyes.

"Why don't you want to hang out with Paul and Jenny?"

"Dimi? She's his ex." Sollen gave an angry glare. Sollen kept quiet, not understanding Dimitri's "insensitivity." She then quickly followed up with, "I was never comfortable with the set-up."

"Didn't you say it was okay with you?" he said, taking a sip from his cup of coffee.

"Well, yeah. Of course I would say so!" Sollen sat up, putting up a defiant face, "I don't want to look like the jealous type *naman, di ba*? And I said it was okay, but we are, like, hanging out all the time." She crossed her arms in front of her chest and finished off with: "like what's that, *di ba*? Are they our only friends?"

Dimi raised one eyebrow. "Have you called Gloria?"

"Glo is on her way." Sollen took a sip from her cup and let out a big sigh. Dimitri brought out his handkerchief and offered it to her and she politely declined. She opened her bag again and rifled through it and brought out some tissue. She wiped her tears from her eyes and face and then blew her nose as quietly as she could. She didn't want to stand up and walk the distance to the comfort room.

"So why did Larry leave you? Is it just because you don't like Jenny?"

"He thought I didn't trust him, that I never felt secure with him."

"Is that true?"

"Of course! He left Jenny to be with me, Dimi. He could do it again," she said, staring at Dimi with disbelief. She quickly added, "but I never gave him any reason to think that I was scared or insecure. I never did."

Dimitri nodded to assure her he understood. He was going to ask another question when Sollen burst into a smile. She stood up and extended her hands, shouting: "Glo!"

"Sol! Oh my God! Can I just tell you?"

The two girls met up beside Dimitri and hugged. Sollen began crying again and Gloria rubbed her back and whispered to her that everything was going to be okay, to hush up now because she deserved better.

When they finally released each other from the hug, Gloria said, "Oh my God! Sol, Dimi, I saw Larry downstairs with Jenny. They were in front of AX and they were talking and Larry saw me, and he didn't say anything. So, *siyempre, hindi ko siya pinansin* (naturally, I ignored him). Why should I, *di ba*? Then Jenny waves at me and says hello. The nerve, no? So I snubbed her also. I just came straight here."

"They're downstairs?" Sol said, tears forming in her eyes.

"Yes, Sol," Gloria said looking very serious, "he's such a pig."

"Oh my God! Glo, can I just tell you? I was telling Dimi just a while ago that he left me because we had a fight over Jenny. I just told him I wasn't comfortable hanging out with them always and he got mad. He said I didn't trust him *daw*."

Gloria covered her mouth with her fingers, exclaimed, "My God! What a jerk!"

Sollen sat down on her chair and saw her cigarette had died. She lit another. Gloria kissed Dimi in the cheek and exchanged greetings.

Glo looked at Dimitri. "Where's Lian?"

"She's with her mom. They went to Rustan's. There is a sale there *daw*."

"Oh my God, Sol! He's right. That is why it was so hard for me to find parking *kanina*. Let's go?"

"After my cigarette?"

"Sure. I'll get coffee."

The three friends walked to U, just a short distance from Starbucks. Both girls walked side by side. Gloria informed Sollen about all her suspicions over the "Larry situation." Sollen kept agreeing. "I know, I know, Glo, I should have seen it coming," she repeated.

Behind them, Dimitri carried two shopping bags. Gloria had bought two pairs of jeans and Sollen had bought a belt. "Shit *talaga*, Glo, I feel so bad. It's like he left Jenny to be with me, just so Jenny would get jealous. I feel so used."

"I know; he is such a jerk." Gloria emphasized her statement by wrapping her arms around Sollen.

Dimitri added, "I am sorry, Sol, but I told you. You shouldn't have got together. There was something fishy about it."

"You didn't say anything like that, Dimi." She stopped to stare at Dimitri who was now looking at a shop window.

"Yes, he did, Glo. You weren't there, but I heard him."

While Dimitri was studying a shirt, his cell phone rang. He held out the screen of his cell phone, which said, "Larry."

"Don't answer it!" Sollen ordered.

"Answer it," said Gloria, "but pretend you don't know anything."

Dimitri looked at Sollen and she nodded.

"Hello? Larry? What's up?" Silence. "Really?" Dimitri rolled his eyes, as if disbelieving what he heard. "No, Lian is with her mom at Rustan's. Yeah, the sale. No, the shirt is at four hundred pesos *na lang*. Yeah, worth it *talaga*." Then Dimitri's eyes bulged and he began to stammer, "Um . . . uh . . . keep you company? Now? Um . . . " He began to stall as he looked at Gloria and Sollen for a way out.

"Tell him you're supposed to meet up with me and Sol in five minutes."

"I am going to meet up with Sol and Gloria in five minutes. Yeah." Dimitri let out a sigh of relief. "Sure. Later. I'll get the boys; don't worry. Yeah, just us. Yes, I won't bring Lian. *Sige*, 'bye."

"What did he say?"

Dimitri gave Sollen a piercing look. Silence.

"What did he say, Dimi?" Gloria interjected.

Dimitri remained silent for a moment.

"Larry said you broke up with him. You got jealous *daw* of Jenny."

"What a liar! Gloria, he's lying," Sollen exclaimed, looking at Gloria. Her world was slowly crumbling and she felt a little dizzy. She held on to

Gloria and Dimitri for some support. She closed her eyes to regain her sense of balance. Tears began falling from her eyes. She turned to Dimitri, "Do you believe him?"

Dimitri hesitated, "Sol, you know I don't. You are my friend. I'm here with you."

"My God! He is going to tell everyone I broke up with him. He's turning this all around. He's lying!" Sollen sat down on a couch; her eyes were full of tears.

"No, no, honey, stop crying. No one will believe him," Gloria told Sollen as she sat beside her and put her arm around her. "Right, Dimitri?"

"Yeah, of course. Everyone knows he's a liar."

Sollen began to cry harder. Gloria looked up at Dimitri. He raised his hands and shook his head. He was out of ideas. Sollen's crying was becoming uncontrollable. Gloria turned to Sollen, "Sol, sweetie, let's go downstairs to Essences. Let's buy some make-up, c'mon."

Sollen held back her tears and spoke, between her sniffling, a rather weak, "Okay."

"Okay, good," Gloria said, helping Sollen up. She turned to Dimitri and spoke, "You buy that shirt, then follow us downstairs, OK?"

"Sure."

Later as Dimitri got off the escalator, he found the two women laughing as they were trying different shades of lipstick and eyeliner. He let out a deep breath and smiled. He approached them and asked, "What's so funny?"

"Dimi, my God! There was this girl *kanina* and she took off her shoe and tried the nail polish on her feet. How gross!" Sollen let out a laugh. "She is so *kadiri*! I swear. She even took some of the lotion and massaged the sole of her feet. It was so gross."

Both girls began to laugh and playfully bump into each other. Dimitri continued smiling and turned away to stop from laughing very hard. When the laughter began to die down, he turned to them and said, "Get what you want *na* and let's go. I'm hungry."

"Where do you want to eat?"

"Anywhere. I'm just hungry." He raised his free hand and motioned to both of the girls, giving them the freedom to choose. Both girls looked at each other.

"Cibo's?"

"Ate there yesterday. Can we just go to Italliani's?"

"Sure. My treat, girls."

"Oh, Dimi, you are so sweet! Thanks." Sollen replied, affirming the compliment with a hug.

"*K lang*, you are grieving *naman, di ba?*"

"Yeah, you guys are so sweet. I am so glad I have friends like you. I wouldn't know what to do without you guys."

Gloria approached the counter to make her purchases and raised her voice to be heard, "Yeah, I know. Imagine what would we do in the mall if we were all alone?"

"Yuck! How boring!" cried Sollen. She realized she was in a better mood now. She glanced at a mirror and saw her reflection. She saw that her cheeks were flushed from laughing and also from the make-up that she had tried on. She was glowing. She didn't look like she had been crying at all. In fact, she was actually very pretty, and from some angles could be considered very beautiful. She admitted to herself that she was pretty lucky, despite the circumstances. She was doing well in school. She had enough money to buy anything she wanted. And most important, she had good friends who took very good care of her. "Yes," she said to herself, "I don't need Larry. I'm a very lucky girl."

(2002)

Gilda Cordero-Fernando

Born 1930, Manila, Philippines

About the Author

Gilda Cordero-Fernando was born and raised in Manila, Philippines. She received her B.A. and B.S. in Education from St. Theresa's College; and her M.A. from the Ateneo Graduate School. She wrote short fiction in her "early housewife" years, from 1952-1970, then put it behind her to go into nonfiction and publishing. Her most recent collection is entitled *Story Collection* (Anvil, 1994). As publisher, Gilda trailblazed with big and beautiful illustrated Filipiniana volumes such as *Turn of the Century*, *Culinary Culture of the Philippines*, and *History of the Burgis*. She was the *Patnubay ng Sining* awardee for literature in the 1993 *Araw ng Maynila*, and the Cultural Center of the Philippines' *Gawad* awardee for literature and publishing in 1994. She has also produced children's books; she has painted; she has organized fashion shows—Gilda's ways for artistic expression is boundless.

Philippine Schools

Soon after the Philippine-American War (1898-1901), the American government established schools in the Philippines. In 1901, the U.S.S. Thomas brought 1,000 American teachers to the Philippines; the name "Thomasite" became generic for all American teachers in the Philippines at the time. The first Normal School was opened in Manila in 1901. In 1902 the Americans established a system of public high schools concentrated in cities and principal towns. In 1909 the first school of arts and trades opened. More schools were opened subsequently.

Aside from these public schools, private Catholic schools proliferated. The schools, such as the Ateneo and Letran, were generally inherited from the Spanish period; although some were established during the American period, such as St. Scholastica and San Beda. As a whole, the children of the affluent attended and continue to attend private schools.

The Eye of a Needle

— Gilda Cordero-Fernando

When I was a little girl and in school, we all had a very strong sense of sin. If you so much as borrowed a crayola without permission, you could feel God the Father's eye in its triangle above the blackboard following your every move till you put it back. We avoided "occasions of sin" like standing before the mirror too long, and going to movies with kissing scenes, and we practiced all the virtues—humility, fortitude, temperance and chastity. We were always very careful not to lie and not to steal, not to commit adultery and not to kill. I didn't know exactly what chastity meant but it had something to do with having your skirt two inches below the knees and minding the way you sat—legs uncrossed, knees together, and not a wisp of underwear showing, because such carelessness, we had painfully been made to understand, was a grievous sin. We were Grade Four and whatever the nuns said was law—you obeyed or went to hell, it was as simple as that.

At one minute to seven, Madame Ludmilla stood in the gray light of the drafty Assembly Hall, and we were expected to fall in line, throw away our bubble gum, stop fidgeting and sweating. Madame Ludmilla was a cold Teutonic nun with a face as cheerless as a chopping board. No morsel of love ever fell from the tight zipper of her mouth. She could swoop down from her perch on the teacher's platform and shake the living daylights out of you. She could leave you crucified against the blackboard with a dictionary on either palm. With the end of her long pointer, she had a way of flicking an offensive bow off a pigtail or a flower off a collar. She was bleak and righteous and pure and germless.

Blessed are the poor in spirit, Madame Ludmilla was fond of intoning, for they shall possess the kingdom of heaven. And our eyes automatically strayed to where Socorro sat in her mended uniform, scratching a scab off her ankle. We, the children of the privileged, who rode flashy cars to school, who had money to waste on candy that rots the teeth and forgot to turn off the tap in the lavatory, we had as much chance of entering that kingdom as a camel passing through the eye of a needle. And as we bowed our heads in sorrow and shame, Madame Ludmilla walked swiftly down the aisle to collect our recess money for the father of Socorro who was dying of TB in a charity ward.

I rode to school with Father who had no sense of time and consequently was always late in the mornings. He took an eternity to shave and to choose his tie while I waited in the car and honked and honked. It was all right for Father. He only went to the courthouse. He wouldn't have to feel the pointer at his back propelling him to a corner, or to have to tell in front of the class (stuttering and crying while everyone tittered) why he was late again: "Because my father, Madame." I was "Miss Because-My-Father," the world's champion late-comer, and Madame Ludmilla sucked in her breath and began the moral about the man who was too late to meet St. Peter.

Sometimes if Madame Ludmilla was busy at the blackboard (she liked to write and to draw maps) I could sneak in late without being noticed. That is, unless Socorro, who sat behind me, was in a holy mood and told. Socorro was a large simpering girl with chopped bangs and a cough in her voice, and she was Madame Ludmilla's spy. She was forever hiding behind doors to see who talked or read comic books or wore colored socks. Upon my back, she heaped endless indignities—flicking my braids like horse reins or dipping the ends of them in her horrid sea-green ink. I can still see the plump red meat of her tongue lolling wetly between the white fence of her teeth. I hated and feared her almost as much as I did our teacher, but we were doomed to each other's company, bound alphabetically together by our surnames (which both began with C) and I endured my appointed desk before this bully, who remorselessly controlled me by the docile ends of my braids.

We used to wait for our cars at five p.m. on an open porch in front of Home Economics. No one ever fetched Socorro but she always sort of stood around hoping someone would give her a lift home. Sometimes we played jackstones. You could stand at the top of the stairs and look down to the Maypole, over to the drinking fountains and the cluster of glider swings where the collegiates sat gossiping, and clear down to the curve of mossy convent wall which enclosed the nuns' vegetable garden.

I remember it was a particularly windy day and I stood at the top of the stairs holding on to my school bag. Suddenly a big wind came swooshing over the playground, lifting my skirt up like an inverted parachute, ballooning it up and over my red-hot ears. Desperately, I struggled to keep my skirt down, but for what seemed like an eternity I was exposed to merciless view—my knobby knees, my thighs, my cotton panties.

The moment I had control of the situation, I looked quickly around to see if anyone had witnessed my humiliation and met Socorro's eyes twinkling mischievously over the rim of a melting popsicle.

"I saw!" Socorro chanted, making all sorts of horrid faces, covering her eyes with her stubby-nailed fingers and peeking through them. "I saw, I saw and I'm going to tell!"

"It wasn't my fault!" I cried. "You know it wasn't my fault!"

"What a mortal sin!" laughed Socorro. "What a great enormous, seditious mortal sin!"

"You're not going to tell are you?" I asked anxiously, "Madame would think I was careless on purpose."

Socorro nodded her head with enthusiasm. "Boy, if there's anything Madame hates it's immodesty."

"Please, Socorro," I begged. "She already hates me. If you tell her—"

"Boy, I bet you get locked up in the broom closet. You heard about that girl Madame locked up there last year and forgot? Boy, they had to bring her out on a stretcher! She was black and blue. She was green and white. Oh boy, what if they expel you?

"Who cares?" I made a face and looked away.

"You said that! Remember you said that, too. Who cares! Oh boy!"

Just then the car came sweeping down the driveway and I had to go home.

Perhaps if there had been no Madame Ludmilla, or if she were more like the kinder teachers of the succeeding grades, Socorro would not have been such an ominous figure in my memory. A trifle rougher, a bit bossier than the others maybe, but someone you dismiss in adulthood with a sigh and even a little pity. Perhaps you'd bump into her twenty years later, carrying a market basket, with a brat squalling at her skirt and she'd have lost her menacing qualities—she'd be just an old schoolmate you couldn't immediately place, but were quickly glad to note hadn't got on in life any better than you. But there was Madame Ludmilla, spewing righteousness and brimstone, they complemented each other like hook and eye—and the nun's bigotry brought to the surface Socorro's subtler qualities.

The next day I tried to talk to Socorro but she refused to answer and turned her back on me. But I could sense from the square of her shoulders and the giggle convulsed in her cheek that she was still going to tell. I didn't say a word when she knotted my braids and stuck a paper flap into them. I didn't flinch when she dipped the ends of them in her sea-green ink. During Geography I caught a glimpse of Socorro drawing something on her pad. I saw her write my name at the bottom of it and then it dawned on me that she had drawn the figure of a girl with her skirt flying up. The paper made its way down the second row and the girls held on to their bellies in silent mirth. By recess time the drawing had made its way back to Socorro and I tried to grab it but she was too quick; she danced away, waving it above my head.

I wanted to walk away, to join the others at handball, but I didn't dare lose sight of Socorro. I sat on a stone bench and unwrapped my sandwich. At my back I could feel Socorro watching me unravel the paper napkin with interest. "What have you got in it?" she asked, throwing the crumpled drawing into the gutter among the dead leaves. "Want to swap with mine?"

Dumbly, I handed my neatly-trimmed ham sandwich over to the enemy. Socorro always had one of those hard buns you get from the Chinese store at two a centavo and it always had margarine and brown sugar in it. Bitterly, I sank my teeth into the hard brown bread.

"Go buy me a soft drink to go with it," said Socorro, licking her fingers greedily. I ran to the canteen.

Socorro didn't tell Madame Ludmilla after recess either and at five o'clock I gave her a lift home.

"You're really confusing me," said Socorro the next day as we stood in the Assembly Hall waiting for Madame Ludmilla to collect our library books. "You know it's my duty to tell. After all you were immodest beyond words."

"But you mustn't," I begged. "I don't know what she'd do."

"I shudder to think about it," Socorro said, riffling in her grimy basket of books. "Boy, I'm all out of pad paper. Lend me ten centavos, will you?"

In the middle of the week Socorro borrowed my fountain pen, a nice new Waterman I had gotten for my birthday, and never returned it. I don't know whether she did it on purpose or merely forgot that it was mine because she used it in class constantly. Each day she also borrowed ten centavos on some pretext or another, and she was still going to tell Madame Ludmilla. I was beginning to learn that there are two kinds of people in the world: the pushers and the pushed, and it wasn't very hard to see where I belonged. I suffered my scratchy old pen, hating myself but never daring to say a word.

If Socorro wandered away for ten minutes I broke out in a nervous sweat and bit my thumbnail to ribbons. Once I had to go to the canteen for a notebook and when I got back I saw her talking to Madame Ludmilla. Afterwards I asked Socorro what they had talked about and she shrugged her shoulders and walked away. I followed her. She had gotten a gold star for Arithmetic that morning and I told her she was the best darned mathematician in the Philippines. Socorro picked up a ball from under the swing and started to bounce it against a wall. When it bounced out of her grasp, I ran to retrieve it. "When I grow up," Socorro said, "I'll be a business woman and own a big dry goods store. Like my uncle. He's got a refrigerator and a radio and everything. They have pancakes everyday." The ball rolled away. I scurried after it. "And you know what you'll be?" she looked down at me contemptuously. "You're going to live in a *barong barong* and be very poor."

After a while she threw the ball across the playground and sat down on a bench and I sat down too. She pinched the pus off a sore on her knee and winced. "Say, have you got that red thing you put on wounds?"

So when the car came I took her home with me to put mercurochrome on her wound. "Did you tell Madame Ludmilla?" I asked at last.

"Quit pestering me, will you?" she said. We went to my room and sat on the bed and then she lay down for a while because she said she liked the feel of the quilted cover. Then we played monkey-monkey but it was no fun at all because Socorro was always cheating. I showed her my Shirley Temple album. She messed around with my box of hairbands and tried on some of them. She was particularly impressed by the pair of pearl earrings I used for special occasions which my uncle had sent me from Japan.

Once I failed to give Socorro my daily allowance and she threatened to go straight to Madame Ludmilla till I promised to give her thirty centavos the following day. "Maybe I don't even have to tell Madame Ludmilla about your mortal sin," she said. "Maybe she already knows."

"Then how come she hasn't called me or anything yet?"

"She's like Dick Tracy—you know—suspense and all that." She laughed and dug me with her elbow because Madame Ludmilla was walking by just then with an armload of confiscated comics.

"You must realize what a big favor I'm doing you," said Socorro. "Because I commit mortal sin too by delaying, and what thanks do I get? You don't care for me at all, so why should I worry about you?"

"You must never tell, Socorro," I said anxiously. "Haven't I always done what you told me?"

"Pooh," said Socorro, "you even miss out on a measly ten centavos."

"I promise to give you thirty tomorrow."

"Besides, I'm getting tired of your ham sandwich."

"I can tell them to put cheese—"

"You don't give a hoot. You bother with me only because you're scared."

"But I do. You're my best friend now, you know that."

"Honest?"

"Cross-my-heart-and-hope-to-die."

"And you'd give me anything in the world I ask?"

"Anything."

"Oh, skip it. You couldn't give me what I really want."

"Why not?"

"Because you're a 'fraidy cat, that's why. You're scared of your mother."

"No, I'm not."

Socorro's voice dropped to a low wheedle. "Then give me your pearl earrings," she said. "And I'll never tell."

I stared at her in horror. "Not my earrings! Mother would—"

"I thought so," said Socorro, kicking the crossbar of the seesaw angrily. "I should have known. So from tomorrow on, no more skeletons in my closet." She flounced away.

"Wait—" I called faintly, but Socorro had already crossed the street.

I don't know why I never told my parents about Socorro, but I think I was afraid they'd made a big fuss and I'd be in an even worse fix. Mother liked scenes. I remember what a big fuss she created in Grade II when I was made a mushroom in the school play when everyone else was a fairy or at least an elf. Mama stormed into the classroom and asked Madame Alice why wasn't I a fairy or an elf. "A mushroom!" she snorted at the little nun's face. "Imagine—a mushroom!" I could just see Mother barging into Grade IV and shaking Socorro until her teeth rattled. I could just see her giving Madame Ludmilla a piece of her mind. Only Madame Ludmilla wasn't the sort you gave a piece of your mind to. Vengeance would fall like the walls of Babylon upon my head. I would be the butt of the pointer, the target for her barbed jokes. Why, she would surely pin my skirts up to my blouse and make me walk around the playground with a placard.

The following day Socorro pocketed my thirty centavos and walked away without saying a word. She was also getting meaner. During volleyball she tripped me and I pitched forward against the net. She told the girls I had a crazy uncle in Japan. She rolled my Waterman over her desk and kicked it under my chair. In the corridor, at dismissal, I overheard her tell Madame Ludmilla she wanted to talk to her about a shameful matter concerning one of the girls. I stood outside the door, cold with fright, and heard Madame answer that she'd see Socorro first thing next morning.

So at recess time I told Socorro I had decided to give her my earrings. "Then see that you bring them tomorrow without fail," she said, "because I'm sick to death of you and I'll never give you a chance again."

What would I tell Mother? That I wanted to wear my earrings to school and then that I had lost them? That they were sucked down the drain of the bathtub? That a bad man took them from me at the school gate?

Carefully, I tiptoed into the bedroom where Mama was taking a nap on the double bed. I knew exactly where the earrings were, tucked in a blue velvet box in the top drawer of her dresser. Softly, I turned the tiny key hanging from its lock.

"What on earth are you looking for?" Mothers annoyed voice called from the tumbled pillows.

"I—I was hunting for—for a pencil."

"Well that's not the place for pencils. Go ask Clara. Or Daddy. Anybody. Shoo!"

I ran out of the room.

The next morning, as soon as I had alighted from the car, Socorro beckoned me to the lavatory. She bolted the door and leaned against it.

"Well," she said eagerly. "Give them to me."

"I wasn't able to get them," I said, "but I'm sure to give them to you tomorrow."

"Why you double-crosser!" Socorro's face shaped itself into an ugly scowl.

"I almost had them but my mother—"

"I should have known. Honestly, I don't know what to do with you any more! Now I'll be forced to keep that appointment with Madame Ludmilla."

"Don't be mad, Socorro," I said. "It's only until tomorrow. Here—" I fumbled in my pocket, "I've got a St. Christopher medal—it's new—you can have it if you want it."

Socorro snatched the medal from my hand, threw it contemptuously into the toilet bowl and flushed it down. The sound of the rushing water echoed in my ears. Her eyes were suspiciously rimmed with red. "I'm so sick of you I could retch!"

The bell rang. "Please, Socorro," I begged, clutching her sleeve in fright. "Tomorrow morning . . . If you don't have it by then you can go to Madame and I won't even try to stop you. I'll surely have it by then."

Socorro pushed me roughly against the washbasin. "All right," she said wearily. "Tomorrow at eight a.m. But if you double-cross me again you'll really get it from Madame Ludmilla and me." She walked out of the lavatory, banging the door after her.

Mother was playing a valse on the piano when I arrived home. I brushed a kiss on her cheek and went swiftly past her to the bedroom. Slowly, I pulled opened the top drawer of the dresser. Mother's fancy combs and brooches, her fans and her veils were there, but the little blue box wasn't! Feverishly, I rummaged through the other drawers but the earrings weren't in any of them either.

I walked to the *sala* and sat on the edge of the rattan armchair. Mother looked up from the piano. "Aren't you dressed yet?" she called over her shoulder. "We're having an early supper because Papa promised to take you to the circus, remember?"

The circus! It had come to town the week before and most of the girls had already gone to see it and in school no one talked about anything else. Mother didn't usually approve of circuses ("It's dusty and all the children who go have colds and what if the tent collapses?") but there it was right on my lap—elephants and lions and clowns and all, and I couldn't even be happy about it.

Over our early supper I asked casually, "Where are my pearl earrings, Mama? I want to wear them."

"What for? It's only a circus."

"It's a big occasion for me," I grinned, trying to swallow a big mouthful of mashed potato.

"You can wear them some other time," said Mother. "I've sent them to the jeweler for cleaning. They'll be back in a week or two."

There is something very sad even about elephants. When you sit in the gallery all you see is the glorious spectacle—the pachyderms with their bells and bright saddles going through the ritual of their slow dance with confetti of light spraying over them. But when you are in the privileged seats, close to ringside, you don't miss a thing. The trainer's sticks are tipped with steel hooks and as they goad the lumbering beasts you notice that their rumps, especially those of the younger ones, are full of healing hook marks. I hugged the folding seat and cried for the baby elephants. "Silly!" Mother scolded, and father laughed out loud.

I couldn't sleep that night. I wanted to crawl under the covers and die. There was a mass murder of elephants under my bed and Socorro's laughter hung like a steel hook from the ceiling. I went to the bathroom and leaned over the tub and tickled my throat, hoping I'd get sick or something. At five o'clock the sun rose, shining fiercely over the fence of brilliant bougainvillea.

The bell had already rung when I got to school, but on Fridays Father Charlie took over the religion class and he couldn't keep track of who was late because he had one glass eye. Quickly, I looked through the door and saw that Socorro had not yet arrived.

After a while a pair of girls sneaked in through a side door and I crossed my fingers hard. Surely, surely, one of them would be Socorro but neither was.

Father Charlie, the chaplain, was talking about the fires of hell. He drew three pancakes on the blackboard. The first he surrounded with shining rays because it was the Soul in the State of Sanctifying grace. The second he covered with spots because it was the Soul in Venial Sin. The last he shaded all over because it was the Soul in Mortal Sin. The period was almost over. I glanced over my shoulder and still Socorro's seat behind me was empty. She had never been that late before. Maybe she was sick. Maybe she was even going to be absent!

Then the period was over. Father Charlie shuffled out of the room and everyone started talking all at once until Madame Ludmilla's shadow darkened the threshold.

Madame came into the room and laid her books carefully on the edge of the table. At the back of the room a couple of girls were whispering together, but she did not scold them as she always did. Her face was drawn and pale as if she had been crying or something.

"Children," she said gravely, "I have an announcement to make. There has been a tragedy amongst us. Yesterday afternoon, while crossing the street in front of our school, Socorro was run over by a speeding automobile." The girls began to babble all together. I dropped limply to my seat in relief and exhaustion, as if I had been walking a long, long distance.

School was dismissed in the afternoon to give us a chance to view the body which was placed in state in the incense-filled chapel. Class by class, we filed silently through the paneled doors, head bowed, silver rosaries twinkling. Between the branched candlesticks, amid the covey of weeping angels, at the end of the aisle lay Socorro in a satin-quilted bier. As we each paused a minute before the open coffin, I looked into the familiar face, so sphinx-like, so solemn, and shed a tear for a dear departed friend.

(1962)

Cristina Pantoja Hidalgo

Born 1944, Manila, Philippines

About the Author

Cristina Pantoja Hidalgo has published two novels—*Recuerdo* (1996) and *The Book of Dreams* (2001)—four collections of short stories, six collections of creative nonfiction, and two collections of literary criticism. Several of these books have received Philippine national literary awards, including the Carlos Palanca Grand Prize for the Novel, the Manila Critics' Circle's National Book Award, the University of the Philippines Chancellor's Artist of the Year Award, etc. She has also been awarded the *Gawad Pambansang Alagad ni Balagtas* by the *Unyon ng mga Manunulat sa Pilipinas* (Writers' Union of the Philippines) for her fiction in English. She has worked as a writer, editor and teacher in Bangkok, Seoul, Yangon (formerly Rangoon), Beirut and New York City. At present, she teaches creative writing and literature at the University of the Philippines, where she is also Director of the University of the Philippines Press. She is married to Antonio A. Hidalgo and has three daughters.

Christmas in the Philippines

The celebration of Christmas in the Philippines starts as early as October, with Christmas decorations appearing on streets and storefronts, and Christmas songs blaring from radios. In the provinces people hear early dawn masses called *misas de gallo*. Many people attend the midnight mass on Christmas Eve, after which they gather for a late meal called *noche buena* or *media noche*. Gift-giving is also part of the tradition.

The Magic Glasses

— **Cristina Pantoja Hidalgo**

I remember that Christmas very well because it was our first Christmas in the New House.

When we talked about it in the family, we always referred to it as the New House. We were very proud of it. It had two stories and large windows, to let in the sunlight and the breeze. It also had a garden, with many flowers, and a hammock hanging between a *sampaloc* tree and a mango tree, and a little wading pool at the back, in the shade of two *santol* trees. School was now walking distance from home, which meant I could stay in bed thirty minutes longer in the morning. And the convent of the Carmelite nuns was even closer. So Mama and Lola could hear mass before breakfast every day.

Mama promised me that I would get stronger and healthier in the New House, because it was in a quiet, clean street with lots of fresh air. Our old house had been in a busy part of town, with the noise of passing cars and jeepneys coming in from the street, and dust settling on the furniture right after it had been cleaned. When we had first moved in, just after the war, Mama had kept the front door open, as the *sala* was rather dark. But one day, a peddler selling pails and basins had come clattering and stamping up the front steps right into our *sala*, and had frightened me so much that I had nightmares about him for many months after. Since then, the front door was always kept tightly locked. And I was not allowed to go out of doors much, except when Carmela, our maid, finished her chores early and could push me up and down on the swing.

I did not have any real friends at school. But somehow, I thought that moving into the New House would also change things for me. It seems strange now that I should have thought this, since I didn't even know how to bring up the subject with my classmates. And I doubt that anyone would have cared if I had. Certainly not Honey Topacio, the most popular girl in

Grade II. And certainly not Edna Duarte, Honey's best friend and the meanest girl in Grade II.

"What does that mean—that Honey is 'popular'?" asked my father, who worked in a bank, where such things did not matter.

"It means that everyone wants to be her friend, doesn't it, hija?" my mother said.

She said I shouldn't worry because I too would become popular soon. And Papa said that I shouldn't worry because popularity wasn't important. They didn't ask me what it meant that Edna was "mean."

I could have told them that I had seen Edna pinch Mary Lou Cepeda for just sitting in her seat by mistake. And that I had seen her hide Zeny Arceo's *baon* during recess and tell Zeny later that it was Cookie Vergara who had done it. Cookie had gotten really mad about that. She and Edna had a big fight and got in trouble, because someone told Sister Sabina, and Sister Sabina made them both stand in the corner with their backs to the room, as punishment. But when Edna did something like that to me—hid Tessie Zapanta's Arithmetic book and told her it was I who had done it—I was too scared to tell on Edna. So Sister Sabina made me stand in the corner with my back to the room.

The mystery to me was why Honey wanted Edna for a best friend when she was so nasty. I think now that it must have been because Edna was always very nice to her, and that was all that mattered to Honey.

One reason Honey was so popular was that she was so good at games like *piko* and jackstones and pick-up-sticks and the yo-yo, better than anyone else in our grade. And, because I was so bad at them, I admired her fiercely. I used to watch furtively, as she played with Edna and her other friends during recess. Honey was so much better than everybody else, that I would wonder if there was a secret I needed to learn, a secret that would make me as good as she.

After a while, I came to the conclusion that Honey was as good as she was, not just because she was naturally talented, but because she played the games with such wonderful things. That had to be it. In my favorite fairy tales, wonders happened because of magical things, didn't they? Fairy-godmother wands, gold thimbles, crystal keys, flying carpets, pumpkins that became carriages, old lamps that hid genies. . . . Now, Honey had several sets of jackstones—silver and gold and rainbow-colored. She had a creamy white yo-yo, which made everyone else's brown-and-black ones look like poor relations. Her set of pick-up-sticks came, not in a cylindrical cardboard box like our sets did, but in a flat, shiny green box with a gold clasp. But best of all was her hopscotch *pamato*. Before the appearance of that *pamato*, everyone would simply pick up whatever flat stone she could find in the schoolyard before playing a new game of *piko*. The point was just to pick stones different enough from each other so that one wouldn't make a mistake. And then one day, Honey brought her own personal *pamato* to school. It was a blue octagonal stone, smooth and glossy, and beautiful as a jewel. I can see it even now, and even now I remember the marvel with which I first beheld it.

After that, it was imperative that anyone who wanted to play a respectable game of *piko* had to bring her own *pamato*. We scoured the schoolyard, our own gardens, the roads through which we walked on our way to school, to find a stone worthy of keeping company with Honey's blue stone. But, of course, no one ever found anything to match it. I would watch that blue *pamato* go sailing through the air and land unerringly on the square patch of ground Honey had aimed it at, and I would sigh wistfully. There was no doubt about it; the blue stone had magical powers. I coveted that stone with all my heart. I told myself that if I owned it—or something like it—things would never be the same again for me. I would become quick and nimble like Honey. Honey herself would welcome me into her circle of friends. She would draw me to her side and call me her best friend, and Edna Duarte would be left out in the cold.

And then Christmas came—our first Christmas in the New House—and I received a wonderful surprise: a pair of glasses, with dark green lenses and a bright red frame. They came in a candy-striped box tied with a glossy red ribbon. I had never seen anything so beautiful! At first, I couldn't believe they were for me. I just sat there staring at them, where they rested on their soft white bed inside the candy-striped box. Dark glasses were for grown-up ladies, not for small girls like me. But Mama said, "Try them on, Trissy." So, very gingerly, I picked them up, and put them on. Mama asked Carmela to go fetch her hand mirror from her dressing table, and then she handed it to me, saying, "Look at yourself, hija."

"Doesn't she look pretty?" Mama asked my father and my grandmother. And they agreed, I did, indeed. I looked very pretty, they said, like a movie star.

So I looked in the mirror, and to my amazement, I saw an entirely different person! I had been transformed, like Cinderella, after her fairy godmother had waved her magic wand. I had become pretty and mysterious and glamorous. I had become . . . yes, a movie star! Why, my glasses were better than Honey's magic stone!

I turned to Mama and asked eagerly, "Can I bring them to school?"

"Well, I don't see why not," Mama said.

Ah, I thought, my time has come!

On the very first day after the Christmas holidays were over, I announced to Carmela that I would be wearing the Magic Glasses to school.

"That's nice," Carmela said, picking up my school bag.

I must have looked rather funny, walking to school that day—in my starched navy blue skirt that nearly reached my ankles (my school uniforms were always made a size larger so I wouldn't outgrow them too quickly) and my starched white cotton blouse and my white socks and black patent leather shoes, and those big dark green glasses with a bright red frame covering half of my face. But I was more pleased and proud of myself than I had ever been in my life.

As soon as Carmela had set down my schoolbag in its usual spot—on the stone bench under the pine tree nearest to where Grade II pupils lined up for flag ceremony when the bell rang—I looked around for Honey Topacio. She was standing with a group of girls on the driveway, to one side of the canteen, comparing Christmas presents.

I skipped up to them, and said more loudly than I would ever have dared before, "Hi, Honey."

Everyone looked up. I stood there, breathlessly waiting for the magic to take effect.

I saw Honey's eyes widen in surprise. And then, I heard her say: "Hey, nice glasses."

My breath came out in a quick spurt. It was working!

Honey came closer. There was a gleam of admiration in her eyes. She hesitated a bit. Then, she said slyly, "Want to trade?"

"Trade what?" I asked.

"The glasses for my *pamato*."

I caught my breath again, not quite sure that I had heard right. Honey was willing to give me her magic stone . . . But was I willing to part with my Magic Glasses, especially now that I knew they were magical?

"I . . . don't think . . . so, Honey," I said. "My mother wouldn't like it. They were her Christmas present. But—but you can borrow them if you want."

"Okay," Honey said. "You can borrow my *pamato* too."

It had happened! Honey Topacio was going to be my friend. I was going to be part of the group of popular girls in Grade II.

Made reckless by my triumph, I turned to Edna Duarte and asked, "Do you like my glasses, Edna?"

Edna stared at me with pure hatred. "No!" she spat out. "I think they're silly. I think they're ugly. They don't even fit you. They're too big!"

Suddenly, her hand shot out and grabbed the glasses from my face. And before I, or anyone else, could guess what was about to happen, she threw them down to the cemented driveway, and stamped on them with one foot . . . once, twice, thrice . . . crushing them to bits.

We were all too stunned to move.

I stared at my Magic Glasses, now just a little heap of broken glass and plastic, and burst into tears. I knew I was disgracing myself, proving myself to be a cry-baby in front of Edna and Honey and everybody else. But I didn't care.

I whirled around and ran away from them. They were mean and spiteful and I would never ever talk to them again, as long as I lived! I ran blindly, the held-back tears from all those days of being excluded, of being not there, gushing out and streaming down my cheeks. If Sister Gertrude, teacher-in-charge of Grade III, hadn't been standing there, about to ring the bell for flag ceremony, I might have run out of the gate and into the street and all the way home . . . and perhaps been hit by a passing car, and killed.

Sister Gertrude caught me, and took me to Sister Sabina, who brought me into an empty classroom, and wiped my tears with her own clean hankie, and asked me gently to tell her why I was crying.

I don't recall what happened afterwards. I think someone brought in Edna, who, by then, was also in tears, and made her say she was sorry. And someone handed me a paper bag into which the broken pieces of my dark glasses had been stuffed. Or maybe the bag was given to Mama, who came to pick me up some time during the day, having been called by the Sisters. And maybe Edna was made to stand in the corner with her back to the room. Or maybe she was made to skip recess. I was too upset to notice. I know now that I was as much shocked by Edna's violence as I was hurt by her cruelty and dismayed by the loss of my brand new present. And, long after that, whenever Sister Sabina talked about the Devil as she prepared us for First Holy Communion, I would see Edna Duarte, with beady eyes and horns and a tail, clutching a pitchfork and stamping on my beautiful green glasses with the bright red frame.

But the biggest pain of all was the discovery that my Magic Glasses were not magical after all. And that if I hoped to become popular like Honey Topacio, I would have to do it on my own.

(1999)

Edgar Poma

Born 1959, Sacramento, California

About the Author

Edgar Poma received his B.A. in English Literature from the University of California at Berkeley in 1983. His plays have been produced in San Francisco and Los Angeles. Some of his short stories appear in *Flippin': Filipinos in America* (Asian American Writers Workshop, 1996), and Cecilia Manguerra Brainard's *Contemporary Fiction by Filipinos in America* (Anvil, 1997). His poetry has appeared in *Without Names: Anthology of Filipino American Poets* (Kearny Street Press, 1986). Poma received a California Arts Council Grant for playwriting in 1994. He's at work on a novel and children's book project, both of which are set in migrant camps in California's Central Valley. He works for the San Francisco Department of Public Works.

Filipino Americans in Migrant Camps

My story, "The Slumbering State," is set in a migrant camp in Northern California, specifically the Sacramento River Delta. The first levees in this area were built by Chinese laborers in the 1870s. Filipino laborers arrived in the mid-1920s to the early 1930s from Hawaii to work in the Delta's fields and orchards. The camps continue to this day, almost eighty years later. Having lived in a camp from birth to around age twelve, having visited camps well into adulthood, I know the beauty and sadness of their isolation, their haunted house quality, their slumbering state—and yet I would not trade the experience for anything in the world, since I believe it made me a writer.

While the story is fictional, there are certainly some autobiographical elements. If your parents, grandparents or older relatives ever drove, years ago, on the east side of the Sacramento River north of Locke, and happened to see a group of Filipino kids in a pear orchard running toward the pot of gold at the end of a rainbow, that was us.

The Slumbering State

— Edgar Poma

Every year, the entire camp pitched in to make Cornelia Valiente's slumber party a shining success. The younger kids in the camp formed a litter brigade, starting from the levee and working down. Their moms cleaned the windows of their little cabins with vinegar, and hung curtains that were freshly washed and pressed. There were five cabins that surrounded the bunkhouse, spread out from one another, four of them on hillsides. The cabin that Cornelia and John lived in was the only one on the flats, and nearest to the bunkhouse, since their dad supervised the workers who picked the pear crop, all of whom were *Pinoy*, like they were; many of whom were, surprisingly, American-born, like they were; and yet at varying stages of poor.

Some of the workers wheelbarrowed in fill for the mud puddles and the ravaged sections of gravel and dirt road that led from the highway along the levee to the camp and the orchard. The clotheslines were kept bare, the old jalopy cars moved out of sight or tarp thrown over them. In the tiniest of the six cabins and the furthest away, Reggie, who was thirteen, and who was quite effeminate, had spent nearly two weeks crafting a WELCOME SLUMBER GIRLS cloth banner as he had done for the past five years, producing a new one each time, and which he always strung up between the porch posts.

In Cornelia and John's cabin, their mom shook out rugs and aired blankets and scrubbed floors. She carefully checked seams in the mattresses and box-springs for bedbugs and bedbug eggs. She had borrowed some bed frames from the bunkhouse to attach to an old foldout sofa in the living room to form one giant bed. In the bathroom, she replaced the crocheted emerald dress of a doll, the kind that fitted over a spare toilet paper roll, with a yellow dress, because she changed the covers for special days, like priest vestments.

At the bunkhouse, Cornelia's ninongs, or godfathers, offered to butcher a goat for the occasion, but Cornelia assured them that she and her mom were cooking more than enough food, and she would be sure to send some over for them to taste. She was true to her word: on the morning of the slumber party, she and her mom sent John to the bunkhouse with a large aluminum pan overflowing with fried chicken backs and *lumpia* and *pancit* and barbecued turkey tails.

The camp dogs, of course, followed him as he made his way along the back path between the cabin and the bunkhouse, in case he should slip on the wooden planks laid over the mud and spill his delivery. This was before their owners tied the dogs on long leashes to the back of the concrete lavatory facility outside the bunkhouse so they couldn't roam about and tuck their noses up the skirts of the visiting girls.

Some of the workers teased John and told him in their Ilocano dialect, which John spoke and understood, "How do your sister's classmates look this year? Are they prettier?" But, at age twelve, as interested in girls as he was, those who came to his sister's slumber party every year had become like *manangs* to him, older sisters, and he was far more interested in being their bodyguard and chaperone than a potential date.

The day before the party, he helped his father wash the family car, a used green Oldsmobile station wagon called a Vista Cruiser, because the routine was that the guests would be driven to the camp and dropped-off by their parents in their beat-up cars, and then Cornelia's father would take all of them home the next day in *his* beat-up car. John cleaned the car's interior with a hand broom, and used a cloth to polish the saint statuettes and small crucifixes that were fixed to the metal dashboard by slivers of magnet. They were placed in tight rows, like chessboard pieces crowded together. Normally John lined them up facing one another like warring armies, but he wanted to be on his best behavior this weekend. The slumber party meant too much to his sister.

As usual, he looked forward to the party, and he could hardly sleep the night before. When the day arrived, he bathed and put gel in his hair and combed it carefully and dressed neatly like he was going to church. Then he went to the bunkhouse and asked one of the workers to clean inside his ear with a bobby pin because his mother was too busy and his father had gone into town to buy some pipe tobacco.

"Aren't you old enough to do this yourself?" the worker said in the dialect with pretend annoyance. The men in the bunkhouse were like extended family; they were like John's army of grandpas and uncles. This particular uncle was rough and tough from years of field work and chronic illnesses and fighting over women and spending much of his wages gambling in the closest Indian casino, thirty-five miles away, and plying himself with drink there and often driving home to the wrong migrant camp but forcing his way into a bunkhouse and onto a bunk anyway—but with John's ears, he was supremely gentle.

When Cornelia's friends arrived, Mrs. Valiente held the screen door open and complimented them on their dresses and smiles. She served them popcorn drizzled generously with hot pork fat, which the girls looked forward to every year. When the popcorn completely ran out, one of the girls asked, "Mrs. Valiente, is there any more pork fat?" As the party got underway, John looked on quietly from a corner as the girls played assorted games, nothing risque. They all led very clean, simple lives, spending the days in camps or towns that were quickly becoming ghostly, and as if a bad thought or action on their part would force God to send in the tumbleweeds. John liked being around their innocence, and yet he knew there was something self-congratulatory about them embracing their dreary everyday environments without complaint or yearning, leaving only to go to school or church or a slumber party with the same people.

John shadowed them when Cornelia took the girls on a tour of the camp, showing them the shared vegetable gardens and the fighting rooster coops, as if they had changed very much since last year. Outside the bunkhouse, each girl got to strike the dinner gong once. One delicate girl missed the gong completely when it was her turn, which astounded John because the target was an enormous rusty griddle that hung motionless from a thick pear tree branch, and the striking object, an iron pipe, was as big as an Olympic torch. But he made sure to stifle his laughter.

Another girl struck the gong repeatedly when it was her turn, and shouted, "COMMMMME ANND GIIT IIIIT!!!" John couldn't suppress his laughter, which didn't matter because everyone cracked up too.

As the group proceeded to the bunkhouse kitchen, Cornelia made a signal to her brother as if she were picking her teeth. John raced into the kitchen before them to remove the novelty toothpick dispensers on the long wooden table at which the workers sat on both sides, on benches, for their morning and evening meals. The dispensers were in the shape of a crouching woman; at the press of a button on the pedestal, a toothpick appeared between her buns. As John picked up the dispensers, they almost slipped from his hands due to the layers of lard built up over the past year. When Cornelia entered the kitchen with her pals, she pointed out a new double-long rolling pin that the cook had just purchased, and the girls politely pretended to care. After the group passed through, John returned the toothpick holders back to their spots.

The group went on to a small fenced-off oval of quicksand adjacent to the three rows of bunkhouse clothesline. It had appeared suddenly, freakishly, the year Cornelia was born. A geothermal scientist from the state, whose name was Reggie Denhiltz, had been sent to the camp to study the quicksand for a couple of months. He rented the Gorospes' cabin during his research. Mr. Gorospe stayed in the bunkhouse temporarily while Mrs. Gorospe stayed with the Valientes, because she was about to give birth, as Mrs. Valiente had done several months before. The difference between them was that Mrs. Valiente had given birth to Cornelia when she was in her mid-thirties, while Mrs. Gorospe was seventeen when she delivered a boy. Mrs. Gorospe named him Reggie, in honor of the scientist.

All these years, the quicksand remained there, a dull and embarrassed gash. As she did every year, Cornelia handed out large rocks from a pile that her guests could toss into the mire, then watch them slowly and strangely bubble under.

They made a stop to see Reggie's sign, and John obnoxiously ran through it like he was breaking the string at a finish line. He was feeling brave because he did not see Mr. Gorospe's car anywhere, which meant that he had probably gone to town to gas up or buy groceries. Mr. Gorospe usually didn't want Reggie to have contact with anyone, and John believed that it was because the dad—and he wasn't old by the way, he was just under forty—was ashamed of his son's . . . excitability. However, Reggie acted perfectly nonchalant as he sat on the porch steps reading a book. The problem was that it was upside down. John noticed it right away, sidled over to him and whispered, "You aren't fooling anyone, dude—you know you waited for us all day."

Reggie entertained the group by playing the piano—the Gorospes had a used upright, with some keys missing—but he had to do so quietly, because his mother apparently was asleep, and yet loudly enough while he was being watched and heard through the screen door. The Valientes simply didn't allow their children to go into the Gorospe cabin. It was common knowledge that Mrs. Gorospe made her body and her services available for a fee now and then, strictly to workers from other camps, preferably during the day, and that Mr. Gorospe encouraged it because his family had debts and needed to make ends meet. He never mentioned, though everyone knew, that he had had assignations with women in nearby distant towns over the years, and had quite a number of kids, of all ages, to support.

Occasionally, to give Mrs. Gorospe and her customer privacy, and because the cabin was so cramped, Mr. Gorospe and Reggie walked over to the bunkhouse with their pillows and blankets to spend the night there. But John knew that this snoring chamber was not quite the slumber party that Reggie longed to be part of.

At the piano, Reggie was thrilled to have an audience, but uncharacteristically made a lot of mistakes, and then insisted on stopping and starting over each time. The girls began to look at one another as if they were being forced to listen to someone scraping his fingernails across the length of a chalkboard. John didn't laugh out loud, but the girls knew by his tremors that he was laughing, and it was infectious. When the girls eventually left the porch, covering their mouths, Reggie stopped playing and remained inside, on the piano bench.

John saw Reggie burst into tears through the screen door and said to him, "Oh, get over it—you didn't play so bad."

"It's not that," Reggie said. "I wanna go to the slumber party too."

"I know you do, dude, but you can't."

Every year it was the same thing. Reggie wanted nothing more than to attend Cornelia's slumber party, and every year, he prepared a bedroll and laid out his pajamas and kept them close by, in the wings, hoping Cornelia would allow him to camp on the porch and listen to all the fun through the screen door. John knew all this, and felt sorry for Reggie, and sort of hinted to his sister every year, but Cornelia would tell him sensibly, "I don't have a problem with Reggie coming over, but there are some things that he can't do and will never be able to do because he's not a girl. He might as well get used to that now."

When John caught up with Cornelia and the others, Cornelia took him aside and told him she wanted to invite Reggie to the house. So while the girls took turns playing on a tire swing, the brother and sister returned to the Gorospe porch. Mrs. Gorospe, who had since awakened and was speaking to Reggie in Ilocano from the bedroom, gave Reggie permission to go, but said he had to come home when his father came home.

Knowing the exact moment when that occurred would be easy enough. Whether they were indoors or outdoors, all the camp kids knew by now which workers—their workers, that is, and not the workers that Reggie's mom enticed—were coming or going by the sound of the cars and trucks that they drove. And of course they knew the sound of the vehicles that visited routinely, like the Vegetable Man or the Goat Man or the Ice Cream Man or the Donut Man. They recognized the hum of the engine and the crunch of the tires of the Donut Man, say, even without hearing his horn that played different tunes like "Are you Sleeping, Are you Sleeping Brother John?" On this day, he played "The Farmer in the Dell."

From the sidelines, Reggie and John watched when the Donut Man, whose van visited the camp every weekend, arrived, and Cornelia and her guests got to order whatever treat they wanted from the various sliding drawers. Mrs. Valiente stood nearby, ready to pay. When the Donut Man saw Reggie out of the corner of his eye, he said, "Hey, how's it goin', faggot?" And Reggie was so embarrassed that he ran home, in his gal gait, even before his father's return. John felt bad when the Donut Man caught his eye and winked, as if to say, "Aren't you lucky you turned out normal and not like him?"

John tried to convince himself that he didn't care all that much that Reggie had left. He was, after all, irritated by practically everything about Reggie, from his mannerisms to his stringbean body. He ignored him as much as possible, at school and in the camp, even though, being a year older than John, Reggie had to be treated with respect. But then John never once thought of him as an older brother: he knew that he would never call or regard Reggie as his *manong*.

It was a long time back, when they were kids, that John realized that Reggie was, well, different. No, weird. An Avon Lady came to the camp, and the boys were sitting on their mothers' laps while their mothers were trying out samples. When the Avon lady passed around a vial of papaya cold cream, John stuck his finger in it and put the finger in his mouth to taste, like any curious, normal, dumb young male child would, while Reggie took a curl of it with a few fingers and rubbed the stuff on his face and gushed to the Avon Lady, "It's simply fabulous, darling!"

John despised Reggie increasingly through the years and he particularly despised him during various times of the year, like Valentine's Day, when he signed all his homemade cards, "Love, Reggie," like a girl would, rather than "From ________" like a boy. Every summer, after pear harvest, John's parents invited Reggie and other camp kids along when they took their own children to the State Fair in Sacramento. And when each kid could pick a souvenir to take home—the Valientes treated—Reggie always picked something feminine, like a parasol, which he lay down with at the back of the station wagon so it wouldn't hit the roof while he practiced twirling it.

On Easter Sunday, at the camp's annual egg hunt, Mrs. Valiente always prodded John into helping Reggie, because he was hopeless when it came to finding any eggs hidden in the grass or hedges or on window ledges. On Halloween, Reggie was the only person John knew who would say "Trick or Treat" with a lisp. On Thanksgiving Day, at the bunkhouse, Reggie was completely useless when it came to the post-meal arm-wrestling contests.

At the donut van, Cornelia and the girls were so preoccupied sampling and ordering and eating that they didn't notice Reggie's absence. "Oh, these are for you guys," Cornelia said, handing John a white paper bag, containing two frosted cupcakes with sprinkles, assuming that Reggie was hanging out nearby. John thought about going to the Gorospes to give Reggie his share, but decided to eat them both. Later he had a stomachache, from guilt.

It was noisier than usual at the Valiente house, with the girls taking turns at karaoke, not to any current songs but the old Tammy Wynette country and western ballad, "Take Me to Your World." Then they got under the sheets and got all cuddly cozy and swapped ghost stories, letting out screams here and there, and hiding under the blankets. In the next room, John slept in his bed with cotton balls in his ears. In the morning, he got up early, at the same time as his father. In fact, they pissed together in the same toilet. Which to an outsider might seem odd, but it was a father-and-son sort of thing, and harmless, and certainly not, as John thought, the kind of dirty, gay business that Reggie would be capable of later, if not now. In the kitchen, John's mom, who had gotten up even earlier than her "boys," made them leftover rice coated with beaten eggs and fried up with fatty bacon pieces and a teaspoon or two of *patis*, or fish sauce. The wonderful scent woke up the girls, and they preferred having a Filipino soul food breakfast rather than cream cheese and bagels.

When it was time to bring the girls home, John sat up front and gave his father directions like he did every year, since he knew from his and Cornelia's school-bus route exactly where all the girls lived. When they returned home, they got ready for church. After church, John and Cornelia helped their mother put the house back in order. Then they folded the sofa and sat upon it, exhausted, and then practically folded into one another and fell asleep.

Six months later, Mr. and Mrs. Valiente had to take one of the older workers, who was one of Mr. Valiente's late father's *compadres*, a man he worked alongside with in fields and orchards, to the airport in San Francisco, because he wanted to go home to the Philippines and spend his last years there. They were staying overnight in the Bay Area with one of the old man's relatives. John and Cornelia wanted to go to San Francisco too, but their parents didn't want them missing school. Though John and Cornelia thought they were old enough to stay home by themselves, their parents insisted that they stay with their ninongs, so the siblings agreed to divide their time between the cabin and the bunkhouse in their parents' absence.

When John, Cornelia, and Reggie came home from school in the afternoon, they felt what seemed to be an extra layer of heat in the air, and it turned out there was a fire roaring two or three camps beyond. From the levee road, where the school bus dropped them off, they could see the black smoke rise in the distance over the orchards. They made sure that the younger kids in the camp were safe inside their cabins before heading to the bunkhouse, where one of the workers' wives, Mrs. Labrada, who lived in one of the cabins with her husband and two dogs but no children, intercepted them by honking the horn of her decrepit Cadillac. Mrs. Gorospe was in the front passenger seat and Reggie ran over to her.

"I'm responsible for you kids," Mrs. Labrada said to John and Cornelia. As she explained, the bunkhouse was empty since all the workers, even the cook, had gone over to help put out the fire. John and Cornelia's ninongs asked Mrs. Labrada to look after the kids. Mrs. Gorospe had a medical appointment to go to, but since her car had broken down, Mrs. Labrada offered to take her. Mrs. Labrada didn't want to leave the kids with other folks in the other cabins, so she told them to get in the car. Reggie, of course, piled in too. All the kids were sort of intimidated by Mrs. Labrada, because she was a heavyset Hawaiian lady with a mean look; whatever she said, they pretty much did. She was actually a very sweet person, and very mild, but when she got upset, like if her car port was blocked or if someone came into her house and didn't take their shoes off first, she had a fit and screamed with such ferocity that she was heard all over the camp.

John didn't mind going out for a drive. He rested his chin against the open window and allowed the air, which was heavy with heat and flakes of ash, lash his face once the Cadillac began to cruise along the winding river road.

The doctor's office was in a lone, run-down trailer on the other side of the river. To get to it, they drove on the highway for a stretch and then dropped to a parallel road cutting through an orchard, then onto a dirt road, then off another dirt road where there were no longer fruit trees but a stand of weeping willows. Reggie's mom gave directions from notes she had on a piece of paper. This was definitely not the doctor that the Labradas or the Valientes or even Reggie had ever gone to.

"I'm sure you know what you're doing," Mrs. Labrada said in the bits and pieces of the dialect that she had picked up over the years, "but are you sure this is someone who can help you with whatever it is you have?"

"I'm sure," Reggie's mother said in the dialect.

"And you sure it's something minor?"

"Something minor."

"I don't feel good about this place. Why aren't you seeing the doctor in town?"

"This doctor is just as good."

"That's not what I asked."

"It won't take long."

"I'm worried about you."

"I'll be fine."

After they parked alongside a pickup, the only other vehicle around, they went inside the trailer and sat in the small waiting area. Mrs. Labrada was so large that the trailer seemed to shake every time she moved or breathed.

The doctor, who was tall and pale, came out of a back office to escort Reggie's mom to her treatment. His assistant, a woman who seemed to have varicose veins on her face, sat at a table with a taped-up leg and guarded the door to the office. She was reading a magazine and ripping out recipes.

"Be good now," Reggie's mom said in the dialect as she group-hugged the kids. "And don't worry about the fire—it's not going to spread." She opened her purse and took out rosary beads, which she cupped in her hand, and some sugar cookies in a Ziploc bag for them to snack on. "Offer some to Mrs. Labrada," she told them, "and the lady over there."

Reggie was too chicken to offer the assistant a cookie, so John went over to her with the bag, but she waved them away. A half-hour passed after Reggie's mom had gone in with the doctor, and the kids started to get restless. They sat in folding chairs that directly faced Mrs. Labrada, and it had not occurred to any of them that they could move the chairs so they wouldn't necessarily have her as their landscape.

Eventually she fell asleep and began snoring louder than Cornelia and John's father, and Reggie's father, combined. John was bored and tried to nap with his eyes open. Cornelia and John had left their homework in the car, but they quizzed each other anyway to prepare themselves for a Spanish test.

Another fifteen minutes passed before the doctor, who looked more pale, came through the door and made eye contact with his assistant. She folded and pocketed her recipes, took an armful of folders from a file cabinet beside her, and followed the doctor out of the trailer. They drove off in the pickup in such a hurry that they clipped Mrs. Labrada's car.

John, Cornelia and Reggie knew that something had gone terribly wrong. They went past the nurse's station and opened the door to the back office where they found Reggie's mom stretched out on a table, naked. Her rosary beads seemed to be dripping off the table with her vomit. Cornelia went to alert Mrs. Labrada. John tried to push back the blood flowing from between Reggie's mom's legs. He sensed that life was draining out of her quickly, and he knew that Reggie felt the same thing too, because he was holding her head with both hands and saying, "Mommy, take me with you . . ."

Mrs. Labrada came in and almost slipped on the blood and slime on the floor and said, "What happened here? What happened here?" She saw

Reggie's mom lying there, near death, and said to her, "What happened to you? What happened to you?" She took off the muumuu she was wearing and wrapped it around Reggie's mom's body, then tightly between her legs, then she scooped her up in her huge arms. She was so powerful and in such shock that she had swept up Reggie as well. Wearing only her slip, she carried them out of the trailer to the car, screaming "Doctor!" thunderously the whole time, as if she thought her voice would somehow freeze the pick-up in its tracks, wherever it was by now. She lay Reggie's mom gently on the backseat and then she screamed to the kids, "GET IN!!!!" and then she took the wheel.

The kids didn't want to crowd Reggie's mom in the backseat, so they awkwardly knelt on the floor, facing her. She bled through the muumuu, and John, who was closest to her legs, felt as though the blood started to soak through his skin into his body. He was sickened by the scorching, creepy heat of it, and the smell reminded him of goats and chickens being butchered in the camp before they were cleaned, feathered or shaved, then cooked, to celebrate special occasions. Reggie and Cornelia were sobbing and wailing. Mrs. Labrada drove in jerks and wild turns, as if trying to avoid other cars, though John looked up once or twice and saw that the road into town was nearly empty.

Weeks later, in the camp, when Mrs. Labrada hung out with the workers and her husband on the porch of the bunkhouse like one of the guys and exchanged stories with them, she said that she knew that Reggie's mom had died in the car because she kept seeing her standing in the middle of the road.

"Did she want you to drive into the river and drown?" one of the workers asked.

"I thought that's what she wanted at first, like she was dead and she wanted company," Mrs. Labrada said. "But I realized later she was just saying goodbye. I don't think she liked the camp, even if it was her home. She didn't want to return there, even in death."

This haunted John, so much more somehow than the adult talk of the "doctor" having experimented with different methods to induce an abortion and failing every time. After the burial, as folks carpooled back to the camp, one of the workers remarked, in Reggie's presence, referring to his mom, "Sometimes, loneliness makes you do all the wrong things."

Before, during, and after the burial, Reggie's cabin was visited by relatives and friends who took over the kitchen and either cooked or reheated food at all hours. And then as quickly as they came, they were gone. Several months later, Reggie's father served notice that he was giving up the cabin, that he was eventually moving himself and Reggie to a camp in

Washington State. They would start out picking apples. Since his wife was no longer around to bring in some money, Reggie would have to make work, and not school, the priority. Mr. Gorospe then asked the Valientes if they wanted to buy the piano, and they bought it just so that the father and son had a little extra money for their move.

John and Cordelia sat down with their parents and asked if there was any way that their parents could adopt Reggie or at least allow him to stay with them. The parents thought it was a bad idea, then changed their minds and consulted Mr. Gorospe, who said no at first, then said he would leave it up to Reggie.

It was Reggie who made the decision to stay with his dad. "We're not close at all," he admitted to John and Cornelia later, "but he doesn't have anyone else other than me." Then he vowed, "I'm not giving up school, though. No way. No matter what he says. He should tell his girlfriends to get jobs. 'Cause I'm not dropping out of school, like he or my mother did. 'Cause it's not loneliness that makes you do the wrong things, it's ignorance and being stuck in a place you don't want to be because that's all you know. I wanna live in a world where we've figured out a way where the fruits and vegetable can pick themselves. That's all I want."

It seemed clear to John that Reggie had grown older and wiser in a brief amount of time. But a month later, days before he was to leave this camp forever, he had not become old enough or changed enough to pass up an invitation to attend Cornelia's slumber party. Unlike Cornelia, the girls seemed initially taken aback by Reggie's participation, but it wasn't long before they opened their arms to him, while in the next room, John, who was almost thirteen now, lay in his bed in the darkness, and for a moment wondered what it would be like to be with one of his sister's friends, the cutest one, kissing her, or what it would be like to be with any girl, and whether or not it would be easy and exhilarating the way he thought it should be or ought to be, like slipping into quicksand and just letting it pull him slowly into the depths, all the way into another world, but he was sure that none of this could ever feel more satisfying, none of this could ever feel more cuddly cozy, than the knowledge that his *manong* was feeling, for an overnight at least, an unrelenting joy.

(2002)

Mar V. Puatu

Born 1937, Manila, Philippines; immigrated to the U.S. in 1977

About the Author

Mar V. Puatu is a six-time winner of the prestigious Palanca Awards in Literature in the Philippines. He is the author and editor of several books, including the novel, *Grandfather, the King* and *The Girl with One Eye and Other Stories*. In addition, he wrote, produced and directed for radio and television; and he also wrote for the cinema. He resides in Sun Valley, California.

Metropolitan Manila

Manila, comprising 38.3 square kilometers is the core city in an area called Metro Manila in 1975, by presidential decree. Metro Manila is a sprawling polluted area with horrific traffic. But Manila has many interesting sections such as Old Manila or the Intramuros which still reflects Spanish colonial days. And you have many shopping districts in Metro Manila, depending on what you want. You can find swanky department stores in malls, and you can still find flea-market type sections where you have to haggle for fabric, or food products, or household goods. In Manila you can find extremes in wealth and poverty.

It's a Gruen

— Mar V. Puatu

"It's a Gruen!" The lady's wristwatch gleams inside the pawnbroker's glass display. It glitters among other timepieces, rings, necklaces, flags, samurai swords, and other World War II souvenirs. Outside the store, my cousin Jimmy points out the heart-shaped watch. "That's your mother's."

The veins at his temples throb. He's very handsome, darn it. At nineteen, he must feel superior, being a college boy. I'm six years younger, in high school.

His tone accuses me. "How much did you get for it?"

"Two pesos," I whine.

He knuckles me. "Two pesos!"

"Ow . . . " I jump away from him.

"It's worth twenty." His curly hair gets in his eyes. Steamed, he brushes it and drags poor, helpless me inside. Ah Suang, the Chinese owner, eyes us, then glances at a calendar on the wall. It's 1948.

Jimmy points to the watch, "How much?"

The pawnbroker's eyes turn beady. "It's brand new."

"I know," I moan.

"Ah, yes." He recognizes me. "*You* sold it to me. Weren't you with another boy?"

"How much?" Jimmy demands.

The pawnbroker lifts his eyebrow. He must have an abacus in his head. I hear his mind click, click, click. After half a second, he announces, "Fifteen pesos."

"Wha . . . " I begin to protest. Jimmy pushes me outside and tweaks my ear.

"*Aray* . . . " I yelp.

"What did you do with the two pesos?"

I sniff. "I rented DC comics, you know, *Batman*, *Superman* . . . "

Jimmy knocks my head. "*The Green Lantern*, *Tales from the Crypt* . . . why do you waste time reading American comics? And you assist Mass on Sundays, and you're a Boy Scout too?" His finger thrusts at me. "You're proud of that, huh?"

My nose runs.

"Use your undershirt." He grunts.

We leave the Quiapo district. The buildings are still pockmarked with bullets three years after the war. Walking on Raon Street, we see surplus stores selling World War II blankets, uniforms, and other keepsakes. Still wearing their uniforms, veterans litter the road. Some beg for food. Others sleep on the street.

"Where to?" I ask. We cross into the Sampaloc district.

"To the Congress," he smirks. The Philippine Senate is a stone's throw away from the tenement where we live. "Home, lame-brain!" he says. "Where else?"

"Can I go to the Congressional Library first?" I ask. "I have to read Tiffany Thayer . . . "

"Yeah, yeah," he says. "And S. S. Van Dine and *The Arabian Nights* . . . you're a real bookworm, huh?"

"But I've got to make a report . . . "

"You better not hang out with Eufemio," he snaps. "You two are always peeping at his sister."

My classmate's sister, Lolita, is beautiful. Wow! One night, Eufemio dragged me over the tin roofs of the tenement. We spied on her and her boyfriend. Boy, her skin glistened in the moonlight, her hair fluttered in the wind! She hugged and kissed her boyfriend under the clotheslines. My heart got stuck in my throat. It thumped, thumped, thumped. I looked at Eufemio. His hands were busy inside his pants! What a pig! His own sister!

"He put you up to it!" Jimmy hits his open palm with his fist. "You stole Auntie's watch just to rent comics books?"

"Eufemio said we'll get it back." I cower. "Originally, we wanted to buy a crystal-radio and listen to *Prinsipe Amante*."

"You listen to that garbage?"

"I love adventure on the air waves," I protest. "DZRH is . . ."

"We have to get the Gruen back." He raises his hand. "We—all her relatives—gave it to your Mamang for her birthday." He sticks his fist at my face. "And you're going to help me."

"H-how?"

"Leave that to me, altar boy," he says.

We cross Morayta Street to the Laperal Apartments in Padre Paredes Street. Before entering the alley to our apartment where my mother is cooking supper, I hope.

"Tomorrow is Friday. Be here after your class." Jimmy kicks my butt. "Don't forget."

Ow, I massage my backside. I raise three fingers. "On my Scout's honor." Water forms in my eyes.

The next day, scared of facing my cousin, I sneak into the Assembly after school to listen to the debates. Claro M. Recto thunders, thrashing President Roxas. Wow, I love to hear the fiercest orator in the Senate! I giggle at old Senator Jesus Ma. Cuenco dozing in his chair! The big clock at the Afable building overlooking the Congress and our tenement tolls 6:00 p.m. With legs of cement, I trudge over to Jimmy's apartment.

"You're late." Jimmy chews me out.

I stare at the tear in my rubber shoes, and scratch my head.

"Come on . . . " He drags me along to Apartment 394-B. "We're playing mahjong."

"With Major Aquino?" I ask.

He nods. "And his boarder, Attorney Guzman. They can't play without a quorum."

I have second thoughts. "Why me?"

"You got yourself in trouble, cousin, and you're helping me to get you out of it," he says. "Beside, I taught you mahjong. Don't tell me you're not itching to read the tiles."

"How about your *barkada*?" I ask.

"The gang's out." His voice lowers. "We're lying low."

"The Major's wife?" I hold on to his *maong* jeans.

"Manang Anita and Mama . . . " He's referring to Lola Luz, his adoptive mother. ". . . are spending the weekend at their sister Loring's mansion."

"And Lolo Leon?" My knees quake, just saying his name.

"Don't worry 'bout Papa," Jimmy shrugs. "He's working overtime."

Leon Pascua, my maternal grandmother's brother, laid the NAWASA, National Waterworks, pipelines all over the city. At more than 6 feet tall, he has gone to the United States, mastered Engineering at the University of Chicago, and had a beautiful American woman as his girl or so I have heard. His protruding eyes could stare me down. His lion's mane would shake, his voice thunder.

I swallow hard. "What about capital?"

Jimmy overturns his pockets. Nothing.

"We don't have to show our money," he says, stabbing the air with his finger. "If we win."

Great, I think. *Really great.*

Major Roman Aquino's eyes scan us with suspicion. We sit at the table. The ivory tiles are piled, one on top of another, into four walls.

"Can't we get somebody else to play?" he nudges Jimmy.

"My *barkada* is out," Jimmy says.

"So we're stuck with this boy," Attorney Guzman says.

"He can beat you." My cousin looks him in the eye. "Wanna try?"

The Attorney's face reddens.

"Shall we roll the dice?" Jimmy says.

We play the whole day Sunday until it becomes dark again. Little by little, our opponents chip away at my winnings. The Major makes *escaleras*, cards in successive numbers. His boarder engineers two pairs back-to-back winnings. They wind up getting *coriando*, double payment, when they win five games in a row.

I can hardly keep my eyes open. My mind pleads, "Mother of God, how can I pay for my losses?" I glance at my partner. His tight mouth doesn't show it, but I bet his stomach's churning.

The Major has pulled down the blinds and locked the door. It must be Monday . . . I yawn. Monday! Oh, my gosh, I'll miss my classes. What will my mother say?

A banging on the door jolts everybody.

"Jimmy . . . !" Lolo Leon's voice booms. Holy God, the lion has tracked us down!

Major Aquino lets him in. "Leon . . . "

The old man does not look at his brother-in-law. He takes out a 1-inch piece of *yantok*, and lashes at Jimmy.

"Arghhh . . . " Jimmy defends himself with his arms.

"Ingrate!" Lolo Leon snarls. He cuts my cousin down—again and again and again. His face bleeds, his body torn. Jimmy runs away. Lolo Leon faces me. I crouch behind a chair, sobbing.

"Your mother will take care of you," he thunders. He pulls me from my hiding place, and shoves me out.

"Gambling. Missing classes. You're only thirteen. Go home!"

I run . . . oh, boy . . . if only my feet could fly! Faintly, I hear the Major apologizing to Lolo Leon. All I can think of right now is my mother. Am I going to get it! I sneak into bed and pull the blanket over me. I lie there, sucking my thumb. "When will my father come?" I cry. My eyes close and after a while, I fall asleep.

When my father comes from work, Mother holds my hand and tells him what I have done. Father, tired and, I guess, disappointed, sighs. He coughs a little. His handkerchief shows blood. Must be because the Japanese tortured him in the war. Father tenses his body and unbuckles his 3-inch leather belt.

I stare at his face. It looks sad. He has never laid a finger on me, even though I was naughty when I was younger.

I bite my lip, and pray, "Mother of God, I deserve this—but please, don't let my father hit me!"

"Bend over," Father orders.

"*He won't hit me.*" I pray, closing my eyes.

"Bend over," he repeats.

Sobbing, I turn my back and lower my pants. "Mamang . . . " I plead to my mother. She shuts her mouth tight and wraps her arm around me.

Whack . . . Oh, that hurts! Whack . . . my God, he's really hitting me! Whack . . . my backside feels like chopped meat! Whack . . . I feel blood oozing! Whack . . . tears blind me!

"No more, Papang," I beg. "I won't do it again!"

Mother nods. My father clutches his chest and goes to the bathroom. I hear him vomit.

"Good!" I cry. How can he do this to me!

Mother sees the hate in my eyes. She slaps me. "Your father loves you!" She follows my father to give him a towel.

For a week, I walk with a limp. I avoid Jimmy, wondering if he had suffered more than I did. He bumps into me in school and hands me a package.

"Your mother's watch," he grins.

My eyes open wide. "How . . . "

"The mahjong game," he shrugs. "Return it, and don't ask, okay?"

I hug him.

"Hey," he pushes me away. "People might think we're gay!"

"Ugh . . . !" I gag.

"You want to boogie?"

"Do I?" I hop. "A jam session . . . you bet!"

"I got extra tickets for the Valentine's party tonight. At my school. Auditorium. Eight sharp." He ruffles my hair. I hate it, but what the heck, he's my cousin. He points to his friends. "The *barkada* will be there too."

With a click of his shoes—he punches me . . . oh, it hurts! I'm joking, of course . . . and he joins his gang.

That night, I creep into Mother's room, find her purse, and replace the watch. I look for her in the kitchen. She's frying moonfish for supper. The cooking oil sizzles. It splatters. "*Aray*!" she exclaims. "Ouch!" It burns her wrist. I rush to the medicine cabinet and hand her some violet liniment.

She soothes the burn, eyeing me as if I were going to ask for a favor. "You're all dressed up."

I kiss her on the cheek. Surprised, she fingers my kiss. "What is it? Go ahead . . . you need something, yes?"

I hug her. "I'm going to National University. Valentine's dance."

Mother bandages her wrist. "You got a partner?"

"Jimmy invited me." I hug her. "He'll take care of me."

As I reach the door, Mother says, "By the way . . ."

"Yes, Ma?"

"Have you seen my watch lately?" She holds on to her wrist.

I stop, a lump as big as a billiard ball stuck in my throat. "It's . . . uh . . . have you tried looking at—

"Where?" she asks. "I've looked everywhere."

"Uh . . . maybe you overlooked it . . . your purse?" I go to the door.

"Well," she smiles, and calls out, "Fix your collar. And your hair . . . *ay*, Santa Maria!"

At the auditorium, Jimmy dances with every girl in the hall. I know every girl wishes he'll pick her to be his Valentine. His skin is whiter than a pearl. He wears a scarlet jacket over a yellow shirt, making him look like a playboy.

"How cute!" The school's beauty queen tweaks his dimples. Jimmy kisses her hand, dips her, whispers—I can read his lips say . . . "*Besame Mucho*." The girl blushes. Jimmy sways with her. The bolero is so romantic.

"*Palikero*!" Narding, one of his *barkada*, whistles. He's a bookkeeper.

"How can he deny all the girls?" Julio combs his hair. He is always combing his hair even when he wears his security guard's uniform at the San Miguel Beer compound.

"What's a Don Juan to do?" Eddie gulps his coke, spilling it on his Hawaiian shirt. I suspect it's laced with gin. He gives a thumbs-up.

Jimmy whispered to me once that Eddie had to quit his job at a printing press because the authorities were after him. They accused him of knifing a man over a girl. Wow!

Jimmy twirls the beauty queen. He waves at us. Everybody cheers. "*Guapo, Guapo, Guapo!*"

"Yeah, Jimmy's handsome all right." I mutter over the band. I fidget. The mirror on the auditorium's wall attests to that. My suit, two sizes too big for me, makes me look dopey. And my dark complexion—oh, boy, I think of black coffee. Jimmy's girls would prefer cream, I bet. I look at my black-and-white shoes. Damn, they're not as shiny as his! And the socks I'm wearing—one is red, the other's green! Damn you, Jimmy! Why do you have to look like Valentino? No one wants to dance with me.

"I was sweet and gentle," the vocalist sings. "Strictly sentimental."

With this, Jimmy cha-cha-chas with my chemistry teacher . . . She's not teaching in N.U., but, he invited her too, I guess. What gall . . . my *teacher, my* teacher!

"Mambo . . . " the band plays afterwards, "Jambo!"

Jimmy chooses a girl who wears glasses as big as dining plates as his partner. I recognize her—she's class valedictorian at my school. Aw, I sit down and cup my chin with my hands.

"*Un poquito de tu amor,*" Jimmy sings as he rhumbas with another girl. "A little of your love," he croons to her ears. From where I'm hunched, I hear him. I wish the roof would fall down on my head.

"Hey, dzing . . . " He calls me like a real tough guy.

"Yeah, what?" I turn my face away.

"Stop moping," he yanks me to my feet. "Take this beautiful girl . . . " He takes his arm from the girl's waist and pushes her to me. "Now, dance."

I open my mouth. He shuts it down.

"Dance with Elisa." He glowers at me.

I swallow hard. Jimmy has told me that Elisa's the president of their Debating Team. She fills her gown like an over-stuffed chicken. Do I want to dance with her? Do I want to kiss the Pope's ring?

The drums boom-boom-boom. The *Apalachicola*. God, I don't know how to dance that! Ready to cry, I look down at Elisa's bosom and kick myself.

Jimmy signals to someone in the band. His friend, naturally. Suddenly, the band changes tempo. They're playing *The Loveliest Night of the Year!*

I waltz Elisa round the crowded auditorium. She holds me tight. I think I'll die. I'm floating the whole night. Her body is softer than a baby's. Her breath smells of *dama de noche*! I'm in paradise! She whispers.

Something. What? She must be joking! I'm more of a man than my cousin is? No way.

"You're kind . . . " She kisses the air near my ear. "A gentleman."

Oh, boy, I'm in heaven!

After the jam session, Jimmy and his gang—I include myself—walk home. I can almost hear the roosters crow, but I'm not sleepy. The Chinese *sari-sari,* general store at the front of Laperal Apartments building is still closed.

Jimmy kicks an empty can. It rattles on the deserted street. "Did you have a good time?" he says to me.

"I . . . I . . . " My tongue is stuck in my mouth.

"The kid's in love!" Eddie puts his thumb on his nose and wiggles his other fingers. I step away from him.

Julio jives me. "Where'd you find the glue?"

"What?" I knit my forehead.

Narding answers, "No one can separate you from that girl."

They yell and hoot. I'm crushed.

"Forget her," Jimmy says, tap-tapping the bongos his friend in the band gave him.

How can I forget Elisa? She's a dream. The girl likes me.

"Don't be an idiot," my cousin says. He concentrates on the rhythm.

Julio stokes the fire. "You don't belong to the same school."

With a crooked smile, Eddie says. "You'll never see her again."

"Ah," Narding adds, "there are more fish in the ocean."

Eddie points to my pants. They're baggy and touch the ground.

"But you got to dress better than that."

Damn his *barkada*. Must they laugh me to death?

Jimmy slaps the bongo, a signal to sing, "A-cumba-cumba-cumbachero!" The *barkada* harmonize. "Cumbachero, cumbacherooooo . . . " They're off-key.

"Shhh . . . " I caution them. I can hear a window open in the tenement. Pretty soon, the neighbors will be pouring water on us—something that doesn't taste like water.

"Isn't Gene Kelly great?" Jimmy gushes. "You guys see him in *American in Paris?*" He rolls up his low-cut jeans, shows his white socks, and tap dances on the street.

"I'd rather be in the U.S.," Narding says. "There, money grows on trees."

"Yeah," Julio says. "The streets are paved with gold."

"We'll drive a Buick," Eddie says. "We'll steal one."

"Nah," Jimmy shakes his head. "We'll buy one."

"First, we have to learn how to drive," Julio says.

"I know how to drive," says Narding.

"You don't own a car," Eddie says. "Nobody here owns a car. We're too poor to have a car."

"We can dream, can't we?" Julio says.

"A Studebaker," Jimmy muses. "Dzing, it's sleek. Makes love to the road."

"De Soto's elegant," says Narding.

Jimmy leads them away towards España Boulevard. He sings on top of his voice, "Tico-tico . . . " He bangs the bongos. "Tico-tico . . . tic—" The *barkada* sambas with him. "—tico-tico . . . tac."

Eddie hugs a lamp post, and dreams about some movie stars, I guess.

"Ouuumh, Lana Turner . . . " He takes his fan-knife, stabs the post, then kisses it.

Narding sniggers. "You wanna make that post pregnant?"

"Oooh, yeah . . . " Eddie makes a wolf-whistle. "Gimme her sweater."

"And Jane Russell, huh, huh?" Julio shapes her figure with his hands. "That's an outlaw I want."

The gang laughs. They move a shout away. They continue talking about Burt Lancaster and Victor Mature.

"Good night," I wave at them. "Or good morning." I'm about to enter the alley to our apartment when I see the outline of two men—one short and fat, the other tall and thin. Can they be Oliver Hardy and Stan Laurel? Oh, oh . . . these guys are pissing near the alley. They zip up and swagger out of the dark. "Hey, b-boy . . . " The fat man crooks his fingers, calling me like a dog. That ticks me. The streetlamp focuses on his face. It looks like a rotten tomato.

"Y-yes, sir?" I approach them anyway.

"W-where are the w-women?" His breath knocks me down!

I cover my nose.

"You know . . . " His companion swishes his hand. He looks like a scarecrow disguised as a girl. Except that his hair is put on backwards and colored green. How funny!

"The w-women!" The fat man belches.

I don't know what he means. Women? The only women I know are my aunts, my mother, my little sisters, and . . .

"Forget the women . . . " The scarecrow grabs me in the crotch. "I like boys."

"Jimmy . . . !" I yell.

My cousin hears me. "Hey . . . " Jimmy shouts. "Shit," he calls his *barkada*. "They're molesting the kid!" The gang runs after him.

"Let's teach these guys!" Julio waves his fist. Eddie brandishes his *balisong*.

Narding tries to hold him back. "No killings, man!"

The scarecrow lets me go. He runs. The fat man waddles after him.

Jimmy holds me. "What?"

I'm shaking. "They're looking for . . . women?"

"Shit!" he explodes.

Some windows of the tenement open. People shout, "What's happening?" Other apartments light up. "It's three o'clock, for heaven's sake!"

Jimmy calls out to the gang. "Stop Eddie!" Then, he turns to me. "Go home!" He gives me a push. "Sleep."

"O-okay." I shrug. "Thanks."

As I enter the alleyway, I look back at Jimmy. He runs after his *barkada*. I hear Eddie curse, "*Putang'na n'yo*, sons of whores!"

Did they catch these men? I wonder.

Two days later I read on page 6 of the *Manila Times* the news about two men—one obese as a barrel, the other thin as a reed. They were found in an *estero*, a foul-infested drainage ditch along Morayta Street. The police said they were stabbed, probably by a fan knife. Eddie comes to my mind. "Mother of God!" I make the sign of the cross.

On his twentieth birthday, Jimmy runs into me. I keep mum about the incident and he seems to have forgotten it. He says his gang got hold of a converted army jeep, courtesy of Narding who does bookkeeping for an Indian businessman. That night, we cruise the city. Upon reaching Luneta Park, we stare at the U.S. Embassy on Dewey Boulevard. Narding says, "Someday I hope to be called for an interview."

"Fat chance." Eddie knocks the baseball cap on Narding's head.

Julio puts his hand over his heart. "You wanna be a second-class citizen?

Everyone laughs. We drive along the boulevard, gawking at the lights of the ships anchored at Manila Bay.

Eddie perks up. "There's a barbecue stand."

The stall moves when the police harass the owner. The toothless hag waits for us in front of Bayside Night Club. Uniformed attendants park

Cadillacs and Mercedes Benzes in the lot. We can hear the sound of a live band playing inside.

"Sounds like Perez Prado," Jimmy does Mambo #5. "Must be Tirso Cruz." With a low, moaning voice, he sings, "It's cherry pink . . . "

The gang sings along. "And apple blossom white . . . " They're off key.

Chuckling, Narding stops the jeep. Eddie orders fried squid. Julio throws me barbecued dried mackerel, while Jimmy chews on jumbo shrimps.

"Yeah, hooo!" Eddie shouts like the Andrews Sisters, "Drink rum and Coca-Cola . . . " He drinks, I guess, what else, Coca-Cola mixed with rum.

Everybody toasts my cousin. "Happy birthday, Jimmy!"

Somebody hands me a drink. The joyride makes me giddy. But I accept, eager to taste alcohol. It's my first time.

"Uh, huh . . . " Jimmy takes the bottle away. "Are you eighteen already?"

I make a face. He rubs my face and laughs.

"Get in the jeep." Narding jostles us.

"Where to?" Julio whoops.

"Where else?" Eddie crows. "To Zapote!"

In thirty minutes, we cross a narrow bridge outside the city. We find ourselves in a hidden barrio in neighboring Cavite's shore. The streetlights are posted every quarter of a kilometer, so we have a tough time looking for the house that Eddie boasts he frequented when he ran from the law. At last, we see the red lights burning at the house. We park on the sandy ground near it. The door opens and women prance out, their half-slips showing off their bodies. Black brassieres cover the upper parts.

"Eddie!" They embrace him.

He gestures to Jimmy. "He's the birthday boy."

The women transfer their kisses to my cousin. They slobber all over him.

My tongue reaches the ground. Jimmy shuts my face. "Stay here," he orders.

"Aw, Jimmy . . . " I plead.

A girl—not a woman—I guess she's fifteen—sidles up to me. "You're cute." Before I can react, she pulls up her skirt and shows her . . . oh, my Lord . . . ! I hold on to the wheel to steady myself. She puts her arms onto my neck like a vise.

Jimmy tears her hands away from my throat . . . damn him. "He has to watch the jeep."

The girl huffs. "Maybe next time?" I nearly faint when she jiggles those two, inviting hills. She turns around and wiggles her bottom.

"Yeah." Jimmy elbows her inside the house. The red light displays the sign of the house: *Hacienda.*

Hell! I bang my fist on the wheel. Jimmy, one of these days, I'll get even with you, I swear. Oh, when will I be eighteen!?

A year later, Lolo Leon checks in at the F.E.U. Hospital. Jimmy and I visit him. The old lion's eyes come to life when Jimmy and I enter.

"*Mano po,* Lolo." I place his hand on my forehead, then kiss it.

With a trembling hand, he blesses me. "I want . . . to talk . . . to Jimmy." His voice quavers. I retreat to the shadows and let Jimmy sit by the bed. He places his ear close to Lolo Leon's mouth. Jimmy listens then looks away. He seems bored or angry or something.

"*Sin verguenza!*" Lolo Leon slaps him. "Don't turn away!"

Jimmy's face is red.

Embarrassed, I look up at the fluorescent light. The bustle of the traffic filters in through to the open window. My eyes shift down to the linoleum floor. Butterflies make up the design. Are the butterflies floating?

After fifteen minutes, Jimmy nods and leaves to wait for me outside. I move my feet to follow.

Lolo Leon calls, "Help me." He motions his head to the toilet. He puts his arm on my shoulder. I worry, how can I support a giant's body? But now he weighs like balsa wood . . . How extremely thin he's become! His body has shrunk like a dead spider. His bones are brittle, his skin sallow. The odor of disinfectant clogs my nostril as he leans on me. It takes us ten minutes to travel from his bed to the urinal. Each step registers pain on his face.

"Do you still . . . " he glares at me. ". . . play mahjong?"

"No, sir . . . " I ease him down at the bowl.

He snorts. "Don't be like your cousin." He pushes down to clear his bowels. "Gambling . . . " He pushes harder. I can see his face in pain as he struggles harder. HARDER. "Women . . . " Down come his feces. It stinks. He gives out a biiiiig sigh. "He's not a big, big hero, you know."

Jimmy and I return to the apartment on the second level near the P. Paredes entrance. A maid is sweeping the floor, working around us. Lola Luz hired this sixteen-year-old *probinsiana* before she went to Mangaldan.

I notice her well-scrubbed face. Her hair is cut short in the manner of Prince Valiant. She has a lot of lipstick on her mouth and her nails are manicured. Her dress is almost transparent I can almost see her nipples. The hem reaches up to her buttocks I can almost touch her butt. I'm feeling warm! Good gosh, my eyes tell me she wears no underpants! I'm hot, by golly! She even smells of Chanel No. 5 . . . Boy, this maid must have stolen money in the apartment while we visited Lolo Leon! How else can she afford this expensive perfume? Oh, uh . . . she's making eyes at my cousin!

Jimmy takes off his shoes and lies on his cot, the lower bunk of a double decker. Pheuuw, his socks smell! I open their ice-box, take out two Cokes, and hand one to Jimmy. The maid steps in between us. I give way so she can finish her job.

"What did he say?" referring to Lolo Leon, I quench my thirst.

Jimmy shrugs. "Nothing. I'm going back to my real parents."

"Yeah?" Mother told me Jimmy was adopted from her oldest brother, Manong Alejandro and Manang Magdalena. They were saddled with five children and were expecting another one.

"Tell me," I say to Jimmy. "Why'd he slap you?

Jimmy plays with his cheek. "What'd you think?"

"He told me not to be like you," I say.

"Ptuiiii!" He's really pissed.

The maid quickly mops the spit.

"Could you put this on a hanger, Violeta?" Jimmy removes his shirt, exposing his body. He swims everyday in the city's pool in Balara. God, why wasn't I born with his muscles or Johnny Weismuller's!

"Of course, Mister Jimmy." The maid flicks her eyelashes. She steps on Jimmy's cot to reach the hanger, her well-formed legs brushing my cousin. His hand creeps up the maid's skirt.

"Mister Jimmy . . . !" the maid blushes. Her eyes flutter. A low, harsh sound comes from his throat. "Lock the door . . . " He means me.

I explain, "But, Lolo Leon may die any moment and . . . "

He raises his voice an octave. "NOW!"

Ow, the heck with him! I turn my back and slam the door shut. Outside, I slump down the steps. My heart pounds . . . ke-dum, de-dum, de-dum. I hear giggling inside. I cover my ears. There is a bulge in my pants. Damn you, Jimmy!

Jimmy and I lose touch and we go our separate ways. I get married, have two children, get divorced, and immigrate to the United States. Jimmy's sisters, Noemi and Fe, visit me from the Philippines. We sit down in my little garden reminiscing about my handsome cousin. After Lolo Leon died, Jimmy went back to his birth-parents. He got married, had a son, left them to work in Guam, lived with a common-law wife with whom he had more children, went back to the Philippines, lived with another woman who bore him other children, had a liver ailment which proved fatal.

"Manong Jimmy wanted to give you this," Noemi says.

She hands me a lady's old wristwatch.

I shake my head and smile. "It's a Gruen!"

(2002)

I cannot speak of the beauty of love without wonder.

— Jose Garcia Villa

M. Evelina Galang

Born 1961, Harrisburg, Pennsylvania

About the Author

M. Evelina Galang is the author of *Her Wild American Self*, a collection of short fiction. She has been widely published in journals such as *Quarterly West*, *American Short Fiction*, *Bamboo Ridge Press*, *MS Magazine*, *Mid-American Review* and *Calyx*. Her collection's title story has been short-listed by both Best American Short Stories and Pushcart Prize. A multi-award author, she has taught at the School of the Art Institute in Chicago, Goddard College, Old Dominion University, and Iowa State University. During the fall of 2002, she joined the creative writing faculty of University of Miami where she has been at work on her novel, *What is Tribe*; screenplay, *Dalaga*; an anthology of Asian American Art and Literature called *Screaming Monkeys*; and *Lolas' House*, a book of essays based on the experiences of surviving WWII Comfort Women. In 2002, she was named a Senior Research Scholar by Fulbright.

Manilamen in Louisiana

According to researcher/historian, Marina Estrella Espina, eighteenth century Filipino seamen abandoned the galleons where they worked in order to escape their harsh Spanish masters. Some of them settled in the Louisiana area, founded St. Malo, Manila Village, Camp Dewey, and other sites in Louisiana. Considered fugitives by the Spaniards from 1765-1803 (when Louisiana was under Spain), these Filipinos hid in the bayous where they lived off the wilderness, hardly socializing and consequently not marrying. Many died without descendants. Some married Cajun women. These Manilamen introduced the process of shrimp-drying to Louisiana. They traded their catch in the market of Vieux (the French Quarter of New Orleans). There is evidence that Filipinos fought with Jean Lafitte against the British during the Battle of New Orleans in 1815.

Her Wild American Self

— M. Evelina Galang

It's like my family's stuck somewhere on the Philippine Islands. My grandmother, Lola Mona, says that I'm as wild as Tita Augustina. That I have that same look in my eye. A stubbornness. And if I'm not careful I will be more trouble than she ever was. She says her daughter was a hard-headed Americana who never learned how to obey, never listened. Like me, she says. My family believes that telling her story will act as some kind of warning, that I might learn from her mistakes.

When she was young, Augustina wanted to be chosen. Maybe it was all those movies about Teresa and Bernadette, flying off to heaven, but she imagined she would be a modern-day saint from Chicago's north side. Sitting at her window before bedtime, she'd divide the night into decades and mysteries. The moon was a candle offering and she surrendered prayers to Mary by that light.

When she was eleven, Augustina wanted to be an altar girl. In a red robe and white gown, she dreamed of carrying the Crucifix down the aisle. Her mother wouldn't hear of it. "God loves your devotion, hija," she'd say. "He loves you whether or not you carry Him down the aisle at church."

To rebel, Augustina stopped going to Mass with the family. "God loves me," she'd tell her mom. "Whether or not I show up on Sundays."

Augustina's dad, Ricardo, clenched his jaw tight, spitting words through the space of his gold-capped teeth. "How can you do this to your mother?" he demanded. He gestured a bony brown finger at his wife who was collapsed on the living room sofa sobbing.

"How will this look?" her mother cried. "My own daughter missing Sunday Mass. People will talk."

Augustina tried bargaining with them. "Let me be an altar girl, let me keep playing baseball with the neighborhood kids and I'll keep going."

Mona let out a little scream. "Even worse!" she said. "Your reputation, anak!" Mona dramatically curled her palm into a tight little fist, and pounded her chest, keeping time with the painful beat of her heart.

Ricardo placed Augustina into the back seat of the car, threatening to send her to the Philippines for lessons in obedience. The threats meant nothing to her. She sat in the car all during Mass, making faces at the people who'd stare into the windshield. Next Sunday, her parents let her stay home alone.

This did not sit well with the family. When Mona and Ricardo moved to America, they brought with them a trunk full of ideas—land of opportunity, home of democracy, and equality—but God forbid we should ever be like those Americans—loose, loud-mouth, disrespectful children. Augustina was already acting wild, and stubborn, opinionated too. To tame her, they sent Augustina to all-girl Catholic schools.

On her first day at Holy Angels, she walked into the cafeteria with her cold lunch—a tupperware of leftover rice and fish. There was a long table of girls sitting near the window. Recognizing some of them from class that morning, Augustina walked over to a space at the end of the table and as she got nearer, their voices grew silent. She greeted the girls and they smiled at her, they nodded. "Mind if I sit here?" she asked. They stared at her as if Mary Mother of God had swiped their voices. They just stared. Augustina sat with them anyway. Then Colleen Donahue said, "This school's getting cramped." She was talking to the girl across from her.

"Yeah," the girl answered. "What *is* that smell?"

"God," Colleen said. "It's like dead fish."

Augustina scanned the table—the girls were eating oranges and apples. Some sat with nothing in front of them. She was the only one with a tupperware of food. Then she said to the girl sitting next to her, "What kind of lipstick is that? It's wild." But the girl turned her back on Augustina as if Our Lady had plagued her.

"I think it's coming from her," said the girl as she held her nose.

Augustina looked down the row of milk-white faces, faces so pure and fresh, it was hard to tell if they were born that way, or if they'd simply scrubbed the color out of them. She looked down at her hands, at the red nail polish peeling, at her fingers stretched out stiff in front of her. She would never have a single girlfriend among them. In fact, they say that Augustina's only real friend was her cousin Gabriel.

When Augustina got home that first day, she begged her mother to let her transfer to the neighborhood school, but her mother wouldn't listen. Instead she sat Augustina down on her bed, brushing the hair from out of her face and told her, "Your father and I work very hard to keep you in that school. It's the best, hija," she told her. "You'll see."

So she started hanging out with her cousin Gabriel in places they'd find disturbing. We have pictures that Gabriel took of Augustina dancing among tombs and statues of beautiful women saints at Grace Cemetery. In many of the photos, her image is like a ghost's. There's the snow-covered hills and Augustina's shock of black hair, her elephant-leg hip-huggers, moccasin-fringed vests and midriff tops, the scarves that sailed from the top of her head, the loose beads and bangle earrings flipping in the wind. They say her cousin Gabriel was in love with her, that he was what made her wild.

Mona used to complain to her husband, "Why does she always have to go to that place? Play among those dead people? Maybe we should have sent her to public school after all, Ricardo, or maybe we should have encouraged her friendships with those children, those boys next door." Her father, a hardworking surgeon, denied there was anything wrong. "Nonsense," he'd say, "She's a girl and she should act like one."

One night, when Augustina was sixteen, she locked the door to her bedroom, hid away from everyone. Her room was a sanctuary where Gabriel's photos plastered the walls, a row of votive candles lined her window ledge, and post cards of Lourdes and Fatima decorated her bedpost. She had built an altar of rocks from the beach up on Montrose, a tiny indoor grotto where she burned incense. She put on an old forty-five. Years later, Augustina would sing that song—about Mother Mary and troubled times and letting it go, or was that *be!* whatever at parties and weddings and funerals and any event where she could bring her twelve-string guitar.

Lighting a cigarette, Augustina waved a match into the air. Then she slipped a hand underneath her pillow, pulling out a fine silver chain. At the end of the chain was a small medallion, oval like a misshapen moon and blue like the sky. From the center of the pendant rose a statue of the Virgin Mary, intricate and smooth like an ivory cameo. Augustina had taken the necklace out of her mother's jewelry box and kept it for herself. She believed it was her lucky charm.

She held the necklace between her fingers, rubbing its coolness into her skin, begging the Virgin to hear her. You were young, she whispered. You know what it's like to love a boy. She imagined her mother's swollen heart bursting and water spilling out, cascading down her tired body, mourning as though her daughter were dead. She'd never forgive her. After all the trouble her parents went through to keep her away from the bad crowd, the boys and lust in general, Augustina still managed to fall in love.

Her mom stood at the door, knocking loudly, but Augustina pretended not to hear. She took another drag of her cigarette, then snuffed it out in the cradle of a votive candle. Reaching to the side of the table, she lit a stick of incense, disguised the smoke with the scent of roses. She slipped the pendant under her pillow and held a picture of her sitting on the rocks at Montrose Harbor. She was wrapped in the cave of Gabriel's chest, curling her body tightly into his. The waves were high and one could see a spray of water falling onto them. Her mother would die if she saw that picture. "Augustina," her mother said, "Open up, hija, I want to know what's bothering you."

"Nothing, Mama," she answered. "I'm just tired."

Her mother jiggled the door. "Open up. Let me look at you, you were pale at dinner." She waited another moment and then asked, "Why don't you talk to me, Ina? Let me know what's wrong."

Talking to her mother was like talking to the house plants. With good intentions, she would sit, gladly nodding, smiling, but she wouldn't hear. Like the time Augustina tried to tell her mother about the nuns, how they pointed her out in class, saying things like, "Thanks be to God, Augustina, the Church risked life and limb to save your people, civilize them. Thank God, there were the Spanish and later the Americans." All her mother said was, "She meant well, hija. Try to be more patient."

The next morning Sister Nora gave her annual lecture to the sophomore class. Standing against a screen, a giant projection of the world splattered across her face and the gym at large, she waved a long pointer in the air, gestured at the map. "There are cultures," she said, "that go to great lengths to keep their daughters chaste." Augustina envisioned a large needle and thread stitching its way around the world, gathering young girls' innocence into the caves of their bodies, holding it there like the stuffing in a Thanksgiving turkey. She had to excuse herself.

The heat in the building was too much, too suffocating. Every time she closed her eyes she saw her mother's image on the screen before her or she'd picture the girls in South Africa, their stitches bursting wide open. Augustina ran out. She sat on the curb, cupping her hands against the wind, her thin legs sprawled out in front of her. She slipped a cigarette between her lips and listened to the girls' voices wafting out of the building. She hated everyone at that school.

A low-riding vehicle, brown and rusted, snaked its way along Holy Angel's driveway. Augustina took another drag from her cigarette. As she moved away from them, she could hear the girls howling.

"It's her sexy cousin," yelled one girl. "The Filipino houseboy."

"You'll get caught," Colleen said plainly.

As she climbed into Gabriel's Mustang, Augustina swore under her breath, and asked, "Yeah, so what's it to you?"

He drove uptown, taking side streets, weaving the car about pedestrians. His camera, a thirty-five millimeter he had inherited from his grandfather, was carefully placed next to him on the seat. It was his lolo's first possession in the States. Reaching for it, Augustina played with the zoom, slipping it back and forth, in and out like a toy.

"Don't break that," Gabriel warned.

The light from outside framed his profile. She could see the angle of his cheekbones, how they jut from his face, the slope of his nose and the dimples that were set in his half-smile. She snapped a picture of him, click, rewind, click. Snapped another. She pointed the camera out the window and watched the streets through an orange filter. They rode most of the way in silence and then he finally said, "So did you think about it?"

"Yep," she sighed, "it's all I can think about."

"Me too," he said.

"Maybe we should stop hanging out so much," she said. "Maybe that would help."

But Gabriel shook his head. "That's not right either."

The window was splattered with slush from the streets. Through the viewfinder, she caught a girl carrying a baby. The infant, dressed in a light blue snowsuit, draped its body across the girl, curled its head into the crook of her neck, slept comfortably amid the winter traffic. Click, she snapped another picture.

Augustina thought the girl carrying the child looked like Emmy Nolando. Apparently, Dr. Nolando refused to give his daughter birth control and when she came home pregnant, the Nolandos sent her to a foster home in town. Disowned her. Augustina's parents milked the story for almost an entire year:

"Can you imagine," her mother whispered as she leaned over her bowl of soup. "The shame of it."

When Augustina asked why Emmy was sent away, her father shook his head, and muttered, "Disgraceful."

Ricardo leapt into a long lecture concerning those loose American girls and their immorality. "She's lucky she's not in the Philippines," he said. "There she'd have that baby and her parents would raise that child as their own."

"That's stupid," Augustina said.

"Oh yes," Mona said. "That baby would never know who his real mommy was. That's how it's done back home. That's how they save the family's reputation."

Even though Emmy had spent her pregnancy in a foster home, and even though she gave her baby up for adoption, Augustina was still not allowed to speak to Emmy. No one did. The Filipino community ignored her. "Better not be wild, better not embarrass the family like that girl. Better not, better not, better not."

Of all their hangouts, Grace Cemetery was their favorite. At Grace, the sun shattered into a thousand bright icicles, splintering branches into shadows, casting intricate patterns on hills of white. New fallen snow draped the statues of saints and beautiful ladies like white linen robes. They stood at the doors of these tombs and they prayed for souls. They stood guard no matter what—storms or drought. Once a twister ripped across Grace Cemetery and trees broke in half—a couple of tombstones even uprooted. But these women stood strong.

She sat at the foot of St. Bernadette's statue, gathering snow into little heaps. When Bernadette was visited by the Blessed Virgin back in Lourdes, they thought she was crazy. They didn't believe her. But Bernadette didn't give a fuck what they thought. She just kept going up that hill, praying, talking to Holy Mary like it was nobody's business. Augustina ran her hands along the statue's feet, tracing the finely etched toes with the edge of her finger. She listened to the wind winding its voice through the trees like a cool blue ribbon.

Gabriel fiddled with his camera, flipping through filters and lenses. She watched him sitting on a hill, his long body bent over the camera, his hair falling to either side of his face, shining midnight under the hot winter sun. Augustina believed Gabriel was an angel in another life. She could tell by his pictures, black and white photos of the city and its people. He once told her that truth cannot possibly hide in black and white the way it does in color. Colors distort truth, make the ugly something beautiful. She considered him brilliant.

"Bless Gabriel," she told the statue. Augustina looked up at the saint's full cheeks which were round and smooth like the sun. Her eyes were carved into perfectly shaped hazelnuts—so lifelike that from here Augustina could see the definition of her eyelashes.

"Augustina!" Gabriel yelled. "Look up." He jumped up onto someone's tombstone. The light from behind him glared at Augustina, forming a haze of white around his black mane. "This light's great," he said. "Your eyes are magnificent."

"I'm squinting," she said. He leapt from the side of the tomb, and leaning over her, he tugged at the ends of her hair.

Augustina placed a cold hand on the side of his face and he shivered. "What would your parents say," she asked. "What would we do?"

He stared at the graves. The sun slipped behind a crowd of clouds and suddenly it was cold out. Augustina lit a cigarette and offered him a drag. He buried his face in his hands as he pushed her away.

Getting up, she walked underneath the rocks that formed an archway where Mary stood serenely veiled in paint—skyblue and gold. Tossing her cigarette to the ground, Augustina walked past the bench, pushed up against the iron rail, leaned her pelvis into the gate and pulled at one of the rods. She stared at the thick wooden rosary that draped Mary's white hands. Augustina told the Lady, "It feels natural. Why not?"

She had not meant for any of it to happen. A few weeks before, *The Chicago Tribune* awarded ten prizes to the best high school photographers. A manila envelope came to Gabriel's house thick with a piece of cardboard, his prize winning photo of the Rastafari woman on Maxwell Street, and a check for two hundred dollars. Second prize. The letter that came with the announcement talked about Gabriel's use of light, texture and composition. The judge said Gabriel's intuitive eye was not only a gift but a way to see the world. Gabriel should develop his potential.

When Gabriel showed his father the letter and winning photo, Uncle Hector blew up. Told Gabriel he was wasting his time again, taking risks with his life, traveling into dangerous neighborhoods and for what? A picture? "Don't be stupid," Hector told him. What if something would have happened there on the Southside? He could have been mugged or knifed or beaten. He could have been shot. Was he crazy, Hector wanted to know. Grabbing Gabriel's camera, Hector shook it over his head like a preacher with a Bible, its strap casting shadows on his face. "Enough of this," he said. "Stop wasting your time." As he threw the camera across the kitchen, the lens popped open, came crashing on Tita Belina's marble floors and shattered.

That night, Augustina had sat on the rocks at Montrose Harbor, holding Gabriel's head on her lap, brushing the hair from his face, wiping the tears as they rolled from the corners of his eyes. "Count the stars,"

Augustina whispered. "Forget him." Augustina felt so bad for him, so angry at her uncle. And when Gabriel glanced up at her, she leaned down to meet him and kissed. She let her lips rest there, held onto him, and something in her stirred, some feeling she was not accustomed to. She let go a long sigh, let go that little bit of loneliness.

Augustina thought she saw the Lady smiling at her, looking right through her. Okay, she whispered, I can't stop thinking about him. Am I bad? At night she imagined the weight of his body pushing down on her, covering her like a giant quilt. She saw his eyes slipping into her, his beautiful face washing over her in the dark. She tried to remember the feel of his hair, how the strands came together, locked around each other. Sometimes she thought she could smell the scent of him, there at the lake, a fragrance of sandalwood, a breeze from Lake Michigan. I'm crazy, okay, she thought. A tramp, if you will. But he loves me, Mary, doesn't that count?

She thought of Sister Nora and the girls whose parents made sure of their virginity. How they'd mutilate them in the name of chastity. And does that operation keep those girls from love, she wondered. Does it keep them from wanting him? Sister Nora would find out and tell everyone. Use her for an example. No, she'd rather die. She imagined her body floating, swelling in the depth of the lake. She imagined herself swimming eternally. Augustina closed her eyes, putting her face to the sky. The sun came out every few seconds, ducking out of the clouds so that Mary appeared hazy and kind of aglow—but only for seconds at a time. "Hail Mary," she said. "Hail Mary, full of grace, the Lord is with thee, so please, please, please, put in a word for me, Hail Mary." She was so deep in prayer, she didn't even hear Gabriel sneak up behind her.

"Are you worried?" Gabriel asked.

"A little," she said. He put his arm around her and they embraced. Kissed. Slowly fell into that long black funnel, slipping across borders they had never crossed till now. They spent the rest of the day lying under the branches of the grotto, watching the changing sky and waiting for the sun to sleep. Neither one of them wanted to go home.

The house was locked when she got there, so Augustina fumbled for the key she wore around her neck. When she opened the door, the symphony from her father's speakers rushed out to her like waves on Montrose beach. Music filled the house so that when she called out to her mother, her voice was lost and small.

Mona stood at the stove, her feet planted firmly apart, one hand on her hip and the other stirring vegetables. Augustina snuck up behind her and kissed her softly on the cheek. "Hi, Mommy," she whispered. Mona continued to mix the stir fry, beating the sides of the frying pan with quick movements. Beads of sweat formed at her temples as she worked. "Do you want me to set the table?" Augustina asked. Turning, she saw the table was already set. Four large plates, a spoon and fork at each setting, a napkin, a water glass. "Okay," Augustina sang, "Well maybe I'll wash up and I'll help you put the food out."

The music was blasting in her father's room. She popped her head in and waved at him.

"Hi, Dad!" she called. He was reading the paper and when he didn't look up she tapped him on the knee. Leaning over, she kissed him.

"Sweetheart," he said. "Is dinner almost ready?"

"Yeah, Dad. In a minute."

She felt as though she had been up all night. Her body ached, was covered with dirt from the cemetery. Gabriel's cologne had seeped into her skin, and she was afraid that her mother had sensed it. So instead of simply washing her hands, she bathed.

The cool water, rushing down her body, washed away the cigarette smoke, the cologne, the dirt. She could almost feel the water coursing through her, washing over her mind, cleaning out her tummy, circling about her heart.

When she got back to the kitchen, she found she was too late. Her mother had placed a huge bowl of rice on the table, a plate of beef and vegetables and a tureen of soup. "Sorry, Ma," she said, as she grabbed a cold pitcher of water. "I just needed a shower."

"Is that all, Augustina?" her mother asked as she looked up from the sink.

"What did you do today? Ha? Where were you?"

She felt her face burning bright red. "At school," she answered, "Where else? Then Gabriel and I went to the mall."

"School?" she whispered. "They were looking for you at school." Augustina stared at the table, ran her fingers around the edge of the water pitcher. It was cold and moisture shivered from the pitcher's mouth and ran down its sides. Her mother's voice was low and angry. "How many times do we have to go through this, hija? Why can't you just stay in school?"

"But I was feeling sick," Augustina said.

"So you had Gabriel pick you up and the both of you were absent?" Her mother threw a dish rag on the counter. "You were at the cemetery again?" She pulled Augustina close to her. "Do you want your father to send you to the Philippines? Maybe that would teach you how to behave." Her parents often threatened to send her there, to all girl convent schools, where nuns pretended to be mothers. "If you think the rules are strict here, wait till you have to live there."

"Sorry, Mom," Augustina whispered. "But the truth is that Gabriel had another fight with Uncle Hector and he was upset. He came to get me so we could talk."

"Still, hija, that's no reason to be absent from school." As Mona brushed the hair out of her face, and kissed the top or her forehead, Augustina's father stepped into the kitchen.

"Ano ba," he asked. "What's going on?"

Mona tucked her hair behind her ears and told him, "Nothing, nothing, Ricardo. Dinner is ready. Come sit. Ina, call your brother."

Augustina spent the next two days locked up in her room, blasting her record. The needle slipped over that old forty-five, bumped along the grooves and scratches, whispering a mantra. "Mother Mary," she sang along. "Comes to me." An old church organ cranked a sacrilegious funk, a honky-tonk that seemed to fade into the slow rise of the electric guitar's bridge. She played around with Gabriel's photos. She mounted them on cardboard and painted borders around them—daisies and rainbows and splotches of love and peace and kiss drawn in giant bubble letters. Her mother stood at the door, knocking, forever knocking, but she pretended to not hear. "I'm not feeling well," she had told her mother. "I don't want to go to school." Bile rose up her throat, churned in her stomach, swamped up against her the cavern in her chest.

Her family came to the door one by one. First her mother, then Dad. Even Auntie Belina, her cousin Ofelia and Uncle Hector came knocking, but the door was locked and there was no opening it. When Gabriel stood at the door, she whispered through a crack, "I'm sorry, I can't let you in. They can't know."

When Augustina finally went to school, Sister Nora stood in front of the classroom, whacking her giant pointer stick across the blackboard. "There has been disgraceful conduct. Sin, sin, sin. Apparently, the story of the young girls and their experience with genital mutilation has not taught you anything. You girls must be punished."

Augustina thought the nun knew, was about to expose her when Sister ordered the girls who attended Kat O'Donel's slumber party to step forward. Apparently the sisters found a video tape of "Marlin the Magnificent" dancing in his elephant mask—and that was all he wore—a mask. The tape was found lying in the Cathedral—second to the last pew, across from the confessional. Fran Guncheon, class librarian, and Augustina were the only ones not in attendance, so they were given permission to leave. Augustina took this opportunity to run to Grace cemetery.

The clouds drifted north, slipped by fast like the second hand in her grandmother's wristwatch. Her body was numb, frozen like the Ladies in the court. She thought they had grown sad. Her constellation of saints, like everyone else in her life, had stopped listening to her. Snow melted around St. Bernadette; the sun burned holes in the ice underneath her. Augustina smelled the earth, seeping through the slush. It was sweet and fertile. A trickle, a tear, maybe the snow, slipped down Bernadette's face. Inside Augustina, something grumbled, roared. She had stopped praying weeks ago. God confused her.

Augustina looked up from the statue and saw her mother climbing over the hill. The sun shrouded her in light. She wore her off-white cashmere coat, the one that fell to her ankles because she was so short. She wrapped her black hair in a white chiffon scarf that trailed past her shoulders, followed the wind. There was a cloud of white smoke trailing from her breath, rising up and floating away from her. When she came near, her mother said, "She's beautiful."

"She's strong," Augustina answered.

"So this is where you go." She tugged at Augustina's braids, examined her face, kissed the top of her forehead. Then, pulling the chain from Augustina's neck, she said, "Where did you get this, hija?"

"Isn't it my baby necklace? I found it in your jewelry box."

Her mother shook her head. "I got this from my godmother. You shouldn't have taken it without asking."

Slipping her head onto her mother's shoulder, Augustina felt her body soften, the energy draining from her. She considered telling her mom about Gabriel. Would she understand? She closed her eyes and fell in time to her mother's breathing. Maybe, she thought. Her mother embraced her and told her, "Whatever is troubling you, hija, don't worry. Family is family."

Of course, Lola Mona never tells me that part of it. The story goes, that Tita Augustina went to the Philippines six months later. Some of the relatives say it was to have a baby, others say it was to discipline her wild American self. Still stuck back on the islands, they tell me, "You're next. Watch out." Even my mother thinks her older sister was a bad girl.

"How do you know," I ask her. "You weren't even born when she left. You hardly knew her." My mother always shrugs her shoulders, says she just knows.

Last time I went to see Tita Ina, she held out her tiny fist, wrinkled and lined with blue veins, and slipped me the Blessed Virgin dangling from the end of a fine silver chain. "Here, hija," she said, "take this." I placed the necklace up to the light. The paint was fading and chipping from its sky blue center, but still there was something about Her. The way her skirts seemed to flow, the way her body was sculpted into miniature curves, the way the tiny rosary was etched onto the metal plate.

(1996)

Cecilia Manguerra Brainard

Born 1947, Cebu, Philippines; immigrated to the U.S. in 1969

About the Author

Cecilia Manguerra Brainard is the award-winning author and editor of ten books, including the internationally-acclaimed novel, *When the Rainbow Goddess Wept*, and her second novel, *Magdalena*. In 1998, she received the Outstanding Individual Award from her birth city, Cebu. She has also received a California Arts Council Fellowship in Fiction, a Brody Arts Fund Award, and a Special Recognition Award from the Los Angeles City Board of Education for her work dealing with Asian American youths. In 2001, she received a *Filipinas Magazine* Award for Arts and a Certificate of Recognition from the California State Senate, 21st District, and others. She teaches writing at U.C.L.A. Extension and University of Southern California. She has a website at http://www.ceciliabrainard.com.

Filipino Games

A popular game in the Philippines especially in the provinces is *buwan-buwan*, which translates into "moon-moon." It was a game we used to play when the moon was full and the weather was good. Around a dozen children—and sometimes grownups—would gather outside under the full moon. Pouring water on the ground, we created a huge circle and marked its diameter. There was an "It" who had to try and catch others while he ran along the circumference and the diameter. The person the "It" caught became the next "It." We spent many happy nights playing this moon game.

Another favorite pastime at night was storytelling; and invariably the stories involved ghosts and scary creatures from Philippine folklore. Still another activity was singing—and it always seemed a person or two had a guitar to play. This was before the days of karaoke and the Internet.

The Last Moon-Game of Summer

— Cecilia Manguerra Brainard

Summer vacation is ending. While the moon is still large, we decide to play another moon-game, the last this summer. Jorge offers to go to his house to get buckets filled with water. As he's leaving, my cousin shouts, "Go help Jorge!" She's been teasing me ever since our last moon-game when Jorge held my hand. I'm burning with humiliation, but Jorge simply smiles.

We're walking down the cobble-stoned street when a warm breeze blows, stirring up the dry leaves, whipping my long hair around. I reach into my pocket for a rubber band to tie my hair back, confine all that wildness. I'm struggling with my unruly hair, when Jorge stops me. "It's nice like that," he says, taking the rubber band from my hands. I feel embarrassed; I feel grateful. This attention makes me feel funny, and I start running. He runs after me, and together we race down the street.

Jorge's house is tall and dark, reminding me of an abandoned cemetery. The first floor is made of mossy bricks that need patching so badly. The upstairs is made of wood and the windows are the old-fashioned sliding kind, made of capiz. The white squares of capiz shells give off a strange luminescent glow.

The front doors were originally carriage doors, very wide, with a smaller door cut-out on the one side for people to use. There's an antique brass door knocker colored green from age, which amuses me greatly; I pound it several times until a servant opens the door.

It occurs to me that finally I'll see the inside of his house. It's two blocks away from our house, but until Jorge held my hand, I'd dismissed this house as another decrepit mansion in Vigan. These past nights I've slipped away from my bedroom to head for the verandah. Standing on tiptoes, I stared across our neighbor's backyard to study the peak of Jorge's roof. I wondered where his bedroom was, how it looked, if he had a desk with books, or a side table, if he kept his books on the side table as I do mine. And I wondered if he was already asleep, or if he was reading, or if he was thinking of me as I was thinking of him.

When we're in the house, Jorge's demeanor changes. He becomes solemn and serious, and I wonder if I played with the knocker too long, or if I said anything wrong. He whispers, "Papa is sick."

People in Vigan say his father is a descendant of a man from Canton, China who made a lot of money from cotton. But Jorge's father and his brothers fought over money and inheritance. His father drove away the brothers, and for that, God punished him and he developed a rare disease and has been bedridden for years.

I, too, assume a serious face. Jorge leads the way upstairs. There is a huge living room, which is dreadfully quiet. The windows are shut and the only source of light comes from double doors that are ajar. "Wait here," he says and he disappears behind the doors. The room is really quite dark and I feel frightened.

I see a huge framed picture of a Chinese man in Mandarin garb. The portrait hangs on the wall from a long cord attached to the ceiling. The man has a drooping Fu Manchu moustache; his eyes are piercing, and his expression so stern that I think this man never laughed. I wonder if this is the man from Canton, Jorge's ancestor. He reportedly came to Vigan in the late 1700s with a bundle of clothes and his abacus. With the cotton boom, he was able to build this house and marry a Spanish *mestiza*. His imperial glare makes me sit on the edge of a plantation chair and fold my hands on my lap. I look around at Viennese mirrors, marble-topped tables, and other portraits of people long dead. When Jorge returns, I point at the man's portrait, and he acknowledges he is a great-great-grandfather.

"I'll show you around," Jorge says. He leads me to another sitting room with a grand piano and harp. Pretending I'm a famous harpist, I stand next to the harp, my spine exaggeratedly erect, and with great flare I run my fingers over the strings. "Bravo!" Jorge says, clapping, "You look good doing that." I give a little curtsy and we both laugh.

"I'll show you something," he says. He takes me to the library, which has enclosed lawyer bookcases. He opens a case and pulls out a book. He lays it on a desk and opens it. I catch the title: *The Discovery of the Moluccas and the Philippine Islands*. Then he points out a date: 1708. I've never seen a book that old. "Can I touch it?" I ask, in great awe. He hands me the book. As I reach for it, our fingers touch. Flustered, I almost drop it.

I remember the night he held my hand. We were playing the moon-game on my aunt's driveway. We had created a huge circle on the ground, using water. The "It" ran along the circumference and diameter, chasing the others who raced in and out of the circle. I stayed outside the circle, where I felt safe. "Come in," the others shouted in sing-song, "come in. Don't be afraid," and reluctantly I ran into the circle. I was breathless with laughter and fear that I would be caught. The "It" singled me out in his pursuit. Like tentacles, his long arms waved toward me. My heart knocked against my ribs as I shrank away. The others shouted at me to run out of the circle, but I was afraid I'd get caught. I stood there, paralyzed. Jorge ran back into the circle, grabbed my hand, and pulled me out. He continued holding my hand. We were safe. I was safe.

"It's very old," I say, trying to hide my thoughts from him. I run my fingers over the old parchment paper. Avoiding his eyes, I fix my gaze on the book; I know he's watching me.

"Look at this drawing," he says, his hand brushing mine as he flips the book. He singles out an illustration of some natives next to a tree. He's standing close to me and I can feel the length of his body near mine. Our heads are so close together, I can feel his breath. We continue to pore over the book, but all I'm thinking about is Jorge next to me. I've spent nights dreaming something like this would happen; and now that it's happening all I can do is stare at an old book.

After we've scrutinized all the drawings, he leads me to a chapel full of antique ivory statues. The statues are dead-white with movable glass eyes and dark brown wigs made from human hair. I shiver and tell Jorge I don't like statues and dolls with real hair. He laughs.

"Do you want to see my room?" he asks. Without waiting for my answer, he leads me past the dining room to a room that must have been a smoking room in the past.

While the rest of the house has a dusty and moldy quality, Jorge's room is airy and light. The brightness comes from a wide window that opens out to the upstairs verandah. There's a bed, side tables, large desk, armoire, and cabinet. I walk past his bed and study an oil painting on the wall—a landscape painting of women threshing rice. "It's by Juan Luna," he says. I nod in recognition of the master painter's name. He tells me he used to have another room, beside his parents' bedroom, and that he moved into this room recently.

He sits on his bed and moves over, as if to make room for me. It's a four-poster bed with rich green velvet bedspread. I'm thinking we should hurry back to the park, but it feels right to be with Jorge. I sit beside him. We stare out at the verandah. There's a dry fountain in the middle, and scattered all around the tiled floor are Chinese dragon pots crammed with aloes and sword plants, tenacious plants that need little care.

All this time, we have been talking in whispers, but here in his room, his voice becomes normal again. He tells me about a sparrow that built her nest on the fountain, and how he watched her lay her eggs, how she sat on them until they hatched, took care of her babies until they were old enough to fly. "It was wonderful," he said, "Life just yards away."

And then I do something strange: I throw my head back and laugh.

"Why are you laughing?" he asks.

"It's silly, the bird with her babies, right in the middle of the verandah where everyone could see them," I reply, still laughing. I'm not making sense—I know that—and I wonder what's come over me. I look at Jorge wondering if he thinks I'm being foolish, but he takes a strand of my hair and pushes it back. He says, "I like to hear you laugh."

He lies back on his bed, closes his eyes. He's smiling; he appears content. He runs the palms of his hands on the bedspread as if rubbing the fur of an animal. "Of all the colors, I like green," he says. I remain seated although I'm tempted to curl up beside him, rest my head on his chest, listen to his heartbeat.

"Why do you like green?"

"It reminds me of Abra," he says. And he continues to tell me about the forest that he visited when he was seven. The caretaker of their house brought him to the mountaintop of Abra, where the forest was so thick there was hardly any sunlight. I have not been to Abra, but have heard of its remoteness, of its strangeness. Many years ago, the people there were headhunters; I have seen sketches of tattooed warriors holding human heads.

In this perpetual green, he looked around and felt God. "Do you believe in God?" he asks.

I pause, uncertain how to answer him. I hear running water and the rattling of pans from the kitchen. I know what he wants to hear. A part of me says I ought to tell him, yes, and in the Holy Trinity. Be done with all of that. Instead I say, "I'm an atheist." I say this softly, but with some defiance. I'm certain he will find me repulsive, he will never see me again.

He is not shocked. He watches me. "Why not?" There is curiosity in his voice, not judgement.

"I can't say; it's too much to explain."

"You go to St. Catherine's, and I've seen you in church."

"I do all that, but I just do them, I don't believe." I check his face and find a furrow between his brows.

Fingers pressed together as if in prayer, I add, "But I was a good Catholic before my father died. I said all my prayers and went to Mass." I describe the Sacred Heart at the landing of the stairs and Our Lady of Perpetual Succor in the hallway. I tell him about the holy cards I collect, some of which I keep in my missal. Before the First Friday of each month, the nuns herd us to the Redemptorist Church. "I learned to invent sins for some man I couldn't see eye to eye," I tell Jorge.

"Ah, I know about your father," he says, "the plane crash in Mount Manuggal. With President Magsaysay."

I fidget. I don't want to talk about *that*. It's too difficult to even think about all that. I hear sizzling and smell fried garlic. I didn't cry when the nun told me about the plane crash. I dug my nails deep into my flesh as I clenched my fist. Dear God, I prayed, let there be a mistake, let him have missed the flight. I made deals with God: I'd hear Mass everyday for the next month. But it didn't matter. Pieces of his body were sent to us in a closed coffin. I never saw his body before the burial, never saw what God did to him.

After the funeral, I used to play near the gate with my father's two police dogs. When a car drove by, the dogs barked and we raced to the gate, expecting my father.

"I didn't become an atheist just like that," I explain, snapping my fingers. "I didn't just say, now I no longer believe in God. Things just didn't make sense. The nuns talked about purgatory, which is temporary. Then there's hell, which is forever. Then there's another place called limbo, where unbaptized babies go. I see no justice in placing babies in such a place. Could God be so unfair?"

Jorge sits up. He strokes my hair back. I can feel the warmth from his hand. "You've been hurt," he says. "You're angry at God. One day you will realize that He loves you. And one day, I'll take you to Abra. It was there in Abra that I knew God exists." Then he adds these words, softly, but I hear him: "I felt it inside, as surely as I know I love you."

He lifts my chin and I let him. My eyes are open; I do not know what to do. He presses his mouth to mine. I am surprised at how soft and moist a mouth is. It makes me think of that green forest in Abra, that mountaintop of Abra where he found God.

It makes me realize even though we'll go back and play the moon-game, and later my cousin and I will walk back to our house, and I'll sleep in the same four-poster bed, and wake up in the morning and do the same things I've been doing all summer, that somehow things will never quite be the same ever again.

(2002)

Marily Ysip Orosa

Born 1947, Manila, Philippines

About the Author

Marily Ysip Orosa attended St. Theresa's College, Quezon City and Maryknoll College where she got her B.A. in Communication Arts. She is a writer, graphic designer, and has been president of Studio 5 Designs since 1979. She spearheaded the publication of award-winning coffee table books such as the centennial books (*In Excelsis, The Tragedy of the Revolution* and *Visions of the Possible*), which were accorded the prestigious Philippine National Book Awards for Biography, History and Best Book Design. She is married to businessman and banker Jose S. Orosa who shares her love for books, Filipino art and culture, and her passion for great designs. She has five children (Jerome, Justin, BG, Chino and Rica) by her late husband Jet Hernandez.

Dating in the Philippines

There is no hard and fast rule on dating in the Philippines. Depending on the parents, Filipino teenagers have been allowed to go out alone or with a group of friends to various social events throughout the decades. In the '60s, the younger teenagers did not date. They went to dancing parties called *jam sessions*. Curfew was usually midnight or one in the morning. Most of the young girls had a chaperone, usually a sister or brother, many times a maid. Those with more lenient parents had permission to be picked up by their friends. Going to parties in groups was advised. In the '70s, teenagers went to discotheques and music lounges. Dating then became prevalent. Curfews were extended but were still implemented. Today, they seek the nightspots in Malate, Manila, where a variety of eating, drinking and dancing places abound. They hang out in malls just to chat, people watch, see a movie, or take a quick bite. Many frequent both high-class and small, intimate bars in Makati, the premier Philippine city, or play billiards, computer games or just chat in the new watering holes in Quezon City. Even in Cebu, the oldest city in the country, teenagers have places, which are a "must" to visit during the weekends.

The Curfew

— Marily Ysip Orosa

I *glance at the bedside clock. It is 12 midnight, the witching hour. The room is dark except for a tiny night lamp that mercifully breaks the blackness. I get out of bed and don a well-worn robe.* With a small flashlight in hand, I quietly make my way to the living room. After pacing up and down the *sala*, I settle on a rattan lounge chair, my husband's favorite. I wonder what is keeping her? Only sixteen and she is out on a date to a young boy's senior ball. He is a friend's child, but nowadays no one can fully trust these young kids.

Earlier that evening, I insisted that she decide on the chaperone of her choice: a maid or her dad. She winced. Please Mom, I'm old enough, she said. The kids at school start going out on dates at fourteen. *Madre mia*, I mutter. Are all sixteen-year-olds this stubborn? Is this an omen of a difficult adolescence in the offing?

All right, I acceded. But you have to be home at 12 sharp. That's your curfew, take it or leave it. After deciding briefly whether she'd make a fuss or not, she reluctantly agreed. I was grateful she didn't put up a fight.

It is now 12:10. She is ten minutes late but I decide to be generous and allow her a grace period of thirty full minutes. My husband's extraordinarily loud snoring shatters the silence of the house. I talk to myself to assuage the fear of being alone.

I am not going to be like my mother, I remind myself. How I disliked her waiting up for me whenever I went to parties when I was young. On stocking feet, I would tiptoe into the house many times after my 12 o'clock curfew. Like a mother owl that sees her prey clearly in the dark, she would always spot my hunched shadow as I made my way in. Her words would pounce on me, "Aha, you are late again. Your curfew is at 12," and then the famous penalty is declared, "You are grounded for a month!" Hurtful words that stood as monument to my painful teen years.

I vowed I would never be like her. I would be a reasonable mom, open and flexible, I promised. My teenagers would have a pleasant adolescence. In fact, I prophesied, I would even enjoy their teen years with them.

It is 12:20. Should I get nervous? Where is she? And why am I so upset? Why am I so untrusting?

I clutch my robe closer to my body to keep away the chilly night wind that has seeped through the window screens. Staring out into the night, I reluctantly allow my mind to slip back to a summer twenty-seven years ago when I was sixteen. My best friend had invited me to spend a week with her family in Cebu. Mommy allowed me, though hesitatingly, after being told that her parents were going to be there too. I was going to be safe, she was assured. Dad, the fun-loving person between the two, said sure. It is time for her to see the world. Cebu was a worthy stepping-stone.

In Cebu, we had a ball. Night after night we attended *jam sessions* and showed off the latest boogie and shimmy steps to an admiring young party crowd. It was a dream come true. Parties galore with great music from live combos. Dancing till the wee hours of the morning. No one to tell us when to stop.

Best of all, no curfew.

On our last night, we dared go out on a double date with two good-looking bachelors, both of whom were six or eight years older than us. These are not boys, I told my best friend. These guys are men. A still small voice inside me warned that we should not be out with them. I turned a deaf ear to that whisper.

Little did we know that these scions from good families had "plans" for us Manila girls. Our dates were the perfect gentlemen during dinner, and later they suggested a quick tour of their city. There was this exclusive subdivision high up in the hills, they said, where one could see the entire city bathed in lights. Even before we could answer, the four-door Mercury headed for this new destination.

Up on the hills, the view was a sight to behold. Cebu was indeed a beautiful city especially at night. We drove on, and soon the car stopped in front of an eerie old house. Say, they asked, are you girls afraid of haunted houses? I honestly said I was. Naively thinking we were just going to have a lively and innocent discussion on whether one should be afraid or not, the unexpected happened. My date suddenly put his hand on my lap, gently caressing it at first, then insistent after. I shoved his hand away. His answer was a tight embrace, and a frantic tugging at the buttons of my blouse. I pushed him away with all my strength. He was strong and continued to hold me tightly against his muscled body. I turned my face away as he brusquely tried to kiss me over and over again. But he managed to land a passionate kiss on my firmly closed lips. It was repelling. I kicked, pushed and scratched, bravely fighting for my dear life. The muffled noises in the front seat told me that my best friend was having the same nightmare with her date. Dear Lord, I prayed, help us!

In the struggle, I felt something near my hand. It was a big flashlight. I hit my date hard on the knee with it. He let out a loud cry. Taking advantage of his momentary shock, I hit him again this time in the face, and managed to break loose. Quickly, I dashed out of the car and ran out into the black night. My friend did the same and was fast on my heels. Together, we headed for the haunted house, in our minds now, our only hope for a safe and peaceful refuge. Choosing between ghosts or our beastly dates, we opted to be with the former. Shaking, we huddled in the safety of darkness inside the old ugly house. Fortunately for us, our dates did not follow. We heard the Mercury speed down the hill. Tomorrow, I said to myself, these jerks would have a lot of explaining to do when their parents and friends see the scratch marks in the light. But they will laugh, shrug their shoulders and say, they are nothing but "love" marks from two Manila girls who could not resist their charms. Ugh! I could hear their husky voices and evil laughter as they regale their gullible audience with horrible lies.

An hour passed, maybe two. In the company of night rats scurrying for food, we waited until our frayed nerves had settled. Then we bid the haunted house goodbye and hurriedly walked down the hill. I took one last look at the view of the city. It had ceased to be beautiful. The once-cool soothing air had become biting. Under the cloak of darkness, we hid our fear and trembling. I vowed under my breath never to return to this place.

I never told Mommy about the incident. Not even my faithful diary was told about our initiation into the real world. I decided I would not immortalize the memory of that night by writing about it in my private journal.

The antique clock beside the sofa says it is 12:50. I am getting nervous and worried. Her date is two years older. What if my sixteen-year-old does not have the good fortune of finding a big flashlight in the car as I did when I almost got raped?

My husband's snoring ushers me back to the present. Surprisingly his snoring gives me a sense of security, assuring me of his calm presence nearby. Tonight it is a welcome sound, and is music to my ears. This is the 21st century, his snores like short messages in Morse code tell me. Forget the boring '60s, they cajole. Values, especially curfews, are different today. Oh, if only I could tell him about that night in Cebu.

I surrender to the beckoning of the past. Mommy was my age when I was sixteen. Forty-two, a mother of five girls, still slim and sexy and attractive. She seemed so untrusting of the boys who came to the house. I often wondered why? I venture to think she may have had a similar experience in the '40s. The American GIs were terribly handsome, friendly and glib-tongued. Did she succumb to a young GI's amorous demand? I pray that she too was spared like I was.

It is now one in the morning. Funny how much blacker the night is at this time. But I am now comfortable with the dark and the silence. It is the waiting that is cruel.

As I turn on the lamplight, my daughter finally comes in. Like a mouse trying not to be heard, she tiptoes in but the clickety-clack of her high heels on our wooden floors gives her away. Seeing me, she immediately says in a soft voice, careful not to awaken her sleeping dad, Hi, Mom. I'm sorry I'm late. But the dancing started at 11 and the band was so good. I wanted to dance forever.

I look straight into her dark eyes, and like black crystal balls I read them. She is telling the truth about the dancing. But they are saying something more. No, they are not charged with fear, as my eyes were that infamous night in Cebu. I spot a certain softness in her eyes that comes from having experienced the thrill of a first kiss.

Ah, I'm sure of it—my little girl's lips have been kissed, hopefully just innocently. But my worrying turns to anger at her insensitivity for making me wait and worry unnecessarily. For making me remember a revolting incident that I had already consigned to oblivion. For bringing back the fear and anger of almost having lost my innocence in such a callous and despicable manner.

I throw all my promises to the wind. Promises to be open and flexible and reasonable. You are late, I bark. Your curfew is at 12. You are grounded for a month, I angrily shout. Words that I had heard over and over again when I was a teenager, I now spit out with impunity. Amazing how much I mean each one of them tonight.

My daughter approaches me and says tenderly, I understand, Mom. I know you mean the best for me. It will never happen again. She hugs me and heads for her room. I watch her and notice lightness in her steps.

It is 1:30. Tired but relieved, I walk towards my room, still clutching my old robe like a security blanket. I am glad the long one-hour wait is over. There will be many more nights like this. This is not the end, I warn myself. But I quietly whisper a prayer of thanksgiving to the Lord. Thank You for keeping my baby safe and sound. And, yes, thank You for giving me only one girl, I hastily add.

As I slip back to bed, and gather the soft comforter around me, I see the chubby face of a little girl in pigtails who tagged along everywhere I went. How quickly the years have gone by. I realize that she is so like me, unmindful of the passing hours when dancing is involved. Yet so unlike me, because she is quick to admit and apologize for a lapse in her behavior or a shortcoming.

As I close my eyes and invite sleep to take over, my thoughts are of the coming morning. Soon, a new day will dawn. A new opportunity will be available to my daughter and me. We will both have a fresh chance to start all over again. She, to make her curfew. Me, to be open, flexible. And reasonable.

(2002)

Anthony L. Tan

Born 1947, Siasi, Sulu, Philippines

About the Author

Anthony L. Tan was born and raised in the small island of Siasi, Sulu, the fifth of eleven children. He attended college in Zamboanga City and has a master's degree in creative writing and a Ph.D. in British Literature. He has taught at the English Department of Silliman, and currently teaches in the English Department of Mindanao State University-Iligan Institute of Technology. Anthony Tan published two books: *Badjao Cemetery and Other Poems* (MSU-IIT, 1985) and *Poems for Muddas* (Anvil, 1996). He also co-edited four titles related to the Iligan National Writers Workshop. His work has been published in Philippine and international literary journals. He has received literary awards from *Focus Philippines*, *Home Life Magazine*, and Don Carlos Memorial Awards.

Sulu, Southern Philippines

Siasi, Sulu lies at the southwestern tip of the island of Mindanao. It is an island, which like the rest of the Sulu Archipelago, is surrounded by many deep seas. In this place where there is more sea than land, a small group of people has been living for hundreds of years. They are known as the Badjao or the Samal. The Samal is an indispensable citizen because he catches the fish. In a materialistic world, however, he is looked down upon by the people from the other groups like the Tausug, the Christians, and the Chinese. He occupies the lowest rung of society because he hardly owns anything, and being in that position he has no one to look down upon. His role in society is limited to supplying the needs of people for fish (which in this part of the country is an excellent source of animal protein), but people hardly think that it is important enough. His small house is on stilts and made of very flimsy materials. Some of them who are still nomadic live on their small fishing boats. The sea is the world to him.

Sweet Grapes, Sour Grapes

— Anthony L. Tan

La belle dame sans merci
Thee hath in thrall!
—John Keats, "La Belle Dame Sans Merci"

Many years later I was told that there are two kinds of grapes. The sweet grapes are table grapes, the sour ones are wine grapes. The wine grapes are crushed by feet or winepress to extract the juice. The juice is stored in casks for fermentation. After several years it becomes wine. The older the wine gets, the sweeter it becomes. If you take wine in excess, you will get intoxicated.

I don't know if all this is true. I have never tasted wine. But I guess it's true. Sour grapes can intoxicate. And they don't have to be made into wine to do that.

One Christmas night, which now comes back to me as a splinter of a remote wound, the sour grapes I wanted to offer to Ruby Elena did intoxicate me.

My real problem started when I saw her. She was bewitchingly lovely. Her head was well-shaped, and the skin around her neck was smooth as a cultured pearl. She always looked fresh like the morning sky after a downpour. If I had been told that she descended from a fairy, I would have readily believed it. I once read in high school a story about seven fairies who went swimming in a stream in the middle of a forest. To swim they had to take off their wings, which they left on the boulders by the stream. A brave and crafty hunter accidentally found them and hid a pair of wings. When it was time for them to go, each fairy put on her wings, but the youngest and the fairest of them could not find hers. She was left behind as her sisters had to fly back home. She was forced to live with the hunter for whom she bore many beautiful children. But one day, as she was cleaning the cottage, she found her wings. Without saying goodbye to anyone she flew back home somewhere between heaven and earth. If Ruby Elena was one of the daughters of that fairy, it would not have surprised me. For everything about her showed some form of the supernatural. Her beauty was divine. But perhaps I was just blind, and blindly in love.

How would I tell her of my love? The thought scared me more than Professor Sabolboro ever could. The fat professor in speech continually berated me because I couldn't pronounce the English words properly. I always confused the *r's* and *l's*, and he mimicked my *p's* and *f's*, saying, to the jocose delight of my classmates, farty, stufid. Because I couldn't properly aspirate the initial *th* and *sh* sounds, he would look at me with an impish grin, and he would look at the ceiling and then back at me, and he would bellow at me *Das a las a nonsense*. No matter how I tried, I always addressed him as Plopesol Sabolbolo. At the end of the term, the most that he could give me was a C minus, C, he said, as in *consuelo de bobo*, for trying my best. Or for the fact maybe that once I made him laugh when I said that Jacqueline Bouvier was "instlumental to the plesidential erection of John Kennedy." I didn't know why the class laughed with him. I was only quoting from the newspapers.

I thought of writing Ruby Elena a letter, but I wasn't good at writing anything. I couldn't visit her at the dormitory, either. She didn't know me.

Besides, I had this problem with my pair of Esco shoes, my only pair of shoes, which was given to me by the school principal upon my graduation from high school. You see, I received the Loyalty Medal Award, and this pair of shoes went with it. It was a multi-purpose pair of shoes, like the multi-purpose government building back home in Muddas. I wore them to school, to social gatherings, to convocation and R.O.T.C. class. Once I wore them to a picnic because my roommate in the dormitory had hidden my pair of slippers. The tread on the soles was wearing out, and the heels were getting uneven. I told myself I should stop the habit of walking around the city at night. I should avoid getting them wet. Walk only when necessary, I said, so they would last until summer.

So I stopped walking around the city. It was crowded anyway with busy people going everywhere and I didn't know where else. And the glitter of the neon lights from tall buildings and movie houses confused me, too. In the fishing village where I came from, we had no street lights. We had Coleman kerosene lamps for the house and for fishing, but no electricity. So I wasn't used to very bright lights. My friends and I walked at night when there was a moon, or when the sky was brightened by a million stars, as on a summer evening. Otherwise, we stayed mostly at home, singing *tenes-tenes* and boat songs about sailors braving the stormy seas on their way to faraway lands like North Borneo and Celebes. We listened to the waves and the sound that strong winds made on nipa roofs. We often wished we were in the big city of Zamboanga or Sandakan. Only the sentimental melody of the boat songs could measure the depths of our longing.

My troubles with my pair of shoes were not that bad, though. I managed to get through high school with slippers and rubber shoes. In fact, by comparison, I was luckier than my father, who had nothing but his bare feet to get about on. Well, of course, what did he need a pair of shoes for? Most of the time he was spear fishing, and his feet were as large as rubber flippers.

I was doing well in all my subjects, except in R.O.T.C. where I was regularly getting 5-point demerits on account of my "unauthorized shoes." But the A minuses in Math, Natural Science, and Physical Education were more than enough to make my parents and three sisters happy. Of course, there was a B in Pol Sc and C minuses in English Composition and Speech. But that was all right with me if only Professor Sabolboro would stop berating me.

Could I tell Ruby Elena of my love? I was told that many boys visited her in the ladies' dormitory. If I wanted I could join the long queue of visitors, but I didn't have the courage. "No guts, no glory," I always heard it said, applied to me, I guess. I was very shy, awkward, and barely seventeen. I stooped when I walked as if I was always looking for some lost coins. Maybe I developed the stoop because I swam a lot. That was how I got the chance to study at the university: I swam. I was the varsity's long-distance swimmer: 800-, 1,000- and 1,500-meter freestyle, and 400-meter butterfly were my forté.

Since I first saw Ruby Elena, I had thought and thought of her. I invented stories to entertain myself, and every story ended with her in my arms. Nights became longer as my stories followed winding routes and tortuous byways, but at the end of these there was always Ruby Elena. There was no end to my imaginings as I added variations here and there. I began to have insomnia. One day I noticed my haggard face. I decided that indeed I was in love.

Days dragged on. Nothing happened to my love. Professor Sabolboro and the R.O.T.C. officers continued to harass me. In the dormitory after supper, I sought refuge in my imaginary stories. I neglected my studies. All my grades plunged below C level. My athletic scholarship was threatened. There was only one consequence of this falling down, I said to myself. I would end up pearl diving like my uncle. In pearl diving, falling down would help.

But I wasn't destined to be a pearl diver, my father said. The high school principal also said I could be a lawyer, and then later become a justice of the peace, and I would settle the problems of other people. I didn't know how this was going to come about, but that was what he said, and he was an educated man, and I respected him. My biology teacher said I was good at memorizing facts. I could become a doctor and cure the diseases of my fellowmen and relieve them of their pain. I had wanted to become a doctor because I wanted to cure grandfather of his coughing. He coughed too much at night, especially when it was cold. But I changed my mind after he was lost in a storm off the coast of Palawan.

Since his death there was less noise in the house at night, except for the sound the wind and the waves made. Uncle became less and less interested in pearl diving. One day he just stopped. He said he was afraid that at forty- feet deep the ghost of grandfather would suddenly appear to him. For a while my uncle shifted to dynamite fishing. I didn't know if he did that to blast away grandfather's ghost. Then he got into trouble with the law and was imprisoned for six months. He nearly died in prison. When he came out, he was so thin he looked like the ghost of grandfather. He left for Davao and never came back.

He was a stubborn man, sometimes unreasonable in his insistence on what he thought was right. Once he found a pearl, smooth and round as a glass marble, nearly perfect but for one small black dot. He demanded 450 pesos for it, plus the usual extra payments of one sack of rice, a sack of sugar, another sack of flour (part of which would be given as offerings to the sea god who guided him to the precious pearl), two reams of Union cigarettes for himself and father, three packages of safety matches for the household, and a half-kilo of lime for grandfather's *mamah*. But the Chinese merchant would not pay him more than 200 pesos and all the extra things uncle wanted. The merchant said the pearl was not worth much because the small black dot went deeper than it appeared. Would my uncle want him to prove it at my uncle's risk? He would scrape off the dot, and if the dot disappeared, he would pay the price my uncle was asking for, plus a new Coleman lamp as an incentive. He said the pearl was lighter than it should be, which meant that it was hollow inside. My uncle said the tiny dot was nothing, that it was just like the mole on the face of a beautiful woman, that, in fact, it made it more beautiful. The merchant would not listen to that kind of argument. My uncle kept the pearl for over a year. The dot had grown bigger. He went back to the merchant, but by then the crafty Chinese would no longer pay the initial value he had given the pearl. My uncle was defeated, went home, and in his madness hurled the flawed pearl back into the sea, cursing the merchant and all his kind.

When grandfather got lost in the storm, father cried and cried like a child. He said the sea was cruel. It gave us many things to eat, but it took grandfather away from us as if grandfather was some form of payment for what it had given to us. And we loved grandfather in spite of his endless coughing.

So when I left the island to study in college, I didn't know whether to study law or something else. All I knew was that I wanted to live in the city. I would fulfill the wild longings embodied in the boat songs. I was lucky. To be in the city was more fascinating than to find a pearl as big as your thumb. I decided to study in college, and at no expense from my father, who could not, of course, support my studies beyond high school. As the principal said to my father, I could swim my way through college.

For a time I was satisfied with myself. Until Ruby Elena came into my life. After that I was like a pearl diver who only expects to find oysters but gets angry when the oysters do not have pearls in them. Desire is like the horizon, mother said. It seems only as far as the eyes could see, but, no, it recedes endlessly as we get nearer, and it is never there for us to reach, and we are sailors on a frail *vinta*. The first semester ended. I was glad I passed all my subjects, getting only two A's in Math and P.E.; and the rest C and C minuses. But, at least, I was free from the fat professor.

Christmas came, and with it the desire for Ruby Elena increased. How in the world was I going to tell her? All those imaginary meetings never took place. She never walked with me in the rain under a wide black umbrella. For one thing I never actually owned one. She never borrowed any of my books where I could slip some notes or letters or a rose petal. When we met in the cafeteria, she was always surrounded by a group of handsome and rich-looking boys, different faces each time. If I could only get near her and talk to her, if I could only visit her in the dormitory, if I could only do that and do this, if I could only, if I could, if I, if . . . if . . . I got confused thinking of the thousand possibilities.

I have always had a weakness for fruits. It probably started on one of those stormy days when father had a meager catch. It was too risky to go far out into the open sea when the *habagat* wind blew. He would fish closer to home, in shallower water, somewhere around the bend of the island where the fishes were small and were not too eager to snap at the baited hooks. And, of course, in the wind-whipped rain, father could not fish as long as he would want to, as he would during summer or sunny days. And probably the howling wind, the incessant creaking of the anchor rope on the cathead, and the endless chattering of his teeth made too much noise, bothering him and driving away the timorous fish. I knew when father had a meager catch because he would bring home thin sticks of sugarcane, young coconuts, overripe mangoes and guavas, instead of rice or even ground cassava for lunch. And so we would eat the meat of the coconuts with brown sugar and wash it down our throats with coconut water and sugarcane juice. I knew he had not sold the small fish he had caught but only bartered them for the fruits of poor farmers who could not afford the bigger fish. Eating these fruits for lunch so often made me like them, and later, from habit, I would skip lunch in order to buy expensive fruit like *durian*, *marang* and *mangosteen*.

That Christmas was a season of grapes, sweet grapes, sour grapes. In one clean portion of the market the stalls were full of them. The vendors knew how to whet the appetite. They simply hung the grapes in clusters for everyone to see, admire, desire and salivate over. I remember how my mouth watered when I saw those tear-shaped globes, bursting ripe, each grape a translucent, succulent purple. I would have wanted to buy some if I had the money. I simply swallowed my saliva. It tasted sweet.

The grocers, I was told, had better ideas of "special packaging" than the vendors. They put the grapes in small, perforated cellophane bags—each bag weighing a quarter of a kilo—for those who could not afford to buy them in larger quantities. They put these bags in open freezers, I was told, so that when you buy them, each bag had a misty aspect to it, and it would remind you that Christmas was a cold season.

A cold, wet Christmas was not unusual. For I remember my high school English teacher, he who was fond of idiomatic expressions, talking about heavy rains every time it was Christmas season. For four high school years I heard him describe a particularly rainy day as "raining cats and dogs." I thought then, in those dark days, that all the cats and dogs in the fishing village had come after a downpour. Years later I learned that it wasn't so, that cats and dogs were not like mushrooms and artists. Anyway, that cold Christmas season brought certain moods appropriate with gusty rains.

In my love for Ruby Elena I became very religious. In fact, over-religious, if there's such a thing. Anyway, I prayed more than the average person did because I prayed to two Gods. I prayed to Allah to help me, and then I prayed to the Christian God on behalf of Ruby Elena. To both Gods at the same time, I also prayed that they would devise some common means to make her love me. I guess they never came to the conference table to talk about my problems, or, if they ever did, they could not agree on a common solution.

So days rolled on like the ocean, huge and opaque, unchanging and unknown. If you have lived as I have, close to the seashore, you would know what I mean about the ocean. But you wouldn't know about the days being like the ocean unless you have loved Ruby Elena. But a lot of boys in the dormitory knew her. In fact, they knew a lot about her. They talked about her. Often when my fantasies met a blind alley, some over-heard comments about her brought my fantasies back to life. They would escape from the maze of variations and end with Ruby Elena shining like a lighthouse on a stormy, pitch dark night. It was a relief to find my foundering fantasies saved by the boys who knew her. But I was envious of the good fortune of these boys. Sometimes angry, too. For instance, one night as I was starting to weave one of my elaborate fantasies, I overheard two boys in the next room talking about her.

"Did you see her at the party last night?" one of them asked the other. There was a malicious tone in his voice.

"Yes, my friend. She wore a backless dress, you know." It was the freshman law student who had just transferred from a school in Manila. "And, you know, I danced with her."

"No kidding, Steve. You did, ha?"

"Oh, yes. You ask Rocky. And that's not all. We took her out after the party."

"Where?"

"Where else? The place you told me about."

"Well, how was it?"

"A long story but we had a good time."

"How, how?"

"A long story, my friend."

I could not make out what exactly they were talking about. All that I gathered was that it was about Ruby Elena and a party and a car and their going out with her. I didn't want to believe whatever suspicion flitted through my mind. But I kept thinking of the place they went to and what they did. I kept thinking until I felt like crying and wanting to smash the wall to pieces. I wanted to smash their mouths to pieces, too, so they would stop talking about my Ruby Elena. I thought then about my uncle's fish dynamite in beer bottles. I wish I had one of those bottles. I would have thrown it into their room to stop them from talking that way about my Ruby Elena. I went to bed feeling as if all my entrails were gone.

That Saturday, a week before the Christmas break, I decided to see Ruby Elena. At the university convocation two days before, she had smiled at me. There was a man with her, but she smiled at me. I took that as an indication that somehow she had known I was crazy about her. At last, I said to myself, the sound waves, or light waves, had carried the spirit of my pure love to her, and she was responding to it. My love was pure as light, and as long as she was human, she would open her eyes to it. She couldn't help it any more than she could help being Ruby Elena, or seeing the light of the sun. She knew it now, at last. Her smile was an invitation.

So I decided it was time I told her about my love. I polished my shoes until they shone like new. The trouble was they had very pointed toes, like dancing shoes, and my large plebeian feet could not fit comfortably into them. For this reason my shoes curled upward as if they were afraid to touch the ground.

I pressed my khaki trousers and white polo shirt. I spent half an afternoon trying to straighten the starched lines of the trousers. They became so stiff and sharp they could cut lizards in half, although I didn't have time to verify that. I asked my roommate to spare me a few drops of his Royal Pub Cologne. They did not mix well with the smell of cheap pomade that greased my crew-cut hair. But it didn't bother me. I wasn't too particular about the odd mixture. It was enough, I thought, that I didn't smell of brine.

I decided, too, to spend my last fifteen pesos on a gift for her. I thought of those purple grapes at the grocery.

I felt light in spite of the rain. Christmas songs and jingles were in the air. They colored my world. On my way to the grocery I side-stepped the puddles as much as I could. I didn't want my shoes to be plastered with mud. The puddles were colored. They reflected the colored light bulbs and blinkers from the houses of the rich. My world was like the puddles, suddenly transformed by the colors of Christmas.

I bought the grapes. Two small cellophane bags cost me twelve pesos and fifty centavos. The salesgirl put them in a larger, brown paper bag. I tucked it under my shirt so it wouldn't get wet in the rain. I wanted to taste the grapes to see if they were sweet, but there was no way of getting at them through the perforations without breaking open the cellophane bags. And I didn't want to defile my gift by eating a part of it. Grapes, after all, were foods of the gods and goddesses, some books say. But I must confess my mouth watered for the juice and succulent flesh of the fruit. But I was hurrying. It was already seven-thirty in the evening, and the rain made me hurry. I was also rehearsing my lines, turning the words over and over in my head.

I reached the ladies' dormitory. My shoulders were damp. Is Ruby Elena here? I asked the girl at the desk. Take your seat, she said. Then she called her through the intercom. Ruby Elena, personal call. No answer. Ruby Elena, personal call. Still no answer. I was beginning to feel warm. Ruby Elena, personal call. Out. I heard the shout through the intercom. She's out, the girl at the desk repeated to me. She looked at me and smiled. I couldn't tell whether it was out of pity or not. Maybe she thought it was funny, seeing me standing there with one hand holding the bag of grapes under my shirt. I said I would wait for Ruby Elena.

The lobby of the dormitory was spacious and full of students. They were talking, giggling, chattering, laughing, doing all sorts of nonsense to make themselves happy, or simply to kill time. Some lovers were holding hands, looking contented like married couples in portraits. A green, synthetic Christmas tree stood in one corner. Around it, on the floor, was a pile of boxes, brightly wrapped with colored paper and conspicuous ribbons. Each branch of the tree was covered with cotton to simulate snow. Decorative balls of diverse colors and Christmas cards hung from the symmetrical branches. Coiled around the tree was the wiring of the blinking bulbs. Now the blinkers lighted the electric clock and the silver star on top of the tree, now they didn't. Off and on, off and on, went the lights, blinking like stupid eyes. After a while they began to bother my eyes. I must have sat there in the lobby for over an hour. For when I looked at the clock again, it was past nine. It had stopped raining. I felt for the bag of grapes under my shirt. The paper bag was damp with my perspiration, and its bottom was giving way. I took it out. I must have shuffled my feet noisily. Those near me saw me crumpling the paper bag in my hands. I felt harassed by their furtive glances and whispers. I felt like an intruder, crashing into their little circle of happiness, or worse like one with a dreadful, incurable skin disease. I stood up and started to leave.

I had not gone far from the dormitory when two heads of brilliant lights suddenly flashed full on my face. It was a car running fast towards me. The light blinded me. I stepped aside quickly. I closed my eyes a full minute, but still I could see two bloody balls of light. I heard the screech of tires, and the water from the puddles splashed on me, soaking half of my body. I opened my eyes and caught a glimpse of a well-shaped head and a long neck looking out from the car window, turning her head to look at me, long and hard, as if she was concerned or worried. Yes, she waved to me as if I were an old friend. I brushed the muddy water off my shirt. The horn blew, and there was laughter trailing out from the car. The tail-lights turned orange. I could make out the heads of several men in the backseat.

I hurried back to the men's dormitory. I didn't forget to look up at the sky, at all the starry glitter high, high up. Imagine a seabed with a million oysters, and each oyster was open, each showing one large pearl in it. The night sky was like that. It was like a summer evening in the fishing village back home. It was a time for singing boat songs, a time for dreaming of faraway lands. I couldn't see the puddles ahead of me. I stepped into many of them. Water seeped through my shoes and socks. I made lapping sounds with my shoes as I limped my way across the R.O.T.C. parade ground. When I reached the yard of the dormitory, I looked up at the sky once more. I raised my arms and crushed the bags of grapes in my hands. I crushed them hard until my fingers ached. The juice ran down my arms and onto my shoulders and down to my belly. I didn't let go of the bags of grapes until there was no more juice to squeeze from the fruit. Like a baseball in my right hand I hurled each bag against a clump of Japanese bamboo that stood near the door. Each time I didn't forget to curse the devils.

I climbed the three flights of stairs up to my room. I passed by the bathroom to piss. I licked my fingers to find out if the grapes were sweet. They were sour.

(1979)

Ruth T. Sarreal

Born 1979, Manila, Philippines; immigrated to the U.S. 1980

Brain Drain

In the 1960s many Filipino engineers, doctors, nurses, scientists, and other professionals immigrated to the United States seeking a better life. There were so many of them that they were referred to as "Brain Drain" in the Philippines. The increasing turmoil brought about by the Marcos dictatorship drove even more Filipinos away, some seeking political asylum in America.

About the Author

Ruth T. Sarreal studied Corporate Communication and English at the University of Texas at Austin. She has lived in the United States and Hong Kong. She writes short fiction and poetry, and enjoys traveling to new places. She has been spotted crossing Abbey Road, crawling through the Cu Chi tunnels, and riding an elephant in India.

Short Answer

— **Ruth T. Sarreal**

How does it feel to watch him hold her hand? How does it feel when he puts his arm around her but looks back to see if you are watching? Do you let him know that you are watching? Are you really seeing? Are you looking at him or at her? Are you wishing you were her?

What did you do when you first noticed him noticing you? Did you blush? Did you feel awkward? Did you say something to him? Did you look away and shake your hair into your face the way you do when you feel shy? Or did you look him in the eye and give him your sweetest smile?

How did you feel when you first heard about your mother? Did your heart come up into your throat and choke you? Why did you say nothing, cry no tears? Did you hold your sister as she cried no, no, no! Did you see your father reach for the bottle of scotch he keeps on the top shelf in the kitchen pantry? What did you do when he locked himself up in their bedroom that whole week? Who made sure he ate? Who made sure you ate? Did you eat?

What is it about sitting in the middle of the grassy area on campus that makes you happy? What gives you that sense of peace that lets you almost relax? When you sit there, under the shade, and the wind is blowing so gently, and you lean your head back and close your eyes, are you sleepy? Is that your happy face?

What is that scar on your left foot from? Why do you wear sandals even in the dead of winter? Did your mother give you the handkerchief that is always in your backpack, wadded up under your copy of *The Republic*? Have you read that book? Do you plan to?

What's the most fun you've had over a summer? Why do you like being in the water? When did you learn how to swim? How long have you wanted to join the swim team? Why haven't you ever tried out? What makes you think you wouldn't make it? Why listen to what your father says? Where is your father?

Why don't you listen to music when you drive? How can you stand the silence? Why do you speed so fast? Who are you trying to leave? Where are you going? Are you scared it will be gone before you get there? Why can't you say no? Why don't you speak up for yourself? Why don't you speak up? Why do you speak so softly? Why be so timid? What are you afraid of? Why are you so uncertain? Why can't you help it?

Where were you last night when we called you? Why didn't you come watch a movie with us like we had planned? Do you think he's better company than we are? What did you do instead? What time did you come home last night?

Who is that in the picture on your dresser? Where did you meet Jen? How many times have you gone to summer camp with her? Will you be her best friend in ten years? Twenty? What do you hate most about her?

Why do you get so jealous? Do you feel insecure? Why is it so hard to be happy? Does it hurt you to smile? Are you melancholy? Are you sad?

Why don't you eat meat? Why can't you stand the smell? Where do you get your protein? What do you eat instead? How come you don't drink milk? Why don't you work out?

When was the first time you broke up with him? How many more times did you break up after that? Why do you always fight? Why don't you put up more of a fight? Why haven't you left him for good? Who cares if he finds someone new? Why can't you be stronger?

Why do you pray so earnestly? Are you praying those times when you're staring off and your eyes are blank but your lips are moving, soundless? For what are you praying? To whom do you pray? Are your prayers answered? Why don't you go to church?

Why don't you ever want to have children? Don't you think your husband will? Why don't you think you'd make a good mother? What makes a good mother? What was yours like? Did you pray for her? Did it help?

Have you tried drugs? Which ones? How did they make you feel? Which did you like best? Where do you get them? Why aren't you addicted? Are the highs worth the lows?

What is that song you always listen to? How does it go . . . say you'll stay / don't come and go like you do / sway my way / yeah I need to know all about you . . . ? Why do you always listen to it? Don't you care that it annoys your roommate? How close are you to her? How come you didn't even notice when she got her hair cut? Why don't you talk to each other anymore? Will you later? How come it's so hard for you to talk?

Do you feel your hands shaking before you go on stage? Does your stomach feel empty even though you've eaten? Does it make loud, rumbling noises? Are they all you hear as you play the first few notes? When do you lose the uneasy, nervous feeling? Has he ever come to hear you perform? Does it make you feel better knowing that he is not watching?

What did it mean when you slammed the door so hard that a framed picture fell off the wall this morning? Why did you leave in such a rush? Why did he look angry and sad and like he had tasted something sour as he watched you drive off? Where did you go? What was there?

Why do you have bags under your eyes? Why don't you sleep more? Does studying really take up that much time? Where do you study? Why do you study? What do you study? What's your major? Is that the right one for you? Why do you have to settle? Why don't you go for what you want? Is he what you want? Are you what he wants?

(2002)

HOME

They were the same streets, with the same houses painted white and blue, the white-washed walls painted in fresco in bad imitation of granite.

— Jose Rizal

Rogelio Cruz

Born 1976, Manila, Philippines

About the Author

Rogelio Cruz has a B.A. (Psychology) from the Ateneo de Manila in 1997, and is an M.A. candidate (Psychology) from the same university. He is also now part of his own research consulting group. His fiction has been published in *Heights, The Philippine Graphic, Likhaan*, and *The Literary Review* (U.S.A.). At the moment he is about to venture into writing his very first novel.

Old Manila

The name "Manila" originated from the "*nilad*" or rushes found in the swampy areas of old Manila. "*May nilad*" meaning "with nilad" eventually became "Manila." The Spanish Miguel Lopez de Legazpi founded the City of Manila in May 1571 upon the ruins of Rajah Sulayman's kingdom by the Pasig River. The medieval walled city of Intramuros (meaning "within the walls") was created. Many other settlements grew outside the walls (Extramuros), including San Miguel, Sta. Cruz, Quiapo, and Binondo. Because the sprawling City of Manila fronts a bay and has the Pasig River running through it, many areas are prone to flooding.

Most of what I've written in my story is real. The flash floods are real, and, stuck in one of those floods a couple of years ago, I really saw a yellow kayak sailing down an avenue. And the old pillared buildings and bridges and broken railways really do seem to tell about a city where people lived handsomely; but today, Manila is tired and old. Its air is the most polluted in Southeast Asia. To keep it barely alive, people are beginning to tear down historic pieces of architecture one by one, replacing them with shopping malls, or other more practical structures.

Flooded

— Rogelio Cruz

Manila was strange. It yielded not the usual parallel city streets and consecutively numbered blocks, but triangles, circles, and other haphazard spaces that brushed at the ends of one's nerves pleasantly. Fritz suspected that the original plan, a century ago, was affluence: sparse black-and-gray vehicles trudging narrow roads on a damp and drowsy Sunday morning, open-air orchestras, an aviary, the Sky Room. The skeleton of it was still there; but its once white and pastel flesh was now bloated with the sweet-rotten color and smell of poverty, of phlegm and urine in the open gutters. The dainty roads now proved to be traffic hell; the corner statues and whores were curses to each other—because of one, the other had too little space. Worst of all, when the rain struck it blind and flushed all the filth the cavities of its dying buildings never ran out of, the city drowned in a sick fluid the color of coffee and milk.

Fritz and Jan were caught in the flash flood. When they left Rizal Memorial after watching the basketball tournament, it was sunny and humid; then the sun died like a lighted match thrown into a ditch, and the slick, damp, rueful silver of rain clouds drained everything of all their color. The view from their windshield shifted quick as the next slide on a carousel, with a blinding white sheet of rain the intermediate frame: the next thing Jan knew, he was keeping his foot on the gas so the water wouldn't get into the muffler as they trudged Rizal Avenue. Along its deepest portion they even saw a yellow kayak speeding past them. The chaos of the city and the chaos of the weather were one. It signified the nearing of the end, they thought, when God just might opt to destroy this pathetic place, and start all over again.

They ended up at Gov. Forbes. It was strangled with cars, and they didn't move for an hour and a half. Jan decided to create a counterflow. He wedged his car out sharply from the gridlock and sped down the opposite lane, but to no avail: the intersection was impossible to pass, and he had nowhere else to go. He retreated.

This lane of Gov. Forbes was empty. It was the only road that was passable at all; and though it led away from Jan's and Fritz's destination, and to unlit, stranger parts of the city, it gave, especially if one did not stare out too far, the illusion that it was the way home. For a moment, Jan seemed to have given in to this illusion: he sped down the lane, until he reached the end of the paved part. Then he hesitated as he realized they were about to enter a colony of shanties, that seemed to be slowly sinking into mud, lighted only by whatever threads of blue moonlight could escape from the dense sky.

"Maybe we should just stay in one place until the floods subside," Jan told Fritz.

Fritz sighed deeply and stretched inside the car. "Damn. Don't expect us to be home before tomorrow, then."

Jan feigned banging his head against the steering wheel. "I want to go home, man."

"Me too," Fritz said.

Jan calculated a possible route. The car, this homunculus he controlled with his hands and feet, skated around the deserted road, jutting its nose into this corner or that, while Fritz froze and frowned in his seat. If he were asked for an exemplar of a face that kept cool in any situation, he would give Jan's: as he played the wheel, the pedals, and gears like a skilled instrumentalist, he kept his already thin lips terse, but not too tense; strength reserved itself in the sinews of his neck as he turned back to look or peer forward, while his almond-shaped eyes remained in their elongated state, as relaxed as his limp bangs. Fritz himself looked at the side mirror and saw his own face in the half-dark, eyes perpetually in shock, lips forever in an anxious pout. He was beginning to feel useless.

Jan turned to a side street, where a few men idled in front of a lit *sari-sari* store. He asked for directions; a skinny, greasy man told him that the road led to where they wanted to go. It would bring them, he said, to Felix Huertas, which would then bring them to Antipolo, then Retiro, then Amoranto, and they would end up sweetly redeemed at Araneta Avenue. The man waved to the direction in front of them, assuring them the flood on this street was only shallow.

The two friends stared at the lake of brown water in front of them.

"What do you think?" asked Jan.

"It's worth a try," Fritz said.

"How deep is it there?"

"The man said it's not that deep."

A passenger jeep emerged from behind them, moved ahead, and plunged into the flood. It shook at the impact of the invisible potholes, and its tires completely disappeared into the water. Jan backed out frantically. They were driving on Gov. Forbes again, though they didn't know where to go.

"There's another street over there," Fritz said, pointing to another dark alley, where another skinny, greasy man stood. When they reached it, Jan rolled his window down again and asked.

"*Saan ba kayo papunta* (Where are you going)?" the man asked him back.

"Quezon City, *ho*."

"*Pwedeng Dimasalang* (Dimasalang is OK)," the man replied. "*Kaliwa kayong Elias, kanan kayong Blicera . . . Dimasalang kayo.* (Left on Elias, right on Blicera . . . Go to Dimasalang)."

"You're more familiar with Dimasalang, aren't you?" Fritz said.

"Yeah," Jan said.

"*Diretso lang kayo dito* (Go straight here)," the man said.

Jan looked intently out the windshield. "*Hindi naman ho baha* (It's not flooded)?"

"*Hindi naman* (Not really)."

They thanked the man and moved. There was indeed, no flood. The end of the street, however, where they had to take the left, was blocked off, and men were signaling them to take the right instead.

There was water where they turned. "It's getting deeper again," said Jan, looking hard out the windshield, afraid to move on. He was revving the motor up again in fear.

"Probably won't get any deeper than this," Fritz said. "Look, all the cars are going that way anyway. Just go on." A few other vehicles were trudging ahead of them, and one or two would appear from behind them, all going forward.

It was also true that there was no space for any of them to back out. Jan followed the queue of cars and when he turned right, the car sank deeper into water. "Shit," he curtly exclaimed. The street was totally dark.

"Shit," said Fritz. "But go on—look, all of them can go through it. Don't stop. Go on. Just go."

In fact the queue roared on, and Jan stepped on the gas. The black car sliced through the black water, sparking froth at its fringes. After what could have been no more than thirty seconds, but what felt like an entire long minute, the water subsided and they hit another intersection.

"There," Fritz said.

The street was not flooded, but he didn't know where they were now. The car in front of them held up only enough to get out of danger and now gave. They deftly overtook it and brought their own car to an abrupt stop.

The two of them puffed air out their cheeks. Barefoot soaked men rushed to the broken car and tried to help the owner, inspecting it, shouting orders and signals to others approaching them, gesturing with their hands to guide the unstranded vehicles to another brightly lit intersection. The cars were lining up once more in front of Jan; there was another gridlock.

"*Manong, ano hong kalye 'yang nasa dulo* (What street is that up ahead)?" he asked a man who had been barking directions to the motorists and shaking a can of coins in one hand. Jan pointed at the cars.

"Forbes," the man said. He looked away and resumed his calling out and can-rattling.

"*Putik* (Mud)," Jan muttered.

"*Ano bang kalye gusto ninyong puntahan* (Which street is your destination)?" the man asked, returning.

"Dimasalang," Jan said.

"*Ay, dito puwede* (This is fine)," he said, and motioned to another narrow side-street to their left. "*Deretsuhin n'yo lang 'to, Dimasalang na* (Go straight and you'll get to Dimasalang)." The muddy water in it sparkled under the car's headlights.

"*Malalim 'yata ho ang tubig diyan* (The water looks deep)."

"*Hindi, mababaw lang* (No, it's shallow)," the man insisted. "*Eto, o* (There)." He pointed to his companion emerging from the cavernous, totally unlit side-street, the water reaching only up to his ankle. "*Kaya 'yan* (The car can make it)."

"*Sigurado ho ninyo* (Are you sure)?"

"*Oo* (Yes)," said the man, his voice lilting in reassurance.

The men helped Jan maneuver the car into the small space and manage the sudden rocky decline at the start of the sidestreet. While Jan was busy he asked Fritz to produce a five-peso coin, or something, to give to them. As the two started to advance, Fritz dropped two five-peso coins into the man's can.

Halfway through the water deepened again; Jan clicked his tongue in ire and stepped on the gas, and Fritz unconsciously clung onto the overhead hanger on his side. The street was an excuse of a passage between two endless firewalls, a suffocating channel almost too narrow for the size of their car. If someone came from the opposite side, they were dead. The farther they got into it, however, the clearer it was to them nobody was with them here.

"Where's Dimasalang?" Jan said gravely.

It was possible that Jan saw ahead what Fritz would himself in a second. "Dimasalang's at the end of this," Fritz said, "the man—"

And then they were stunned: "*Puta!*"

The revelation was both majestic and frightening: getting out of the alley, they had entered the sea, its darkness one with the sky's, its surface quivering in its depth. The stone buildings were but islands; the water seemed to stretch a thousand kilometers. A distant glow of headlights to Jan's right urged him to steer there; but he didn't have any choice.

"They fucking said it wasn't flooded!" Fritz cried.

"He's going, Fritz, he's going," Jan said, referring to the car. They turned the air-conditioner off and opened the windows. The engine bellowed like a half-slaughtered beast, then finally died. "There you go."

Jan turned the keys to click off the already dead vehicle, and sighed; and the two froze, unable to look down, only too aware of the water's surface already tickling their waists, the innocent yet vulgar smell of earth and sewage.

"Fuck," they recited again in unison. The car rocked gently to the undertow. They could hear only sea-sounds: the absolute stillness of the air around a stranded boat, the collected swish-swash of vehicles sailing far away. For a moment they heard the solitary laughter of some street-children playing in the muck, coming their way; this faded as they swam on and left them. A second set of splashing sounds came nearer as another drenched half-dressed man appeared in front of Fritz's window. "Boss *tulak natin* (Boss, shall I push it)?" he offered.

"*Tutulak din kami* (We'll help push)," Jan said. The two abandoned passengers opened their doors heavy against the water and stepped out.

"*Huwag na, ako na lang* (I'll do it)," the man said. "*Baka mapasma pa kayo* (You might get sick)."

"*Tangina,*" Jan said, "*para naman kasing di pa kami basa* (It's not like we're not already wet)."

The two pushed from either side, holding the arch of their doorways, while the man pushed from behind.

"*Liko natin d'yan sa kanan* (Let's push to the right)," the man told them, "*bababaw d'yan sa may* St. Jude (It's shallow over at St. Jude)." Jan did as he was instructed and steered to the right at the corner of Dimasalang, waiting for the promised end.

"Jan," Fritz called soberly. He flashed at him. Jan stared back, held his gaze, his eyes still the narrow slits that looked like they were closed. "Do you know what's happening?"

Jan looked away and laughed. He laughed through his windpipe, laughed like he was almost choking. His laughter made Fritz feel light, with both gladness and fear: that what had happened to them was not as fatal as it seemed, that it could have been his fault, but he seemed forgiven anyway. As they approached the corner of Dimasalang the water subsided, the heavy resistance against their legs gradually being dispelled until Fritz was merely kicking diluted mud out of his way. The dry strip was filled with stranded vehicles like theirs; they wouldn't be able to get out of it not until tomorrow, probably—but compared to the thought of drowning, it was an oasis, and they probably would want to stay there.

(2002)

Connie Jan Maraan

Born 1959, Annapolis, Maryland

About the Author

Connie Jan Maraan teaches fiction and creative writing with the Department of Literature and Philippine Languages at De La Salle University (D.L.S.U.). Her collection of short stories entitled *Transient: Stories 1977-1994* was published by the D.L.S.U. Press in 1995 and nominated for the Philippine National Book Award that same year. She was holder of the Henry Lee Irwin Chair for Creative Writing at Ateneo de Manila University for school year 2000-2001. She is working on her first novel.

Manila in the 1980s

This story was written about and against the backdrop of downtown Manila in the early 1980s. It describes the "common man's" mode of transportation, the jeepney, known locally at that time as "the King of the Road." The title of the story, "The Boundary," refers to the percentage of a day's earnings that a jeepney driver must turn over to his employer; metaphorically, it is a reference to the "limit" the main character reaches before arriving at her epiphany.

What perhaps attracts the character of Lisa Bernal to the city is its diversity—Quiapo, the opening setting, is home not only to the Church of the Nazarene and its patrons, but to the Muslim quarter as well. It is also in close proximity to two of the oldest commercial centers in the country, Escolta and Sta. Cruz; and is linked to C. M. Recto Avenue, the city's University belt.

The Boundary

— Connie Jan Maraan

"Summer's Here" was the music blaring from a jeepney stereo one particularly steamy day in April on Taft Avenue. It was one of several dozen beach-flavored tunes being revived by a Top Forty–oriented radio station in its bid to relieve listeners of the sweltering heat, but the idea behind it was nauseating enough to make even the most dedicated sun-and-surf harmony lover swear-off radio altogether. To make matters worse, the disc jockeys persisted in making their fake American-twanged voices heard over the rip-tides, reaching the height of tropical monotony, and landing a direct hit upon the ears of a Filipino American kid named Lisa Bernal. Sneaker-clad and starved, she was programmed to attack a cheeseburger and fries—to go.

The music of "Summer's Here" was part of an unconscious ploy among the jocks, with their repulsive twangs, to be tragically hip in celebrating this, Bernal's ninth year of serving time in the Philippines. Having lived on this rock anchored deep beneath its waters, she somehow knew that the Philippines would forever remain fixed upon the sea floor, never to drift out into the Pacific blue and crash unexpectedly—but with precision and accuracy—upon the California coast. In spite of her certainty, however, this scenario and other similar phenomenal occurrences were frequent features in the cinema of her sleep, vital parts of the irony made only more vivid by the sounds of "Summer's Here."

The signs were everywhere—not only in the music blasting out in super-treble from a jeep, but elsewhere as well. Skinny brown boys wore black hi-tops, Levi's, and brightly-colored tees announcing "Property of the L.A. Dodgers"; many proclaimed "I've Been to Disneyland," or were emblazoned with the words "Universal Studios"; and The Cities—New York, San Francisco, Boston, Maui, Detroit, Miami, Chicago, D.C., Dallas, Atlanta, and Baltimore—were all accounted for. Bernal cringed and thought, "Ugh—how shallow!" but she could not deny that it was familiar, just the same; and, being familiar, it created a longing.

She often wished she could rid herself of that longing. It was a ghost that had come to haunt her more and more as the years passed, preventing her from fitting in. Relatives, neighbors and classmates had come and gone or remained permanent fixtures in her life, but there was not one among them with whom she could relate with completely. The ghost shattered any hope that she might someday find someone who would understand.

So it was not unusual for her to run off to be alone and be comforted in her solitude. She turned away from people and in a kind of madness searched for things familiar. These she found in the Levi's and tees, the costumes of the streets. And there were more—khaki and fatigues, nautical stripes and marine sweatshirts, most of which had belonged to servicemen who had sailed off to The Continent in search of The Legal Tender. It was all so absurd, everyone trying to create some sort of image of themselves, but it was a false image, and yet it was not intentional. It was just a tragedy, a curse that fell upon people who wore brown skin, and lived on a rock anchored deep beneath its waters.

The jocks would not let Bernal forget that curse, and she knew it. The Americanized twang and catch-phrases were becoming increasingly pronounced, in more radio-station formats. It angered Bernal and added lines to her forehead. "Why do they refuse to use their own language?" she asked herself, she who struggled to make that language her own. "Why don't they play more of the local stuff?" she prodded. "Even if it hurts their ears and egos . . . even if it makes them wince . . . well, at least it would be true."

She had decided that the problem of metropolitan programming was an overabundance of American pop, sabotaged by brown-skinned lyricists and performed by brown-skinned vocalists. The sad state of popular music depressed her, and she knew that if people would stop and think about it long enough, it would probably cause them great pain as well. But in a moment, her agony had subsided, and a smile came upon her lips as she toyed with the idea of how wonderful it would be, "if someone could produce a hit that featured a bamboo orchestra."

Bernal's mood turned ethnic as a sudden mess of music—a confusing mix of what blasted out the jeepney speakers and what was forming in her melodic imagination—provided the perfect accompaniment to the "making movies" effect of watching people whiz by while one was seated in a moving vehicle. Having traveled though the grime arising from the construction of the city's light rail transit system, as well as from the drainage and communications projects, the jeep was now fast approaching its destination: Quiapo. Bernal enjoyed what remained of the ride, as the jeep sailed over the Pasig to the sound of a hundred and one bamboos.

Stepping off the jeep at a point just before the overpass, her feet landed on familiar turf. Out of all the urban districts Manila had revealed to her, Quiapo was the favored hang-out for this self-proclaimed child of the streets. Every so often she felt the urge to visit its shops and stalls, as there was an unexplained attraction that somehow pulled her toward the district. In its surrealistic madness, it provided an unusual sort of sanctuary, where she could go unnoticed among nameless faces, and invade the streets with joyous abandon, searching for the treasures buried among the vendors' wares.

This was also the place where she had been, in her opinion, educated; numerous brown truths had been revealed to her here, because in the surrealism there were many real things. The people of Quiapo, she later understood, were what drew her to it, the unknowing teachers of this school, who initiated her into the brown world. They were constant reminders of what the world was, as it was, when teachers were also victims, and when what was true was less important that what was false.

In Quiapo there was no Americanized twang, and brown voices sang brown songs from out of kitchenette jukeboxes. The kitchenettes served food that stimulated Malayan senses: as was proper, there were noodles of the Eastern world; and, as was fitting, there were hamburgers of the Western world—spiced up for brown palates. Everything had a taste that was beyond tasty, that was almost an attack upon the tastebuds: it was as if taste had to be intense in order to make up for the lack of quantity served by budget-conscious eatery-owners. And, Bernal was certain, each eatery was self-infested by fat, low-flying flies, just to prove how flavor-laden its dishes were.

But she would not be eating in any of these fly-infested eateries on this particularly steamy April day. On this day, as she had planned for an entire week, she would treat herself to a meal at that world-famous hamburger restaurant, the one that promised "There's a difference you'll enjoy." As she hastened down Quezon Boulevard, the image of cheese dripping over a one-hundred-percent-pure-beef-patty became more vivid, its taste almost upon her tongue; as she shut her eyes, the vision became clearer, so that it was difficult for her to keep her pace down to a fast walk.

As she turned on Recto, however, she began to slow down, disturbed by the number of people that filled the sidewalk—more than she had expected on a Thursday afternoon. As she walked on she found a small crowd trying to squeeze into the entrance of a shopping arcade that sold American goods. A banner over the glass doors explained the crowd's behavior, as it announced a one-day sale on imported canned goods and sundries. A blind man who played on a makeshift instrument for loose change had almost gotten swept away in the rush. Bernal felt her throat tighten and walked faster, moving as far away from the crowd as she could.

In her hurry to leave the crowd far behind, she suddenly found herself at the intersection that would bring her directly to the doorstep of the world-famous hamburger restaurant. Bernal heard a grumble from within.

She had grown hungrier in the rush, and the only thing that had stopped her from running straight across the street was the wall formed by vehicles that sped past on either side. She flexed both feet impatiently while waiting for the pedestrian light to turn green, and when it did, walked quickly up to the doors beneath the golden arches.

As she had expected, the place was filled with people lining up at the counter. The phenomenal thing about the world-famous hamburger restaurant was that there were always as many people behind the counter as there were in front of it. Stainless steel railings had been installed in an effort to keep customers in line, but as they reached the counter all of the lines seemed to merge, causing even more confusion. To ease the situation, attendants armed with pencils and paper had positioned themselves in the throng, and jotted down orders of customers to pass on ahead to the kitchen crew.

Bernal resolved to be patient and soon found herself in the middle of a line. She stood with her arms folded across her chest, thinking in consoling tones as a reply to her stomach's pleading, and hoping that she would have her order within a few minutes. Looking into the eating area she saw students sharing jokes in huddles, parents putting food into the mouths of infants, couples sipping on chocolate milkshakes, businessmen wiping ketchup off their neckties. The ones that she definitely could not avoid looking at were the tourists, who had trekked from their hostels in Ermita to the University belt, in attempts to savor meals that were "all wrapped up and ready to go." Whenever it was possible, they sat themselves in far corners, away from the natives.

It was for this reason that she half-loathed this restaurant, in spite of her love for cheeseburgers and fries. She knew it was the air of spotlessness, the antiseptic white formica tables and bone fiberglass seats, and the absence of flies and fish sauce, that attracted foreigners to it. Americans, basking in the belief that they remained the superior species in a country not their own, were part of the decor, and if there was anything Bernal hated more, it was the sight of Embassy wives running into each other, cloaking their snootiness with restrained voices, their lips drawn in pink *crayola*. Their attire was shamelessly and inappropriately native, the embroidery so obscenely large it practically jumped off the fabric. They never learned that it was tasteless to wear anything so commercially native, especially when the locals refused to do so themselves.

Bernal turned away and felt the hair on her forearm rise. At that moment she despised nothing more than these gaudy Americans. Even more upsetting was the thought that she was, technically speaking, one of them. It did relieve her to know that she did not look like one of them—her features and color guaranteed that much. Yet she could not deny being a bit angry that her only claim to being an American was her passport and fading memories of a childhood spent on western soil.

With a sigh she decided it might be better not to dwell on the issue. Bowing her head she was amused by the sight of a pair of dirty Caucasian feet in huaraches. Her eyes moved steadily upwards, past hairy legs, soiled cut-offs, and an old T-shirt from which bulged a grotesque beer belly. Further upwards lay the wilderness of an untrimmed beard, an offensively large nose upon which rested reflector shades, and a mass of hair that never seemed to have experienced being combed. Bernal blinked at the sight of this average tourist that somehow weakened her otherwise uncontrollable appetite. She turned the other way, preferring not to dwell upon the unpleasant appearance of this literally ugly American.

It seemed as though an eternity would pass before she would reach the counter. She gave in to monitoring the second hand of her outmoded watch, as it moved steadily from the one to the twelve. Counting each person that walked past her with food in hand, she dragged her feet across the stained tiles, wearily approaching the boundary that was the sanitized stainless steel counter. Beyond it, sitting in identical wrappers on incubated shelves, were the rewards of those who withstood the penance: Junkfood for Junkies. Bernal saw them all waiting to be devoured, and felt her mouth water.

She and the ugly American reached the counter simultaneously, but by this time she was so hungry that she did not mind his nauseating presence. Her main concern was getting her order in, taking her food away, and heading home. The counter girls, however, seemed to have disappeared, just when it was her turn.

It was not until she heard him raise his voice that she bothered to look at him. He was apparently angry.

"Hey look," he said to a woman dressed in black who had approached the counter, "would you mind getting in line?" Spit flew from out of his mouth as he threatened her, his Ray Bans seeming to glare. The situation was a common one for Bernal, who had come to find such arrogance quite trite. She could almost predict what would happen next.

"It's okay, sir," said a girl from behind the counter, the one who had come to attend to him. "She's only asking for a packet of sugar." As expected, this girl had been trained to deal tactfully with customers like him, and managed to ease the tension. She reached under the counter for the sugar and gave it to the woman, who mumbled with hostility as she walked away.

"Oh. I didn't understand what she said." The American was not apologetic. "I thought she was cutting in."

They are all so cynical, Bernal thought, disgusted at this man's haughty behavior. As if that were not bad enough, his order would be taken before hers. It had happened again, a scene so familiar to her that smiling waitresses and ugly Americans were stereotypes in her nightmare called life. She was so hungry she was near tears, yet it seemed only natural that no one would notice.

The girl behind the counter smiled, a role model in customer service. No doubt she had also been trained to choose which customers deserved her immediate attention. "May I have your order?" she said to the man.

Bernal, half-starved but still sane, noticed something strange about the way the girl spoke. It barely caught her attention at first, but as the verbal exchange at the counter progressed, it became more evident. She listened intently to the words being spoken, first by the American and then by the girl.

The man slurred some of his words and spoke through his nose. His voice had a tinny quality she could not stand, and she found it to be as repulsive as his ugly appearance.

Then the girl spoke. Bernal strained to hear what she was saying, and with some effort managed to decipher the words being said. It was then that she realized what the strangeness was. She could not do anything but stare at her.

"Could you wait a while?" the girl told the American once he had given his order. "This will probably take a few minutes."

Bernal watched the girl's mouth as it formed the words, and listened to the slur as she spoke. Suddenly, the only sound Bernal could hear was that voice, an echo of the ugly American's, the words running over and over again in her head. This girl spoke through her nose, with an all-too-familiar nasal quality, making awful sounds that rang painfully in Bernal's ears. It was a voice like the voices without faces that spoke through radio speakers, and haunted her in the sweltering heat. It was the horror of hearing that sound, the sound that was forced, that was a lie, that made things strange, that she could not bear.

It was at this point that another girl came up to Bernal to take her order, but she could not bring herself to speak. A twanging sound reverberated in her ears, and her feet brought her towards the door, past the brown faces of those who had stood behind her and now looked at her curiously. Bernal walked and walked, out of the world-famous hamburger restaurant, back into the street, until she was relieved by the sounds of voices and voices, all blending as one, all in the language she wanted desperately to be her own. She slowed down, catching her breath, and wiped the water out of her eyes.

It was still warm in the street, where the afternoon sun poked through holes in rusty old GI sheets above the stalls. Once again, Bernal moved unnoticed among nameless faces, her feet sidestepping cracks in the pavement. She needed the warmth of other bodies pressing past her, the warmth of this mass. She felt safe again.

She was halfway down Recto, walking back towards Quiapo. She saw that the crowd at the shopping arcade had gotten bigger. This time, she did not run away from them. She stopped and watched with pity as women pushed to get inside.

The blind musician was still there and, oblivious to the noise, continued to play on his makeshift instrument. She noticed that he was smiling. There were a few coins in the tin can that sat beside him, and the shine from its base could still be seen.

Bernal stuck her hands into her pockets, her fists pushing down hard and deep, and she shifted her weight from one foot to the other. Digging deeper into one pocket, her hand pressed against something she had forgotten was there. She wrapped her fingers around it, and crumpled it. She bent down and put it into the can.

She stood up and was surprised by the breeze. She let the air fill her. As she headed for home, she was no longer hungry. But she was certain that someone would be having himself a good, hot lunch.

(1983)

Alex Dean Bru

Born 1944, San Juanico, Leyte, Philippines

About the Author

Alex Dean Bru has a B.A. and an M.A. in Business Administration from the University of San Carlos, Cebu, and the University of the Philippines, respectively. He studied creative writing under Alan Dean Foster at the Los Angeles City College, and through the Long Ridge Writers Institute in Connecticut. He graduated with a Business Degree from the University of San Carlos, in Cebu City, and received his M.B.A. from the University of the Philippines, in Diliman, Quezon City. He works as Financial Controller, and lives in Chino, California with his wife, Marietta, and son, Andrew.

Lent: Good and Evil

Up until the 1960s when monumental changes were sweeping the globe, superstition was the norm and the bill of fare in the Philippine countryside. It was for me a kind of childhood journey from darkness to light, and as a youngster I found it enchanting and magical. Like the middle ages in Europe, the church was not only the focal center of spiritual attention, but also a center of visual entertainment where the priest and townsfolk presented spectacular pageantry lifted from the pages of the Bible. This was for me just as fascinating as the theater and the opera. The pageantry of the Holy Week, a celebration of days of colorful tableau and drama, from Palm Sunday to Easter Sunday, observed even now in towns and smaller cities in the Philippines, had over the years pulled ethnic superstition to the center stage, to be confronted and destroyed by the mighty power of the Christian faith—in a sense, the eternal struggle between good and evil. So, it was believed that on Good Friday, Christ died and we were defenseless against the fearsome spirits hiding within our midst, waiting to inflict horrible harm on us, the kind of which, up to this day, one who had fallen prey, has yet to reveal.

The Spirits of Kanlanti

— **Alex Dean Bru**

San Juanico Strait, 1969

It was a time for heroes and supermen when on summer nights, young and old men crowded around a long table where gallons of *bahalina* deep crimson, smooth and fine as vintage from the cool region of Burgundy, *siete viernes* for the discriminating, straight from the cool subterranean jars of Jaro, Leyte, poured freely and drained as quickly as one or another recounted tales of lost honor and redemption, and magnificent men of remarkable existence. It was not a place, nor would there be any that Padre Fabio De Alba would have wished to be, and called to memory because his place, he said, like the wind, was nowhere.

Padre's story began long before our paths crossed, his path already a wide road, mine an obscure foot walk. It is clear in my recollection, that it happened in the fifth year of my schooling because it was when my friend, Romeo, lost his name. In that year, Romeo came to be called "Inglis" after having been caught in possession of a stolen grammar book called *Correct English.* I couldn't know the extent of his embarrassment, but I thought that being one who had lost honor, he would carry this name to the grave, unless of course he grew up, got a job and came up with the money.

My story, which is the lesser one, began on the afternoon of Good Friday of 1955, when on that day an unusual crowd of people marched into the church, which had quickly filled as more inched their way inside. Why only on one day of the year the town would turn out a swelling crowd, wearing clean clothes and hear this—wearing shoes—was a mystery only Padre Fabio understood. It was *Semana Santa* (Holy Week), and it was Padre's display of pageantry, a show kept alive only in the streets of Cadiz, the church and convent furious with activity; men, women, school children, *cantors* and *cantoras*, *cofradias* and *composanteras*, and Man Lucio, *cantor mayor*, inhaling a burning *tostos* as if oxygen had run out. It was open season for sinners and lesser sinners to be seen without embarrassment in the portals of the church, sins forgiven en masse, and absolved even by an affected act of penance, delivered of course with Padre Fabio's blessings.

Clutching a *matraca* under one arm, I drove hard against the crowd that formed a knot at the door and in the process stepped on a fat fish vendor's foot, clumsily tucked in an ancient white shoe still wet with Shu-Milk shoe polish. A soft groan rose and I ducked before she could hit me with the other one. I rushed to post myself on the spot near the altar designated for boys who created the blasting noise of the *Teneblas*.

Inglis was posted behind me and his neck arched forward to my ear, eyes like those of a hawk, hunting for witches and warlocks in the crowd, and the girls that we liked but couldn't recognize because they had scrubbed and fixed themselves. He carried the latest beat in his breath while I carried history to people sitting at home. "Look there." He pointed to the sight; Man Anton hid a long scar on his neck. He had been struck by a sharp *sundang* blade when he snorted fresh blood under the bamboo floor where Agaton's wife was giving birth. He had gone there as a big black pig. There were two pigs that night, but the other one got away. It was Sulima, his wife. The blood on the ground trailed him to his house. That was what Man Anton and Sulima did: they stalked new-born babies, drank their blood, and brought sickness and diseases to them, the reason why many babies died in our town.

Now, roving along the aisle were the Twelve Apostles, who wore false beards and masks, and togas of purple, red, and yellow, and they struck flashes of fear in smaller children who unleashed frightened shrills bouncing up in echoes, around the dome of the unpainted roof. This group of twelve had combed the island since Tuesday like missionaries, praying for the sick, collecting church contributions—*O, hala, penitensya ini* (Well, then, this is sacrifice)—and they even helped celebrate birthdays.

Outside, the hot Pacific sun sent waves of piercing rays that rode upon the humid air and radiated with heat as they hit the rusty roof that had gathered salt from the sea. People and players stood there now, holding their places, and the appointed time came and passed, but Padre was nowhere. He was not inside the convent. So, the waiting crowd murmured, and the women fanned themselves more vigorously blaming it on Padre's broken back and wobbly feet. He was supposed to deliver the *Siete Palabras* (Seven Last Words) at three and lead the procession of the Corpus Cristi and *Teneblas* by nightfall, but as we stood, we faced a foreboding thought that Padre Fabio had gotten lost, so we kneeled and crossed our chests. "I knew this was coming," Inglis said then ran off. I stayed. Mother was in the crowd.

It was only on Palm Sunday when school girls shining in white stood on bamboo towers and flung their arms to the heavens, tossing blossoms and petals of flowers, which descended in a display of mystical showers. Floating above, their voices gathered in a song, Latin and soft in melody: *Hosanna, Filio David, qui veni en nomine Domine.* Padre Fabio, radiant in his chasuble led the walking crowd who brushed and waved leaves of coconut palms of many shapes, bent and folded to form patterns and embellished designs of the Christian cross, some leaves crafted to appear like butterflies and birds in flight. These offerings made for Palm Sunday would be sanctified for their mission, after Padre had rained holy water on them as they waved in the air, holy and powerful. The holy leaves, destined to be enshrined in the pedestals of homes, in the company of saints and God, are kept until their freshness turned to brown crusted twigs—or until Man Suling, the medicine woman crushed them with her callused hands into a blend of incense that exorcised demons. She would burn them to help a mother save a child lying on a sickbed, after a frightening encounter with fearsome spirits that dwelled and sent chilling sounds from the dark side of the huge *rimas* trees.

The day turned into a bright April night. After the sun had sunk into the sea, and a hundred cicadas looking for mates had shrilled, the full moon sprayed its rays on treetops and cast shadows of children playing in the dusty streets, as it sailed across the sky. Above, the rushing breeze from the vastness of the Pacific swept in, filtered in the warm breathe of the tropic sun, and sent waves of gentle ocean breeze upon the coconut palms and spreading *acacia* trees. Flares of torches and lamps lit the island as they scanned the night, but Padre Fabio, perhaps swept away, was some place beyond.

Daylight found him in the sea, like one wounded on the shore, unknowing and alone. A promising sign of life was on his breath, like one who had struggled away in a long and painful journey.

Padre Fabio De Alba walked with a crooked back and a walking stick, and wore a black soutane and a safari hat. His imposing tower of more than six feet and wide shoulders had now been reduced by some physical mutation to match the smallness of the men and women in the island. The years of toil, the foot trips to the villages, and his response to his flock's beck and call had created an irreparable tear. His gait now unstable, called for a walking cane, which he raised to hush up children who had shouted profanities while playing in the streets, and sometimes, to drive away and separate romantically-driven dogs, male and female that had crossed his way without regard for his reverential presence. "*Oy, sin verguenza! Kan hino ini mga ido?* (Shameless! Who owns these dogs?)" Patches of white thin hair and a scraggy white beard had become a shadow of his brown hair and green eyes of his European youth. His skin, now dark and brown, had adapted to the piercing rays of the tropic sun.

Padre had a lost history, so it seemed, as no relation or friend came to visit him, and the postman never brought him letters that were personal in nature. His opinion about this was that he had been sent by One without beginning nor origin, so Padre went in the same way. He never spoke about his home or family. Recollections from him were few and rare, for he wasn't one to look back, and histories and beginnings were of no consequence. He was *Katsila*, a Spaniard, born in a town near Valencia to a family consigned to the church. They had sent him to replace a brother who died in the seminary. His sister, his only living relative, was a nun and the Abbess of Santa Clara Monastery in Manila. He spoke several languages and spoke the dialect of Waray accented, and interjected with Spanish expletives. He thought the way to bring people to God was to retreat from the excesses of the city, and his search ended when he was sent to our parish. With little help from a faithless town, as he would chastise us when he was fasting, he went on to build the church, every rock and stone, carved by his hands, and soon his goodness and purpose won the spirit of the people, and his heart was won by the beauty and pureness of the island.

On the third day the Reverend delighted everyone when he rose from his sickbed and delivered the familiar leaden sermon everyone slept through. He thought he saw the procession leave without him. He kicked his cane and raced toward a cluster of light guided only by his failing eyesight. The brightness came from the fishermen's torches and gaslights that lit the fish traps set around the waters that bordered the bays of the island. From a distance, the parish was a stretch of land that dangled from a hill and gradually dropped to the sea. The tropical rain and showers maintained the lush growth of tall coconut trees and bamboo groves. From the sea at night, amber lights from windows of straw and wooden houses flickered against the shadows of the dark growth of tall trees and green vegetation.

The dark and moonless nights brought stories about stalking creatures and evil spirits that walked the empty streets. But when the moon was round, we became emboldened to recall what we had heard and recount what many claimed to have seen.

Inglis gathered us and anyone willing to listen about Padre's secret meetings with the strange lady and her connection to evil. Gatherings like this drew people, as though tuning in to popular Rafael Yabut on DZRH. Inglis talked about fearsome creatures that dwelt in the dark mountain ridges of Kanlanti: the *agta, kapre, sigbin*, and the ever popular *aswang*, poor old woman by day, queen of the airways by night, and visitors from the north, *manananggal* and *tikbalang* and two imports from Hollywood: Dracula and Frankenstein. In the blackness of night they traveled and came to town to stalk us and frolic with the locals—the *multo*, the *ungo*, *santilmo*, and the *minatay* that parked the coffin in the middle of the bridge, and the domestic *duwende* that struck and dropped *calderos* at midnight. These ghoulish spirits, Inglis said, abducted Padre to convert him, and the timing was more than perfect. It was Good Friday and Christ is dead, the church powerless. It was time for *anting-anting* (talisman), time to make pacts with the devil. They made him fly, only Padre mistook the fishing lights for the procession, so he landed on the traps below, and when they pulled the nets, he struggled with the fish.

The sacristan knew this strange woman had sent Padre bottles filled with mysterious powders. After this woman arrived, people talked about sightings and encounters with crocodiles and snakes. Disaster struck when we skipped school for a swim in the stream, and a crocodile crawled up. We ran and shouted for help, and the commotion brought the principal out. We drove the devil away with rocks and poles but none of us were spared the sting of the schoolmaster's stick. At home, Inglis' mother found a green snake coiled underneath the pillow where his brother slept.

The full moon rose and Querico, who spied the woman from across his house, swore she was a witch from Kanlanti, and the crocodiles her subjects. "The crocodiles hunted for her and she shared their food," he told us, and we spat. When she moved containers and boxes to her boat, we thought it was time to uncover her deadly secret. Querico had in his pocket a bottle containing a potion of roots and oil, which he carried whenever he walked in the woods. The potion could detect evil spirits and witches. If evil was near, the bottle would fizz and sometimes explode. The strange woman saw us and smiled and turned around. We stared straight into her eyes. Witches don't stare back because light doesn't show in their eyes. Some witches don't have pupils. "Must be a bad teacher." Inglis laughed, and got pelted with rocks. We fixed our eyes on her. But she turned away, uneasy now, and spoke again almost upset (the bottle must have been working), "If you young men stop staring and help move these boxes, I would pay you money." We hadn't received such an offer before, so we did as we were told. We also forgot about the bottle. When work was done, we bolted away and feasted on the *siopao* and smoked the sticks of cigarettes her money had bought.

School days were drawing near when Padre was struck down again. He lay inside the convent sinking in silent pain. Inglis pointed out that Padre's condition had become worse now that Sulima cooked his food, sending him dinners of boiled *gabi* leaves at night. Once he dined at the mayor's house and when dinner was over, Padre walked out to the sink to breathe some fresh air. The guests had to assure one another of the clarity of their eyes, because they witnessed a sight most remarkable, that of Padre (right in front of their own eyes—God strike them if they lied, they swore) standing straight, raising his head, and in the light of dusk coughing and a swarm of black wasps flew out of his gaping mouth.

A growing typhoon hovered around, and coconut trees bent, and banana trunks crashed at our feet, and days with dark clouds heavy with moisture and cold air kept everyone inside. Howling winds from the east grew louder, blowing another kind of terror as Padre's condition turned critical. Heavy rains poured day and night, the clouds hung low, followed by blasts of forceful winds. The Reverend went on to celebrate Mass, the last he would ever say, like a performer's final act, a scene on which black curtains must fall. There, inside the dark and empty church where a candle could not be lit, Padre felt the burning pain he had taken for lassitude and the dimming vision that had kept him in bed for days. He lifted the offering of wine as he had done a thousand times and as always, it had been blessed with gifts he gave his flock in silent celebration. But the blessing didn't come that day. Before it could reach the hand of God, the goblet slipped, and later people found the old man soft and silent on the hard and cold cement. They strapped Padre to a chair, covered him with a white sheet, and gently carried him away.

There was a time when the Reverend was always there for everyone, in joyful celebration of birth and marriage, sickness at home and most fearsome of all, when the spirit leaves, and the body becomes lifeless on earth. When this time was at hand, we drew back in fear and chose to look away. It was only from behind his frock and his cross, and the powerful words that came out as his voice, that we were able to look at the face of danger and death, not without fear, but with confidence because he stood by our side. There would be no one as fearless as he had been, to stand by him, now that it was his turn to face the fearsome foe. We recalled how he had driven away the demons that haunted the empty streets at night, which had kept our doors and windows locked, our little lamps burning all night, above the chamber pot, and the terrifying creatures of darkness that roamed in the recesses of our minds. Now greater fear came to possess us for we would have to face many perils and many deaths without his invincible stance that wielded godly power. To a people who feared both life and death, he had shown us in his work how one must live and in what one must believe.

No one in the parish visited our priest, but the kindness of the Strange Woman, who was a medical doctor sent by the Bishop, saw him through in his most difficult hours. She had confined Padre to the convent, and from her we came to know, that he had endured deadly germs and diseases that had invaded his body and lungs, and death was waiting at his door.

By daybreak, the gusts of winds had left, but the sun did not shine to warm our cold spirits and fearful hearts. At the seashore, we brushed coconut palms and leaves in the air, and prayed a hopeful goodbye for Padre Fabio.

Years came and went before I understood what Padre Fabio and his mission had left behind. It was the essence and force of a work of a lifetime, manifested in all the rocks, posts, and stones his hands had built, a monument that stood in the shadow of God. I found the part of his story that had been lost, perhaps lost only in the darkness of our faith, for histories of goodness can be found only by looking into the heart. As he walked with us, a bigger history was unfolding, waiting to be written. He had given us a lifetime, the only one he had, to be in our midst bringing the light he had lit from the Master to brighten the road for everyone to follow. He had said, "The road to God is short and straight, the road away from God, long and endless."

Years later when I left the island for the seminary, they built a bridge shooting like a path of stones, rising from the main and came down on one end of the island, and the concrete pavement carried wires of electric current. The fishermen's torches and gaslights were dimmed in favor of the brightness of mercury lamps, borne by steel beams to spread glowing light on the streets along the water. The streets are still dusty but now quiet and empty, and the children no longer play under the moon. Its rays have grown dull and can't cast a shadow. Even if it were full, they would stay in, and sit with family and friends, all senses attuned to the magic joy coming from the electric box, that shows people speaking the language of the city. Then, the Japanese loggers built campsites on the ridges of Kanlanti, and the tide floated the timber to ships anchored in the bay.

After I finish Mass every Sunday, people linger in the convent, its walls now covered with history, photographs, and pictures of the island. Curious children take time to study the faded photographs of Padre Fabio, searching for clues of black wasps flying out of the old Reverend's smiling face.

(2002)

M. S. Sia

Born 1948, Samar, Philippines

About the Author

M. S. Sia is the author of a novel titled *The Fountain Arethuse: a Novel Set in the Unversity Town of Leuven* published in England.

The Town Called Guiuan

In the southernmost tip of the island of Samar in Eastern Visayas, Philippines is a town called Guiuan. Regularly buffeted by typhoons yet richly endowed with natural beauty, Guiuan has retained its traditional ways of life despite making some progress in many areas. Practically surrounded by water, including the vast Pacific Ocean, it is remarkable for its beaches. Growing up in this town inevitably meant spending a lot of time at sea or on the beaches. Its remoteness also led to much day-dreaming and storytelling among the youngsters as they dreamt of distant shores or better lives. And yet its own attractions also had a way of persuading some to remain or even to return. This fictional story, set in Guiuan, captures the mood and the scene of the early childhood days of some boys in this town. The story is part of a novel-in-progress titled *Those Distant Shores*.

Below the Belt

— M. S. Sia

The gentle breezes that cooled the sandy beach of Dumpao were particularly tempting to the youngsters. It was only a little after eight, but already the sun's rays warming their brown skins forecasted another hot tropical day. It was the kind of day best spent where else? but at the beach.

The signs were there. Even the blue sky was beckoning to them. To the boys the sky was like the ocean itself, with only a couple of tiny "white ships," looking as if they were spots on the horizon, sailing on it. The coconut trees that usually stood like lifeguards scanning the horizon were now, with the help of the sea breezes, more like slaves fanning these boys with their leaves. And, seemingly to pass the time, the foamy waves kept bashing the big boulders. But always being the loser in this combat, the waves, in the manner of paying the price, had to spit their watery wares to cool the rocks and the beach.

The boys had stripped themselves down to their waist and as they lay back on the sand, entertained by their imagination and shaded by "their slaves," they could feel the welcome wind caressing their frail bodies, which were being soothed with the sprays from the sea. And they had the beach all to themselves, with only a bird or two to spy on them. No one could really blame them for spending the day here stretching themselves on the sand, dipping themselves in the water to cool off and then competing as to who could stay underwater the longest, cavorting with the playful waves, and every few minutes, throwing sand at each other just for a change for it was rather too hot for any other kind of activity or game. Theirs was an understandable situation indeed.

Except that the three of them were playing truant that morning. Rodrigo should have been in Mr. de la Cruz's class and at this time of the morning he should have been enunciating his vowels and consonants in the English language. His two companions were supposed to be digging the vegetable plot assigned to them in preparation for planting *pechay*. But these two knew that Mr. Jimenez would be annoyed since they couldn't produce the horse manure they had been told to bring for fertilizer. They had scoured the streets of Guiuan yesterday, but their classmates must have got ahead of them—that was the alibi they had rehearsed together. Unfortunately, it didn't sound convincing even to them since there was no way the streets of Guiuan would ever be manure-free, given the number of *tartanilyas*, those horse-drawn carriages which were a legacy from Spanish times. So they had opted for the beach solution. Why face the ire of Mr. Jimenez as well as spend the morning sweating it out in the garden when they could have this? Anyway, they could prevail on the "genius" of Rodrigo since he had promised to help them with any homework that would be given that morning.

Besides, Monet, a friend and classmate in the same section, was manning the post, as it were. He was to tell their teacher that the two were sick. And they had given him instructions specifically to ask for the homework so that their "illness" would not cause them to lag behind. And if they were ill, they could not be expected to be out gardening either. So it was all arranged: their school matters were taken care of, and they had the beach to enjoy as well.

Juan was clearly enjoying the day. He had his head propped up by his bent right arm. The beads of seawater were trickling down his body into the layer of coconut leaves which he had spread out to protect himself from the hot sand. "Isn't this better than being in class today?" He turned his head sideways to the two, stretched out beside him, expecting immediate agreement with his expression of delight. So he was a bit startled when Rodrigo snapped at him.

"Stop talking about it; you're making me feel bad. It's all your idea, you know." Rodrigo seemed to be having second thoughts after all, and he needed a scapegoat.

"You mean, we shouldn't have come here. Is that it?" He rolled over on his stomach as if to confront Rodrigo.

"No, just . . . you know . . . just that I haven't done this before. Suppose we get caught, what then?"

This time Pepe interjected. "Stop worrying. Are we here to enjoy ourselves or not?"

"That's right, if we're going to talk about school, we should have gone there. Stop feeling bad. You're making me feel bad as well." Juan assumed his supine position.

"Okay, what do you want to talk about then?" Rodrigo concluded that it was the wrong time to share his misgivings about their present adventure.

"What's all this going to school anyway? I don't need all that stuff. I just want to make a lot of money. I don't need to learn all that history. And all that geography—we'll never get out of this town anyway." Pepe looked at his more academically inclined friends.

Rodrigo retorted quickly, "You said you didn't want to talk about school." But then he decided that Pepe's last observation was worth pursuing. "And how are you going to make all that money if you just remain here? Go ahead, tell us." He sat up and faced Pepe squarely. "And are you saying, you want to stay in Guiuan forever and ever?"

No immediate answer was forthcoming from Pepe, so Juan ventured a comment. "Me, I want to see the world. I want to see all those beautiful countries that we only hear about. America, for example. Every time we sing 'Oh, beautiful for spacious skies' it makes me wish I could sing it in America. It must be beautiful over there. And they're all rich. And all that snow as well. I wonder what it would be like. I want to do a lot of traveling. Definitely." And he looked longingly into the horizon and beyond it. Between it and the adventurous Juan, however, lay the vastness of the Pacific Ocean.

"Stop dreaming, Juan, you know there's no way you can afford to do all that traveling unless you win the sweepstakes or join the Navy!" Rodrigo thought that his friend needed to be rattled back to their reality.

"But I want to travel, I just don't know yet how. But give me time. There's nothing wrong with dreaming right now." And he continued to stare ahead of him.

After a few minutes had elapsed, as if it finally dawned on Juan that Rodrigo had a more realistic appreciation of their situation, Juan decided to switch over to Rodrigo's dreams. "What about you? What do you want to become when you grow up?"

Rodrigo didn't hesitate. "I want to take care of Nanay. She has no one else. I'll get a job here."

"But you have the brains, the teachers say that you can go further in your education, you might even go to Tacloban or Cebu," Pepe remarked without any trace of envy while pointing to his head.

"And where will I get the money to do that, tell me?"

"From Pepe, when he gets rich, ha, ha, ha! whenever that will be. You can work for him. Here in Guiuan!" Juan let out a good laugh.

Pepe craftily turned the tables on Rodrigo. "You're the one with the brains, you tell us."

"Well, I'd like to be a teacher."

"You mean, like Mr. Jimenez? Are you stupid? They're not paid well. And imagine trying to teach boys like us? You'll have to be looking for them at the beach!"

With that remark from Juan, the trio burst out laughing. Then as if on cue they all sprinted towards the water, trying to catch the waves beckoning to them as they slipped back into the ocean.

After a few minutes, Pepe and Juan had had enough of the ocean, so they settled themselves again on the sandy beach, leaving Rodrigo to amuse himself in the water.

Much later Rodrigo emerged from the water, intending to shake the drops off his body before joining his friends. The sun was not yet at its noontime position, but already the day had turned much hotter. When Rodrigo stepped on the burning sand, he cried out instinctively, "*Agui!*" Then, while the drops of seawater raced down his shoulders and chest, he hopped to the shady spot where his friends had been resting. The sight of Rodrigo practically leaping into the air the minute he set foot on the sand and then bobbing up and down towards them became a source of entertainment for the two. "It's not funny," protested Rodrigo when he noticed the reaction of his fellow-truants. Then, when they persisted, he added, "*O, sigue*, continue laughing if you like."

"*Ikaw naman.* It was only a joke. You should have seen yourself. You were like a grasshopper!" And they were off again.

"Grasshopper? It shows you don't know your science. You won't find grasshoppers on the beach," Rodrigo gave them an annoyed look.

"O, *ano*, I told you so," Pepe turned on Juan, ignoring the fact that he had reacted the same way. "You shouldn't be insulting the genius."

"But I was only joking, honest," claimed Juan. Then making sure that their academic ace-card would forget the incident, he swiftly added, "Sorry." A pause while Juan checked Rodrigo's reaction. "You'll still help us with our homework?" The threat of the sudden collapse of their well-laid-out school plans was enough for Juan to backtrack.

"Depends," Rodrigo wasn't going to make it easy for Juan.

"I stopped immediately, *di ba*?" Pepe, who had quickly shifted his loyalties, wanted to save his own skin. After all, he couldn't afford being without Rodrigo's valuable help. He didn't relish going to school tomorrow empty-handed. Juan could take care of his own affairs.

Rodrigo had gained the upper hand. In fact, he had them eating out of his hands so to speak. "Okay, I'll forgive you both this time. But you'll help me fight that bully Arsenio. Is that a deal?" He sat back as if to indicate that the matter was now in their hands.

Pepe and Juan were aware of the situation. Because Rodrigo was half-bred, he was the target of Arsenio's taunts. Somehow, he resented Rodrigo's handsome looks since they were very much in contrast to his own; and his way of coping with his own unfortunate physiognomy and of forestalling any jeering of him was to draw attention to Rodrigo's background.

Initially, with as much spite as he could muster, Arsenio kept calling Rodrigo a *mestizo*. But it backfired. Labeling someone with that term, originally used to describe Spaniards born in the Philippines and then those of Filipino and Spanish parentage, was actually to pay a compliment. It had become a term to describe any mixed-blood Filipinos. And in some cases, these *mestizos* were much admired by those Filipinos who are unappreciative of their own racial features. As the mother of one of Arsenio's classmates bitingly remarked, after hearing of his resentment of Rodrigo, "Pity that Arsenio isn't a *mestizo* himself!" When the comment reached his ears, Arsenio changed his bullying tactics. He said that Rodrigo "didn't know his own father." Some of the townsfolk were already talking; but for an elementary school kid to draw attention to it was worse. What was being whispered behind one's back was now being spat out in front. And when it was tainted with the venom of someone like Arsenio it was worse than a snakebite.

And that was why Rodrigo had resolved that he had to do something about it in school. He didn't tell his mother what was happening so as not to worry her. He thought he'd better handle it himself. At first he tried to reason with Arsenio, informing him that his father had died when he was a baby. But Arsenio merely sneered and called him "a souvenir of the war."

Unfortunately for Rodrigo, he was being cast into the same mold as the many children who had been left behind in the Philippines, the consequences of liaisons between native women and American GIs. It didn't make any difference that Rodrigo's father was Irish since to many Filipinos in the country every white person is an American. They would always greet any white male whom they would encounter with "Hello, Joe!" and give the victory sign. So the sad fact of the death of Rodrigo's Irish father, who was not even a soldier, was regarded by Arsenio as a mere cover-up of the plight that Rodrigo shared with the "war babies."

Bribing this ignorant bully didn't work either. Rodrigo offered to help him with his homework: he would spend every night being his intellectual slave if he liked. It was all he could offer since he had no money. That move earned Rodrigo more contempt because, being the only son of a wealthy storeowner in Guiuan, Arsenio despised the *pobres*. Not only was Rodrigo "fatherless" but his mother was also so poor that Rodrigo had no money to buy something off the street vendors who lined the schoolyard during recess-time. If he had, then he could at least pay Arsenio off. Getting his homework done was no benefit to the well-provided Arsenio. Even if he failed in all his subjects, he was going to inherit his father's business anyway. He had no need for any intellectual slave.

It was no use. The only thing left, as far as Rodrigo could see it, was to fight him.

"Fight Arsenio? *Ano ka, loco-loco?* He's bigger than any of us."

"But he has to stop. He's insulting me." There was no masking Rodrigo's annoyance and frustration.

"I don't want to lose any more teeth." Juan showed Rodrigo his missing front tooth. "If I lose any more, I won't be able to eat."

Pepe sneered at him. "And the girls won't be able to look at you without laughing!"

Juan landed a soft blow on Pepe's right shoulder. "The next time it will be you who won't have any teeth!"

"Well, no help, no homework."

A lot was at stake a second time. Juan, it seems, couldn't see that. Pepe, on the other hand, was willing, but hesitant. "How will we do it?"

"You can fight in my place!"

"What? You think I'm the one who's *loco*," objected Pepe this time, shaking his head to emphasize his point.

"Well . . . it's up to you." Rodrigo stood up; he had made his best offer.

"*Anay, anay*. Don't go. Maybe we . . ." Pepe was into strategy-making. "Suppose we all fight him together instead. Juan, let me think, you're the biggest of us three, you can pin him to the ground. Hold him down with all your strength. Then Rodrigo can kick him. Give him everything you've got. For those dirty remarks of his. I'll give him a black eye—just make sure you hold him. *O ano?*" He looked up at Rodrigo to check whether his own latest offer would tempt him.

"And how do I pin this bully to the ground in the first place?" Juan suddenly felt the onerous burden imposed on him. "And what if his gang joined him, what will we do then?"

"Then it'll be a free-for-all!" came Pepe's quick reply.

"And we'll all be expelled," warned the intellectual initiator of the plan to fight Arsenio.

"That means no more homework!" exclaimed Pepe and Juan almost simultaneously. It was an attractive plan after all although not in the way Pepe had envisioned it. They both looked at Rodrigo, whose usefulness would thereby be eroded.

The next move was clearly his if they were to advance any further.

"We need time to think about this. But you promise to help, right?"

When he received the assurance he had asked for, Rodrigo continued, "We'd better get ready to go home. We could already be in trouble." He was unsure of how he was going to get out of both troublesome situations.

"We can't go yet, our pants are not yet dry. They'll know where we've been," Pepe reminded the group.

Suddenly, they heard a noise in the distance. Someone was running towards them. Instinctively they ducked behind some overgrown bushes that were just a few feet away. But then the unexpected arrival seemed to be yelling out their names.

"Quick, let's hide! *Didto!*" Pepe pointed to the large boulder farther away. An hour ago they had been perched on top of it pretending that they were pirates looking out for an easy prey. Now it would serve as their haven.

But Rodrigo stopped them. "Don't panic. If he knows our names, he must already know we're here." So instead of running away towards the suggested hideout, Rodrigo made himself clearly visible. "We're here!" he shouted boldly.

Sure enough, it was their classmate, Monet.

"Monet? What's he doing here? He should be in school!" To which Juan and Pepe should have added, "on their behalf." Now they were really in big trouble. Once again, their carefully planned strategy was in jeopardy. No wonder, once Monet was in sight, they immediately demanded from their classmate an explanation for his unplanned and unwelcome presence.

"I came to join you. I thought you'd be glad." Monet was obviously hurt that his friends were not more appreciative of him. "I won't give you the homework then."

"Okay, okay, we were just surprised." It was the pragmatic-minded Pepe again.

"No homework, and I didn't give your excuses to the teacher either." Monet stood firm.

"Don't be stupid, are you a friend or not?" Juan was less compromising than Pepe.

"C'mon, Monet. Did you or didn't you?" Pepe was starting to fear the worst.

"I didn't. Now are you happy?" With those defiant words, he lifted his T-shirt over his head, hurled it towards Pepe, and sprinted to the sea. Juan ran after him.

"Something's funny here," muttered Rodrigo. "School's not over yet. So why is Monet here?" He mentioned this point to Pepe.

"You're right, you know. Let's go. We'll pump it out of him!"

At the sight of the two fast approaching him, in addition to Juan who was catching up on him, Monet raised his arms. "Okay, okay, I surrender!"

"Well, we're waiting." There was no doubting the impatience in the voices of the three who had trapped him in a circle.

"There was a teachers' meeting. Emergency *daw.* All classes were canceled," he made a dramatic pause, "—and no roll call. So they told us to go home. I came here as soon as I could. So you don't have to be feeling bad."

As only boys will understand, the trio expressed their relief by shouting and then engaging in a mock fight. While laughing loudly, they exchanged blows, at first all three against Monet to show physically their appreciation of the news and then in pairs to show off their prowess.

When enough gratitude and relief had been expressed in this very physical way, they all sat down to catch their breath. Between pants, Rodrigo suggested, "We can have a practice session like this before we challenge Arsenio, how about it?" He rose like a boxer after the gong had sounded again.

Juan and Pepe groaned. Being roped into a fight with Arsenio and his ilk was no laughing matter. They informed Monet about what they had been discussing, including the division of labor.

Thankfully for Rodrigo's sake, before it dawned on the two that the new situation had absolved them of any promise to help him in this matter, Monet, with much enthusiasm, promised his support. His tiny frame was no match for Arsenio, but with four of them . . . terrific, he could do what he had long wanted to do. After all, he too had been a target of the name-calling bully. Monet didn't like being called "skeleton."

"And what will you do? Strike him first so I can pin him down?" asked Juan, as he glanced dubiously at this bold but frail contender.

"Well, all of us together . . . we'll attack him at the same time. No problem there," Monet made it sound so simple. "Like the midrib broom that Nanay uses. Each of the sticks, that's you and me, each one is breakable." He picked up a twig from the ground, then snapped it. "But bind them together and you can't break them." This time he closed the fingers of his left hand and bound them together with an imaginary string. "You see, if all of us joined together, we'll be strong. You know, like the broom. So . . ." and his voice was getting stronger with excitement as he thought of what could be accomplished, "At the count of three, we'll all jump on him." And then dramatically acting out each role, he continued, "Juan, you can hold him down with all your might, okay? Use your legs, if possible, okay? You, Pepe, give him that black eye, okay? He deserves it. Maybe, even two if you feel generous. Rodrigo, wallop him as hard as you can. Tell him that he can meet your father in the next life! Me, I'll . . . I'll pull down his pants!"

'You'll what?" the trio of voices sounded incredulous. Then an uproar.

"I'll pull down his trousers. I've been wanting to do that for a long time. Now I'll have your help." remarked an invigorated Monet. "You see, Arsenio is not circumcised!"

Rodrigo, now in his forties, reclined back on his seat and loosened his seatbelt. He was on a Philippines Airlines flight from Los Angeles to Manila via Honolulu. He could hear himself laughing as he recalled that incident during his schooldays. It certainly put an end to Arsenio's bullying of him or of anyone for that matter. And they didn't even have to engage him in a fight. So there had been no danger of being expelled from the school either.

All they had to do was to converse loudly, in front of Arsenio, about the time they were all circumcised. To Filipino boys who prize this sign of masculinity, Arsenio, who feared the whole process, was definitely out of their league. The boys, particularly Monet, derived much pleasure in meticulously describing how the job is done. Conveniently ignoring the fact that in their case it had been a hospital job and Monet was actually a baby, they talked, between guffaws, about how the old man in Guiuan would stretch out the foreskin, insert a *bolo* inside it, and whack, with a blow of his large wooden stick, would accomplish the feat. According to these know-alls, the job doesn't take long. But it was known that Mang Tonio would sometimes forget to sharpen his *bolo*. So he would need more than one blow. And his eyesight and aim were deteriorating, added Monet. Poor Arsenio—Rodrigo could still vividly picture his face, which had been drained of all color.

And then, like victorious toreadors holding up the ear of the dead bull, these true specimens of Filipino masculinity downed their trousers to show off their own little achievements! Despite the persistent taunts, Arsenio refused to bare his own . . . well, uncut part. Instead it was his secret that was out now. Pinned down, without a struggle. Arsenio promised not to call anyone names anymore if they didn't tell and promptly fainted!

Rodrigo was eternally grateful to Monet, who on that day at the beach got him out of hot water twice. And he wondered how effective their strategy of dealing with Arsenio would be today. It was rather below the belt, but it worked. It emasculated the school bully!

Was he right in believing that sometimes the only language that bullies understand is their own? He heard afterwards that Arsenio became a medical doctor! He had turned his back on his father's business, and obviously on the traditional ways of helping boys into manhood. But was he ever . . . ? Rodrigo laughed out loud again and then abruptly stopped when he noticed the amused look of the passenger next to him. His friends and he never found out because after graduating from the elementary school in Guiuan, Arsenio's father, at his son's urgings, sent him to Cebu for his high school and college education. The four boys kept their word but on a couple of occasions they did dangle their own possessions in front of him to remind him of his promise. And Monet? He went into politics where he was able to put his diplomatic skills to wider use!

(1999)

Erwin Cabucos

Born 1973, Carmen, North Cotabato, Philippines

About the Author

Erwin Cabucos is Australia's newest Filipino fiction writer following the publication of *The Beach Spirit and Other Stories*, his first collection of short stories in 2001. Born and raised in the southern Philippines, Erwin came to Australia first on a scholarship, then after marrying his Australian wife. He has completed degrees in Psychology (cum laude) at Notre Dame University, Philippines, and in Communication Studies at the University of Newcastle, Australia. He lives with his wife and children in Sydney.

Filipinos in Sydney, Australia

Sadly, Filipinos are the fourth largest number of illegal stayers in Australia in the 1999 immigration release. U.K. nationals came first: 5,931. Americans came second: 4,759. Indonesians came third: 3,977. And the Filipinos: 3,796. Consequently, there has been a rigorous screening of visas applied for from the Philippines before gaining entry into Australia. On the bright side of things, visas granted from the Philippines for Filipinos who would like to settle here for good are increasing. As of June 1999, there are now 116,887 Filipino migrants in Australia. In 1996, there were only 92,902. There are more Filipino women (60,617) than Filipino men (32,285).

I'll Be Home for Christmas

—Erwin Cabucos

"Renato," Rebecca whispered, tapping me on my shoulder.

"Yeah." Half asleep, I opened my eyes slowly, squinting. "What?"

"Look." She was pointing out the window of our taxi.

"Look at what?" My brows knitted together. I shook my head a little, trying to figure out where we were. We were on our way to the hotel at which we had booked in for a night before we would travel on to my parents' place in the province. I looked around at the queues of cabs, buses and jeepneys waiting for the traffic to move. The clock in the taxi said six o'clock.

"There's a child outside, singing. He's been there for a while and he seemed to be waiting for something. He's following us. I thought you heard him all along."

"No, I was half asleep."

"What are those things clipped to the tip of his thumbs and fingers? Castanets, that's it! He's hitting them as he sings." Rebecca turned to the boy. "Look at him. I don't think he's going to stop."

"He wants some money for his Christmas carols."

She dug into her jeans pocket. "I have a peso here. This'll do, won't it?"

"One peso?" I snorted. "You gotta give him more than that. Don't you feel sorry for him?"

"How much, then?"

"Give him a hundred-peso note."

"What!" Her eyes popped. "That's too much!"

"Why is it too much? It's what you'd pay for a junior burger in McDonalds in Sydney."

"But compared to the cost of living here, it's a lot, isn't it? You told me a meal here might only cost fifteen pesos."

"It's all right." I bent my head towards her and smiled.

She took out the hundred-peso bill from her wallet, wound the window down and handed the note over to the boy. The child ran to the woman selling cigarettes and candies further along the street and passed the note to her. She waved at us, smiled and caressed the little boy's head. The taxi slowly crawled along with the other vehicles. The traffic cleared gradually and we crept towards the open wide road. We heard the car accelerate and saw the child leaning on the lady, who was sitting on a stool beside the road. As we drove further, their image blurred and was slowly replaced by the blinking lights of billboard ads. The car stereo was on, tuned in to Cebu Mellow Station playing Jose Marie Chan's "Christmas in our Hearts."

I broke the silence. "I used to do that when I was young."

"Really." She faced me. "Did you get lots of money?"

We had agreed to meet at the front of Mrs. Villegas' mixed business shop. We thought it was the perfect rendezvous because the light there was bright thanks to the fluorescent tube that hung on the top of the post. The light was a public display of Mr. Villegas' ingenuity. He had climbed the post the previous week, spliced the live electrical wire that ran through our whole street, attached the thin wire of the fluoro, and his store's front yard became what looked like the centre of our little community. He was a hero to us for bringing us light after the town's only power company rejected our request.

The fluorescent light attracted a lot of mosquitoes, and several kinds of moths were hovering around it. The light lifted the energy of young men in our street in the afternoon, as they played basketball with the iron ring attached to the trunk of the dying *santol* tree. The crowd, composed of younger women, mothers with their toddlers, and grandparents minding their young grandchildren, settled around the playing teams, cheering.

Mrs. Villegas was inside her little shop, picking off tiny horseradish leaves for her fish-soup dinner whilst keeping abreast with the competing scores of both teams. Her eyes moved between the leaves on the plate, the sweaty basketball players a few metres away, and me, her customer, muttering that I would like a pack of Marie biscuits. It cost me twenty-five centavos. I liked the nutty taste of the Marie biscuits. They would tide me over at night if we did not have anything for dinner, or if we only had rice, water and salt.

I was waiting for Gideon, Ricky and Darwin to arrive. They knew they had to come early so that we could cover a lot of houses that night.

The *santol* tree trunk was just about to collapse but no one seemed to worry about it. As long as it could still support the thuds of the ball, why worry? Poor tree. I used to climb it when it was still full of fruit. It was a nice variety of *santol*—a Bangkok one, they said. The fruit had had thicker flesh, thinner seeds and was more flavoursome. Although we were told not to swallow the seeds, I did anyhow. It was last school vacation, after we finished third grade. We climbed the trees in the school orchard. The seeds had slipped smoothly down my throat.

"What, you swallowed the seeds of *Bangkok santol*?" Gideon's eyes had nearly popped.

"Yes. Why?"

"Renato, you can't do that. They could grow inside you and you would die, you know," he said warily.

"That sounds like a Komiks story." I simply lifted my eyebrows. "I'm still alive, though."

"I'm serious," he said.

The guys were still not here. They might still be having their dinner. I went back to Mrs. Villegas and spent another twenty-five centavos on some cold water. I tore the plastic with my front teeth and sucked the icy cold water from it. I could be luckier tonight if we came home with lots of coins. Then I could buy boiled eggs from the sidewalk vendors and munch them with rice on my way home. I wished my father earned lots of money again and was able to buy us nice food every night. I wished I had some toys like those of the kids in the movies. I wished that the *santol* tree would bear fruit again. I wished we also had a glittering and singing Christmas tree. I wished the airport would change its decision to remove all the porters from inside the building.

My four brothers, three sisters and I used to know that my father had had a good day if he came home with boiled eggs or barbecued chicken. Usually, it was because lots of Filipino overseas contract workers had arrived in the airport that day. In ten years of lifting suitcases for these highly paid domestic helpers, seamen and bar entertainers from abroad, my father, to attract tips, had mastered eye-to-eye contact, suitable gestures and well-chosen words.

He had been doing it for so many years that it was a big shock when, one afternoon, he was told that he was no longer allowed to work inside the airport building. Only selected porters, the ones who knew someone in management, were allowed to work inside. My father did not know anyone in the office so he was stationed outside the gate, asking passengers if they needed cabs to go around Cebu. He was disappointed, because the money was not as good. Everyone thought he was a con man. I did not know how to help my father. I wished I could. I now wore some of his porter work shirts, as he did not need them any more. My two younger brothers wore them to school, too.

"Where is everyone?" Gideon asked as he came out of his mum's shop, holding his ukulele in his right hand and a flashlight in his left.

"I'm the only one here," I said.

He handed the flashlight over to me as he tried a few strums. I envied his ability to play an expensive instrument like that. I placed the flashlight under my arm and shook the piece of wood with flattened Coca-Cola caps nailed in it as I tried to do a little jam with him. We saw Ricky coming with two spoons. Darwin was coming in the opposite direction with a triangle and a money tin.

We did not waste a moment. Our first house was the Santos', who we knew had lots of money because they ran a big newspaper shop in town. We positioned ourselves on the leaning trunk of a jackfruit tree from where we could see Mr. and Mrs. Santos' silhouettes behind their windowpanes, as he read and she knitted. The jackfruit tree was actually bearing fruit underground. We could see one fruit breaking the ground and smelling like heaven. Before we started, we looked around to make sure that their dogs were not off the leash. It looked like everything was safe.

"Gregorio," said the wife, "I think there are people outside. Can you check who it is?"

"It could just be kids from our block, carolling."

"Just give them some money now so they can leave early. After all, that's the only thing they want."

"No, let them sing."

"As if you really want to listen to them."

"Let them sing, anyway."

"But they're just going to make noise."

"OK, give me the coin and I'll give it to them later."

We were happy when we heard the word "coin," a guarantee that we would be getting something in the end. Gideon strummed the ukulele, Ricky banged the back of the spoons together, I shook the Coca-Cola caps, we looked at each other and together we sang "Joy to the world, the Lord has come, let earth receive her King." We looked at Darwin and his triangle and wondered why he was not hitting the instrument. He smiled, because he had forgotten the rod which he used to hit the triangle. We continued singing while he bent down, looking for a stone to use instead. Towards the middle of the song, we heard his triangle and we sang louder.

Suddenly, we were surprised to see two dobermans racing towards us. The dogs must have broken loose from their leashes. The other three ran as quick as a flash. I was behind them, catching up. I had only one slipper on. For a moment, I thought I might leave it behind so that I could run as fast as possible, but I remembered it was the only one I would have until my mother could buy me another pair in a few days time. I was limping, when I saw the two vicious dogs right behind me. I still tried my best to push myself forward and I could feel my heart pounding hard. The dogs howled behind me. I closed my eyes and ran as fast as I could.

We reached the bright front yard of Villegas' store, puffing. Gideon, Ricky and Darwin were laughing at my pants nearly dropping, the elastic busted. My Coca-Cola caps were no longer in my hands and my slipper had also disappeared from my foot. Oh well, at least I was safe.

We rested for a while until we were ready to go on to the next house.

We got to the Tolentino's front yard; it was covered with young guava trees. They were the new variety of guavas called guapple, a blend of the guava's citric taste and the apple's succulence. We knew the Tolentinos had lots of money, because he was a high school teacher and she was a midwife. We always saw their daughters at school eating delicious sandwiches at recess. Most of the time I had nothing. To pretend I wasn't hungry, I used to play marbles and holes while my friends were munching banana cue and cheese snacks. When I got home, I used to get angry at my mother. Why did she not give me any money to buy food?

The Tolentino's living room was brightly lit. It had a nice maroon couch which blended with their exquisite hardwood furniture. In the corner stood a tall, fully decorated Christmas tree with statues of Jesus in the stable and Mary and Joseph and the Kings and the shepherds. The Tolentinos were having dinner. The strong aroma of chicken, soy sauce and coconut vinegar made me hungrier.

Gideon started to play his ukulele. We all went, "O holy night, the stars are brightly shining. It is the night of our dear Saviour's birth." Because I no longer had my Coca-Cola caps, I picked up two small rocks from the ground and hit them together in time with the melody. We finished the song energetically and then we started another one. "Silent night, holy night, all is calm, all is bright, round yon virgin mother and child." We sang and sang until we were tired but no one came out to give us anything.

Suddenly, Mrs. Tolentino's head poked out of their screen door: "*Hoy*, here's a peso. Now go home and stop disturbing us. You were here last night, weren't you?

"No, that was a different group," Darwin answered, stepping closer to her.

"Anyway, here's your money," she said quickly.

"It's not enough, Mrs. Tolentino," Darwin protested.

"You should be grateful that I've given you something."

"OK, then." Darwin conceded, scraping the two fifty-centavo coins off her palm.

She quickly turned her back and slammed the door.

We then sang the Merry Christmas tune with revised lyrics: "Thank you, thank you, tight-ass people are you, are you? Thank you, thank you, thrifty clan in hell will land."

Darwin dropped the coins into our money tin; I heard them hitting the bottom. It would have been nicer to hear some jingling of pennies inside. We left that hideous family and continued walking towards the next house. We heard dogs barking—the Santos' two dobermans were still wandering free in our street. We screamed and ran back to the lit electrical post again, yelling, "Mr. Santos, your vicious dogs are loitering dangerously in our street. Mr. Santos!"

I stared at the decorated pine trees in the middle of the road and my mind drifted to the face of that little boy, how his lips stretched and his cheeks lifted when he felt the paper money in his palm. I wished I had experienced the same feeling twenty years ago. I wished I could gather Gideon and the guys again to go carolling. We would sing enthusiastically once more but, this time, I would not be asking for people's money.

"So, did you get lots of money?" She leant her head over my shoulder.

"Sometimes."

"How cute." She spoke softly. "We don't have that in Sydney."

"No, we don't," I sighed.

(2001)

Glossary of Words and Phrases

(Words areTagalog unless indicated as Bisayan or Spanish)

adobo	a popular stew dish
agta	enchanted black giant, from Philippine folklore
agui/aguy	(Bisayan): the English expression is Ouch!
anak	child (my)
anay	(Bisayan): wait; or later
ano	what
Ano ba?	What is going on?
Ano ka, *loco-loco?*	Are you nuts?
anting-anting	talisman
aparador	armoire; cabinet for clothes
aray	ouch
aswang	witch
ate	oldest sister
ay	expression for surprise, wonder, etc.
Ay, Bisaya gid	Oh, a real Bisayan (that is, one from the Visayas islands); in context, derisive
Ay Hesus, Ginoo!	Oh Jesus, Lord! (Ginoo means mister, or sir, or may refer to God)
azucena	a kind of sweet smelling flower
ba	as in "What happened ba?"; an expression meaning "What really happened?"
bahalina	a Philippine native wine made from the sap of coconut flowing from its crown; it is fermented with chips of crimson wood and aged in earthen jars from one to seven weeks
bakla	gay
bakuran	fencing in
balikbayan	visiting Philippine-born emigrant
balisong	butterfly knife
bangus	milkfish
baon	sack lunch or snack
barkada	circle of friends
barong barong	shack
batok	back part of the head
baul	trunk for clothes and other belongings
bistek	beaf steak
bobo	imbecile

bodega	warehouse or storage room
bolo	machete
boto/bototoy	penis
bustipol	a kind of hard hat
calderos	pots and pans
camachile/kamachile	a kind of fruit tree
camposanteras	a volunteer group, typically old women who clear and/or weed tombs, graves, and plots in the cemetery
cantor/cantora/ cantores	male and female singers
cantor mayor	lead singer
carabao	water buffalo
champaca	a kind of flower that smells very sweet
chayote	a kind of vegetable
chicken perdiz	a special kind of roast chicken
chico	a kind of fruit-bearing tree
chongca/sungka	a kind of game using seashells
cochero	rig driver; driver of the *tartanilla*
cofradias	a religious organization or club of women devoted to a particular saint
comadre/compadre	name that godparents/religious sponsors and parents call each other
consuelo de bobo	consolation prize given to a loser
convento	parish priest's residence
coriando	double payment
crayola	crayon
daw	reportedly
dewende	dwarf
di ba	contraction of "hindi ba"—isn't that so?
didto	(Bisayan): there
dinoldog	(Bisayan): a confection of sweet potato, bananas, jack-fruit, etc. in coconut milk
dios ko	my God!
durian	a kind of fruit characterized by its strong odor
escalares	cards
estero	drainage canal
F.E.U.	Far Eastern University

gaba	curse
gabi	taro
guapo	handsome
hagabat	southwest wind that is destructive
hay naku	oh my!
herbalista	herbalist; medicine woman; healer
herbolario	male herbalist
hija, hijo	(Spanish): daughter, son
ho	sir; to show respect
hoy	hey you
hoy barbaro	hey, barbarian; hey, thug
ikaw naman	you also
jam session	term in the 50s and 60s used for dancing parties
jeepney	jeep modified for public transportation
juez de cuchillo	massacre; from Spanish, literally judge of the knife
Ka	sir; comrade
kadiri	gross; disgusting
kagat	bite (down)
kanina	earlier
kapis	shell
kapre	enchanted black giant
Katsila	Spaniard
kundiman	love song
kuya	oldest brother
lang	only
la-us	finished; done-for
leche	milk; but also used to curse, "damn"
leche flan	custard
lechon	roast pig
loca/loka	crazy girl/woman
loco/loko	crazy boy/man
lola/lolo	grandmother/grandfather
lumpia	egg roll
mabolo	a kind of fruit tree
madapaka	motherfucker in a Filipino accent
madre mia	my mother; used as an exclamation
maganda	beautiful

malas lang	too bad (refers to bad luck)
malibog	handsome
mamah	betel nut chew
mamang	mother
man	mister or miss; short form for mang or manang
mana/manang/nang	short for hermana, meaning sister
manananggal	from Philippine folklore; a creature with a head and exposed intestines that flies about at night
mang	mister
mangosteen	a kind of fruit
Mani, mani! Yosi, bos, yosi!	"mani" is peanuts, "yosi" is cigarettes, "bos" is boss or chief
mano/manong/nong	short for hermano, meaning brother
mano po	may I kiss your hand; to show respect to elders
maong	jeans
marang	a kind of fruit found abundantly in Sulu, Philippines
masyadong mahaba	too long or too lengthy
matigas ang ulo	hard-headed
matraca	a noisemaker made of light wood; noise is produced by spinning it on its axis which is also its handle
merienda	snack
mestiza/mestisa	mixed-blood female, generally Filipino and white
mestizo/mestiso	mixed-blood male, generally Filipino and white
minatay	corpse
multo	damned spirit who roams the earth
na	already
na lang	only
naku	an expression meaning "Oh my," showing exasperation
naman	also
nanay	mother
Negro	Spanish or Tagalog for African American
nilagang baka	stewed beef
ninang/ninong	godmother/godfather
nobya/nobyo	girlfriend/boyfriend
Ooy! oy!	(Bisayan): expression for surprise, wonder, etc.
paciencia, hijo	(Spanish) patience, son
pamato	flat stone used in the "piko" game or hopscotch
palabok	a noodle dish
palayok	pounding implement for threshing rice grains
palengke	market

palikero	ladies' man; flirt
palo china	a kind of soft wood
pan de sal	a popular bread roll
pancit	a noodle dish
pasalubong	gifts brought by visiting person
patis	fish sauce
pechay	a kind of vegetable
piko	a kind of hopscotch game
pitimini	a rose variety
pobres	poor ones
polvoron	a delicacy made from butter, flour, sugar, and powdered milk
porbida	(Bisayan) expression of exasperation
probinsiyana	provincial
pukengkeng	vagina
puta	whore
putang'na n'yo	literally your mother is a whore; or son of a bitch
puti	literally white; Caucasian
puwet	ass; buttocks
rebeldes	rebels
rimas	a kind of fruit tree
ron	rum
rosal	gardenia
sala	living room; salon
salamat	thank you
sampaguita	the Philippine national flower; a jasmine variety
sampaloc	tamarind
sandali lang	wait a second; just a moment
santilmo	St. Elmo's fire; spirit of the damned
santol	a kind of fruit tree
sarap	delicious
sari-sari	literally "mix-mix"; refers to a sundries store
Semana Santa	Holy Week
Siete Palabras	Christ's seven last words
siete viernes	(Spanish) seven fridays, referring to a premium quality bahalina, aged to seven weeks.
sigbin	from Philippine folklore; a creature like a huge black dog
sigue/sige	all right; okay
sin verguenza	without shame; shameless
sina	them or those or that

sinigang	a sour soup made with fish, pork, beef, or shrimps and vegetables
siopao	steamed bun of Chinese origin; a popular Filipino snack
Siyempre, hindi ko siya pinansin.	"Naturally, I ignored him."
sundang	large knife or machete
suerte	luck; lucky
'sus	contraction of Hesus; expression of surprise
talaga	really; certainly
tartanilyas/tartanillas	horse-drawn carriages
tatay	father
tenablas	From Latin word tenebrae, darkness. A church rite in lent where candles are extinguished one at a time until the church is in total darkness and the blasting sound of matracas and drums highlight the ceremony.
tenes-tenes	an improvised song, usually in quatrains, dealing with light subject matters
tia/tiya/tita	aunt
tikbalang	from Philippine folklore; creature with body of a human and face of a horse
tio/tiyo/tito	uncle
tostos	cigar
tu-tu	(colloquial) penis
ungo	(Bisayan): witch
U.S.T.	University of Santo Tomas
vinta	a kind of sailboat with bright sails found in Mindanao
yantok	a kind of palm used to make canes and furniture
yaya	nanny

Acknowledgements

GÉMINO H. ABAD: "Houseboy" is part of Abad's first collection of fiction, *Orion's Belt* (University of the Philippines Press, 1996). The story was also published in *Chimera* and *Manoa*.

CECILIA MANGUERRA BRAINARD: "Last Moon-Game of Summer" is part of a novel-in-progress. Copyright 2002 by Cecilia M. Brainard. All rights reserved.

ERWIN CABUCOS: "I'll be Home for Christmas" is part of *The Beach Spirit and Other Stories* (Ginninderra Press, 2001) by Erwin Cabucos. Copyright 2001 by Erwin Cabucos.

LIBAY LINSANGAN CANTOR: "Tea and Empathy" was first published as a nonfiction narrative in the Pinoycentric cultural webzine Native's Wish.Com (www.nativeswish.com) in 2000.

GILDA CORDERO-FERNANDO: "The Eye of a Needle" is part of Gilda Cordero-Fernando's collection of stories, *The Butcher, The Baker, The Candlestick Maker* (Benipayo Press, 1962). It is also part of *Story Collection* (Anvil, 1994).

ALBERTO FLORENTINO: "Indian-Giver" was first published in a chapbook (limited private edition, copyright 1997, New York).

M. EVELINA GALANG: "Her Wild American Self" is part of the book of the same title (Coffee House Press, 1996). Reprinted by permission of Coffee House Press and the author. Copyright 1996 by M. Evelina Galang.

VINCE GOTERA: "Manny's Climb" was first published in *Tilting the Continent: Southeast Asian American Writing*, edited by Shirley Geok-lin Lim and Cheng Lok Chua (New Rivers, 2000).

CRISTINA PANTOJA HIDALGO: "The Magic Glasses" was first published in *Catch a Falling Star* (Anvil, 1999).

OSCAR PEÑARANDA: "Day of the Butterfly" was first published in the *North American Review* (January-February 2001).

RUTH T. SARREAL: "Short Answer" was first published in *Mirror Weekly* (Manila, November 2000).

M. S. SIA: "Below the Belt" is a chapter of a novel-in-progress called *Those Distant Shores*. Copyright 2001 by M. S. Sia. All rights reserved.

RICCO VILLANUEVA SIASOCO: "Deaf Mute" was first published in the *North American Review* (January-February 2001).

ANTHONY TAN: "Sweet Grapes, Sour Grapes" first appeared in *Focus Philippines* (June 9, 1979).

JOEL BARRAQUIEL TAN: "San Prancisco" is part of a memoir in progress. Copyright 2002 by Joel B. Tan. All rights reserved.

LINDA TY-CASPER: "In Place of Trees" was first published in *Hawaii Pacific Review* (1990).

MARIANNE VILLANUEVA: "Grandmother" is part of Villanueva's collection of stories, *Ginseng and Other Tales From Manila* (Calyx, 1991).

ALFRED A. YUSON: "Voice in the Hills" won first prize in the *Asiaweek Magazine* short story competition in 1987; it is part of Yuson's collection of short fiction, *The Music Child and Other Stories* (Anvil, 1991).

Contributors' Additional Information

GÉMINO H. ABAD

Education:

B.A., English, *magna cum laude*, University of the Philippines, 1963
M.A., English Literature, with honors, University of Chicago, 1966
Ph.D., English Literature, University of Chicago, 1970

Publications:

Books Published:

Fugitive Emphasis (poems), University of the Philippines, *The Diliman Review*, 1973.

In Another Light: Poems and Essays (critical essays), University of the Philippines Press, 1976.

A Formal Approach to Lyric Poetry (theoretical work), University of the Philippines Press, 1978.

The Space Between: Poems and Essays (critical essays), University of the Philippines Press, 1985.

Poems and Parables, Quezon City: Kalikasan Press, 1988.

Man of Earth: Filipino Poetry and Verse from English, 1905 to the mid-'50s, Ateneo, 1989 (co-edited with Edna Zapanta Manlapaz).

State of Play: Letter-Essays and Parables, Kalikasan Press, 1990.

A Native Clearing: Filipino Poetry and Verse from English since the '50s to the Present/ From Edith L. Tiempo to Cirilo F. Bautista, University of the Philippines Press, 1993 (sequel to *Man of Earth*).

Orion's Belt and Other Writings (short stories with essays on fiction), University of the Philippines Press, 1996.

Father and Daughter (stories, poems, essays), Quezon City: Anvil, 1996 (with daughter Cyan R. Abad).

A Habit of Shores: Filipino Poetry and Verse from English, '60s to the '90s / The Sequel to A Native Clearing, University of the Philippines Press, 1999.

A Makeshift Sun: Stories and Poems, University of the Philippines Press, 2001

The Annual Likhaan Series of the Year's Best Fiction and Poetry:

- *The Likhaan Book of Poetry and Fiction*, 1995, University of the Philippines Press, 1996 (co-edited with Cristina Pantoja Hidalgo).
- *The Likhaan Book of Poetry and Fiction*, 1997, University of the Philippines Press, 1997 (co-edited with Cristina Pantoja Hidalgo)

The Likhaan Book of Philippine Literature in English, University of the Philippines Press, 1999 (collegiate textbook co-edited with Associates of the University of the Philippines Creative Writing Center)

Awards and Honors:

Various literary prizes from the Don Carlos Palanca Memorial Awards

Prizes from the *Philippine Free Press*

Awards from the Manila Critics Circle's National Book Awards

University of the Philippines Outstanding Faculty Award for 1985-86

Gawad Pambansang Alagad ni Balagtas, 1996

University of the Philippines Alumni Association Professional Award in Literature, 1997

Ellen F. Fajardo Foundation Grant for Excellence in Teaching, 2000-2001

Chancellor's Award for Best Literary Work, 2001

Employment:

University of the Philippines:

Secretary of the University, 1977-1982; Vice-President for Academic Affairs, 1987-1990; Director of the University of the Philippines Creative Writing Center, 1995-1998; University Professor (Department of English and Comparative Literature)

Exchange Professor in Literature, St. Norbert College, Wisconsin, 1998

Visiting Professor, Center for Philippine Studies, University of Hawaii at Manoa, 1991

CECILIA MANGUERRA BRAINARD

Education:

B.A., Maryknoll College, Quezon City, 1968

Graduate work in Film Making, UCLA, 1969 and 1970

Publications:

Books Published:

Woman With Horns and Other Stories, New Day, 1988.

Philippine Woman in America (essays), New Day, 1991.

When the Rainbow Goddess Wept (novel), Dutton, 1994, (first appeared as *Song of Yvonne*, New Day, 1991); Plume paperback, 1995; University of Michigan Press, 1999.

Acapulco at Sunset and Other Stories, Anvil, 1995.

Magdalena (novel), Plain View Press, 2002.

Books Edited:

Seven Stories From Seven Sisters: A Collection of Philippine Folktales, (co-editor) PAWWA, 1992.

The Beginning and Other Asian Folktales, (co-editor) PAWWA, 1995.

Fiction by Filipinos in America, New Day, 1993.

Contemporary Fiction by Filipinos in America, Anvil, 1998.

Journey of 100 Years: Reflections of the Centennial of Philippine Independence, (co-editor), PAWWA, 1999.

Growing Up Filipino: Stories for Young Adults, PALH, 2003

Awards and Honors:

1989-1990 California Arts Council Artists' Fellowship in Fiction
1990-1991 City of Los Angeles Cultural Grant
1991 Special Recognition Award, Los Angeles Board of Education
1991 Brody Arts Fund Fellowship
1992 City of Los Angeles Certificate of Appreciation
1993, 1995, and 1997 USIS Grants
1998 Outstanding Individual Award from City of Cebu, Philippines
2000 Recognition Award, California State Summer School for the Arts
2001 *Filipinas Magazine* Achievement Award for Arts and Culture
2001 Certificate of Recognition from the California State Senate, 21st District

Employment:

Freelance Writer, 1981-Present
Faculty, Writers Program, UCLA Extension, 1989-Present
Adjunct Professor, Animation Department, USC, 2000-Present

LIBAY LINSANGAN CANTOR

Education:

B.A., Mass Communication, University of the Philippines, 1995
M.A., English (Creative Writing), University of the Philippines (in progress)

Publications:

Work anthologized in:

Taxi Signs (Finkomarts, 2000)
Ang Aklat Likhaan ng Tula at Maikling Kuwento 2000, University of the Philippines Press, 2002.
Essays and short stories in English and Filipino published in *Mirror Weekly Magazine, University of the Philippines Sappho Society Online* and *Likhaan Online*, from 1998-present.

Awards and Honors:

Third place for short story "*Si Joe Cool Kasi*" and for short story for children in Filipino "*Si Totoy Sa Gubat ng Diwata*" from 47th Don Carlos Palanca Memorial Awards for Literature (1997)
Honorable Mention Award for screenplay "*Kalas-Kalas, Kabit-Kabit*," from 1998 Film Development Foundation of the Philippines, Inc.

Employment:

Creative Group Writer, Premiere Entertainment Productions, Inc., August 1996-February 1998
Entertainment Editor, *Pinoy Times* daily/special editions, Sept. 2000-Dec. 2001

ALBERTO FLORENTINO

Education:

University of the East, 1948-1956

University of the Philippines (Diliman and Padra Faura-Manila campuses), 1956-1958

Far Eastern University 1959-1961

Publications:

Books Published:

The World Is an Apple and Other Prize Plays, Philippine Cultural Publishers, 1959.

Midcentury Guide to Philippine Literature in English, Manila, Filipiniana Publishers, 1963.

The Portable Florentino: 7 Representative Plays for Stage and Television in English and Filipino [1954-1998], Manila, De La Salle University Press, 1998.

From Book to Stage: Adaptations of Classic Filipino Short Stories, MCS Enterprises, 1972.

Panahon ng Digma: Tatlong Maikling Dula (3 Short Plays), Cacho Hermanos, 1973).

Memento Mori: Three Short Plays, Manila, Pedro B. Ayuda, 1972.

Awards and Honors:

Carlos Palanca Memorial Awards for Literature: 1953, 1957, 1970, 1971

Arena Theater Playwriting Awards: 1959

Patnubay ng Kalinangan (Araw ng Maynila)

Ten Outstanding Young Men Award (TOYM) Award, 1960

Philippine Delegate to PEN World Congress, New York, 1966

Balagtas Award, Institute of National Language

Balagtas Award: UMPIL

Kabataang Barangay for the play "Mariang Makiling"

Employment:

University of the Philippines: Secretary, Office of the University of the Philippines Board of Regents; Marketing Head, University of the Philippines Press; Professorial Lecturer, Institute of Mass Communication Graduate School (ca. 1970s); Professorial Lecturer, University of the Philippines Creative Writing Center, CAL (ca. 1990s)

Filipiniana Book Guild, Assistant Editor to Chairman Carlos Quirino

Editorial Assistant, Macy's New York, 1985-1991

Adjunct Faculty, New York University School for Continuing Education, 1980s-1990s

M. Evelina Galang

Education:

B.A., Communication Arts, University of Wisconsin, Madison, 1983
M.F.A., Creative Writing, Colorado State University, 1994

Publications:

Book Published:

Her Wild American Self (short stories), Coffee House Press, 1996.

Book Edited:

Screaming Monkeys (anthology), Coffee House Press, 2003.

Awards and Honors:

Colorado State University Graduate Diversity Educational Fellowship, 1991-1994

John Gardner Scholar in Fiction, Bread Loaf, August 1994

Wisconsin Library Association Outstanding Achievement for *Her Wild American Self*

Lannan Fellowship recipient for residency to Ragdale Foundation. Lake Forest, Illinois, Summer 1997

"Her Wild American Self" listed as one of *Best American Short Stories*' 100 Distinguished Stories of 1997, Houghton Mifflin Company

Gintong Pamana (Golden Heritage) *Pluma* Award in Literature, *Philippine Time-USA News Magazine*, January 1998

The Filipino American Community of Chicago and Midwest States Philippine Independence Centennial Outstanding Achievement in Arts and Literature, June 1998

Pushcart Prize 1997 anthology short list for story, "Her Wild American Self," Fall 1998

Asian American Institute 1998 Milestone Award for Excellence in Literature. November, 1998. Chicago, Illinois

Illinois Arts Council Grant, January 1999

Fulbright Senior Research Scholar, January 1-May 31, 2002

Employment:

Film Production Houses, Chicago, Illinois, July 1986-present

Colorado Review, Fort Collins, Colorado, August 1991-1992

Colorado State University, Fort Collins, Colorado, August 1992-May 1994

Old Dominion University, Norfolk, Virginia, August 1994-1997

School of The Art Institute of Chicago, Chicago, Illinois, August 1997-1999

Goddard College, Plainfield, Vermont, Spring 1998-present

Iowa State University, Ames, Iowa, Fall 1999-2002

University of Miami, Miami, Florida, August 2002-present

VINCE GOTERA

Education:

A.A., General Studies, City College of San Francisco, 1977
B.A., English, Stanford University, 1979
M.A., English, San Francisco State University, 1981
M.F.A., Poetry Writing, Indiana University, 1989
Ph.D. (double), English and American Studies, Indiana University, 1991

Publications:

Books Published:

Dragonfly (poetry), Pecan Grove Press, 1994.
Radical Visions: Poetry by Vietnam Veterans (literary criticism), University of Georgia Press, 1994.
Fighting Kite (poetry) Pecan Grove Press, forthcoming.

Magazines and Anthologies:

Poems, stories, and essays have appeared in such venues as *Kenyon Review, Liwanag*, and *Connecticut Review*, as well as in such anthologies as *Flippin'*, *Returning a Borrowed Tongue*, and *Bold Words: A Century of Asian American Writing.*

Awards and Honors:

Mary Roberts Rinehart Award in Poetry, 1988
Felix Pollak Prize in Poetry (University of Wisconsin), 1988
Creative Writing Fellowship from the National Endowment for the Arts, 1993
Nominated for the Pushcart Prize three times (1991, 1992, 2000)

Employment:

Editor, *North American Review*, 2000-present
English professor, University of Northern Iowa, 1995-present
English professor, Humboldt State University, 1989-1995
Has also worked as a high-school teacher, an editor/writer, a graphic artist, a civil servant, a soldier, and a musician.

CRISTINA PANTOJA HIDALGO

Education:

Ph.B., *magna cum laude*, University of Santo Tomas, 1964
M.A., English Literature, University of Santo Tomas, 1969
Ph.D., Comparative Literature, University of the Philippines, 1993

Publications:

Sojourns (travel essays), New Day, 1984.
Ballad of a Lost Season (short stories), New Day, 1987.
Five Years in a Forgotten Land: A Burmese Notebook (travel essays), University of the Philippines Press, 1991.
I Remember ... Travel Essays, New Day, 1992.

Philippine Post-Colonial Studies (literary criticism), co-edited with Priscelina P. Legasto, University of the Philippines Press, 1993.

Tales for a Rainy Night (short stories), De La Salle University Press, 1993.

Skyscrapers, Celadon and Kimchi: a Korean Notebook (travel essays), University of the Philippines Press, 1993.

Where Only the Moon Rages: 9 Tales (short stories), Anvil, 1994.

Filipino Woman Writing: Home and Exile in the Autobiographical Narratives of Filipino Women (literary criticism), Ateneo, 1994.

The Path of the Heart (essays/nonfiction), Anvil, 1994.

The Likhaan Book of Poetry and Short Stories 1995, co-edited with Gémino H. Abad, University of the Philippines Press, 1996.

Recuerdo: A Novel, University of the Philippines Press, 1997.

Coming Home (essays), Anvil, 1997.

A Gentle Subversion (literary criticism), University of the Philippines Press, 1998.

The Likhaan Book of Poetry and Short Stories, 1997, co-edited with Gémino H. Abad, University of the Philippines Press, 1999.

Catch a Falling Star (short stories), Anvil, 1999.

Pinay: Autobiographical Narratives by Women Writers, Ateneo, 2000.

A Book of Dreams (novel), University of the Philippines Press, 2001.

Awards and Honors:

Manila Critics' Circle Book of the Year Award, 1994

British Council Fellowhip, Downing College, Cambridge University, United Kingdom, July 10-18, 1996

Carlos Palanca Grand Prize for the Novel (for *Recuerdo*), 1996

Best Literary Composition of the Year (for *Recuerdo*), 1998

University of the Philippines GAWAD Awards, 1998, 2001

Umpil Gawad Pambansang Alagad ni Balagtas for Fiction in English, 2001

Manila Critics' Circle Book of the Year Award, 1998

Employment:

Assistant Women's Editor, Better Living Section, *Graphic Magazine*, Manila, 1964-1965

Instructor, University of Santo Tomas, Manila, 1964-1972

Assistant Editor, *Living Magazine*, Bangkok, 1975-1977

Copy Editor, Yonhap News Agency, Seoul, 1981-1982

Columnist, *The Korea Times*, Seoul, 1981-1984

Lecturer at Hankuk University, Seoul National University, and Sogang University, 1982-1984

Regional Editor for Rangoon, *Lifestyle Asia*, Manila, 1982-1984

Curriculum Coordinator and Faculty Member, International High School, Rangoon, 1985-1989

Editor, Program Funding Office, United Nations Children's Fund (UNICEF), New York, 15 December 1989-1930 March 1990

Director, The University of the Philippines Creative Writing Center, University of the Philippines, 1998-2002

Director, The University of the Philippines Press, beginning June 15, 2002

Professor, Dept. of English and Comparative Literature, University of the Philippines, 1990-present

MARILY YSIP OROSA

Education:

B.A., Communication Arts, Maryknoll College, 1968

Publications:

As Publisher, published the following:

Philippine 2000: A Vision for the Nation, edited by Melinda Quintos-De Jesus, Studio 5, 1993.

In Excelsis: The Mission of Dr. José P. Rizal, written by Felice Sta. Maria, Studio 5, 1996.

The Tragedy of the Revolution: Life and Death of Andres Bonifacio, written by Adrian Cristobal, Studio 5, 1997.

Visions of the Possible: Legacies of Philippine Freedom, written by Felice Sta. Maria, Studio 5, 1998.

Awards and Honors:

Studio 5 Designs, which Marily Ysip Orosa founded and heads has won the following:

Gold Awards, National Advertising Congress: 1985, 1987, 1989

National Book Awards for Best Book Design (*In Excelsis*, 1996), *Tragedy of the Revolution*, 1997), *Visions of the Possible*, 1998)

1997 *Gintong Aklat* Award (*In Excelsis* and *Tragedy of the Revolution*)

Anvil Awards of Excellence for Most Outstanding Coffee Table Book (*Dynamic Partnerships: The Petron Story*, 1999), (*Paragons: 23 CEOs on Corporate Ethics*, 2000)

Bronze Anvil Award for Best Creative Tactic from Public Relations Society of America (2000)

Employment:

President, Studio 5 Designs, Inc., specializing in graphic designs and corporate communications. 1979-present

President, Studio 5 Publishing, Inc., specializing in coffee table books, 1994-present

MAR V. PUATU

Education:

University of the East, 1951-1957

Publications:

Books Published:

Sojourns, Leo Mar Concepts, 1977.

The Girl With One Eye (short stories), LMC Publishers, 1998.

Grandfather, the King (novel), Leo Mar Concepts, 2001.

Awards and Honors:

Carlos Palanca Memorial Awards for Literature: 1960, 1963, 1964, 1965, 1966

Arena Theater Award: 1960

Employment:

University of the East, 1957-1960

J. Walter Thompson, 1961-1965

Great Wall Advertising, 1966-1968

Ace-Compton Advertising, 1969-1971

Pan-Pacific Advertisers, 1972-1976

Rosary Movement, 1976-1977

Richards & Switzer Typographers, 1979-1987

LMC Publishing, 1995-present

ANTHONY L. TAN

Education:

B.A., Ateneo de Zamboanga University, 1968

M.A., Silliman University, Dumaguete, Philippines, 1975

Ph.D., Silliman University, Dumaguete, Philipppines, 1982

Publications:

Books Published:

Badjao Cemetery and Other Poems, Mindanao State University-Iligan Institute of Technology, 1985.

Poems for Muddas, Anvil, 1996.

Honors/Awards Received:

1st Prize, *HomeLife Magazine* Poetry Award, 1994

Carlos Palanca Memorial Awards for Literature, 1991, 1993, 2002

Employment:

Professor at:

Notre Dame of Siasi College, 1969-1970

Silliman University, Dumaguete City, 1970-1983

MSU-Iligan Institute of Technology, Iligan City, 1983-present. Service interrupted when I taught for one term at De La Salle University in 1991

JOEL BARRAQUIEL TAN

Education:

B.A., Ethnic Studies, University of California, Berkeley, 2002
M.F.A., Creative Writing, Antioch University, in progress

Publications:

Monster (poetry), Noice Press, 2002.
Edited *Queer Pilipino, Asian, and Pacific Islander Porn*, Cleis Press, 1998.

Awards and Honors:

Gay Role Model Award, 1993, *L. A. Gay and Lesbian Center and Genre Magazine*
Filipino American Leadership Scholarship, 2000
Markowski-Leach: Horizons Foundation, 2000

Employment:

Program Coordinator, Asian Pacific AIDS Intervention Team, January 1992-July 1994, Community & Board Involvement
Program Manager, L.A. Shanti AIDS Foundation, 1994-1996
Health Education Department Director, Asian Health Services, Inc., 1996-1998
Consultant, Centers for Disease Control/Associated Schools of Public Health's Institute of HIV Prevention Leadership Program
HIV Programs Manager, Asian Health Services, Inc., 1998-2000
Associate Artistic Director, Asian American Theater Company, 2000-2002
Social Services Case Manager, Orange County AIDS Services Foundation, 2002-present

LINDA TY-CASPER

Education:

A.A., LL.B., University of the Philippines, 1949-1955
LL.M., Harvard Law, 1956-1957
Silliman University, 1963
Radcliffe Institute, 1974-1975

Publications:

Books Published:

The Transparent Sun (short stories), Peso Books, 1963.
The Peninsulars (historical novel), Bookmark, 1964.
The Secret Runner (short stories), Florentino/National Book, 1974.
The Three-Cornered Sun (historical novel), New Day, 1979.
Dread Empire (novella), Hong Kong, Heinemann, 1980.
Hazards of Distance (novella), New Day, 1981.
Fortress in the Plaza (novella), New Day, 1985.
Awaiting Trespass (novella), London, Readers International, 1985.
Top 5 Women's Fiction Choice, United Kingdom, *Feminist Book Fortnight*, 1986.
Wings of Stone (novella), London, Readers International, 1986.